CRY BLOOD

On Friday, May 13th, 14-year-old Diana Halloran disappears. She takes a short cut home from school through a wooded ravine, and is never seen again. Months later, her shoes are found in Gary Malone's basement. The police search and find more of her clothing. And that's when Malone's nightmare begins. Malone is a popular young real estate agent, but overnight he turns into a murdering sex fiend. His best friends, Luke and Betty Summer, turn against him. Police Chief Kraft is convinced of his guilt, though he doesn't have enough proof to arrest him. The D. A. is howling for his blood. Even his own wife Ellen shuns him. He is tried by everyone in town and found guilty. The only one who knows that Malone is innocent—is Malone himself!

KILLER IN SILK

When she meets Morgan O'Keefe, he's a writer on a ten-day drunk, verging on the dt's. Irene Wilson takes him in, as she does so many alcoholics, mostly to assuage her own guilt at having accidentally shot and killed her husband, Jay, ten years ago. As Morgan begins to recover, he is introduced to her family: her brother-in-law, Frank, and his wife Glenna. They join Irene for cocktail parties all the while condemning her for Jay's death. Glenna is convinced that Jay's death was no accident. The more Morgan finds out about the events of ten years ago, the more he begins to agree—Jay's death was no accident, but who is the real guilty party in this household of death?

CRY BLOOD

"Dixon goes beyond telling a story of an innocent man wrongly accused…the book deserves a wide audience and should perhaps be mandatory reading for fans of police procedurals."
Reading California Fiction

KILLER IN SILK

"Vernor Dixon is at the top of his game here. The story moves easily and Dixon's prose is, as usual, lean and clean. Fans of crime fiction, both genteel and hard-boiled, are likely to enjoy the novel."
Reading California Fiction

Cry Blood

Killer in Silk

H. Vernor Dixon

Introduction by Donald S. Napoli

Stark House Press • Eureka California

CRY BLOOD / KILLER IN SILK

Published by Stark House Press
1315 H Street
Eureka, CA 95501, USA
griffinskye3@sbcglobal.net
www.starkhousepress.com

ISBN: 1-933586-79-6
ISBN: 978-1-933586-79-3

Book design by Mark Shepard, shepgraphics.com
Cover art by Barye Phillips

First Stark House Press Edition: January 2016
FIRST EDITION

H. Vernor Dixon
By Donald S. Napoli

If you came across one of H. Vernor Dixon's paperbacks in the 1950s, you might have been in for a surprise. The cover foretold a standard crime novel. On the front was a good-looking young woman accompanied by a snappy phrase summarizing the adventure inside. On the back were a couple paragraphs providing more details about the story. But when you started reading, you discovered a few things askew. The leading character was up to no good – not a dedicated crime-fighter with character flaws, mind you, but a seriously bad guy. Yet he wasn't dangerous in the ordinary sense. He didn't rely on violence, but counted instead on his ability to exploit the weakness of a specific target. If there was some sort of mystery to be solved, reaching the solution was not the point of the story. Occasionally the paperback cover proved completely deceptive, and the book was barely about crime at all.

Yet despite Dixon's focus on how a crime evolved rather than how it was solved, he had little trouble commanding an audience among readers of crime fiction. During the period when he concentrated on writing novels (1950 to 1966), Dixon averaged nearly a book a year. The first and last appeared in hard cover before being released in paperback editions. The remaining dozen were published initially as paperbacks, for which print runs reached the neighborhood of 250,000 copies. So altogether Dixon's books sold in the millions.

Harry Vernor Dixon was born in Sacramento, California, in 1908 and lived there until he graduated from high school in 1926. His father, after whom he was named, held several different jobs – painter, grocer, plumber – before settling in as a real estate salesman in the 1920s. His mother had a penchant for dance and a devotion to the Baptist religion. The Dixon family moved around town from one middle-class home to another. Young Harry was a lively young man, performing as traveling piano player before the age of ten and learning to fly bi-planes as a teenager. With the help of his mother, he also became an accomplished dancer. After high school his skill at drawing led him to enroll at the California School of Fine Arts (now the San Francisco Art Institute).

Dixon never lost his interest in art. But a lack of financial resources and (as he admitted) a lack of sufficient talent soon brought his college career to an end. He then worked in a variety of jobs and traveled widely across the country. By the early 1930s he had formed a dance duo with his sister, Dorothy. They played the vaudeville circuits in the eastern United States, entertaining audiences as what one small-town newspaper called "a pair of comedy tangoists." They gained some note on Broadway as well for "eccentric dancing." In 1932 they appeared (without screen credit) in *Blondie of the Follies* for MGM. They may have made other uncredited film performances as well. Dixon was still dancing in the mid-1930s, but vaudeville was fading away and the movies didn't offer steady employment. A new line of work became important, especially after 1934, when Dixon married Dorothy Moriarty, with whom he later had two children.

Dixon always liked to write. He may have had some professional assignments as early as 1929, but he published nothing of importance until *Laughing Gods* in 1935. Employing the ideas of fundamentalist preacher Harry Rimmer, the novel was like nothing Dixon ever wrote again. It tells of a young scientist in New York who comes to reject Darwinism and other aspects of modern thinking. The book, released by a small religious press in Michigan, sold poorly. But it did well enough, Dixon later explained, to let him "plunge self and family into a career of writing."

So Dixon changed his name from Harry to H. Vernor and got to work. During the next fifteen years he wrote more than fifty magazine stories, staying away from the pulps and limiting himself to well known national publications like *Collier's, Cosmopolitan* and *Argosy*. His plots varied in tone and subject, with adventure stories being his forte. A sign of his growing reputation came at the end of World War II when Editions for the Armed Forces collected six of his pieces in *Come in Like a Yankee and Other Stories*. Dixon usually kept to standard magazine length, but occasionally he tried something longer. In 1940 he produced what amounted to a second novel, "The Siren Smiled," as a serial for *American Magazine*. It focused on the rivalry between salvage companies in San Francisco. Although lacking the edge of his later work, the serial rendered both diving sequences and business shenanigans with knowing detail.

Dixon moved around quite a bit before and during World War II. He lived in the Los Angeles suburbs during a brief and unproductive stint writing for the movies. He and the family also resided in San Francisco, New York and the Florida keys before moving to Carmel after the war. Dixon hadn't seen any combat, but he did participate in the military effort by flying for the Ferry Command, helping to design a helicopter, and serving briefly as a naval officer. The relocations and wartime activities did not curtail his writing. In fact, he published more stories at the height of the war in 1944 than in any other year.

It wasn't long, however, before Dixon's career was in jeopardy. The publication of magazine fiction plummeted in the United States after the war, and the demand for short stories almost disappeared. He placed a few more long magazine pieces in the 1940s, possibly seeing them as harbingers of his literary future. In any case, he launched his career as a novelist in 1950 with *Something for Nothing*. It was published in hard cover by Harper and Brothers and reissued in paperback by Bantam in 1951. A French translation appeared the same year. For his next book, perhaps to regularize payment of royalties, he switched to a publisher that specialized in original paperbacks. Fawcett Publications had invented the idea of by-passing hardcover publishers a couple years earlier. Using the Gold Medal imprint, it had already published nearly

200 novels by the time Dixon's book, *To Hell Together,* appeared in 1951. Dixon published his next eight books with Fawcett, ending in 1956 with the two reprinted in this volume, *Cry Blood* and *Killer in Silk.*

Whatever advantages Dixon may have gained with Fawcett, publishing only in paperback did nothing for his literary reputation. The folks supervising America's world of books – critics, librarians, academics – paid almost no attention to paperback originals. They wrote no reviews, made few mentions in bibliographies, and undertook systematic collection only in a handful of college libraries. The results can be seen today. Of Dixon's nine Fawcett paperbacks, for example, only three titles are included among the 39 million books amassed in libraries of the University of California. Other libraries in the state don't have any copies at all. As the present volume illustrates, interest in paperbacks from the past is growing. Readers today have much greater access to the books than readers of only a decade ago. Even so, what's true of Dixon is generally true of other paperback writers. And because they present a less cheerful vision of the country than do their hardcover colleagues, the disappearance of so many of their novels leaves a hole in America's literary history.

For Dixon, once he became a full-time novelist, America meant California. All but one of his novels were set in the state. His favorite setting was Monterey County, home of such famed places as Cannery Row, Big Sur and Pebble Beach. The county is often referred to as "Steinbeck Country," since that author set much of his fiction there. Steinbeck, however, did not exhaust the possibilities for stories in that part of California. The people he chose to write about, primarily agricultural workers or men living together without women, did not represent the county's changing population. True, while Steinbeck was still living there, other authors pretty much left the place alone. Once he made his final departure to the east coast in 1950, however, they began to look at the county in different ways and write about different sorts of people. Dixon, who set more novels in the county than did Steinbeck, led the way.

So what were the characteristics of the post-Steinbeck Monterey residents (and those living in the San Francisco Bay area, where Dixon set the rest of his California novels)? First, they were well off and lived in sumptuous houses often near the ocean. They were well connected socially. Although they had plenty of money, they'd gained it through inheritance rather than work. With no jobs to worry about, they had lots of time to spend drinking, playing golf and going to night clubs. While some were deeply dishonest, more were just oblivious to what was going on around them. Either way, none of these folks cared much about anybody else. Although Dixon's novels occasionally presented an exception, as a whole they don't offer an upbeat view of humanity.

Dixon almost always used the master plot in which an outsider comes to a well-established place. That place was wherever the rich ne'er-do-wells congregated, and the outsider was the novel's protagonist. This fellow arrived without a purpose but soon concocted a scheme to promote his own interests.

Sometimes his plans had an altruistic element, but usually they simply involved a quest for money or social status. The second goal was usually as important as the first. The interloper wasn't planning just to take his cash and skip town. He wanted to become part of the upper crust. His success depended on clever manipulation of the ambient rich. His appearance – tall, well-built, around thirty – helped him get within striking distance. (It should be noted that Dixon himself was more than six feet tall and in his days as an acrobatic dancer, at least, kept himself in good shape.) Since Dixon didn't have the aversion to sex that he did to violence, a good-looking woman soon showed up to move the story along and fulfill the expectation of paperback readers for some sexy interludes. She found the protagonist irresistible, not knowing or caring that she formed part of his target group. No matter how attractive she was, she appealed to him primarily because of a fortune she had just inherited (if middle-aged and recently widowed) or would soon inherit (if around twenty and looking to gain grown-up experience). In any case, she was an integral part of the story and not simply tossed in to add some sexiness. Surprisingly, Dixon created a female protagonist for one of his novels, though she was a nicer person and had less opportunity to exploit her position as an outsider than did her male counterparts.

Like other paperback writers, Dixon strove to keep readers involved. He tried to accomplish this first by tightly focusing on his protagonist. Although Dixon seldom employed a first-person narrator, he put the lead character in nearly every scene and told most of the story through his thoughts. Ancillary characters, meanwhile, remained on the sidelines, and actual antagonists were pretty much non-existent. In addition, Dixon usually succeeded in concocting enough plot twists to keep things interesting but not so many as to confuse readers. He avoided diverting attention with significant subplots. As all paperback writers tried to do, Dixon kept his writing clear and straightforward. An arcane word appeared only in a technical passage. A sentence was easy to follow and usually short, though not conspicuously terse. A scene always had a point and seldom dragged on longer than necessary. Finally, by dispensing with many of the accouterments of crime fiction – detectives, hoodlums, fist fights, myriad corpses – he gave readers a chance to think about the main characters in the book, people who possessed or sought substantial wealth and social status. All this made Dixon's novels entertaining and sometimes thought-provoking.

The novels in this volume, both originally published in 1956, were the last Dixon produced for Fawcett. They came during a period of increasing financial problems. His many talents, interests and hobbies did not include maximizing income. He had a falling out with his agent, moved the family out of Carmel and eventually declared bankruptcy. In the late 1950s he published some short stories and a novella for *Cosmopolitan,* but his only novel was a 1959 "uncensored abridgment" of *To Hell Together.* Then in 1962 came the first of three paperback originals for Monarch Books. The content of the first two was similar to Dixon's previous books. The third went in a completely different direction, telling of a jungle fighter in Malaya who saw himself on an anti-communist suicide mission. In 1966 Dixon produced his longest and least focused novel, *The Rag Pickers.* Published first in hard cover, it depicted the activities of clothes' buyers for a San Francisco department store. He probably hoped for a commercial blockbuster, but the book never cracked the bestseller list. A paperback edition appeared in 1969. Dixon lived for another fifteen years but published no further fiction. He died in San Francisco in 1984 at the age of 75.

Both the novels in this volume show Dixon extending the range of crime stories to cover additional topics.

Here's the setup for *Cry Blood:* Gary Malone is a successful and popular young Morales (Monterey) County real estate salesman. He's lived in Bayside, a small town on the coast, for three years. Like other residents Malone has lost interest in the shocking story of Diana Halloran, the girl who mysteriously disappeared on her way home from high school three months before. Then, unaccountably, his wife finds the girl's gym shoes in their garage. The police renew their investigation. In a matter of hours Malone becomes a suspect in what was probably a horrible murder. Though the public is likely to demand quick justice, the police chief is determined to build a solid case before making the inevitable arrest. Which would suit Malone fine if he were not the putative killer.

This novel differs from the usual story of an average guy getting into trouble. Ordinarily, the protagonist would make a make a minor but disastrous misjudgment. Here he bears no responsibility at all for the mess he's in. Don't feel safe, the author says. This could happen to you. Or, put another way, you may be more of an outsider in your community than you realize. But Dixon goes beyond telling a story of an innocent man wrongly accused. He casts a dark eye at the eagerness of the press to raise public fury through sensationalized reports. He throws doubt on a legal system that tries to convict the obvious suspect rather than conduct a thorough investigation. And he wonders how many friends and family members would stand by an average guy who faced condemnation by the press, public and police. So while this story has a mystery to be solved, it's much more than a mystery story. The novel should perhaps be mandatory reading for fans of police procedurals.

Killer in Silk begins this way: Morgan O'Keefe, an unsuccessful author of grim novels, has failed to overcome his serious drinking problem. After blowing a good-sized royalty check on a long binge in San Francisco, he's given a chance to dry out in the posh Pacific Heights home of a reclusive young widow, Irene Wilson. He soon learns that she shot her husband some years before but remembers little about what happened. The death, which gave her control of the family business, had been ruled an accident, but her brother-in-law and his wife, as well as many of her acquaintances, had suspected murder. O'Keefe doesn't want to go on staying in the house, especially if he's to be patronized by the Wilsons and their rich friends, but he is intrigued by the killing. Without quite realizing it, he becomes determined to find out what really happened.

Dixon is at the top of his game here. His interest is not so much crime as character development. Morgan O'Keefe and Irene Wilson begin the story isolated — he by his anger and alcoholism, she by a fear (or perhaps a realization) that she really did kill her husband intentionally. As Dixon drops in clues about the shooting, he shows O'Keefe's investigation bringing them both out of seclusion. The portrait of O'Keefe is the sharper and more believable of the two. (He ruminates about writing novels, perhaps reflecting some of Dixon's own thoughts, and is arrogantly nasty when dealing with the rich folks.) Modern readers may find an unfamiliarly large amount of psychologizing here: The book is, after all, a product of the 1950s. But the story moves easily and Dixon's prose is, as usual, lean and clean. Fans of crime fiction, both genteel and hard-boiled, are likely to enjoy the novel.

There is much of Dixon himself in these novels. Whether he saw himself as the arrogant and unappreciated outsider or he simply enjoyed creating these characters, he was first and foremost an entertainer: the life of the party, continually on stage, always striving for a dazzling performance. And *Cry Blood* and *Killer in Silk* show Dixon at his best.

—Sacramento, CA
July 31, 2015

Donald S. Napoli has written hundreds of reviews for his blog, *Reading California Fiction*. He is also the author of *Architects of Adjustment*, a history of the American psychological profession.

Cry Blood

H. Vernor Dixon

Introduction

MAY 13, 3:00 P.M. When the bell rang at Bayside High School, on California State Highway No. 1, Diana B. Halloran, fourteen years old, left her seat in the Home Ec. classroom and started down the corridor toward Algebra I, her last class of the day. She was a leggy, medium-sized young girl, with an abundance of dark brown hair that hung about her shoulders, and a warm smile that had made her the most popular freshman in the school. More than one of the upper classmen turned to grin and nod at her. She giggled and hurried on, still more than a little self-conscious about the sudden womanly maturity that was overtaking her.

She was wearing brown and white saddle shoes, white bobby sox, a pleated skirt of Scottish plaid and a green cashmere sweater that had been reversed so that it buttoned in back. She had an Elgin watch on her left wrist, a recent present from her father for good grades, and also a gold charm bracelet, to which she was slowly adding new miniatures on important occasions. A tiny bow of yellow ribbon was tied about a lock of her hair just above the left temple.

What she was wearing that day soon became a matter of national interest.

3:12 P.M. Mr. Nathaniel Rigsby, prominent county rancher, entered the real-estate office of Baker & Allen on Surf Avenue, Bayside's main street. He was pleased to find young Gary Malone going over some papers at his desk by the front window. Gary was trying to make a name for himself as an architect, while making a living as a real-estate salesman, so that he was away from his desk most of the time. Mr. Rigsby remembered later that the young man seemed his usual self, restless, cheerful and full of spirit.

Mr. Rigsby owned a piece of property on Chinmen's Ridge, high up in the Santa Lucia Mountains, about thirty-five miles from Bayside, which he wanted to sell. The land was virtually without value, as there was not sufficient water for cattle, but there was a small cottage with a tremendous view out over the ocean that might have an appeal for sportsmen. There were large herds of deer in the vicinity, and also quail and some doves. Gary had promised before to have a look at the property, but had never found the time for it. On this occasion, however, he did have the time. He had no appointments for that day or the Saturday following and, besides, Ellen, his wife, had gone up to San Francisco to spend the weekend with her ailing mother. He promised Mr. Rigsby that he would leave at once and look the place over.

Mr. Rigsby suggested that he could spend the night at the cottage, if he pleased, as he used it himself now and then and kept it fully equipped. Gary considered the idea for a moment and nodded. It would be good to spend a night up in the mountains for a change. Give a man time to think things over. Mr.

Rigsby gave him the key to the cottage, shook hands and left the office.

Gary cleaned the papers from his desk and walked around the block to where his car was parked, a '53 Ford four-door black sedan. He drove to his home at the southwest corner of Bayside, one block from the ocean, where he raided the refrigerator and found enough food for dinner and breakfast. He placed it all in a cardboard box and then changed clothes.

3:25 P.M. Gary drove away from home in his Ford and headed up the incline of Surf Avenue toward the highway. Friends and acquaintances turned to smile and wave at him from the sidewalks and in passing cars. Gary was well known and well liked. Some of his friends noticed that he was wearing a red-checked sport shirt and an old suede jacket. He was also wearing short ten-inch boots with thick cleated rubber soles and dirty corduroy trousers stained with the blood and grime of dozens of bird hunts in the mountains and valleys.

What he was wearing that day also became a matter of national interest. His photogenic appearance, however, aroused even greater interest and unbridled curiosity. Gary was twenty-eight years old, he was almost six feet tall, his shoulders were broad, his hips were slim and he looked and carried himself like an athlete, which he was. He was top-ranking golfer at the Scenic Heights Country Club, he was an excellent tennis player and swimmer, and at college had been the light-heavyweight boxing champion. But of more interest to the press photographers were his ruggedly chiseled features: high cheekbones, a square jaw, thin, determined lips, piercing green eyes and ruddy complexion, all topped with thick, wiry, unruly auburn hair.

His features were soon known to almost every man, woman and child in the United States.

3:32 P.M. Students of the Bayside High School poured out of the classrooms and corridors and onto the walks and lawns of the grounds, Diana Halloran among them. She chatted for a moment with classmates on the stone veranda overlooking the broad valley to the south, then left them to walk toward the gym adjoining the football field. The classmates later remembered that she had been carrying four or five schoolbooks and a leather binder. Diana entered the gym, where some of the boys were practicing basketball, and went directly to her locker in the girls' section. She took out a pair of month-old shoes, which she intended cleaning over the weekend, and tucked them under her arm with the books. No one remembered her leaving the gym or the school grounds.

4:00 P.M. Diana had crossed the highway to the city limits of Bayside and had walked four blocks to the edge of a wooden ravine that angled down into the town. A well-used path ran down into the ravine, traveled along the bottom, then zigzagged up the other side to a diagonal street that was the beginning of the residential area known as Cliffside, on the north side of the town. She saw a friend of hers, a sophomore named Susan Engler, and stopped to talk with her for perhaps five minutes. Then she waved good-by and left. Susan watched her for a moment as she walked down into the ravine.

Diana Halloran was never again seen alive.

MAY 14, 11:35 A.M. Gary first heard of the missing girl on his way down from the mountains that Saturday. It was a hot day, so he stopped for a beer in the Gold Nugget bar at Valley Center, about twenty miles from Bayside. A number of customers were at the bar, all of them speculating on the girl's disappearance. When Gary overheard the girl's name he was deeply shocked. He had never seen Diana, to his knowledge, but he knew her father slightly and respected the man. He drove away from the bar in a thoughtful mood, wondering what could have happened to the girl.

7:30 P.M. Clarence Smith, a cowhand employed on the Kingsley Ranch, got out of his jalopy at Valley Center and approached the Gold Nugget bar for his usual Saturday night spree. He noticed a book lying on the ground, picked it up and took it into the bar. He handed it to the bartender and said, "Maybe one of your customers dropped it." The bartender opened the cover and saw the printed name inside: Diana B. Halloran. He stared at it incredulously for a full minute before turning to the telephone to call the county sheriff's office.

10:15 P.m. Gary Malone was one of the many men who joined the sheriff's posse to search the ravines and hills surrounding Valley Center. Diana was not found that might, nor did they find any trace of her during their thorough search.

Diana's disappearance was front-page news in the nation's press for a week or more for a number of reasons. Mrs. Halloran's hobby was photography, and the press had hundreds of excellent pictures of her daughter to print in the papers. Diana, herself, was good copy. She had been an honor student; she had been very popular and she had been physically matured.

The region was also good copy. Bayside, about one hundred miles south of San Francisco on the coast, was a nationally famous resort village adjoining the fabulously wealthy estate area of Scenic Heights, which was internationally famous for the great names of society residing there. Finally, Mr. George Halloran, Diana's father, was a prominent attorney who, only the month before, had won a law suit that had received national attention. All of this combined to interest the press, the wire services and the public.

But when May came to an end the last of the "foreign" reporters had left Bayside, and in June Diana's name was no longer found even in the local papers. Searches became desultory and then ended and July passed with no trace of the girl.

August 10. William Kraft, Chief of the Bayside Police, wrote on the face of the voluminous records concerning Diana B. Halloran: Disposition unknown. Case temporarily closed.

He sighed and put the records away in a filing cabinet. He noticed Sergeant Welte watching him and said defensively, "What the hell? We did our best. Maybe we'll never know what happened to that kid. But, by God, one of these days I'd sure like to get my hands on the guy—" He let the rest of it go unsaid.

Chapter One

In the late afternoon of the twenty-third of August, Gary Malone got out of his Ford in front of the Gold Nugget, stretched his arms and legs and combed his fingers back through his wiry auburn hair. He had spent the entire day looking about the old Kingsley Ranch—examining farm buildings, outbuildings, barns, corrals, cattle chutes and mechanical equipment—and he was tired and thirsty. One more day, he thought, and he would be through. Then the ranch could be listed and put up for sale at a quarter of a million dollars. He grinned as he thought of what the commission would be on a sale of that sort.

He brushed dust from his neat gabardine jacket and trousers and turned for a moment to look over Valley Center. It was not exactly a town, but a small collection of business establishments including two bars, two grocery stores and a butcher shop, a hardware store, a beauty shop and a Western-style diner, all in a row. A liquor store and, farther down the road, the adobe building of Boots and Saddles, a popular late spot for dining, drinking and dancing. The summer season was in full swing, so many of the cars parked in front of the various buildings had out-of-state licenses. Others were from Bayside, people temporarily escaping the coastal fogs for the dry heat of the valley.

For the past few years, Gary had had a hand in the development of the valley. He had sold and resold some of the homes, he had been the architect on some of the newer ones, and he had become a specialist in the sale of ranch properties. He regarded the valley as his private baby.

He stamped dust from his moccasins and walked into the Gold Nugget. It was a small room of knotty pine, highly polished, with a bar and mirrors at one wall, a few booths opposite and a circular fireplace at the end of the room. All of the furnishings and decorations were Western, and the bartender-owner wore Western riding clothes with high-heeled boots. He wore them, however, only in the bar, for the titillation of tourists. Herb wouldn't mount a horse for love of money.

Gary nodded at Herb and saw that all the stools at the bar were taken except one at the far end. He slid onto the empty stool, ordered a bottle of beer and watched Herb pour it. The bartender was middle-aged, with thinning blond hair, a bulbous nose and the beginnings of a paunch. The tourists at the bar had been irritating him with their endless questions about the country, but he grinned happily at Gary. He was fond of the younger man and liked especially the bonuses Gary passed on to him whenever Herb gave him a tip on available realty property.

He shoved the full glass and the half-empty bottle toward Gary and leaned his elbows on the bar. "How goes it?" he asked.

Gary drank the glass of beer down without pause, sighed and wiped the back of his hand across his mouth. He poured the rest of the beer into the glass, then looked across at Herb. "Okay," he said. "I've been looking over the Kingsley spread."

"Think you can sell it?"

Gary shrugged. "Who knows? But I think the price is right. Man," he chuckled, "what a fat commission that would be. Biggest thing I've sold so far was that old Beston place for eighty-five grand."

"The one on the hill. Yeah, I gave you that lead." Herb scratched his head, frowned and said, "That Kingsley Ranch, now. Wasn't that cowhand who found the girl's schoolbook out front here from the Kingsley spread?"

"The Halloran girl? Sure. Clarence Smith was his name."

"You got a good memory."

"Good, hell. I got a lousy memory. But I'll never forget anything about that case. I went out with the posse to search for her. And, besides, what else could you read in the papers the next couple of weeks?"

"That's right. I wonder what ever did happen to her?"

Gary finished his beer and ordered another bottle. He drank the second one more slowly than the first, savoring every drop in his parched throat. His green eyes stared thoughtfully into space for a long moment, then he said, "I think it's easy to figure out. The kid was well built for her age, and she always took that same route home from school, down through the ravine. Some sex deviate got wise to her habits—"

"You mean a pervert?"

"Uh-huh. They come in all sizes, Herb. Anyway, this guy intercepted her in the ravine, probably knocked her out and took her up the valley. I suppose he had a car around somewhere."

"You don't think he attacked her and killed her in the ravine?"

"No. The cops made a thorough search down there. They didn't find anything. Not one clue. I think she was taken up here somewhere."

Herb sighed and said, "I don't imagine there's any chance she's still alive."

"Good Lord, no. The kid was probably killed the day she was kidnaped. A funny thing, you know, I was having a beer here with you when it happened. The last time she was seen was about four o'clock on the thirteenth. I was on my way up to Chinamen's Ridge that day and stopped here just about that time for a beer. Maybe," he mused, "if I had been on the road a little later I might have seen them. Who knows what would have happened then?"

Another customer called for Herb and he walked to the other end of the bar. Gary sat there until he had finished his beer, then waved to Herb and walked out. By the time he reached his car he had forgotten about the kidnap case and was considering ways and means of selling the Kingsley ranch.

He drove slowly down the valley toward the coast, appraising the new homes under construction on either side of the road and up in the hills. Santa Isabel was the actual name of the long valley that wound its tortuous way up into the mountains, but no one ever referred to it as anything other than simply the valley. Deer grazed in the meadows and under the oaks, coveys of quail darted across the road, steelheads and trout were found in the Puma River, hawks rode the convection currents overhead and occasionally a mountain lion roamed through the valley on its way to the mountain fastnesses to the south. It was a sportsmen's paradise, yet it was also a valley of many resorts, dude ranches, hotels, roadhouses, farms, working cattle ranches, small estates and a thousand or more ranch-type homes. Coastal fogs that plagued Bayside and other towns during the summer months almost never penetrated the valley. The weather was usually as beautiful as the scenery, so the valley was growing fast. Gary hoped that one day, when he sold his home in Bayside, he would be able to build another far up the valley. Ellen was the catch in that dream. Ellen couldn't stand the valley.

"My God, Gary, live up there with all those hicks? Not on your life," she always said.

Gary left the valley at Highway 1, passed the high school and turned down the hill into Bayside. He saw a bank of gray fog out over the ocean, but the village of about seven thousand people, built among the pines, was bathed in late-afternoon sunshine. As he started down the hill Gary could see over the tops of the trees to the fabulous section of Scenic Heights and its many golf courses and to the exclusive residential area of Cliffside, where Diana Halloran had lived. Gary shuddered as he thought of the girl, and he put her out of his mind.

The beer had refreshed him and Gary was no longer tired. He whistled tunelessly as he drove down Surf Avenue, lined on either side with shops catering principally to tourists. During the three years he had resided in Bayside, Gary had come to feel almost as if he had lived there all his life. He liked the atmosphere, the scenery, the people, and everything else about the area. In Korea he had often dreamed of a place such as Bayside, without knowing that it actually existed. He had discovered it only when he married Ellen in San Francisco and she had informed him that Bayside was a favorite spot in Northern California for honeymooners. He was in the town hardly an hour when he made up his mind never to leave it. He adopted Bayside then and there, and Bayside adopted him.

Gary noticed hundreds of tourists in their shorts and slacks and sandals and bandanas and new vacation clothes as he drove down the main street. He had to park two blocks away and walk back to the realty office on Surf Avenue. All the employees had left for the day, but Mr. Theodore Baker was at his desk near the front windows winding up some late business. His partner, Allen, had died some years before, and Baker himself had had a slight heart attack during the past summer. He was still active in the business, but he was taking it easy and looking forward to the day when he could retire and devote all his time to the gardens of his estate in Scenic Heights—at which point, he had already made up his mind, he intended turning the business over to young Malone. Baker was a tall, spare man with a bald head fringed with gray hair, cadaverous cheeks, shrewd gray eyes, and lips that were always pressed tightly together as if in pain. He was rarely known to smile, yet Gary often made him burst into laughter. Gary was also the only person on the peninsula who called the older man Ted.

Gary nodded at him and threw a handful of papers onto his desk next to Baker's. "That's about it," he said. He crossed to Baker's desk and sat on the edge as he lit a cigarette. "One more day and I'll have it cleaned up. That's the only trouble with these ranch properties, there's so damned much paper work involved."

Baker rasped his throat clear and asked, "Got any leads to sell the place?"

"One. Man and his wife named Colgate. Texans."

"Well, if you need any help, call on me."

"Sure thing, Ted. Anything new in the pot?"

"Nope. Better run along. You know how Ellen is about the dinner hour."

A faint suggestion of a frown crossed Gary's face. Ted was so right. Ellen had a lot of queer ideas, the dinner hour being one of them. She'd make him wear a dinner jacket, if she thought she could get away with it. As it was, he had to be home never later than six, shave and shower and change clothes and mix exactly three rounds of 5-1 Martinis. Dinner was served promptly at 7:30. Not a minute sooner or later. With candles on the table.

"Yeah," he said. "Well, I'll see you in the morning." He started toward the door, but paused to look back at his boss. "By the way, how's Teddy getting along?"

Baker leaned back and drummed his fingers on the desk. "The boy's in Georgia now. He's getting his transitional training in jets." He glanced sharply at Gary and said anxiously, "You were a jet pilot. Tell me the truth. Are those things dangerous to fly?"

Gary chuckled and shook his head. "Believe me, Ted, they're pushovers. Riding a stovepipe is the easiest kind of flying. Don't worry about the kid."

"I don't know much about this jet age—"

"Stop worrying. I'll tell you what. You and the missus drop over to the house tomorrow night and I'll give you the lowdown on what jet flying is all about. Okay?"

"Thanks. It would be a help to know."

Baker got up from his desk, put an arm about Gary's shoulder and walked with him to the door. "I almost forgot to tell you. I saw Halloran today."

"Diana's father?"

"Yes. It must be a terrible thing to be in that man's shoes. They have two other children, you know, a boy and a girl, but Diana was always George's favorite. This tragedy has almost killed him. He's lost weight; he looks twenty years older, and you just can't get him to smile about anything. Today is the first day he's been downtown since it happened."

"It's lousy, all right. And the hell of it is, he knows in the back of his mind that the kid was undoubtedly raped and beaten and probably worse before she was killed. Cases like that—these sex crimes against children—we should take a lesson from the Chinese. When you catch the man he should be spread-eagled and tied down over a patch of growing bamboo. And even that would be too good for him."

Baker ran his hands slowly up and down his face and shook his head. "I don't know, Gary. I've lived long enough to know that there's no such thing as sexual normalcy. Deviations can take a million different directions, some harmless and others cruel and savage. Naturally, we try to curb savagery in all its forms, but I really don't think there's any way to stamp it out when it appears in the sex deviate."

"You gotta do something. You just can't let characters like that run loose."

"No. That's true. Unfortunately, what we can do occurs only after a crime has been committed. We don't yet know of a sensible preventative and I don't think there is one. As long as there are people, sexual deviation is something we have to live with, like weather."

"That's sort of hopeless."

"And so are people." Baker slapped him on the shoulder and shoved him toward the door. "You better run along."

"Yeah. Good night, Ted."

Gary walked back to his car and drove down Surf Avenue to a cypress-lined road that wound along the edge of the sparkling white beach. Taking that route home was a few blocks out of his way, but he enjoyed looking out over the ocean and filling his lungs with the sharp, salt air. Two freighters were dimly visible at the edge of the fog bank far out at sea, and closer inshore a sailboat was beating its way to the north. One day, he thought—but rather hopelessly—he would have his own boat. A ranch home in the valley and a sailboat in the bay— that would be real living. Ellen, however, had no liking for boats.

He left the beach road to swing around the block onto his own street, and grinned with satisfaction as he approached his home. He had designed it himself three years before, and had helped to build a large part of it with his own hands. It was a modern house of horizontal redwood siding, a slanting shed roof that gave it a studio appearance, a long deck across the front and a half-deck at one side, and a fireplace wall of narrow, used brick. There was a patio in back that he had been working on the past few months, a brick barbecue with a protective shed roof and, at one side, an overlarge two-car garage with a workshop in the rear. The land in that area had originally been sand dunes, and so the house was built on a shallow slope with a basement running from front to rear. Access to the basement was had by a door in back and another in front next to the garage. Neither was ever locked.

Gary was proud of his home, but there was one thing wrong with it, which was why Ellen had prevailed upon him to put it up for sale. The house had been designed with children in mind. What would have been a large second bedroom had been divided into two smaller rooms with built-in bunks and closets scaled for small children. Gary had never had the heart to rebuild the rooms. Even the bathroom had a second and lower wash basin for children, all door knobs had been placed lower than usual, and the kitchen refrigerator had been built within a sort of platform so that children could get their own cold drinks. All of which had become useless detail in the home when the surgeon had informed Gary, the year after they had been married, that Ellen would never have children.

He felt again now as he had on that day, but grunted and shook the gloom from his mind as he turned into the open garage. He was whistling as he got out of the car, tucked a package under his arm and turned on the lawn sprinklers while crossing toward the front door. Ellen was in the living room, arranging a bowl of flowers by a side window. She gave Gary a brief smile, but looked hungrily at the package he was carrying. He handed her the present, a new blouse she had seen in a shop window the Sunday before, then kissed her cheek and stepped back with a smile to watch her open the package. She smiled with proper appreciation when she saw the blouse, and returned his kiss. Gary sighed. He had learned long ago that Ellen had the attitude of a child toward receiving presents. He had to bring home something—the item itself was not important— at least two or three times a week, or Ellen would go into one of her long pouts. On the other hand, any sort of present would keep her happy, at least for a few hours.

Gary watched her as she turned the blouse about, examining it critically from every angle, looking for flaws. He thought again of how lucky he was having a wife like Ellen. She was Gary's age, yet her skin was so clear and her features were so lacking in any sort of lines that she seemed hardly to be in her twenties. Strange bartenders often refused to serve her, thinking she was underage, which never failed to delight her. Her long, fine hair was straw-blonde, her large eyes were as deep and blue as a child's, her small teeth were so white they seemed almost unreal and the pink lipstick she used blended exactly with the polish on her long nails. There was rarely any expression on her face other than a light smile or a petulant frown. She was convinced that emotions aged a woman, so she kept a careful rein on hers. She was intensely vain about her figure, a vanity not altogether misplaced. She was of medium height, but she was so slim that she seemed much taller. Her legs were long and slim and delicately rounded, she had the firm breasts of a young girl, and her narrow waist, the envy of all her friends, was exactly nineteen inches.

Gary turned away to head for the bedroom, but she called after him, "Put on your clan tartan jacket, darling. We're having guests for dinner."

Gary hated the silly jacket, but mumbled, "O kay. Who's coming?"

"Luke and Betty."

Gary brightened. Luke Summer was his closest friend in Bayside, and his wife was also Ellen's closest friend. Ellen would probably insist on a few hours of bridge after dinner, as usual, but Gary figured he would be able to get together with Luke before the evening was over to plan a hunting trip in the Santa Lucias. Luke had been born and raised in the Bayside area, and knew all the choice locations on the mountains where deer were to be found.

Gary went into the bedroom, an almost aggressively feminine room that Ellen had decorated, and hurried out of his clothes, which he placed carefully in the closet. He shaved and was singing in the shower when he heard Ellen calling him. He could not hear what she was saying until he had turned off the shower and was toweling himself. He opened the bathroom door a crack and said, "Sorry, baby, I couldn't hear you."

He had a glimpse of Ellen shrugging her arms into the new blouse as she spoke over her shoulder: "The gym shoes," she said. "I was telling you about the gym shoes. Couldn't you hear me?"

"The shower was running."

"Then turn it off."

"It is off. What were you saying about shoes?"

"The gym shoes I found in the basement."

He had no idea what she was talking about, so he said simply, "Oh?"

"Down there between two boxes," she said. "Do you know about them?"

He finished drying himself, slipped into a pair of shorts—nudity shocked Ellen—and stepped into the bedroom. He got a clean shirt out of the bureau and said, "You better start from the beginning, baby. I don't know anything about shoes in the basement."

She appraised herself in the full-length mirror of the bathroom door and was satisfied that the new blouse went well with the black toreador hostess slacks she was wearing. Her figure looked more youthful than ever. She glanced at Gary and wrinkled her nose with distaste at sight of the curling mass of red hairs on his chest. The whiteness of his skin was also distasteful to her. The fact that it was impossible for his skin to tan she considered as a rather personal affront. He could at least try.

She sighed with exasperation and said, "You just don't listen."

"The shower—"

"Anyway," she interrupted, "I was down in the basement this afternoon looking for that recipe book Mother gave me last Christmas. I didn't think much of it at the time, but when I was talking to Betty today she said something about this wonderful cookbook and I remembered that was the one mother gave me. So I went looking for it and found these shoes."

She paused, as if that seemed to explain everything. Gary finished buttoning his shirt, slipped into a pair of charcoal-gray slacks and gave Ellen a baffled glance. "Oh?"

"Yes. They were wedged down in between two of the boxes. Girls' gym shoes, the kind they wear in high school."

Gary was more baffled than ever and continued playing it safe. "Oh?"

"I haven't had a pair of shoes like that in, my goodness, ten years or more. Anyway, they look very new and they're not my size. Now, how on earth did they get down there in the basement? You didn't put them there, did you?"

"What the devil would I be doing with girls' gym shoes? Where are they?"

"In that closet by the front door. I put them there so you can give them to the Salvation Army, or somebody."

"I'll have a look at them. How did they get in the basement, if they aren't yours?"

"That's what I've been asking you."

He chuckled and said, "You've found me out. I wear them when I go to fairy drags."

"Oh, don't be an ass. I detest humor of that sort."

"Sure, baby."

She glared at him and said slowly, "And stop calling me baby. I think that's a frightful habit of yours."

"Sure, sure. Sorry."

She went into the front room and Gary knotted his tie and shrugged his broad shoulders into a jacket of green and blue plaid. Such jackets were apparently the fashion for hosts, but Gary felt that the idea belonged more in Hollywood than in Bayside. He dutifully put it on, however, and tucked a silk handkerchief into the pocket. Actually, with his coloring, the jacket looked very good on him and made his rugged features appear almost handsome. Gary wasn't aware of it.

He walked to the closet by the front door and looked down at the shoes on the floor without picking them up. They were white canvas with thick, black rubber soles and circular pieces of leather at the ankles. Gary stared down at them and scratched his head. They were ordinary gym shoes, a type with which he had been familiar in his own high-school days, but he had never seen that particular pair before. He wondered how they had got in the Malone basement and could find no answer. Well, anyway, the Salvation Army, or somebody could use them.

He went back to the gadget-filled kitchen and proceeded to mix a pitcher of dry Martinis. Ellen was at the sink arranging a plate of hors d'oeuvres, so he asked her, "You say you found them in the basement?"

"What?"

"The gym shoes."

"In the basement, yes. They were on the dirt, sort of wedged in between two boxes. Which reminds me. When are you going to pave that basement floor?"

"Why go to all that trouble when we have the place up for sale?"

"It's so messy, though, all that sand down there."

"Yeah, I know. I thought—" He caught himself just in time and fell silent. What he was going to say was that he had thought a sandy basement would be a good place for kids to play on rainy days. Ever since the operation, any mention of children had been taboo in the Malone household. He continued stirring the pitcher of Martinis, staring vacantly into space.

The Summers arrived and were served Martinis in the living room. Luke was a few years older than Gary, with a wiry, compact physique and a deceptively lazy appearance. He had black wavy hair, warm brown eyes and a smooth olive complexion. He was well over a head taller than his wife, a diminutive, rather chubby young woman who seemed to be made up entirely of soft curves, smiles, lace and bows. She wore her dark brown hair cut in the Italian style about her small head, but spoiled the effect with a small bow tied to a lock of hair that dangled over her forehead.

The Summers had been the first people the Malones met when they arrived in Bayside on their honeymoon. It was Luke who had introduced Gary around the town, got him the job with Baker and Allen, helped him select the lot for their home, sponsored him for membership in the country club and gave him the leads for his first few realty sales. Ellen had been a bit reserved toward the Summers the first few months, but when she realized that Betty offered no competition whatever, and also learned that the Summers were wealthy, with an unassailable social position, she thawed out quickly. The four had become close friends.

They chatted about local gossip, drank their Martinis, had dinner by candlelight, in spite of the fact that the sun had yet to wane, and then sat about a card table in the living room to play bridge. Gary liked to talk, as did Luke, but Ellen insisted on total concentration in their bridge sessions, so the two men suffered silently through the game. Betty also preferred conversation and especially something to laugh about, but inasmuch as the simplest kind of card playing was an effort for her she was forced to concentrate, like it or not.

The game came to an end at eleven o'clock. Gary and Luke wandered out to the kitchen, where they sneaked a couple of quick shots and planned a hunting trip for the following month. They could hear the women talking in the other room, and then Betty calling that it was time to leave. When they joined the women Gary noticed that Ellen was showing the strange gym shoes to Betty.

Ellen was telling her, "It's very queer. They aren't mine and Gary's never seen them before."

Betty stared at the shoes with a rare frown. "They were in the basement?"

"Between two boxes. I simply can't understand who would have left them there."

Luke asked her, "What's this all about?"

Ellen explained once again as Luke walked to the front closet and got his hat. He returned and took the shoes from Ellen to examine them more closely. "Not too old," he said. "They don't look to me as if they'd even had their first cleaning. Small size, too. Maybe some kid was playing in your basement—"

Ellen shook her head. "That I doubt very much. We don't lock the basement doors, but I've never known any children to go in there without permission. I'm bewildered. I just can't think of any logical explanation for their being there. Can you?"

Luke shrugged, still examining the shoes. Gary was getting tired of hearing about them and said, "Look, baby; we'll just give them to the Salvation Army, and that takes care of that. Here. I'll put them back in the closet."

He reached for them, but Luke said, "Wait a minute. I can see some sort of initials stenciled down near the soles." He walked to a bright lamp, held the shoes close to the light and mumbled, "Yeah. They're inked in. DBH. See, here, Ellen? Under the light you can see the initials very well."

Ellen crossed to his side and peered at the initials. "DBH," she said. "Funny I didn't notice that before."

"Well, they're down so close to the soles." He grinned and handed the shoes to Ellen. "Now, all you have to do is think of someone with those initials and your mystery is solved. Simple. All you need in this household is old Sherlock Summer. Do you know anyone with the initials DBH?"

All four were silent for a moment, looking questioningly at each other and away and back again. Betty broke the silence by saying, "Wouldn't it be terrible if—" But she caught her breath sharply, her words came to a halt, and one hand rose slowly to her mouth.

Ellen, too, had thought of the same thing at the same time. She stared at Betty, then sat down slowly on the nearest chair. "No," she whispered. "Oh, my God, no. It can't be. It simply can't be."

Betty had recovered her breath and said quickly, "But it's the same, Ellen. Identically the same."

Luke glanced from one to the other and said, "Okay, you two. I'm damned if I know how a woman's mind works, but there's some sort of rapport between the two of you. Now, what gives?"

Ellen glanced oddly at Gary and said, "Those initials, darling. Don't they mean anything to you?"

He shrugged and frowned at her. "Should they?"

"You were on the posse that searched for her. Do you think it's possible? Do you really— My God, Gary, they're the same initials as the missing girl, Diana B. Halloran. And she was taking gym shoes home that day. I remember. I read it in the papers."

Gary and Luke stared at each other, as stunned and shocked as the two women. Gary took the shoes from his wife's lap and examined the initials, and turned the shoes over and over in his hand, blinking at them with stupefaction. It was a long moment before the shock wore off and he shook his head.

"It's a fabulous coincidence," he said, "but like the man says, it ain't necessarily so. How in God's name could that kid's shoes get into our basement? I can't buy that at all. In the first place, we don't even know the girl, and in the second place, she wouldn't be going by here on her way home. After all, Cliffside is clear over on the other side of town. Strictly a coincidence."

Luke cleared his throat and said, "A damned queer one, though."

"Yeah. You can say that again. Sort of gives me goose pimples even thinking about it." He put the shoes on a low coffee table and scratched his head. "Now, I wonder who else—"

Ellen sucked in her breath sharply, exhaled slowly and said, "There's only one thing to do."

Betty completed the thought for her: "Call the police."

"Yes. They would know and we don't."

Gary grumbled, "Aw, now, wait a minute. Take it easy. Let's think this thing over. It's easy to call the police, but sometimes it's a lot tougher to get rid of them. Suppose we sleep on it? Tomorrow I'll get a city directory and see if anyone in this neighborhood has the last initial H. Then—"

Ellen cut him off by getting to her feet and stating flatly, "I'm going to call the police now. You may be able to sleep on it, but I can't. I wouldn't be able to close my eyes all night, thinking—well, you know—maybe they're hers and— No. Either you call the police, Gary Malone, or I will."

Luke chewed at his lower lip, nodded and said, "She's right, Gary. Maybe it's a coincidence, like you say, but if it isn't you got hold of something mighty serious here."

Gary thought, What a way to end a pleasant evening, but he had to agree with the others. It could be serious.

Luke said, "Better call Bill Kraft, the chief. You know him?"

Gary nodded. "I see him practically every day. Nice guy. He's the one to call, all right—if—well—"

The telephone was in the short hallway between the living room and bedrooms. Gary looked up the number of the police station, called and got a Sergeant Welte on duty. He was informed that the chief was at home. Gary called Kraft's home number, got one of the children, and a moment later was talking to Kraft.

"Gary Malone calling," he said. "Hope I didn't get you out of bed."

He heard a loud yawn and then Kraft said, "You did. Family's up, though. They're watching television. What's on your mind? I hope it's serious," he chuckled, "or, by God, I'll give you a parking ticket tomorrow for getting me out of the sack."

"Well, Bill—" He turned to glance at Luke and the two women watching him tensely, then said, "I hardly know how to begin. My wife found some gym shoes in our basement—"

"And you're calling—"

"Now, wait a minute. If I remember correctly, the day the Halloran girl disappeared she was taking some gym shoes home with her. Right?"

"Well—uh—yes, I believe so. Yes, that's right."

"The shoes my wife found are girl's gym shoes. They're not very old. Down near the soles on each one is inked in the initials DBH. The shoes are strange to us. We've never seen them before. We were thinking—"

Kraft was suddenly wide awake, and asked sharply, "DBH? You're positive?"

"Yes. The initials are small; you need light to see them, but they're clear. DBH. I'm positive."

"And you found them where?"

"In our basement. Ellen—you know my wife—"

"Sure. I see her around."

"She found them. Says they were wedged in between two boxes."

Kraft's voice became even sharper. "You're calling from home?"

"Yes."

"You have the shoes there?"

"Right here."

"Don't touch them again. Hear me? Don't handle them. I'll get dressed and pick up Welte at the station and be right over."

"Our house—"

"I know where you live. On my way in a minute. You wait."

The line went dead and Gary replaced the phone slowly in its cradle. He sat there staring at the wall for a moment, trying to organize his thoughts, but Ellen wanted to know what Kraft had had to say. Gary got to his feet and repeated the whole conversation. He noticed, as he was talking, that Betty was getting restless and was glancing nervously at Luke. For a woman who was always smiling or laughing about something, she seemed suddenly very grim.

As soon as Gary finished, Betty took Luke's arm and said anxiously, "We'll run along, dear. We can hear all about it later." She attempted to smile at Ellen, but failed. "You'll let us know, won't you?"

Luke scowled at her and growled, "This is no time to leave."

She tugged at his arm and cried, "But it's late."

"I don't give a damn how late it is. I'd like to hear what Bill has to say about those shoes."

She fairly screamed at him, "Luke Summer, how can you be such a fool? Do you know what will happen if those shoes really belong to that girl? Do you want our names in the mess? For heaven's sake, Luke, use your head."

Luke understood and the color receded a bit from his olive complexion. "Jees," he mumbled. "I hadn't thought. Say, Gary, how about that? Betty's right. Maybe we had better run along. We didn't find the shoes. We didn't have anything to do with them. You can tell Bill everything he needs to know without us."

Gary bit his lip and ran his hands over his face. "Yeah, I guess so. I wish you'd stick around, though. I'm beginning to feel kind of queer about the whole thing."

Luke glanced pleadingly at his wife; he felt suddenly that if he left he would be running out on his friend. But Betty was tugging fiercely at his arm. He snapped at her with exasperation, "All right, for God's sake. Hold your horses. We'll go." Then he asked Gary, "You'll call me as soon as you've talked with Bill?"

"Sure. I'll let you know."

"Well, then—I guess—Thanks for the dinner, Ellen. Very nice."

He had more to say, but Betty's face had turned almost white and her fingers were biting into his arm. Luke glanced at Gary as if to say, "What can a guy do?" but turned away and followed Betty out the front door. A moment later their car drove away.

Gary looked at Ellen, who was standing rigidly on one spot, frowning thoughtfully, staring into space. He walked by her and went into the kitchen, where he mixed two double highballs in short glasses. He drank his, standing at the kitchen sink, looked at the other and drank that, then mixed two more. He carried them into the living room. Ellen was now seated on the couch, staring fixedly at the white canvas shoes on the coffee table.

Her eyes turned slowly and up to stare with fascination at her husband. After a moment she cleared her throat and asked huskily, but so softly that he could hardly hear, "Gary, did you know that girl?"

Chapter Two

Gary handed a glass to his wife and crossed the room to stand for a moment looking out the windows at the dark street. He could not see beyond the radius of the glow cast on the lawn by the porch light. He thought, Light would be shed on everything when Kraft arrived.

He turned back and dropped into a chair facing Ellen, his features partly in shadow and partly lighted by the yellow glow of a lamp at his elbow. Ellen's face was fully in the light and so he noticed her intent expression and wondered about it.

"Diana?" he said. "No, I don't think I ever knew the kid. I've probably seen her around town, without knowing who it was. Why do you ask?"

"You know her father."

"Just casually. Everyone around here knows George Halloran. I used to see him out at the club now and then, before the tragedy. Famous guy as an attorney, you know, but democratic. Nice person."

Ellen persisted, "You never saw him with his daughter?"

"I'm darned if I know. He has two other children, too, a boy and a girl. Diana was the oldest. I don't remember seeing him with any of the kids, and I'm positive I never met any of them." He sipped at his drink and cocked an eyebrow at her. "Why do you keep asking that?"

The intensity of whatever was bothering Ellen faded and her face was again a smooth mask. She took a swallow of her drink, made a face and shoved the glass aside on the low table, next to the shoes. "Nothing," she said. "Nothing. When do you think the police will get here?"

"Soon, I hope. I'd like this cleared up. The idea of those shoes belonging to that kid is ridiculous. It would be impossible for anything belonging to her to wind up in our basement. It's as if something of mine turned up in Alaska, where I've never been in my life."

"It could happen, though. Anything can happen."

"Oh, nonsense. Cripes, let's talk about something else. This whole stupid deal is getting me jittery."

He got to his feet, switched on the radio and tuned in to a platter program playing popular records of the late twenties and early thirties. Gary grinned happily and stood there leaning on the console radio sipping at his drink and listening to the music. He disliked virtually all current musical hits and was convinced that all good danceable, singable music had died in the Depression. He had once started a collection of early records, but Ellen had not liked them, so that project had come to an end.

Gary didn't blame Ellen for the many things she disliked; he blamed himself. Her womanhood had been thwarted and he knew she was living under a daily strain. Any woman would react in the same way, and perhaps even more so. If only he hadn't been in such a hurry to have children.

Ellen had not wanted children right away. She had wanted security first and some measure of success. Perhaps, too, she had been afraid of losing her figure; Gary had never been quite sure about the latter. But Gary was a born family man and possessed a deep hunger for children of his own. So, in spite of Ellen's desires in the matter, she became pregnant. Gary remembered, still with a sense of shock, how she had reacted to that condition, with pain and tears and hysteria. She had not been able to eat or sleep and in a very few weeks her weight had dropped from a hundred and twelve pounds to eighty-nine.

Ellen's condition had alarmed her doctor and Gary was told that if the situation continued he would lose both wife and child. She was fast losing even sufficient strength to carry a child. The fetus was not yet viable, so the doctor had suggested that it be legally aborted. After a great deal of soul-searching, and a running battle with Ellen, Gary had agreed.

What should have been the simplest kind of operation turned into a nightmare. Ellen's womb had burst on the operating table. Gary learned later that such a freak happening would occur perhaps once out of a hundred thousand or more operations. It was so rare, in fact, that Ellen's doctor had not known what to do about it and had lost his head. Fortunately, there had been another surgeon in the hospital at the time who knew what should be done and so he had taken over. He managed to perform a successful, even miraculous, operation. Ellen hovered between life and death for weeks, but her will was greater than her surface appearance would indicate, and gradually she recovered. In a matter of months she was back to normal, her health recovered and her figure preserved.

The surgeon who had operated, however, had known that the scar would be a point of weakness for a long time to come. The walls would not be capable of distension. Another pregnancy in the too-near future would obviously be fatal for Ellen. So the surgeon had tied off the tubes. Ellen was no longer capable of having children.

Gary had despised himself ever since the operation and so he had become more than normally gentle with Ellen and acquiescent in her wishes and desires. If only, he thought bitterly, he hadn't been so damned anxious to get started on a family of little Malones.

He sighed and had started walking away from the radio to freshen his drink when he heard a car pull up in front of the house. He glanced out the window and saw the red light blinking, so he opened the front door. The huge form of the chief of Bayside police came striding up the walk into the light. He had taken off his hat to scratch his head and looked like a classic Viking; six feet four inches tall, two hundred and forty pounds of hard muscle, hair so blond it was almost white, pink skin and blue eyes and hands like sledge hammers.

He turned to call back in the direction of the squad car, "Get the lead out, Hank," then came on up the walk and shook hands with Gary. "Evening, Gary."

"Hiya, Bill. Sorry I had to get you out of bed."

"Hell, Gary, cops are like doctors. We never know when we'll be called, except that it always happens when we're eating dinner, or in bed, or enjoying a good show. Now, you're sure about those initials on the shoes?"

"Oh, yes. Frankly, I don't think—"

"Skip that. Let's have a look."

"Sure. Come on in."

He left the front door open and led the way into the house and introduced Bill Kraft to Ellen. She acknowledged the introduction, but stared at him and had nothing else to say. Gary waved a hand toward the white gym shoes on the low table.

Kraft asked, "You haven't handled them again since you called me?"

"No."

"Good boy. How many people have handled them all told?"

"Well, I have and Ellen, of course, and Luke Summer."

"Was he here?"

"He and Betty, for dinner."

"Uh-huh. Did she handle them, too?"

"I don't think so." He asked Ellen, "Did she?"

Ellen shrugged. "I don't remember. I don't think so, though."

Kraft squatted down on his heels by the shoes and said, "Well, not more than the four of you, anyway. Narrows the field."

Gary heard someone else enter the living room and turned to face Sergeant Henry Welte, known to the members of the police force as Hank, but known to everyone else in Bayside as a cold-blooded robot who would arrest his own grandmother. He had been on the force for eighteen years and had assumed that one day he would be chief. Kraft had blasted that hope when he had been hired from out of town, so Welte had a deep resentment for the younger man.

Kraft called to him, "Come here and take a look, Hank."

The sergeant squatted down with him. He took a handkerchief from his pocket and lifted the shoes by the edges of their soles so that he and Kraft could better examine them. Welte pointed to the initials and grunted, "DBH. They belong to the kid, all right. No doubt of that."

Kraft turned his head and looked at the sergeant with an amused twinkle in his blue eyes. "There could be plenty of doubt about it, Hank. She wasn't the only person in the world with those initials. Could even be some other kid in town with the same initials."

Gary said, "That's what I've been saying, Bill. It's an utter impossibility for that poor kid's shoes to get in our basement."

Kraft straightened and faced Gary. "Now you're going overboard, too, like Hank. I've seen a lot of so-called impossible things." He turned to the sergeant and told him, "Wrap them up in some newspaper. I don't want any more handling."

Ellen handed a newspaper to the sergeant. He wrapped it around the shoes and replaced them on the low table. Kraft then asked Ellen how she had found the shoes, and she explained in detail.

Kraft wanted to see the exact place, so the four went out the front door and across the lawn to the basement door near the garage. They had to stoop to enter and, inside, had to remain stooping. Gary flicked a switch and a bare bulb flooded the basement with light. It was a long room that ran the full length of the house from front to rear, but was only about ten feet wide. Nothing had been finished and all joists, beams, pyramid foundations and underpinning were exposed. The floor was simply hard-packed sand. Trunks, boxes and empty barrels were stacked to one side. Piles of old magazines were in one corner. Gary's fishing and hunting equipment hung from a number of nails. The basement had never been meant as a storeroom, but it was well filled.

Ellen showed Kraft where she had found the shoes, between two grocer's cardboard boxes about seven feet in from the front door. Kraft paced off the exact distance and jotted it down in a small notebook he carried. He also made a rough pencil sketch of the basement and the placement of the more prominent objects.

When they went out it was Kraft who closed the basement door and noticed the absence of a lock. He asked Gary, "Don't you even padlock it?"

Gary passed around a package of cigarettes and held the match for the others. He took a deep drag of his own, then shook his head. "Never felt the need to lock it up."

"You got some pretty expensive sporting stuff in there."

"Cripes, Bill, you know how it is in Bayside. We don't even lock the house doors."

"Yeah, I know. Not many burglaries in this town. Anyway, anyone who wanted to could go in your basement with no trouble."

"I guess they could. But I don't know why anyone would want to."

"Getting rid of those shoes could be a damned good reason."

"But why in there? I don't mean to tell you your job, Bill, but that idea is silly. Just suppose the guy who kidnaped the kid is someone I know, or someone who lives right in this neighborhood. They're the only two possibilities you can consider. But it still doesn't make sense. The sensible way to get rid of those shoes would be to burn them in an incinerator, dump them in the ocean, or bury them in some remote spot, each one easy to do. Even a moron would do it that way. Leaving them in a basement, any basement, is practically begging for someone to discover them sooner or later. That's why I don't think they're Diana's. I'd be willing to bet ten to one we'll find out they belong to someone else."

Sergeant Welte glanced at Kraft and said flatly, "I'll give ten to one they're the kid's."

Kraft shrugged. "Let's find out."

Ellen led the way back into the house and pointed out the telephone to the chief. He knew the Halloran telephone number as well as his own and dialed it automatically. After a long wait, a maid answered the call. She was reluctant to wake the Hallorans, even after she knew it was the chief of police calling, but she finally consented.

After another long wait, Kraft heard George Halloran's sleepy voice on the wire. "Bill? What's up?" he asked.

"Sorry to disturb you, George, but something important has come up."

"This time of night?"

"Yeah. Is the missus in bed?"

"She is, but she's awake. Why?"

"I'm dropping by in a few minutes. I have something I want the two of you to take a look at."

"Perhaps if you could tell me—"

"I'll see you soon enough. But turn on the porch light, will you? I almost broke my neck on that path of yours one night. See you in a couple of minutes."

"Very well,"

Kraft turned back into the living room and was lost in thought for a few moments. After a while he glanced narrowly at Ellen, then turned his attention to Gary. "It's possible," he said, "that those shoes are really Diana's. The odds favor it, regardless of logic. If they are, it will mean the biggest break we've had in this case. It will also mean that your life will be turned upside down."

Gary blinked and stared at him. "Just because they were found here?"

"That," Kraft said, and then added, "and a number of other reasons. So I want you to do me a favor. Don't either of you leave this house until you hear from me. Understand? And don't go in that basement, and don't let anyone else in it."

Welte said, "You want I should stay and guard it?"

Kraft glared at him. "Gary can do the job."

Welte squinted at Gary and said suspiciously, "But he's the guy—"

"Skip it. You come along with me." He picked up the paper-wrapped shoes, tucked them under his arm and started toward the front door. He paused and looked back at Gary. "One thing more. Do you know where you were the day the kid disappeared?"

"You mean the exact hour?"

"Yes."

Gary frowned, then smiled slightly and nodded. "I know exactly. I was talking about it just today. I was drinking beer with Herb up at the Gold Nugget."

"At four o'clock on May thirteenth?"

"On the nose. I'd left town about three-thirty, on my way to Chinamen's Ridge. I stopped and had a beer with Herb. That's about twenty miles away, and it takes about thirty minutes to drive on that road."

Kraft nodded and looked relieved. "Good," he said.

"I'm glad you can nail it down. You will be too, later."

"You'll let us know—"

"Sure. As soon as I get the word from the Hallorans I'll call you. So long."

Ellen dropped onto the couch, but Gary walked to the windows to watch the lights of the police car disappear down the street. He was beginning to get an odd sensation of heat in his stomach, and his mouth was dry. He turned from the windows and looked at Ellen and again caught that queerly intent expression on her face.

Her lids lowered to veil her eyes and she yawned and mumbled, "I think I'll go to bed."

"It was just a little while ago you said you'd never be able to sleep until you knew."

"I feel different now. I'm sleepy."

"Okay. I—ah—I think I'd better wait up. Bill said he'd call back."

Ellen walked back to the bedroom hallway and paused to look back at Gary over her shoulder. "Don't you know already what he's going to say?"

"No. Why should I?"

"I know. Those shoes belonged to the girl."

"Oh, for God's sake. You women and your damned intuition. Even Bill refused to say one way or the other until he knows for sure."

"But I know, Gary. Good night."

"Yeah. Good night."

He watched her walk into the bedroom, then reached for a cigarette in a silver box. He noticed his fingers shaking and stared at them.

Welte was driving the squad car and Kraft sat back to drag on a cigarette and stare out at the lights cutting through the darkness. The sergeant wanted to talk, but Kraft was not in the mood and silenced him. He was thinking of the publicity he had received in the national press at the time of the Halloran girl's disappearance. Now, if the shoes proved to be hers, it would start all over again. Kraft was a rare police chief. He didn't want publicity and dreaded what he knew would happen.

In many ways, the chief was a great deal like Gary Malone. He was only in his middle thirties, and could have gone far in a large city. But he was also a family man who idolized his children, a boy of fourteen and a girl of twelve, and wanted them to grow up in the healthy atmosphere of Bayside. He had no aspirations greater than the job he was holding, except to improve the force he commanded and show what could be done when intelligence was applied to police work.

He had got into that field quite by accident, simply because of his size. While he had been at base camp, in World War II, his commanding officer had suggested that he would be excellent material for the MPs. Kraft hadn't been too interested, but at the time he had been doing more than his share of KP duty and anything else looked better. He put in his request for transfer and was quickly accepted by the Military Police. He was an intelligent man, with three and a half years of college to his credit, and rose rapidly in the organization. He was a major when the war ended, and completely sold on police work.

He finished his dangling half-year in college, then went on for a two-year course of study with the F.B.I. He could have remained with that organization, but his real interest in police work was at the grass-roots level. He returned to California, where he had been born, and went into the police department at Sacramento as a special officer. Each summer he and his family spent their vacation at Bayside, where Kraft became acquainted with the members of the police force, the mayor, the councilmen and other civic dignitaries. All of them liked him and were well acquainted with his background. When the old chief retired the job was offered to Kraft and he accepted happily. It was the job he wanted, and Bayside was exactly the place where he wanted to live.

He sometimes wondered if he should not have greater ambitions, but whenever he looked about at the tree-covered slopes of Bayside and filled his lungs with the heady salt air he was content. He especially liked the schools his children attended, their playmates, and the atmosphere they enjoyed, that was small-town and yet possessed a cosmopolitan shading because of the heavy tourist trade. He could not think of a more perfect place in which to raise children.

It had not been so perfect for the Halloran girl.

Kraft frowned and swore under his breath. Whenever he thought of the Halloran case his anger boiled and he felt guilty for not having solved it. The only clue that had ever been turned up had been the schoolbook found in front of the Gold Nugget the day after the girl disappeared, but Kraft felt that somehow, in some way, he had failed personally. His first move at that time, of course, had been to round up and question all known sex deviates of the entire peninsula. Each one had had an iron-clad alibi. Kraft finally concluded that the abductor had been a stranger from out of town.

But now, if the shoes were really Diana's, the abductor was undoubtedly not a stranger, and was probably living in town at that moment. The thought didn't make Kraft happy. He felt that he had failed before principally because the person had been a stranger. Now, there would be no excuse for his failure. He felt it more keenly than ever. It almost sickened him.

Welte swung the squad car into the exclusive roads of Cliffside and brought it to a halt before the dark bulk of the Halloran home. It was old Monterey style, set well back from the road, shaded by large gray oaks and surrounded by gardens and paths of white gravel. Lights were on in two of the upstairs windows, and a yellow light was glowing over the massive front door of solid oak.

Kraft got out of the car and told Welte to wait for him. He tucked the bundle of shoes under his arm, walked down a long path to the front porch and rang the bell. George Halloran opened the door almost at once and shook hands with the chief. Kraft had not seen him in a few months and was shocked by the attorney's appearance. The robe he was wearing failed to hide the stoop of his shoulders, and his slippered feet shuffled tiredly across the thick carpeting as he walked. His eyes looked old and vacant, his sagging cheeks were deeply lined, and his dark hair had turned almost solidly gray. He was a rather small man of tremendous vitality who had always walked proudly erect, but now there seemed to be no life in him at all. Kraft watched him and felt a knife twisting in his heart. God, he thought, what if it had been my daughter!

Halloran led the way into the comfortable living room with only one lamp pushing back the dark. Mrs. Halloran was seated on a couch under the lamp watching, without expression, the approach of the two men. The tragedy had not affected her appearance as much as it had her husband's. In her forties, she was still a slim woman with no gray in her black hair, and very few lines in her face. The giveaway was in her hands only, which stirred nervously in her lap. She managed to smile at the chief, but it was a wisp of a thing that faded at once.

Halloran dropped wearily onto the couch at his wife's side and nodded his head toward a nearby chair. He looked curiously at the package under Kraft's arm as the chief removed his hat and sat down.

With the quick sense of a talented legal brain, he asked, "What's in it, Bill? Something to do with Diana?"

Kraft leaned toward the Hallorans. "A little while ago," he said, "I had a call from Gary Malone. Do you know him, the young fellow in the Baker and Allen office?"

Halloran thought for a moment and then nodded. "Rather tall, with auburn hair?"

"Yes."

"I used to see him around the club now and then. Fine golfer, I understand."

"Uh-huh. Well, this afternoon his wife was down in their basement looking for something or other. Between two boxes she found a pair of girls' gym shoes that were strange to her." He paused as Mrs. Halloran closed her eyes with pain and her husband sharply sucked in his breath; then he continued, "The shoes were also strange to Gary. Neither had seen them before. They were going to dispose of them, but this evening they happened to notice some initials stenciled on the canvas. That's when they called me. The initials are DBH. Better have a look." He unwrapped the package, got to his feet and placed the shoes, resting on top of the paper, on Mrs. Halloran's lap. "Don't touch them," he warned. "We may get a print off of them."

Halloran stared at the shoes and nodded, then fixed his pain-filled eyes on his wife. She leaned over to examine the shoes more closely and turned one of them on its side to expose the initials to the light. She remained stooped over the shoes for a long while, then she settled back against the couch and tears trickled slowly down her cheeks.

Kraft said, "I guess that does it." He lifted the shoes by the paper under them, wrapped them carefully and returned to his chair.

Mrs. Halloran said softly, "My baby, my poor darling."

Halloran squeezed her hand tighter. "Now, now, dear. We made up our minds that it's better to try to forget."

She shook her head. "It's never in the past. Every time I look at the front door I expect to see it open and Diana walk in and—and—"

"Now, dear. You torture yourself to think she is still alive. It's impossible."

Kraft swallowed and cleared his throat loudly and looked away from them to hide his own emotion. When he looked back, Mrs. Halloran's eyes were fixed on his and she was nodding. "They belonged to Diana," she said. "I recognize them."

Kraft asked gruffly, "You're positive?"

"I stenciled those initials on myself. I put them low, toward the soles, so they wouldn't show so much. All the young girls in high have to have initials stenciled on their gym things, you know."

"I know."

"These are the shoes she was bringing home that—that day. They needed cleaning, you see. Diana was always such a neat child, and—" But she could not go on. Her body snapped forward, she gasped and threw herself into her husband's arms with loud, racking sobs. He patted her back gently and stared vacantly into space.

Kraft had all the information he needed and got to his feet. He jerked his head at Halloran and walked out of the front room into the hallway. The attorney joined him there after a few minutes. He was wiping his eyes with the back of his hand.

The two stepped outside and paused on the porch, where Kraft said, "You and the missus drop by the station some time tomorrow so we can get your statement on record about the shoes."

"Of course. Anything you say."

Kraft, with sympathetic insight, said, "You don't like this, do you?"

"I'd rather they hadn't been found. Nothing will bring Diana back, I know. But now we will probably have to go through it all again. But I guess there's no help for it. About Gary Malone, though. What sort of people—"

"They're nice people, George. Looks to me like the wife runs things, but that's nothing new in this day and age. She was the one who found the shoes, and he called me about it right away."

"Then you're not suspicious of—of—"

Kraft snorted. "Good Lord no! It's a hell of a puzzle how those shoes got in their basement, but when we track it down the answer will probably be a simple one. Rest your mind about Gary. He knows exactly where he was when your daughter disappeared."

"You've checked?"

"Not yet, but I will. Meanwhile, I have no reason to doubt him."

Halloran insisted, "But you will check."

"Naturally. The shoes were found in his basement, weren't they? That makes him number one on the list. I guess he knows that by now."

Halloran rubbed his hands over his face and squinted out at the police car, then looked narrowly into Kraft's eyes. "Do you know much about sex deviates, Bill?"

"A little. I'm no psychiatrist, though."

"One of the things you can almost always count on with a person of that sort, they hang onto some article of the person they have assaulted, such as panties, or a bra, or a skirt, or even shoes. And generally, too, they keep that article in a convenient place. A basement would be convenient."

Kraft drew a deep breath into his lungs and slowly let it out. "I'll check his story first thing in the morning."

"You see what I mean, don't you?"

"Sure. Well, good night, George. Tell the missus I'm sorry that— It had to be done, you know."

"We understand. Good night, Bill."

Kraft walked out to the squad car and slid his bulk onto the right-hand seat. Welte made a U-turn and started back the way they had come. "Well?" he asked.

"The shoes belonged to Diana Halloran."

Welte grunted his satisfaction. "That's what I said."

"So you did."

"I guess we just run down and put the bracelets on Malone, huh?"

"You know, Hank, you can jump to more conclusions. You heard his alibi for that time."

"Yeah. Do you believe it?"

"I don't believe or disbelieve until I know. I'm mighty curious, though. How about that Herb at the Gold Nugget? What's his last name?"

"Short. Herb Short. He's out of our territory."

Kraft snapped testily, "I know that. There's nothing to stop me from calling him, though. How late does he stay open week nights?"

"One A.M., usually. But if he's got customers he'll stay open until two."

Kraft glanced at the luminous dial of the clock on the dashboard and saw that it was ten minutes to one. "Remind me to call him when we get to the station."

Herb Short had not yet closed the bar when Kraft reached the police station and called the Gold Nugget number. Kraft told him what he wanted and Herb verified Gary's story. "Sure, I know the day and the hour," he said. "Me and Malone was talking about it just today. Refreshed my mind. He was here having a beer with me at four o'clock on May thirteenth."

"You're positive of that?"

"I sure am."

"Good. Then how about doing me a favor? Drop in to the station when you get a chance and dictate your verification for the record."

"Okay."

"Thanks a lot, Mr. Short. I like that Gary Malone. You take a great weight off my mind."

He put his finger down on the phone plunger and turned to look at Welte over his shoulder. "Short just verified Malone's alibi. He's positive."

"I'll be damned. I was almost positive myself—"

"Yeah, I know. How about looking up Malone's number for me? Maybe I can take a weight off his mind, too."

Gary was still in the living room, working on another highball, when the telephone rang. He was in such a hurry to answer it that he almost spilled his drink.

"Gary? Bill Kraft. I just left the Hallorans. The shoes are positively identified as having belonged to Diana Halloran."

Gary closed his eyes tightly and gasped, "Oh, no!"

"I'm afraid so. Rough, isn't it? This thing is going to put you and your wife right smack in the spotlight. You know that?"

"Yes. I've been thinking. Oh, hell."

"My sentiments, too. You have no idea what it's going to be like. Fortunately for you, though, I just verified your alibi with Herb Short. He says you were in his place at that day and that hour. You don't have that to worry about, at least. Most people have a terrible time remembering where they were four months back."

"My memory's not too good, either. It's more or less accident that I remember that day."

"And luck, too. Anyway, you're in the clear."

Gary held the phone away to stare at it, then snapped angrily, "Was there any doubt?"

"Look, Gary, we have to check everyone. As I say, you're the clear. But that basement of yours—"

"What about it?"

"I have a request to make. Do you mind if I come in with some men in the morning and look through your stuff down there and maybe dig up the floor?"

Gary was about to protest, but then realized what the chief had in mind. He said reluctantly, "Okay, if you put things back in order again."

"I promise. Meanwhile, don't go down there yourself for any reason. Tell the missus."

"Sure."

"I'll see you in the morning. Night."

Gary was about to turn away from the phone, but then remembered that Luke wanted to know, too. He dialed the Summers' number and Luke answered on the second ring. Gary told him briefly the information the chief had passed on to him. Luke repeated, "I'll be damned," over and over as Gary was talking.

At the end, Luke said, "Well, anyway, old boy, your alibi for that is solid. Isn't it?"

"Yeah."

"Otherwise, you know, you'd be the number-one suspect. Have you thought of that?"

"I'll say I have."

"After all, finding the kid's shoes in your basement—Even so, you're on a hell of a spot. Wait'll the reporters get wind of this. Man! Uh—by the way, Betty and I were talking—we were wondering if you and Ellen could just forget we were there—You know what I mean."

"Sorry, Luke, but it's too late for that. I had to tell Bill that you were here and handled the shoes. They'll be looking for prints, you know. Sorry."

Luke sighed and said, "Well, I guess there was no help for it. Betty is pretty upset, though. Now, when I tell her the shoes were really the kid's— Nasty mess. You got any idea who could have put those shoes in your basement?"

"None."

"Then you'd better start thinking, and think hard." He paused to yawn, then said, "I'm hitting the sack. See you tomorrow."

"Okay."

Gary finished his drink and went about the house turning off lights, then walked into the dark bedroom. The rays of a high moon flooded in through a window and he could see well enough to get undressed without turning on a light. He could see Ellen's form outlined under the covers of the twin bed against the wall, and noticed that she was lying on her back. He knew that she could sleep only on one side or the other, so she had to be awake. Yet she was not moving and was feigning sleep. Gary shrugged. There would be plenty of time to talk in the morning.

When he awakened in the morning, however, and rolled over to face Ellen, the other bed was empty. He sat up with a puzzled frown, rubbed sleep from his eyes and swung his legs out of bed. It was not like Ellen to leave her bed, for any reason, before ten or eleven o'clock. Gary kicked his feet into leather slippers, draped a flannel robe over his shoulders and padded through the house to the kitchen. Ellen wasn't in the house.

He was returning to the bedroom when he noticed the note propped against a photograph on an end table. He picked it up and read, "I heard you talking on the telephone last night. You know what's going to happen now, what with reporters and all. I just cannot stand that sort of ugliness, so I'm going up to stay with Mother for a few days. Don't tell anyone where I am, or I'll never forgive you. I'll call you maybe tomorrow. Love, Ellen. P.S. Pick up the cleaning at Stein's and send me that chartreuse dress with the white collar."

Gary dropped the note to the floor and walked to a front window to look out at the quiet street. Fog had settled in during the night and was trailing its gray skirts through the damp green pine trees. Gary stared out at the fog and felt a little sick. Ellen had run out on him. But not for the reason she had given in the letter. He knew her better than that. Ellen would welcome a deluge of newspaper men with open arms—especially the press photographers. She was lazy, but he knew she actually loved excitement and she enjoyed having her picture taken, whatever the reason.

The letter was a lie, but why had she run out on him? In Gary's mind, there could be only one answer. She knew what he would soon be going through with the police and the reporters, and she had no desire to stand by his side and take it with him. Or could it be that she doubted his alibi? He shook his head. Impossible. She could never think that way.

Gary, suddenly angry, rushed into the bedroom to get dressed, to drive to Grand Point and catch Ellen before she got on the train. The clock on the bureau stopped him. It was 7:20, and the San Francisco train had already left at 7:15. He thought of intercepting the train at the Los Olas junction, but he would probably be too late for that, too. Besides, his anger faded as suddenly as it had been born. It would be ridiculous to expect her to face what was going to happen.

Gary dressed in moccasins, slacks, and a sport shirt and went into the kitchen to prepare breakfast. He took his time and was still sipping at a cup of coffee when he heard the first car stop in front of the house shortly after eight o'clock. He heard other cars grinding to a stop, a constant string of them, and then the doorbell rang. He opened the door to face Kraft and looked beyond him to two police cars, and saw a light truck and other cars pulling in diagonally to the dirt curb with press stickers on their windshields, and still more cars pouring in to the street from both directions. The whole block was packed with automobiles in almost a matter of seconds, and their drivers and passengers were swarming toward the house.

The chief shrugged and sighed, "Big news, my friend. Plenty big news. I wanted to hold it up another few hours, but Hank gave out the story this morning a couple minutes before I got back to the station. And this isn't half what it's going to be. Wait'll the boys start pouring down from San Francisco from the papers and the wire services. You're in for it, Gary."

"Yeah. Looks that way."

He and Kraft tried to get into the house and close the door, but it was impossible. The members of the press shoved in with them and flashbulbs started popping. Reporters surrounded Gary, trapped against a wall, and fired a steady string of questions at him. He was allowed to relax only after he had told the story over and over again—exactly how the shoes had been found and by whom, who had been present, and what had been said. Photographs were even taken of the note Ellen had left that morning. In less than five minutes, too, all photographs of Ellen and Gary were taken from their places on the bureaus and walls. Gary was annoyed, but there was nothing he could do about it; a slow anger started burning toward all reporters, an anger that would inevitably increase his troubles.

The chief patiently allowed the reporters all the time they wanted; they had their job to do, too. But as soon as he felt that their questions had been answered satisfactorily he broke up the crowd around Gary. He and Gary went outside to face a crowd of curious neighbors standing about on the lawns and hanging over fences, talking excitedly. Gary knew most of them, but when he smiled and waved there was no response, other than curious, granite-like stares.

Kraft got matters organized in a hurry. He stationed policemen at the front and rear of the basement to keep out the curious and sent in Welte and two other policemen to drag all the boxes and barrels out on the lawn. Nothing of interest was found in any of them, and they were all carefully repacked. Kraft then sent two men he had hired into the basement with picks and shovels to dig up the hard-packed sand floor. He went in with them to supervise the work.

Gary stood on the lawn for a while talking with reporters, but the cold fog was chilling him through the light sport shirt he was wearing. He went inside to get a jacket and found half a dozen reporters huddled together in the living room and another using the telephone. Gary realized that most of the men had probably not had breakfast, so told them to help themselves to the coffee in the kitchen. He went into the bedroom, selected a dark corduroy jacket from the closet and shrugged his arms into it.

On his way back to the living room, the reporter who had been using the phone got up and joined him. He was an older man with a wiry build, iron-gray hair, shrewd eyes and a deceptively mild manner. He looked familiar, so Gary asked him, "Aren't you from the Grand Point *Sun?*"

"That's right." He reached out and shook hands with Gary. "Carson's the name. Sam Carson. I'm the editor."

"Oh. I thought—"

"Uh-huh. Two of my men are out front. When a thing like this breaks I get on the job, too." He stuck a cigarette into his mouth and lighted it, his eyes never leaving Gary's face. "Kind of a lousy mess, isn't it?"

"I should say it is."

"You have no idea how that kid's shoes got in your basement?"

Gary sighed and shook his head. "Believe me, Mr. Carson, I'm as much in the dark as you are."

"You know what people are thinking, don't you?"

"Well—"

"You're the guy. Except," he added dryly, "you have an alibi."

"Thank God for that."

"Yeah. I've been wondering about that alibi, though. So's everyone else. That's why I was using your telephone. I was just talking to Herb Short."

"Then he told you—"

"He did. But here's something to think about, Malone. My rag will have an extra out on the streets in about half an hour. So will the others around here. In another hour or so the wire services will have it out in every newspaper in the nation. You know why? This is what you might call a classic case. Prominent people involved, a young, pretty girl and the horrible, macabre thinking of what probably happened to her—element after element of mystery. It's juicy. And you're the guy."

Gary snapped angrily, "Now, just a minute—"

Carson stopped him with a light smile. "You don't get it the way I mean. I'm not telling you that you're the guilty one. How do I know who is? I'm trying to tell you what people are going to think. You're the man in the spotlight and you're the logical suspect. The only thing that saves you is Herb Short. Without him, you know, it's even possible that you could be lynched before the day ends."

Gary felt a cold chill travel up his spine. "You really mean that?"

"You bet I do. People feel pretty strongly about what happens to young kids. I do myself. I got a couple of my own. Frankly, Malone, if I were Halloran facing you right now, even knowing about your alibi, I think I'd have a hard time containing myself." His voice rose a degree as he said, "Those shoes can't logically be explained away. But," he shrugged, "you got a pretty good alibi."

"I keep telling everyone—"

"What you say doesn't count any more. It's only the facts that count. So I got thinking. How could Herb Short be so positive of that day and that hour? Hours and days, to a bartender, must be pretty much alike. I questioned him about who else he had seen that day and he couldn't remember. Why just you?"

"Well, we were talking about it yesterday."

"He told me that. It still doesn't mean that his memory is correct. So I asked him to see if he couldn't nail it down some other way, something more positive, like a big bill he had paid that day, or maybe a fight that had happened in his place, or, better still, something on record. He's going back through his books now. Says he'll call me back here as soon as he discovers anything. You'd better start hoping he nails it down."

"I see what you mean."

"Sure. A district attorney could take that memory of his to pieces and throw it out the window. I'd cross my fingers, in your shoes."

Gary started to say something, but was suddenly conscious of a difference in the atmosphere. He knew suddenly what it was: before there had been considerable talk and hubbub outside; now there was an eerie, deathly silence. Gary frowned and turned away from Carson as Kraft came walking through the front door, followed by Welte. The chief was pale and looked a bit ill. The two men were carrying a number of sand-covered articles, which they placed carefully on the floor; white panties, saddle shoes, a skirt and sweater, bobby sox and a collection of schoolbooks. Gary stared at them and had difficulty to keep from throwing up.

Kraft straightened and faced Gary and said hollowly, "We dug these things out of your basement. The only things missing are a little ribbon she was wearing in her hair, and a bra."

Gary stared at the articles on the floor and swallowed and dropped heavily into a chair. "Diana's?" he asked in a whisper.

"No doubt of it. We'll make positive identification later, but there's no doubt in my mind." His normally pink face turned beet-red as he roared, "By God, Malone, it's almost impossible for me to believe— How in the name of common sense did these things get buried in your basement if you didn't put them there?"

Gary shook his head slowly back and forth and said huskily, "I don't know. I can't explain it. I don't know, I tell you." He was conscious of reporters flooding into the room and flashbulbs again popping, but his eyes were fixed rigidly on Kraft. "I don't know.'

"Uh-huh. So you don't know. Your own house. Your own basement. And that was the afternoon you took off to the mountains, according to your own story."

"Bill, I don't know. Maybe— No, that couldn't be it."

Kraft stepped toward him and bellowed, "Maybe what!"

"I just had an idea. Maybe it's no good. You remember when the girl disappeared. The following week there was a city election. I think it was the following Tuesday."

"They're always on a Tuesday."

"Yeah. Okay. There was this election. Our garage was used as a polling place. A lot of people were in and out during that day. I wasn't home. I was working."

"So?"

"So any one of those people could have slipped into our basement during that day. It's never locked, you know. I don't say that's when it happened—I don't know—but the more I think of it—" He looked away from the chief and stared into space, turning the idea over in his mind.

Kraft glanced at Carson, and said, "Now we got hundreds of suspects. Do you remember that election, Sam?"

Carson nodded and chewed thoughtfully at his lip, then said, "That was May seventeenth. Strictly a local election for assemblymen and that school bond issue. I remember it. There was a young gal running for assembly."

"Uh-huh. Now I remember. She didn't get in."

"No. I don't think many people turned out to vote, though, so the list of voters who used that garage shouldn't be too long."

"Yeah, and still have to look up every one of them. And even then it doesn't make sense. Say the guy we want was one of the voters that day, which would make him a resident of this neighborhood. So he comes here to vote and notices the basement door is unlocked. The stuff we found would have to be in his car. So he goes out and loads down his arms with the kid's things and buries them here in the basement."

The chief turned to address the balance of what he was saying to Gary: "Does that make sense to you? It doesn't to me. Consider the chances the guy is taking. People are going in and out of the garage to vote. The basement door is in plain sight. It's also in plain sight of your neighbors living across the street. It would almost be impossible for him to go in and out of that basement without someone seeing him and wondering what he was carrying. I think even a moron would have better sense than to run a risk like that when it would be so easy to get rid of the stuff elsewhere." He paused to scratch his head, squinted at Gary and suggested, "Unless it was done deliberately to pin the whole thing on you. How about that? You got any enemies in Bayside?"

Gary looked up at him and, in spite of the sickness in his stomach, he had to chuckle. "There's an old lady who threatened to sue me once. She didn't think I deserved my commission because the first person I showed her house to bought it. That's about it. No enemies."

"Well, it was a farfetched idea, anyway." Kraft turned to Welte and told him, "Take the exhibits up to the station. Call the Hallorans and ask them to drop down and identify them at once. I'll call City Hall and ask them to dig out a list of the people who voted in this garage."

He helped the sergeant gather the articles together and placed them all in a pillowcase Gary brought from the bedroom. He slapped the sergeant on the back and shoved him out the door, then stood for a moment staring at Gary, re-appraising him—nice guy, liked by everyone, powerful build, nothing physi-cally wrong with him and, as far as he knew, nothing mentally wrong either. He seemed to be a well-adjusted person who knew exactly where he was going and how to get there. He had none of the apparent frustrations that most sex devi-ates seemed to suffer from and was not obviously a neurotic. He shrugged and sighed deeply. Right when everything seemed to be opening up the case was get-ting more mysterious than ever.

He walked back to the telephone, called City Hall and asked the registrar to find the list of people who had voted in the Malone garage on May seventeenth and send it to him at the station. He placed the phone back in its cradle and was turning away when it started ringing. He picked it up automatically, before Gary could move, and barked, "Yes?"

Herb Short asked, "Who's this, Mr. Carson?"

"No. This is Kraft, Chief of Police."

"Oh. Kraft, huh? Say, what's going on there?"

"Why do you ask? Who's calling?"

"This is Herb Short at the Gold Nugget. Mr. Carson called a little while ago about that alibi of Gary Malone's. Maybe I'd better tell you instead of him."

"You told me last night."

"Yeah, I know, but I was wrong. I was talking with Gary yesterday and he said something about being here when that kid disappeared and I just sort of took his word for it and figured this is where he was. It wasn't so much that I re-membered, you see. It was just sort of casual-like and I figured he knew what he was talking about. But I was wrong. He couldn't of been here that afternoon."

Kraft's hamlike hand closed tightly about the telephone and he had difficulty keeping his voice level. "What changed your mind?"

"Well, that call of Mr. Carson's. He asked me to try and nail down the date with something else that maybe happened that day. I been looking through my books. Something else did happen. The joint wasn't even open the afternoon of May thirteenth."

Kraft felt as if someone had stuck a pin into his body and all the air was run-ning out, like a balloon. He dropped his voice to a whisper and asked, "You're sure of that?"

"You bet. It's in my books. I keep records, you know. You gotta in this busi-ness."

"All right. All right. What happened?"

"I'm getting to that. Because of the State law, you know, I gotta serve food in my joint, so I got a little range for cooking hamburgers and hot dogs and stuff like that in the back. Sometimes grease collects behind it. There was some there that day, and it caught on fire. I put it out with a fire extinguisher, it wasn't much of a fire, but the fire chief out here made me close the joint for the afternoon while all the grease was cleaned out and the back wall was washed down with some kind of chemical stuff. Anyway, I got it right here in my books. On May thirteenth the Gold Nugget was closed from about one to five P.M."

"And you're positive you served no customers during those hours?"

"The front door was locked. I didn't allow nobody in."

"I see." He dropped his voice to where it was barely audible over the wire and whispered, "Now, listen closely. This is damned important. I want you to keep that information to yourself until I tell you otherwise. Got that? Don't let it out to anyone."

"Not even Mr. Carson?"

"No one. Understand? If he calls back, or anyone else, just stall them off. Say you're still looking up the records. Don't give out that information to anyone. Believe me, this is the most important thing that has happened in the case. Now I think I can crack it open, with your cooperation. Can I trust you?"

Herb was pleased to be the chief's ally and replied enthusiastically, "You bet you can, Chief. Count on me."

"I intend to. Now, just sit tight. I'll call you later in the day. Be seeing you. And thanks for what you've told me. Thanks a hell of a lot."

Kraft put the phone down on the little table in the hallway and glanced into the living room. The reporters were all huddled together in an exchange of ideas, but Gary Malone was looking curiously in the chief's direction. For a split second, Kraft almost admired the man he now thought of as a killer. He had come very close to getting away with a perfect alibi.

But now his own lie would send him to the gas chamber. And even that, Kraft thought, is too good for him.

Chapter Three

When the chief turned from the hallway into the living room, Carson was suspicious and asked him who had called. Kraft mumbled something about one of his men calling from the station and walked away from the editor. He went back through the kitchen, where a couple of reporters were talking and drinking coffee, and on to the back windows overlooking the rear yard. He could see half a dozen pine trees, border gardens, a patch of lawn, the brick barbecue and a new patio perhaps twenty feet square paved with redwood slabs.

Kraft was turning a gruesome idea over in his mind. Gary Malone had lied about his whereabouts on the fatal day, and he had also been stupid enough, or confused enough, to bury the evidence in his own basement. So, although it wasn't logical, it was possible that he had also buried the girl's body on his own property. Perhaps he had not gone to the mountains at all that afternoon, as he claimed. Where did he say he had gone? Oh, yes. Chinamen's Ridge. Maybe he was lying about that, too. Maybe he had intercepted the Halloran kid at the ravine, or somewhere else, and had taken her here to his own home, where he could have assaulted and killed her. That could explain the reason for the kid's things being found in his basement. He hadn't yet had an opportunity to get rid of them, or perhaps lacked the courage to move them.

Then he sighed and shook his head. The idea didn't make sense. After all, Mrs. Malone lived in the house, too.

Kraft spun about on his heel and hurried back to the living room, where the crowd was now thinning out a bit. The reporters had phoned in their stories long before, but some of them had left to file in person. Gary was sitting on the couch talking to Sam Carson, who was standing rocking back and forth on his heels. Kraft nodded at the two of them and dropped into a nearby chair. He waited a moment before speaking, to control himself, to keep the hate and the rage he was feeling out of his voice.

He leaned toward Gary and said, "Suppose you tell me again the time you left for Chinamen's Ridge, why you were going there, and when you came back. Fill in some of the details?'

Gary looked at the watch on his wrist and saw that it was a few minutes after twelve. He had been subjected to a steady barrage of questioning for four solid hours. He was getting tired, and hungry and thirsty. He told Kraft to wait a minute and went into the kitchen, where he opened a can of beer and threw together a cheese sandwich. He wolfed down the sandwich on his way back to the living room and dropped back into the couch sipping the beer,

"Okay," he said, "but let's make this the last time around. I'm not too positive about the timing involved. After all, Bill, I'm trying to think back four months. Anyway, here's about as close as I can figure it. You know Nathaniel Rigsby, the rancher?" When Kraft nodded he continued, "Well, he dropped by the office about three o'clock that day and asked me to run up and look over a beat-up old ranch he owns on Chinamen's Ridge. I told him I'd do it and came home here to change clothes. I guess I left town about three-thirty—somewhere around that time. I went up the valley and stopped at the Gold Nugget about four o'clock, where I had a beer wih Herb, then I drove on up to Chinamen's Ridge. I guess I got there maybe a little before five. Mr. Rigsby has a cottage there and I had the key, so I looked the property over and spent the night there."

"Did anyone see you up there?"

"I don't think so. I don't remember seeing anyone. Anyway, I stayed up there in the morning, too, and drove away about eleven."

"That's May fourteen."

"Yes. I stopped at the Gold Nugget about noon, on my way back, and that's where I heard about the girl's disappearance. I came straight home. Later that evening I joined the posse to look for the girl up the valley." He took a swallow of the beer, smiled wearily and said, "That's the schedule. Incidentally, Bill, I don't mind you asking these questions. You got your job to do and, naturally, you have to suspect everyone."

Kraft nodded and said dryly, "Yeah. That's good of you. But how about Mrs. Malone? Didn't she object to your going off that way to spend the night in the mountains?"

"Ellen? Gosh, no. If she had been here I wouldn't have gone up there."

Kraft tensed and asked, "She wasn't here?"

"No. Didn't I tell you before? She'd gone up to San Francisco the day before to spend the weekend with her mother."

"You—you mean—" Kraft swallowed hard and said, "Look; let's get this straight. You were home here alone?"

"Sure." Gary gave him a puzzled look and asked, "Why?"

"On the day of May thirteenth—now, think about it—no one was here with you at all."

"No. Well, for that matter, I wasn't here either. I'd gone to the office first thing in the morning, I came back at the time I said to change my clothes, and I wasn't back here again until the next afternoon. The house was empty."

Kraft gasped involuntarily. "My God, it could be. The kid could have been killed right here."

Gary stared at him as if he had lost his senses, then cried, "No, Bill. Good Lord, no! You're way off base. How would the guy who did it know that this house would be empty that afternoon? I don't buy that at all."

Sam Carson moved a few steps to his left, where he had a better view of the chief's face. He squinted narrowly and saw something that Gary had not noticed. The chief's normally pink face was flushed red with anger and he was obviously having a difficult time keeping his expression smooth as he talked to Malone. Carson had a hunch. The chief knew something no one else knew. The editor decided to stick close.

Kraft got to his feet and paced the floor until he had his emotions under control. Then he stopped and faced Gary.

"I got a request to make, Malone. You can deny it, but if you do I'll go through channels and get it done, anyway."

Gary realized suddenly that the chief had not addressed him by his first name in quite some time. He wondered about it as he said, "What's on your mind?"

"I'd like to send my men out to dig up your back yard." Gary's own anger, that had been building for some time, exploded. He slapped his hands on his thighs and jumped to his feet. "What the hell's the matter with you?" he shouted. "I always thought you were a pretty smart cop. Now you're talking like a dumb hick. That kid could not have been on this property, can't you get that through your head? If you'd only use your, brains—" He paused as an idea crossed his mind and the anger faded a bit and he mumbled, "Mr. Rigsby knew I wasn't going to be home. He also knew my wife was away. I guess some others in the office knew, too. But they're not the kind of people—" He stopped again and frowned, lost in thought. It was getting more complicated. You could say no one knew the house would be empty that day, but when you stopped to think about it a number of people knew. Black was suddenly white, or at least gray.

Kraft had no way of knowing what he was thinking and leaped to the wrong conclusions. "Do I have your permission?" he asked.

"Well—Bill, I've spent a lot of time working in that yard. I just put in that new patio the last few months—"

Kraft interrupted by asking sharply, "Since May thirteenth?"

"About that time, and since then, yes."

"We'll have to tear it up."

"Aw, hell, Bill. The yard will be ruined. I'd like to cooperate as much as I can, but tearing up the yard—"

"You'll get it back in good condition. I promise."

"It won't be the same."

"We'll do our best. Do I have your permission, or are you going to force me to throw my weight around?"

Gary walked away and to the front windows to look out at the crowds of curious gathering on the street. The extras were out, and most of them clutched papers in their hands, talked excitedly together and pointed at the house. Gary was disgusted and turned away from the sight.

"Okay," he said. "You'll never be satisfied until you make sure and, in a way, I guess maybe you're right. Go ahead and dig it up. But tell your men to be careful, will you?"

Kraft was astounded and momentarily puzzled. The idea he had had at the kitchen windows had seemed, after all, to be the correct one. But if the kid was really buried in the back yard and Malone was the guilty one it wasn't reasonable to expect his cooperation in digging up the place. On the other hand, how could anyone ever really know the workings of that sort of brain? There was only one way to find out.

Kraft went out front, where the two men he had hired to dig up the basement were standing patiently on the lawn. He called to the men and led the way around the side of the house to the back yard, where they were joined by two policemen and Sam Carson. Kraft explained what he had in mind and all of them searched about the yard for spots that might indicate recent digging. Nothing was found, other than the obvious fact that there was always digging around the flower beds. Kraft turned his attention to the patio.

He told the diggers, "Pull up the patio first. Be sure you stack those redwood blocks neatly. Hear? They have to be put back again. Then probe around under there and dig down a couple of feet at least. You don't have to go too far. Just be sure you dig down to undisturbed earth." He looked the yard over and could see that there was a long job ahead, so he told one of his officers, "You take charge, Frank. I got work to do at the station. Give me a ring—and fast—if you find anything."

He started back to the house with Carson at his side. The editor stopped him at the rear steps. "All right," he said, "what gives? You've made up your mind Malone is the guy. Right?"

Kraft said, "I haven't made up my mind about anything."

"You're not digging up this yard for no reason. You don't think someone else did the job. You think it's Malone. Look, Bill; I'm no child and I'm not a cub reporter on my first beat. No one other than Malone would bury that kid in this yard. I know it and you know it. It's stretching reason too damned far to expect anyone else to use this yard for a burial ground. Now, what have you got on Malone? Come on. Give."

Kraft shook his head and said stubbornly, "Not now, Sam. Sorry. You'll get it when I'm ready to give it out."

"That alibi?"

"I said you'll get it when I'm ready, not before. Don't foul up my work, Sam."

"Well, promise me you won't give it out unless I'm around, or one of my men."

"That's a promise."

"Good enough. Any idea of when?"

Kraft jerked his head at the men already prying up the redwood blocks. "It depends on what they find."

"Yeah. See what you mean." The editor's shoulders quivered and he looked chilled. "I don't think I'll stick around. Some things I can face and some I can't. This one I don't like even thinking about."

"That makes two of us. Good God, Sam, whatever could inspire a man to attack a kid like that?"

Gary was standing at the back window of the master bedroom watching the workers prying crowbars under the heavy redwood slabs and lifting them out of the loose ground. He had just come to the same conclusion Carson had reached. He was worried, puzzled and angry. Bill Kraft apparently did not believe his alibi, and thought that he could be the guilty one. There was no other reason for digging up the yard. It was preposterous to think anyone else could have buried the girl back there, especially under those slabs. If such had been the case Malone himself would have noticed long ago that the slabs had been disturbed. Besides, who else would have had the time and opportunity to dispose of the dirt displaced? Kraft suspected him.

Gary remembered a similar circumstance when he had been a young boy in grammar school. One of the pupils had brought a book of prized stamps to school to show to the class. The book had been passed from desk to desk and then had simply disappeared. The teacher determined the progress of the book by questioning each pupil who had seen it, and came at last to Gary; he evidently was the last one who had handled it. The teacher questioned him severely as to what he had done with the book. All Gary knew was that he had passed it on, but the boy occupying the desk to his rear denied having seen it, nor had anyone else further back in the line. The teacher dismissed the rest of the class and questioned Gary over and over again for a matter of hours. The book was eventually found on the ground outside, and it was learned that the boy to Gary's rear had tossed the book through an open window in a spirit of mischievousness. The teacher apologized to Gary, and that should have been the end of the matter.

During those two hours of questioning, however, Gary had suffered torture. He had known he was innocent, but the teacher had known equally well, in his own mind, that Gary was guilty. The boy's protestations of innocence had succeeded only in arousing the anger of the teacher, and had reduced Gary to a sobbing, tear-streaked, frightened child. Even the later apology did little to assuage his emotional damage. He had not been able to return to school for two days, and for many weeks after the incident he had an odd feeling of guilt and fear whenever he faced the boy who had owned the stamps.

He felt very much as he had at that time. Kraft had not said that he suspected Gary, but now Gary remembered how his attitude had changed after the finding of the girl's belongings and that telephone call, whatever that had been. There was no longer any doubt that in the chief's mind Gary Malone was the one and only suspect. It was horrible that anyone would suspect him of such a loathsome crime, but it was also baffling. After all, Kraft knew very well that he had been at the Gold Nugget at the time the girl disappeared. Herb Short had already verified it.

Gary thought of Herb and of what Carson had had to say about his conversation with him, and suddenly his heart was pounding and he was short of breath, as if he had just finished a long run. He understood, for the first time, what Carson had been getting at. Why, indeed, should Herb remember that he had been in the Gold Nugget that day and that hour and not remember anyone else who had been there? Carson had been right. That alibi would have to be nailed down in a much firmer manner.

He left the bedroom and was walking toward the telephone when Kraft came in through the kitchen and the living room and saw him in the short hallway. When Gary reached for the telephone the chief moved quickly, took it out of his hand and replaced it in the cradle. "Who did you intend calling?" he asked.

"Why—why, I was going to call Herb Short, is all."

"Why?"

"Because he's the only one who knows where I was at that time. It's getting pretty damned obvious to me that you don't believe me any more."

"But why call Herb Short?"

"Because I'd like to make sure he knows absolutely I was having a beer with him that day. It's getting more important every minute."

"Yeah. It sure is, isn't it? But there's no use calling him now. I was talking with him a few minutes ago. He's looking through his books to peg down the day and the time. He—ah—he said he'd call me at the station later on."

"Oh. Well, in that case, I guess I'll have to wait, too. Meanwhile, I think I'll run over to the office—"

"Hey, wait a minute. There's nothing you have to do that's as important as this case. I want you to come along with me to the station."

Gary stiffened and asked, "You're arresting me?"

Kraft glared at him and was silent for a minute, then managed to force a smile. "Don't be a damned fool. What have I got to arrest you on? I'm just asking for your cooperation, that's all. We have to get this whole thing down on paper, witnessed and signed and so on. It's quite a bit of work. I'd appreciate it if you'd come along and help me out now. The sooner we get this phase of it over with, the quicker we can get on to more important matters."

Gary thought that over, and agreed. He telephoned the office to talk to Mr. Baker, but he was not in, so Gary left a message with Baker's secretary that he would drop in later in the afternoon. The girl had already seen the papers and started questioning him excitedly, but Gary simply hung up on her. Kraft was impatient to be on his way, but Gary went into the bedroom and changed his sport clothes to a shirt and tie and a gabardine suit. He brushed his auburn hair carefully, adjusted a narrow-brim hat at a cocky angle on his head, and then joined the chief.

They made their way through the spectators out front and into the chief's car, then drove uptown to the police station, a block away from the main street. It was a small building on a corner, and designed to look as little like a police station as possible. It looked more like one of the quaint shops on the main street. There was a small reception room and a broad counter over which one could see into the even smaller radio or dispatch room. Beyond was a large room with lockers and benches and two doors in the end wall. One led into the lavatory and the other into the single cell the station possessed. Except for heavy steel mesh at the windows, the room looked very unlike a cell. It was used as a place of only temporary detention. Whenever a cell was really needed, which happened rarely in Bayside, prisoners were taken over to the jail at Grand Point, which had formal cells with real steel bars.

The only other room in the station, with the exception of two storage rooms, was the chief's office, a comfortable room about eighteen feet square with a large desk, a number of chairs, a long leather couch, a gray filing cabinet, a closet, and some pictures on the wall, including some photographs of the Kraft family.

Kraft led the way into his office and nodded Gary toward the couch; then he dropped into the swivel chair behind his desk and faced Sergeant Welte, who had followed them in. "You got a stenographer?" he asked.

Welte nodded. "Jane Bestor. She's in the other room transcribing some of her notes. You want her now?"

"Uh-huh. You come back, too. Did you call the Halloran?"

"Sure. They just left. They identified the kid's belongings and signed an affidavit to that effect. That's why I got Jane over, to take it down."

"No mistakes about the kid's things?"

"Nope. Mrs. Halloran broke down. We had to get a doctor over to help her home."

Kraft glanced hatefully at Gary from the corners of his eyes, then looked back at Welte. "Call Luke Summer and his wife and tell them to get over here to the station as soon as they can. He owns that brokerage office over on—"

"Hell's bells, Bill, I've known Luke ever since he was a kid."

"I keep forgetting you people around here have known other most of your lives. Sorry, Hank. Anyway, tell them to get over here. Then you come back in with Jane."

Hank closed the door as he went out. The chief leaned back in his chair and swung partly about to face Gary. "I got a telephone here," he said. "You can use it."

"For what?"

"Call your wife at her mother's place and tell her to get back down here either tonight or tomorrow morning, but better tonight."

"How did you know where she is?"

"You really have a lousy memory, don't you? Don't you remember the reporters found her note to you?"

"Yeah, that's right. But she's not going to like this."

"She really has you under her thumb, doesn't she? It surprises me; you look to me like a man who wouldn't stand nonsense from any woman."

Gary was lighting a cigarette and held it away to snarl, "Our private life is none of your business."

"No? You'd be surprised how much that private life of yours is going to be everybody's business. Just a minute. I'll give you an idea."

He got out of his seat and left the room, to return after a moment with the Grand Point *Sun* extra. He tossed it onto Gary's lap and dropped back into his swivel chair. He propped his elbows on the desk and placed his fingertips together at his chin as he watched Gary read the paper.

Gary gasped with shock and disbelief as he scanned the first page of the paper. The headline read, DIANA HALLORAN'S SHOES FOUND, and underneath that a sub-line that read, WAR HERO QUESTIONED. He read the rest of the story, which gave in detail all that had taken place prior to the finding of Diana's other effects in the basement. That would be later news, already being readied for other extras. The report was amazingly accurate in every detail, but the fertile imagination of a reporter had been at work and the account was loaded with gruesome implications and dangling questions concerning one Gary Malone. There was always a shift away from libel, however, with the constant repetition of "it is alleged." Gary also read a brief history of himself since the day he had been born, the schools he had attended, his marriage and his exploits in the skies over North Korea, where he had shot down one MIG jet and two propeller-driven YAKs. The report almost made it appear that Gary was indeed the guilty man, but only almost. His alibi was at the very end.

Gary shoved the paper aside and stared across at the chief. "I'll be damned," he mumbled. "A war hero, yet. That's a laugh. But where did they get all that stuff about my life, and so fast?"

"You're in the newspaper morgues. Didn't you know? I checked myself last night and early this morning. You were local news when you joined Rotary. You were small news again when you made a speech at a Kiwanis luncheon, then again when you gave that talk before the American Legion. You're also an up-and-coming young businessman. The local sheets keep their eyes on guys like you. So they collected the details of your history long ago and stuck them away in the morgues. Now they got a reason for dragging it all out. And this is only the beginning. You'll be reading stuff about yourself you don't even remember any more."

"But a war hero! That's really stretching it."

"Yeah. Makes good reading, though. But now you can see how it goes. Your wife will get a big play, too. She's the one who found the shoes and, besides, the press is going to love her because she's photogenic. So you'd better get her back right away. I need her statement, and you need her help."

Gary was still puzzled as to why Ellen had sneaked off the way she had, though he would not admit to himself that it went any deeper than a desire to avoid unpleasantness. But he wanted to talk to her as much as the chief did, so he took the telephone from the desk and dialed Long Distance. He gave the San Francisco telephone number of his mother-in-law to the operator and a minute later had her on the wire. He could visualize her in the neat Marina apartment overlooking the Golden Gate, a plump, gray-haired, motherly-looking woman with a poisonous tongue and the striking of a cobra.

"Mom?" he said. "This is Gary. Look; I'm calling from Bayside. Things are a little hectic here, and—"

"Gary Malone!" she screamed. "You dare to talk to me —you—you—"

He stiffened and snapped, "No, I don't care to talk to you. Put Ellen on the phone."

"You—you—" she sputtered. "I've been reading the papers, you— Reporters are all over the place here; they're even in my bedroom. Oh, that poor girl. To think you—"

"For God's sake, put Ellen on the phone."

"She's not here, thank the Lord. She was here this morning, poor baby, but she didn't stay more than half an hour. To think what you've done to her—"

"Doesn't surprise you, does it? You always did say she was stupid to marry me."

"If I've told her once I've told her time and again—"

"Oh, skip it. Now, you listen to me. I have to see her and the chief of police down here has to talk to her. Where can I get in touch with her?"

She laughed shortly and said, "You can't get in touch with her, for which I thank heaven. She said she was going to hide out somewhere for a few days. Even I don't know where she is. I offered to go along with her, where ever she went, but she wanted to be alone. She was like a broken doll. Simply like a broken doll, the poor child. To think of the suffering you've heaped on her, that horrible operation that was all your fault, and now—"

Gary held the phone away to stare at it for a moment, then dropped it into its cradle and replaced it on the desk. He sat back on the couch and lit a cigarette, conscious of Kraft's hard gaze fixed on him.

"Ellen cleared out somewhere," he said. "Even her mother doesn't know where she went and, believe me, that's something new in this family."

Kraft asked, "You got no way to get in touch with her?"

"No. I may get an idea later where she might be, but right now my mind's a blank. Anyway, I think she'll be calling me sooner or later."

"Yeah. She sure ran out on you, didn't she? Doesn't that impress you as being pretty unusual?"

Gary glared at him, but had nothing to say. It was even more unusual than the chief realized. For Ellen to make any move without her mother was virtually a miracle. But what, he wondered, is prompting her to run this way?

Sergeant Welte came into the office followed by a young woman with a pencil and stenographer's notebook. Kraft introduced them, "Miss Bestor, Mr. Malone," but Gary merely nodded and looked away.

Welte grinned and told the chief, "It's breaking big now, Bill. Reporters and photographers from the San Francisco press and the big wire services just arrived. They want a talk with Malone as soon as you can spare him."

"Sure, sure, Did you call Luke Summer?"

"He's busy right now, but he says he'll get in touch with his wife and come over here as soon as they can make it."

"No word from Malone's house?"

"Frank called. They're still digging."

"Okay. Let's get on with this deposition." He watched Welte fold his arms and lean back against the wall, saw that Miss Bestor was ready, then turned his attention to Gary. "What I want from you," he said, "is a straightforward statement, with as much detail as possible, on where you were the day of May thirteen and that night and next morning, including as many people as possible you talked to or who saw you, and the approximate times. Got that?"

Gary crushed out his cigarette and took his time lighting another to compose himself, then said, "Aren't you supposed to ask me if I want an attorney?"

"Not necessarily. You aren't charged with anything, you're here of your own free will and you can say nothing at all and walk out that door, if that's the way you want it. But if you think you need an attorney—"

Gary shook his head. "No, no. If I had anything to hide I'd be the first one screaming for a lawyer, but there isn't anything like that. Let's get on with it."

He closed his eyes and turned his mind inward to recapture as much as possible of the day in question, then started talking. He retold everything, then was questioned briefly by the chief, especially concerning the time he had spent with Herb at the Gold Nugget. Gary opened his eyes to frown at the chief, curious as to why he was belaboring the point, but Kraft at that moment brought the questioning to an end. Gary noticed that he seemed smugly satisfied as he told Miss Bestor to type the statement in the other room and bring back an original with three copies.

She had just opened the door to leave when an extremely angry district attorney burst into the room. Scott Douglas was a short, chunky man with heavy shoulders and a long torso which was out of proportion to his short arms and legs. He had beetling brows, a perpetual scowl and a lantern jaw. Still in his thirties, he had his eye on a judge's bench in the next election. He wanted to be the youngest judge Morales County had ever known, and was not likely to allow anything to stand in the way of that ambition.

He slammed the door to the office, glanced briefly at Gary, and then leaned his fists on the desk to glare down at the chief. He roared belligerently, "What the hell do you think you're up to, Bill? I heard about this thing at ten this morning and I've been waiting in my office ever since for a ring from you."

Kraft hid a smile and said mildly, "You could have called me."

"So that's it, huh? You're on top of something big, so I come running to you."

"Now, Scotty, it's nothing like that. I've been busy, as you can well imagine."

"Oh, sure. I understand you even knew about the shoes last night. That's when you really should have called me."

Kraft leaned back and placed his fingertips together. "Call you about what, Scotty? This is straight police work. Even now I don't have anything for the D.A.'s office."

Douglas blinked at him and swallowed hard and shouted, "You don't have anything! What's all that stuff they're printing in the papers? And now another extra on the way about the rest of the kid's stuff being found in Malone's basement and your men out digging up the back yard. What am I supposed to think they're doing out there, amateur gardening? Look, chum, let's get something straight. This Halloran case is the biggest thing ever to hit this county, and everything that happens and every move you make, or anyone else makes, is a matter of vital interest to me. Do we understand each other?"

He stood there glaring at Kraft, breathing hard, and the chief had to stifle the laughter that was welling in his chest. For once, he had the D.A. exactly where he wanted him and, he had to admit truthfully to himself, he had done it deliberately, to reduce the man's self-importance.

Douglas sensed the entertainment he was affording the chief and exerted masterful control over his anger. He turned to appraise Gary, who knew nothing of the antipathy existing between the two men. The D.A. remembered having met Gary a year or so before and also of having seen him here and there. However, he had heard a great deal about Gary Malone, that he was a ball of fire in the real-estate business, that he was a rising young architect, that everyone liked him and that in time he would be a man to be reckoned with in the local political field. But, he thought, he doesn't look like much now. He looks downright scared.

"Kind of a mess you're in," he said.

Gary dragged at his cigarette and nodded. "I'm not enjoying it."

"Uh-huh. I'm Scott Douglas."

"I know. What do you have to do with this case?"

"Don't you know much about the workings of the law?"

"I haven't needed to, until now."

"Well, in case of prosecution, you know, I have to be the wheel behind the wheels."

Gary shrugged. The statement meant little to him, but he said, "I see."

Douglas turned back to Kraft and asked to be briefed on everything that had taken place. The chief had had his moment of fun and also knew that Douglas could make matters extremely uncomfortable for the Bayside police if he became too angry, so he decided to cooperate. But he did not care to talk in front of Gary, and asked Welte to take him out to the other room.

The moment Gary stepped out of the office he found himself the center of a mob of reporters and photographers from the bay area. Flashbulbs went off in his eyes and he was again subjected to a steady barrage of questioning. He tried to shove his way through the crowd, but it was impossible. He tried to ignore them and found that, too, to be impossible. Gradually he started giving answers to their questions and talked steadily for a solid hour, usually repeating over and over again details that had already been explained. He talked automatically, almost without thought. But the constant weight of the questioning that had been going on steadily since eight that morning was beginning to exhaust him. Welte noticed his haggardness and became alarmed enough to rap on the chief's door.

It was a relief for Gary to get back into the sanctuary of the office and drop onto the couch again. He accepted a glass and a small pitcher of water from Welte and drank it down almost without pause. He closed his eyes for a moment and nearly fell asleep, but shook himself awake when he heard the door open and close again. Jane Bestor had returned to the office with the typed deposition.

Kraft took the papers from her, handed a copy to Douglas, now relaxed in a chair at his side, another to Welte, and the original to Gary. All of them sat back to read and there was a heavy silence in the office. When Gary had finished he glanced across at the chief, who had also finished his copy and was watching him narrowly.

The chief asked, "Satisfied with it? No mistakes?"

Gary rubbed his hands over his eyes and blinked at the chief. "No mistakes that I could find. It's the way I dictated it."

"Then you don't mind signing the one you have and the copies?"

Gary noticed the chief's tension and the note of eagerness in his voice, and had a hunch that something was wrong, that perhaps he should not sign. He glanced through the papers again and could find no reason for his odd hunch. Miss Bestor had taken down his conversation and the chief's questions verbatim. Everything seemed to be in order.

"No," he said, "I don't mind signing. They're my words. Why should I mind?"

Kraft handed him a fountain pen and Gary signed the papers he held, and the copies as they were passed to him. Welte and Miss Bestor signed their names as witnesses, after which Miss Bestor quietly left the office. Kraft heaved a great sigh of relief, stacked the papers together and placed them in a fresh folder on the face of which he marked Malone, Gary. He put the folder away in the filing cabinet and dropped heavily back into his chair.

Kraft's features underwent a sudden, marked change. His lips thinned, his face darkened and all the hatred he had been feeling and suppressing flooded into his eyes and voice. He slammed his big hands palms-down on the surface of the desk, leaned toward Gary and snarled, "Now, you lying son-of-a-bitch, where have you buried the kid's body?"

Gary had started to lift a cigarette to his mouth, but paused halfway and stared into the chief's eyes. He thought for a moment that he had not heard right, but when he realized that he had, his temper exploded like a rocket. He snapped to his feet and made a wild dive for the chief. He managed to get in a hard left blow on the head that knocked Kraft out of his chair and back against the wall, but that was as far as he got. Welte and the D.A. fell on top of him and the chief was instantly on his feet and wrestled Gary back to the couch. Kraft took great pleasure in using his huge bulk and power to slam Gary down so forcefully that the whip of his head almost snapped his neck. Kraft went back to his chair, pulled it upright, and dropped down again facing Gary.

"Okay," he said. "Now you got that out of your system, let's have it. Where is the kid's body?"

If the two had been alone, Gary would have gone after him again, but he realized it was hopeless. "You go to hell," he snapped.

"We'll get it out of you, you know, one way or another. I'm the first guy in the world to stick to ethical police procedure ninety-nine times out of a hundred, but this is that one time that's different. Anything that happens to a bastard like you is too good for you."

Douglas had returned to his own chair and asked excitedly, "What have you got on him, Bill? You must have something."

"I have. But you keep out of this."

Gary picked up the cigarette he had dropped to the floor and took a long drag of smoke deep into his lungs. He blew it out slowly and said, "You're convinced I'm guilty; I've known that for some time. Why has that stupid cop brain of yours made up its mind that I'm guilty? Or is it some deep, dark secret?"

Kraft picked up a pencil and turned it slowly about in his fingers, his eyes never leaving Gary's. "Nothing secret about it," he said. "Not any more. Now that I have your signed statement down in black and white. I'll tell you, you bastard. At first, it never entered my mind that you could be guilty. Stupid as I am, I always kind of liked you. Even finding the shoes in your basement didn't put the finger on you. I was set back on my heels when we found the rest of the kid's stuff, but even then you were mostly innocent in my mind. You see, I believed that alibi of yours. Even Mr. Short confirmed it. What the hell? I figured you were in the clear. But Short called back again, while I was at your house. Your alibi exploded like a punctured balloon."

"You're lying."

"Oh, no. You've been doing all the lying. Herb Short checked through his books. He found that on the afternoon of May thirteenth he had a small fire and his place was closed from one to five P.M. Neither you or anyone else was drinking beer with him at four o'clock that day."

"But that can't be. Herb and I were talking about it just yesterday. He remembered me being there that day."

Kraft shook his blond head slowly back and forth. "You were the one who brought it up, which was pretty clever of you, I admit. He assumed you knew what you were talking about. When he checked his books, though, he found that you were all wrong. He knows, now, that you could not have been in his place at that time. Now he really remembers the day. He'll swear by it. And I have your sworn lie in my files. How do you like that?"

Gary was suddenly confused, as well as frightened. He sat back and tried to think of how it had been on the fateful Friday and could remember definitely starting up the valley road at about three-thirty and passing through Valley Center somewhere around four o'clock. He thought he had stopped to have a beer in Herb's place, but it could easily be that he had confused that day with the time he had stopped at Herb's on the way back the following noon. Three months had passed. It was almost impossible to remember something that had been so trivial at the time and yet was now of vast importance. The more he thought of it, though, the more he realized that he must have been mistaken. Probably, though he couldn't remember it, he had stopped at the Gold Nugget, but, on finding the door locked, had simply driven on. That was undoubtedly what had occurred and why his memory had played a trick on him.

"Well," he said, "I guess you're right, at that. I suppose I did stop, but then drove on. So I made a mistake."

"You mean you were deliberately lying. And I got your signature on that lie."

"Look, I tell you it was a mistake. For God's sake, you can't expect a man to be accurate about every beer he drank and where three months ago. I thought I had stopped there. Maybe I did, but I couldn't get in and drove on. Now that I've been thinking of it I don't really remember."

"You mean you've got a convenient memory, now that you're trapped in a lie."

Trapped. That was it. He looked about at the three pairs of eyes staring coldly into his and knew how an animal felt in a trap. He also realized the futility of argument.

He sank down limply in the couch and mumbled, "God, I wish Ellen was here."

Welte had been watching Gary with a savage look in his eyes, but now he turned to the chief and asked, "Shall I book him?"

Kraft asked mildly, "On what charge, Hank?"

"Why, murder, of course."

Douglas turned to stare at the sergeant and exploded, "Don't be an ass, you ass. Murder! How do you know a murder has been committed? Can you prove it? It's even possible that kid could be alive somewhere. Can you prove she isn't?"

Gary whispered, "We all know better than that. She's dead, all right."

Kraft asked, quickly, "You got a statement to make to that effect?"

"As I said before, you can go to hell. I wouldn't know that poor kid if I tripped over her. I never met her in my life and I don't even remember seeing her around town, though it's possible I did. No, I don't have any more statements to make. But I think we all know she's dead."

The D.A. nodded. "Yeah. No doubt of that. She couldn't be alive and hidden away somewhere this long, anyway. Besides, we got her clothes. She's dead, all right." He glanced at the sergeant and growled, "But damn it all, man, you have to prove a thing like that."

"Then how about holding him on suspicion of murder?"

"Murder! Murder! What murder? Can't you get it through your head that the law has to have proof of murder? We have a moral certainty that murder has been committed and we're morally certain we have the man who committed it, but that isn't enough to convict a man before a jury."

Gary said, "You'll have to charge me with something, or I'm going to walk out of here. I've had enough."

Kraft smiled icily. "You aren't going anywhere, Malone, and I'm not charging you with anything, at least not for the present. You're going to stay right here of your own free will."

"In my hat. I'm leaving."

"No, you're not. Ordinarily, I'd keep that lie of yours locked away in my files, but now I have to use it to keep you sitting right on that couch. I'm going out in a minute and tell the reporters all about it. When that lie hits the front pages you won't dare walk on the street without police escort. We haven't had a lynching in California in a good many years, but that's no guarantee we couldn't have one if you start walking around loose. You sit right there."

Kraft took a copy of Gary's statement out of his files and walked out of the office to join the crowd of reporters. Gary could hear the roar that went up through the closed doors when the chief informed the press that Gary's alibi had been completely punctured.

Douglas said, "You hear, Malone? Your life isn't worth a plugged nickel from this point on. You're free game for anyone."

Gary tried to think of it from that angle, but succeeded only by concentrating on someone else being in his shoes. Then he could understand it. He realized that he, too, would convict a man in his own mind with the few facts presented so far if he read about it in his newspaper. It was not logical to assume that anyone else would run the risk of burying the girl's belongings in another person's basement. Then there was the big lie. No one would think of it as a simple mistake. It had become the big lie and that it would remain.

"Yeah," he said. "I see what you mean. In a way, though, it's funny. I'm the only one who knows I am innocent and that doesn't count."

Kraft came back into the room, closed and locked the door and took his seat behind the desk. He had two new sheets of paper in his hands, in addition to Gary's statement, and studied them for a few minutes before looking at Gary.

He rattled the papers and said, "This is the list of voters who used the polls in your garage on May seventeenth. Twelve women and eight men. I think we can forget the women. It isn't their type of crime. So we have eight men, any one of whom you claim could have gone into your basement."

"I don't claim anything. I just say it's a possibility."

The D.A. asked, "What's this all about, Bill?" and Kraft explained about the Malone garage being used as a polling place the Tuesday following the Halloran girl's disappearance.

"We have to check every angle," he said. "Eight men. It shouldn't be hard to find out where each of them was on May thirteenth. Then that escape route will be closed."

Douglas asked Gary, "Who else had access to your basement around that time?"

"Anyone who walked by, I guess. We never locked it. But let me think a minute." He was silent for a moment, then said, "Well, there's the grocery delivery boy. We always put empty bottles in the front end of the basement for him to pick up. His name is Jerry something-or-other. Works for the Flightway."

Kraft wrote it down on a pad and mumbled, "I'll have talk with him. Who else?"

"We also had something wrong with our plumbing along about that time. I'm not sure of the date, but it was around the middle of May."

"The plumber was in your basement?"

"Yes. He had to shut off the water. The main cutoff is down there."

"Name?"

"I think it's Franklin. He's a good man. Works independently and does some small contracting."

Welte said, "I know him. Bert Franklin. He lives up on Ridgeway with his wife and a whole passel of kids. Want me to question him, Bill?"

Kraft nodded. "May as well. Better have him come down here, though, and we'll get that out of the way. We'll need signed and witnessed affidavits if we're going to present this to the Grand Jury."

Douglas said, "The Grand Jury is in session now."

"I know."

Gary stared down at the floor for a long while, then looked up at the chief to say, "Luke Summer, too."

"What was he doing in your basement?"

"Well, the trout season opened in May and Luke borrowed a spinning reel of mine to try it out. He got it out of the basement. He didn't like it much, though, and put it back."

"You mean he got it out of the basement or you got it out for him?"

"He got it himself and put it back himself. He knows where I keep my stuff down there."

"Okay. He should be along any minute. I'll get his statement. Anyone else?"

Gary thought again for a long while, but finally shook his head. "That's about it. The basement is just kind of a storage place. Except for the grocer's boy, hardly anyone else ever goes in there. No, I can't think of anyone else. But it doesn't have to be one of them, you know."

"Who else, except you? We'll run down each of these people because the Grand Jury won't be satisfied unless we do. But you and I know it's a lot of waste motion. Don't we? Why don't you come clean, Malone? Everything we've turned up so far points straight at you. You had the time, you had the opportunity, you had the house to yourself that weekend and you're strong enough to subdue a healthy, fourteen-year-old girl."

"Oh, God. Even to think—"

"Then there's all the stuff found in your basement and the vital fact that you lied about where you were at that time. Cripes, Malone, all we need now is the body. Practically everything else is complete. So why don't you come clean and save us a lot of trouble and yourself a lot of additional grief? Where did you bury her?"

The chief asked the same questions, phrased differently each time, over and over again. When he got tired Welte took over the questioning and when he became tired of it Douglas asked questions. It went on until a few minutes before six in the afternoon. It ended then only because everyone was hungry and because Gary made a suggestion that rather staggered the other three.

"Look," he said; "none of you are ever going to believe I'm telling the truth about anything. So why not put me to a test? How about these lie detectors I've heard about? Are they any good?"

Douglas blinked and said, "They work damned well in the hands of a skilled operator."

"All right. Then you get a skilled operator and one of those machines and I'll answer any damned question you can imagine."

Kraft did not know where such a machine could be had, but Douglas thought that he might be able to borrow one from the San Francisco police. He went into another room, to use a telephone in privacy, then returned with the information. "They'll send a machine down to us from the city tomorrow. Also an operator, Inspector Richtof."

Kraft asked, "Who were you talking to?"

"The chief. We've done them a few favors down here. Besides, they're all excited about the case, too. Oh, yes. The chief says some psychiatrist from the University of California will be coming along with Inspector Richtof. Big deal, huh?" He yawned and stretched his arms. "I think I'll be running along. Nothing else breaking right now. How about that digging in the Malone yard?"

"It's still going on. I called Frank a little while ago to put on a new shift of diggers and keep it going all night if necessary. They can rig up some lights out there."

"Good idea. Let me know if anything breaks. And as for you," he said, turning to face Gary, "it will give me great pleasure to take you apart piece by piece in court one of these days."

Gary gritted his teeth and told him, "It will also give me great pleasure to pin your damned ears back when you find out how wrong you are."

"I should live to see that day."

He jerked his head at the two officers and they started out of the room with him. Kraft paused to tell Gary that he would have some dinner sent in, then went out and closed the door.

It was the first time Gary had been really alone since eight that morning. He sagged back in the couch and closed his eyes and thought of the nightmare that had overtaken him. He had to open his eyes and look around the office to assure himself it was not all a bad dream, that it was truly happening to him.

Because he was alone he was suddenly aware of all sounds and noises outside the room he was in. He could hear Kraft talking to someone and reporters arguing and the buzzing of the dispatch radio and sounds of cars out on the streets. He also heard something else strange in his experience, a deep, low rumbling that seemed to be everywhere in the air, but was most likely from outside the building. He walked to a window that had glazed glass on the lower half and clear glass on the upper. He stood up on a chair and looked out the window and his heart started pounding wildly.

As far as he could see the streets were packed densely with people. They were milling about and talking loudly, which accounted for the rumbling noise, and their faces turned constantly toward the police station. And in every expression was hatred and rage and the lust to kill. For me, he thought.

He dropped quickly away from the window before he could be seen and leaned back against the wall. There had not been a lynching in California in years. But he had seen those faces. They were the faces of a lynch mob.

Chapter Four

Gary was able to eat very little of the dinner brought in by one of the policemen, and when he ran out of cigarettes he became almost frantic until another pack was brought to him. He paced the floor, endlessly smoking cigarettes, turning over in his mind everything that had happened and trying to resolve it into a sensible pattern.

Gary put it off as long as possible—he hated to face the people outside the office—but he was finally forced to use the lavatory, which was at the other end of the building. He stepped out of the office and the excited conversations buzzing about the building came to a dead halt. Every eye turned in his direction and every face became a smooth, cold mask. Men were packed in the small reception room and the hallway and the air was blue with smoke. Some of them were writing in notebooks and others had portable typewriters propped on loose chairs and even the dispatch counter. All action halted as Gary made his way through the clusters of men and on into the police locker room. His progress was followed by whispered curses and his spine felt as if it had turned to ice.

He had almost reached the lavatory when he was intercepted by a strange policeman who wanted to know where he was going. Gary told him, and received the information that Kraft had gone home for dinner, had then gone out to Malone's house to see how the digging was going, and would be back at the station in a few minutes. Gary glanced at his watch and was surprised to find that it was almost eight o'clock.

He went into the lavatory and heaved a sigh of relief at finding it empty. He was washing his hands and dousing cold water on his face and hair when he heard Kraft's voice in the locker room. He paid little attention until he also heard a familiar woman's voice. He dried his face and hands and hurriedly combed his hair, then stepped to the door. He pulled it open a crack and looked out into the locker room.

Kraft was standing a few feet away from the door, his back to Gary. Luke and Betty Summer were standing before him, and Jane Bestor was seated on a chair close by taking down their conversation. Everyone else had been cleared from the room. Luke's features looked drawn and tired. His face was pale and he kept wetting his lips with the tip of his tongue. Betty's rather chubby face, on the other hand, was colored with excitement and her usually mild eyes were blazing with anger that seemed tinged with fear.

She was stating flatly, "That is exactly the way it happened. We had nothing to do with it at all. Nothing."

Kraft asked, "Then you weren't actually present when the shoes were found?"

Luke said, "I think you were told before that Ellen—Mrs. Malone—found the shoes some time during the afternoon. We arrived at the house just before dinner. Afterwards we played some bridge. It was not until we were leaving that Ellen mentioned anything about the shoes. I was out in the kitchen with Gary. Betty knows more about that angle."

"Well," said Betty, "there isn't much to that. She just happened to mention finding the strange shoes, and she brought them out to show to me. Luke and Gary joined us about that time."

Kraft nodded. "All that checks. What I would like to know is Malone's attitude at the time."

Luke looked uncomfortable as he said, "That's hard to say, Bill."

Betty's anger flared and she snapped, "Oh, don't pussyfoot around protecting him. You remember he got mad about the whole thing. He even tried to take the shoes away from you so you wouldn't see the initials."

Luke sighed and said patiently, "You don't know it was for that reason, dear. I think he was just fed up hearing about them. He was as surprised as anyone when I found the initials."

The chief's pale eyebrows raised with surprise. "I didn't know that. You were the one who noticed the initials?"

Luke answered reluctantly, "Yes. They were pretty hard to see, so small and down near the soles that way. I held the shoes under the light and made out the initials DBH. Betty and Ellen guessed almost right away that they probably belonged to the Halloran girl."

"Uh-huh." Kraft glanced at Miss Bestor and she nodded that she was getting everything down. "So," he said, "what happened then? Was that when Malone called me?"

Luke appeared more uncomfortable than ever and mumbled, "Uh—let me see—just about, I guess."

Betty cried, "That isn't so, Luke Summer, and you know it." She looked back at the chief, her eyes blazing more fiercely. "You can't listen to him," she said. "I'm afraid my husband has a distorted sense of loyalty. We've been arguing about this thing ever since it happened, and I don't mind saying I'm practically on the verge of hysteria. All this publicity and now our names in it, and this questioning—"

Kraft said soothingly, "Sorry, Mrs. Summer. I know how you feel. Now, you were saying—"

Luke glared at her, but she refused to face him and said, "I'm just trying to tell you the truth of the way it happened. I don't care what my husband says, I know very well Gary was badly upset by the whole thing. He wouldn't listen to reason at all and wanted us to forget the whole thing, with those initials staring us right in the eyes, mind you, and he kept saying it was coincidence and he was going to get rid of the shoes and——"

"In other words, Mrs. Summer, he had no intentions of calling me."

"I should say he didn't. Ellen was the one who practically forced him to call you."

"Oh?"

"She just said she wouldn't be able to close her eyes without knowing, and insisted that he call the police. Even then he stalled, trying to tell her that he'd look for someone in the neighborhood with the same initials. Imagine!"

Luke stared at his wife with pain in his eyes, then told Kraft, "She isn't putting exactly the right construction on this. Gary was bored with the whole business and, besides, he just couldn't believe it was possible that the shoes would belong to the Halloran girl. I don't think he was deliberately stalling, or being evasive, or anything like that."

"Then you deny what your wife has just said?"

"Well, no. It did happen that way, but—— It's the way she said, I mean the way it happened, but when it comes to his attitude——Oh, hell, I don't know. I'm getting confused myself."

"Well," Betty snapped, "I'm not confused. His attitude struck me as being very odd even then. That's why I made Luke leave as soon as you were called, Mr. Kraft. I didn't wish to get mixed up in it. I had a feeling right then he was guilty, by the way he was acting." She looked at Luke and demanded, "Didn't I? Didn't I tell you on the way home I'll bet he's the one?"

"Oh, for God's sake, Betty. Please! We're talking about Gary—Gary Malone—not some stranger."

Kraft nodded at Miss Bestor to close her book and smiled and said, "That's all, folks. You've been a great help, and I appreciate it. Miss Bestor will have your statement typed in the morning, so drop around any time tomorrow and sign it, will you? Incidentally—about the reporters—you can say what you please, everything you've told me, for your own protection, just remember that there are laws concerning slander and libel. Malone hasn't been charged with anything yet. Be careful."

Luke nodded and growled, "I'd like to shut her up with a gag in her mouth."

Betty was on the verge of snapping back at him, but movement caught her eye and she turned her head and gasped as Gary pulled the lavatory door all the way open and stepped into view. Gary paid no attention to the others, but stopped in front of Betty and whispered huskily, almost without emotion, "You dirty, rotten bitch."

Kraft stared at him, then snapped his eyes toward Luke and stepped back out of the way. It was obvious, by his action, that Luke had the chief's blessing to take a swing at Gary if he wished. Luke, however, looked into Gary's eyes with shock and what seemed to be a tacit plea for understanding. Then he turned slowly and closed his fingers in a grip of steel about his wife's arm. She winced with pain, but when Luke spun her about she went with him meekly enough, glad to get away from the rage and accusation in Gary's hot eyes. They reached the crowded reception room and were immediately overwhelmed by reporters. Betty had regained her composure by that time. She glanced back once at Gary through the glass partition, then she started talking.

Kraft shrugged and said, "Well, anyway, you can't hear her any more. Did you hear most of what they had to say?"

"I guess."

"I was hoping you would."

"You mean you knew I was there?"

"Sure. I was told. That's why I brought the Summers in here. Your best friends, aren't they?"

"Luke is."

"Not Mrs. Summer?"

Gary bit his lip, then admitted reluctantly, "She's my wife's closest friend."

"Uh-huh. A close friend. And you heard what she had to say. Can you imagine how a jury would react to her testimony? Look, Malone; doesn't this prove to you that you haven't a prayer? Even your wife's closest friend is a hostile witness. Now, why don't you come clean and give me the whole story?"

"What's the matter? Haven't you found any bodies in my back yard?"

"Well, not under the patio, anyway. The men are now digging up the rest of the yard. We'll find what we're after. You can bet on that."

"Oh, sure. And you still have the wrong man. How about the other people who had access to our basement?"

"We're checking. Let's go back into my office."

"Are you asking or ordering?"

Kraft stared at him narrowly, then smiled thinly. "I'm still asking."

"Okay."

They made their way back to the chief's office and closed the door against the reporters who were insatiable for more information. Gary stood on a chair and again looked out the window to the street. It was twilight and darkening fast under the tall pines, but Gary could still see the crowd, thinner now, milling about.

Gary remarked about it as he stepped down from the chair and dropped back on the couch. The chief settled his big bulk in the swivel chair behind the desk and nodded.

"Mobs like that," he said, "don't stay steamed up too long. They got other things to do. But if they'd had a leader it could have been pretty rough. Did you know we got state cops out there keeping things in order?"

"No."

"A couple dozen of them are patrolling the whole town."

Gary ran his fingers about his throat and swallowed hard.

He had left half a pot of coffee on the chief's desk. It was cold, but he poured it into a cup and drank it down. Kraft shoved a decanter of water and a glass toward Gary's side of the desk.

He took some papers from an inside pocket, sat back to look through them, then said, "Well, here's the score so far. Jerry Smith, the grocer boy, was questioned by Welte a little while ago. He knew Diana Halloran; in fact, he went to the same school. He was a senior then, and graduated in June. On May thirteenth he left school at about three-thirty and drove downtown in his jalopy. He wasn't feeling good, so he didn't go to work that afternoon in the grocery store. He says he took a ride down the coast with some friend of his—he doesn't remember who it was, but it will probably come back to him. Then he went home."

"Can he prove where he was and who he was with?"

"His memory isn't too clear. He just remembers being sick that day."

"Does he go for a ride every time he's sick?"

"Oh, stop playing like a detective. The kid's all right. It isn't too easy to remember exactly what you were doing three months ago."

"That's what I keep trying to tell you."

"Yeah, yeah. Anyway, Welte told him it was important and he'd better give it a lot of thought, so he will undoubtedly come up with the answers. Welte says he's a shy sort of kid."

"I know. I don't think he has many friends. I was always nice to him, but he never had much to say."

"Uh-huh. So the next is your friend, Luke Summer. He remembers borrowing the spinning reel, but not the date."

"I didn't hear him in the other room—"

"I ran into him outside. He was telling me about it on the way in. Anyway, he remembers when he put the reel back. He remembers it well, because it was the morning after the kid disappeared."

"May fourteenth?"

"That's right. He says he went by your place to give it to you, but you weren't home—"

"I didn't start back from Chinamen's Ridge until about eleven."

"—so he took the reel down to your basement himself and left it there. He says that was about ten in the morning. As for May thirteenth itself, he isn't too sure of his actions. The New York ticker goes off in that brokerage office of his at twelve. He says he usually knocks off for lunch about an hour and a half, goes back to the office to clean up some paper work for maybe another hour, then sometimes calls on a few clients. He doesn't really know what he was doing that particular afternoon, but he's going to look through his records tomorrow and says he'll let me know." Kraft put the papers aside for a moment and looked quizzically at Gary. "Do you think he's a suspect?"

Gary snorted, "Don't be a fool. Luke isn't that type any more than I am."

"So now we got a certain type? Interesting." He glanced at the papers again and continued, "Then there's Bert Franklin, the plumber. Hank called on him, too."

"That sergeant gets around."

"All on overtime. I told him to knock off and get some rest, but he's got his teeth in this thing and wants to see it through." He looked off into space and said musingly, "Kind of a lousy cop, some ways, but other ways he's a real bird dog. Anyway, he saw Franklin. The plumber remembers doing some work for you, but he doesn't remember dates or anything else. He's looking through his records now. Hank told him to be sure and check on May thirteenth, too. We'll have his answer tonight or tomorrow. That's the works."

"How about the eight men who voted in our garage that Tuesday?"

Kraft gave him a pitying look, then growled, "Knock it off, for God's sake. Who are you trying to fool? We'll look up all these people eventually, because we have to, but, believe me, I'm not losing any sleep over them. Which reminds me. You'd better spend the night here. You can use one of the cots in the cell." He added dryly, "The door won't be locked."

Gary's greatest desire of the moment was to leave the police station and go home. He had talked so much that his jaws ached, his eyes were beginning to water and his body felt as if someone had been pummeling on it for hours on end. He wanted to crawl into his own bed and simply die. He knew, however, that it could not be done. There was the temper of the people to consider.

"How about a hotel?" he asked hopefully.

Kraft chuckled hollowly and shrugged. "Take a chance if you want, but I'm not detailing anyone to protect you."

"Why not?"

"Because I don't give a good goddam what happens to you, that's why. Understand? Stay here or not. Make up your own mind. I'm leaving pretty soon myself. I'm beat."

Gary thought of going to a hotel and then of what he might run into if he stepped out into the street alone, and fear was again a hard knot in his stomach. He mumbled weakly, "I'll stay here."

"Yeah. I thought you would."

There was a knock at the door and Welte entered with Bert Franklin in tow. The plumber had a ledger and some envelopes under his arm. He was a small man, about five-six, with a round, moonlike face, thinning hair that was bald in back, square, calloused hands, a sensitive mouth and a weak, receding chin. He was an excellent plumber, but he resented orders from anyone else, so years before had gone into business for himself. He was wearing dirty corduroys, short boots, a T shirt and a leather jacket.

He looked with open distaste at Gary as he shook hands with the chief and placed his ledger and papers on the desk. Gary had started to smile—he had always rather liked the plumber—but when he saw the hostility in the man's eyes his own expression froze.

Welte told Kraft importantly, "This guy's got something to say, so I thought I'd better bring him down here."

Kraft reminded him mildly, "I told you to bring him down here in the first place." He smiled pleasantly at the plumber and asked, "What's on your mind, Mr. Franklin?"

The plumber cleared his throat and answered in a high-pitched voice, "Well, a couple things maybe you should know. But first things first." He pointed at his ledger and said, "It's all in there, the work I did for Mr. Malone. I was in his place twice, down in that basement, I mean; once in the morning at eight-thirty and again in the afternoon a little before five. I ain't sure, exactly, but it was close to five. Anyway, I went in there first to fix a bad leak in the main, but I didn't have the right stuff with me, so I had to shut off the water for the whole house. Then I come back about five, like I say, and repaired the main. That's the whole job and that's the only time I been in there."

"I see. I suppose the sergeant explained to you that anyone who had access to that basement is a suspect of sorts?"

"You mean like the guy who done it?"

Kraft hid a smile and nodded. "That's right. How about the thirteenth of May? That was a Friday."

Franklin stiffened and said spiritedly, "You don't have to tell me. I know what day it was. And I looked up the record. You'll find it all in them receipts and stuff. Friday the thirteenth. Jeez, that was sure one unlucky day for that poor kid. I ain't never been superstitious myself, but when a guy thinks of a thing like that—" He paused and shuddered, then continued, "Well, anyway, I looked up where I was that day. I done a job for Mrs. Trent. You know the old lady who judges all them fancy dog shows? Well, sir, I finished that job at three o'clock. She was home, so you can check with her. Then I left her place and went over to the new house John Bergstrom was building in the dunes. You know Bergstrom, the contractor?"

The chief thought a moment and nodded. "I believe I've met him."

"Yeah. He cuts them bids of his awful short and then he's gotta cheat somewhere to make good, but he's a crackerjack contractor. I do lots of work for him. Anyway, I got there a couple minutes after three and installed a new water heater. Took me just two and a half hours. You'll see the charge there in my books and stuff. Then I headed home for dinner—"

Kraft interrupted with a wave of his hand. "That's all that is necessary, Mr. Franklin. The main thing is that on the thirteenth of May you were working at Mrs. Trent's home until three in the afternoon and then on the Bergstrom job until about five-thirty."

"Yes, sir. You can check with Bergie. I got it there in my stuff the hours that heater was installed, so it's more'n likely it's in his books, too. In this business a man's gotta keep track of things like that, you know. Just forget once and these contractors will cheat a man out of his eye teeth."

"Well, that's out of my line. Anything else?"

"There sure is." He turned and scowled at Gary for a moment, then looked back at the chief. "Now, this you can take for what it's worth. I didn't pay it no mind at the time, but I did notice it."

"What's that?"

"Well, like I say, I was in that basement at eight-thirty election day, when I shut off the water. I noticed something. There was a place the dirt was dug up— fresh dug up, I mean. I work around dirt a lot. I know when it's fresh dug. This was fresh and I sort of wondered about it, but, like I say, I didn't really pay it no mind. But when I come back about five that day this place that was dug was all smoothed over and you couldn't tell it from the rest of the dirt and sand."

The chief sat up straight and asked tensely, "Do you remember exactly where that dug-up spot was located in the basement?"

"I sure do. It was right under where some fishing rods was hung on racks."

"You're positive?"

"It's in my mind like I seen it yesterday."

Kraft smiled and leaned back in his chair with a deep sigh of satisfaction. He winked at Welte and nodded and said, "That fixes it, Hank. That is the precise spot where we dug up the Halloran girl's belongings, right under those racks of fishing rods. Now we know definitely that those things were buried in there some time between May thirteenth and eight-thirty on the morning of May seventeenth. What a break this is."

He got to his feet and walked around the desk to pump the plumber's arm. "You're a great help, Mr. Franklin. You have no idea."

"Well, now, I didn't know it was that important."

"But it is. Fixing time is always difficult in police work. This information of yours can save us a lot of unnecessary work. I'm grateful." He laughed and slapped the plumber's shoulder and said, "Next time you get a ticket bring it in to me."

"I don't get no tickets. I'm real careful about things like that."

"Well, just in case, then." He eased the plumber out the door and into the hallway, where he asked, "You're ready to swear about that place that was dug up, and the date and the time?"

"Sure."

"No doubts in your mind at all?"

"Now, you look here. I wouldn't of said nothing if there was any doubts. I seen that dug-up place—"

"Good. Good. You may have to give your testimony to the Grand Jury, you know."

The plumber's little eyes gleamed with interest and excitement. "That's all right with me."

"Fine. And thanks again for your help. We'll keep in touch with you."

"Yeah. I guess maybe you better."

Kraft watched him leave, then turned back into the office and faced Gary. Gary's head was bowed and he was staring down at the floor, his eyes half-closed with fatigue.

Kraft said, "Kind of stacking up on you, isn't it? That little guy's statement rules out all the voters who used the polls in your garage after eight-thirty that Tuesday. We're getting it narrowed down to where it belongs—you."

Gary looked up and stared at the chief and shoved himself to his feet. "How about that cot?"

"Can you sleep with what you have on your conscience?"

"As I have said before, but it can bear repeating, you can go to hell."

Welte grabbed Gary's arm and shook him and scowled at the chief. "Why don't you paste the bastard one in the mouth?"

"Leave him alone."

"I wouldn't take that kind of talk from him."

Gary looked into Welte's eyes and said, "You can go to hell, too. In fact, I'll give you ten seconds to get your filthy hand off my arm or I'll paste *you* one in the mouth."

Kraft moved in between the two of them fast and shoved them apart before anything could happen. He hustled Gary out of the office and away from the few reporters still standing around and on into the locker room. He opened the door to the cell and saw that one of the cots had two blankets and a pillow.

"Better leave the door open," he told Gary. "You can turn off the light, though."

"I'm also closing the door. I'm a guest here. Remember?"

He staggered into the room, threw his coat on the other cot, stepped out of his trousers and dropped them on top of his coat. He sat down on his own cot to remove his shoes, but his eyes closed and he fell back sound asleep with one shoe still on. Kraft removed it for him, pulled one of the blankets out from underneath his inert form and tossed it over him. When he went out he left the door open.

Welte was standing in the locker room. Kraft called him over and said, "Let him sleep about thirty minutes, then wake him up and question him for fifteen minutes or so. I don't care what you ask. Just keep him awake for a while. Then you go home and get some rest. But pass on the word to the rest of the night shift to wake him up every half-hour or so and question him."

"What's the idea?"

"Well, I want him to get a little rest, but not much. I want him still pooped tomorrow when he takes that lie test."

"Low resistance?"

"That's the idea." Kraft scratched his head and said admiringly, "The guy's got a lot of stuff in him. You have to admit that. He's gone through plenty today and yet he's still ready to take on the whole force. We have to break that down. It all depends on him."

"Not if we find the body."

Kraft was thoughtfully silent for a moment, then squeezed Welte's arm and said, "You know something, Hank? I got a hunch we're not going to find that body. He made a mistake when he buried that stuff in his own basement, but I don't think he made any other mistakes. That body is not in his yard."

"How about Chinamen's Ridge? That's where he says he spent that night."

"I know. I wanted to go through the yard first. That should be cleaned up tonight. Tomorrow I'll get in touch with the sheriff and we'll have a look around the Rigsby place at Chinamen's Ridge. That has always been the logical place in my mind, anyway, an isolated cabin up in the mountains and all. But I don't know. I just don't know."

"What's the matter?"

"Well, there's something about that Malone. Some ways, he's so damned sure of himself. Like volunteering to take that lie detector test. He has a lot of guts. But I think I know why. He's not worried about anyone finding that body. And if we don't find it, well—" He sighed. "Me for the sack. Remember. Tell the boys to keep him awake most of the night. We have to break him down."

"Yeah."

Kraft started walking away, then came to a halt and stood there for a minute, then turned about to look at Welte. "Hank."

"Uh-huh."

"Are you convinced that Malone's guilty?"

Welte stared at him with surprise. "Hell's bells, yes. No doubt of it. That's a silly question to ask."

"I guess you're right. I'm a little pooped myself. Well, good night."

The chief's orders were carried out. All through the night, every half-hour, one of the night force awakened Gary and asked questions for ten or fifteen minutes. Gary was so drugged with fatigue and the bit of sleep he was getting, that he hadn't strength enough to protest, or sufficient mental awareness to know what was being done to him. He was always allowed to drop back to the cot and fall asleep again before his mind could become fully awake. It went on all night.

Only at dawn was he left alone, and then he slept without moving, breathing deeply and loudly, for not more than an hour and a half. He was awakened a few minutes after seven by someone shaking him. It took a tremendous effort of will for him to force his eyelids open, but he was suddenly wide awake when he looked up in the gray light coming through the window and saw Ellen bending over him. He sat up quickly and wrapped his arms about her legs and buried his face against her. His emotions almost went out of control for a few seconds, and he came very close to sobbing, but he held to her tightly until the moment of weakness was gone and he could feel strength ebbing back into his body.

"Thank God," he mumbled, "you're here. You have no idea what it's been like. They think I'm the one. Can you imagine anything so ghastly? I'm supposed to have killed that poor kid. My God!"

There was no response from Ellen. She simply stood there, waiting patiently, and at last he was aware of the rigidity of her body. His arms fell away and he sat back to look up at her. She shook herself and smoothed the dress down over her hips. Ellen looked as beautiful to him and as coolly contained as ever, but he noticed faint circles under her eyes and a bitter twist to her mouth.

"At least," she said, "you've been getting some sleep. That's more than I can say."

He looked beyond her and saw a policeman watching them through the open door. He grunted and got to his feet and slammed the door, then quickly got into his trousers when he saw the expression of distaste in Ellen's eyes. He got out a crumpled pack of cigarettes, lit one and inhaled deeply as he dropped back to the cot. Ellen sat on the cot across from him, her legs crossed to reveal slim knees and the long, smooth line of her calves. She was wearing a skirt that fitted tightly about her hips and thighs and a sheer white blouse that accented her breasts. Gary grinned as he thought of what the press photographers would do with her.

"Where have you been?" he asked.

She sat stiffly and proudly erect as she replied, "Mother's, of course. But one of her friends called—"

"I didn't know she had any friends."

Ellen's eyes blazed and then calmed. She was afraid she might have to frown. "Oh, you— Anyway, this friend called and asked if I was there, so I knew it was in the papers. Honestly, Gary, couldn't I even trust you to keep that to yourself?"

"I didn't give it out. The reporters found your letter."

"Well, you could have done something about it. But I knew what would happen and it was no good staying there. I went downtown and rented a car and drove to Sacramento. I checked into a motel there. But then the later papers were out and there was my picture, the one I always keep on the bureau, right on the front page. What on earth ever prompted you to give that to the papers?"

"You think I gave it to them?"

Her back stiffened another fraction and she asked imperiously, "Who else?"

Gary slumped back on the cot and puffed at the cigarette and stared at Ellen and thought of what he had gone through and suddenly was vastly irritated with Ellen and her attitude. For the first time since the operation, he felt anger stirring.

"Sure," he said. "Sure, I gave it to them. It's typical of me. So then what?"

"Well, naturally, I was recognized right away. I left that motel and went to another, but right after dinner someone else recognized me and before I knew it reporters seemed to be coming out of the walls. Really, it's the most horrible experience I've ever gone through."

"Uh-huh. But they weren't accusing you of murdering a child, were they?"

Her finely plucked eyebrows lifted and she stared at him blankly. "I don't understand."

"Skip it. Go on. What else?"

"Well, my God, it's just that they wouldn't leave me alone from then on and no matter what I did I was surrounded by crowds and I couldn't get away. You can't imagine. It went on all night."

Gary lifted his wrist watch and glanced at the time. "You must have left there pretty early. Do you still have the rented car?"

"Yes."

"It's about a four-hour drive from here to Sacramento. So you left there at two or three in the morning. How come?"

"Well—" She tried to face him and could not. Her eyes slid away as she replied, "No one would leave me alone and, anyway, I realized it was useless trying to hide out anywhere. So I decided to come on home. One of the Sacramento reporters was nice enough to drive down with me."

"Yeah. Real nice. And I'll bet he kept you talking all the way."

"It wasn't a man, it was a woman. I guess what you call the sob-sister type. She was very kind."

"Uh-huh. You know something, Ellen? You're lying."

"Lying!" she gasped. "Why, how dare you—"

"Believe me, baby, the shape I'm in right now I dare anything. I say you're lying. You're not very good at it, which is one of the things I've always loved about you. Whenever you lie about anything you can't face me. You're lying about why you came back. Would it lower that phony pride of yours too much to admit that maybe you came back to help out the man you're married to? Is that it?"

Her head lowered and her hands twisted nervously in her lap. "Of course," she said. "Naturally. If there is any way I can help—" But she could not look at him and he knew again that she was lying. In the next moment, though, he knew why she had returned. Her head came up and she looked into his eyes and could no longer repress a frown of annoyance. "Is it true," she asked, "that the police are digging up the back yard?"

"Sure. They're looking for a body."

"They're digging up everything?"

"That's right."

"But they have no right to do that," she cried. "Our beautiful garden—the patio—you could have stopped them."

"I gave them permission."

"You! After all the work you've done out there. How utterly ridiculous. You must have been out of your mind."

He stooped over to pull on his shoes and asked suspiciously, "When did you find out about the garden?"

"Why, not so long ago. Just before I left Sacramento."

"So that's why you came back."

She got to her feet and flipped a lock of blonde hair back from her high forehead. "I'm going home right now," she said, "and put a stop to this nonsense. Why, the very idea, digging up that beautiful garden. Honestly, Gary, I can't understand why you would allow a thing like that."

He stood up, too, and nodded and said wearily, "Sure, baby. You run on home. Give 'em hell. That's a pretty important thing, that garden of ours. You run along." He opened the door for her and stood aside, but she stood there for a moment staring at him, knowing that he was angry and wondering why. "Incidentally," he asked, "are there any crowds out in front of the police station?"

"Crowds? I didn't see anyone when I came in. Just some policemen and a few reporters. Why?"

"It was jammed out there last night. People all over the place. They were pretty mad. There could even have been a lynching."

Her lips parted to form a round O and for a second or two her eyes mirrored sudden awareness of the realities of the situation, but then she snorted and flipped her hips about to walk by Gary. "A lynching," she said. "Indeed! That's even more stupid than digging up the garden."

"Yeah. That's what I kept telling myself. But run along and take care of the daisies and the roses. I'll be seeing you."

She paused again to stare at him, but then she shrugged and brushed her fingertips lightly across his cheek and walked away. Gary went into the lavatory and doused his head under the cold water faucet and toweled his face vigorously. He felt a little better, but not much, when he went back into the cell and slipped into his coat.

He had another cigarette and stood at the window looking at the blank wall of another building. He faced at last what he had known all along, that Ellen was emotionally and mentally immature. It was not a product of the operation. She had always been that way. She was spoiled and arrogant and selfish and vain and self-centered, and none of it was new. At no time during her brief visit had she displayed any concern about his predicament, or even questioned him about it. That, however, had not been simply oversight. That was much too abnormal to accept. She had deliberately not wished to burden herself with his problems. What sort of a wife was she?

He was afraid he knew the answer to that question. She was the clothes she wore and the house she lived in and the fashion magazines she read and the movies in which she lost herself and the advertisements that catered to her and the car she drove that was built to please her and the liquor she drank that had been altered and blended to her tastes and the tobacco she smoked that was made milder and even milder for her and the insurance policies in her name and the laws that protected her and the perfumes and powders and ointments and scents and soaps she used and the mink coat she wanted and the Cadillac she wanted and the mansion she wanted and everything else she wanted. But she was not a wife. She was Rita Hayworth and Lana Turner and Grace Kelly and Miss Rheingold and Miss America and the latest mannikin on the current issue of *Vogue*, but she was not Mrs. Gary Malone.

Gary swore under his breath and rubbed the heels of his palms into his eyes. It was no good thinking of her now. She was worried about the garden and he was alone and needed her, but it was no good thinking of her. He would have to think of her later. He would have to take her apart and put her together again and really think of her, but later. He could no longer bear thinking of her with everything else boiling in his mind. Later, he sighed. Later.

He spun away from the window and walked out into the locker room. A policeman standing there tried to stop him and question him, but Gary impatiently brushed him aside. He went out to the reception room, where a couple of reporters were comparing notes, and faced the radio dispatcher across the counter. The dispatcher worked for the force, but he was more a clerk than a policeman. He wore the khaki shirt and black tie of the force, but otherwise he was not in uniform. Gary asked him if the chief was around and learned that he had not yet come in, nor had Sergeant Welte. In fact, except for the dispatcher and the single policeman in uniform and the few reporters, the station was virtually without life.

Gary opened the front door and cautiously peered out at an empty street, then turned back to the dispatcher. "I've been cooped up long enough," he said. "When Kraft comes in tell him I've gone over to Dan's Place for breakfast. From there I'm going home for a shower and a change of clothes. I'll telephone from the house."

The dispatcher look suddenly worried; no one had told him what to do in case Gary decided to leave. He wanted Gary to wait a few minutes while he tried to get in touch with Kraft, but Gary brushed that off, too. One of the reporters grabbed his arm to ask a question, but Gary shook him off angrily.

Gary stepped outside into a cold morning fog and walked briskly toward the main street. There was practically no life in the town at eight in the morning. None of the stores or places of business opened until nine; the citizens rarely came into the business section before then and the tourists usually slept late. Gary crossed Surf Avenue and walked diagonally over the grass of the town square toward Dan's Place, a block away. He saw a few cars going up the main street, but otherwise there were few people around, for which he was grateful.

Dan's Place was a small brick building on a corner, with a long counter and red leather stools, a few knotty pine booths, a kitchen grill and a large magazine rack. It was the only place in town that stayed open all night and did its biggest business, mostly bacon and eggs and black coffee, after the bars closed at two A.M. At that time of morning there was only one car parked at the curb.

Gary went in and was happy to see that Dan, himself, a large, beefy man with a booming voice and jovial manner, was behind the counter in white cap and apron. Gary had a habit of dropping into the place often for doughnuts and coffee and looked upon Dan as one of his close friends in Bayside. Dan had never been in the Malone home—Ellen was openly hostile toward anyone who worked behind a counter—but he and Gary had many times gone fishing and hunting together and had a warm respect and liking for each other.

Dan was not happy that morning when he looked up from the single customer he was talking to and saw Gary drop onto a stool at the counter. His broad grin faded at once and a worried, haunted look crept into his usually amiable eyes. Gary noticed the change and bit his lip, but turned to look at the other customer, Sam Carson. The editor blinked at Gary, raised his eyebrows with surprise, then shoved his coffee down the counter and dropped onto the stool next to Gary.

"Aren't you taking a chance?" he asked.

Gary turned and looked out at the street and the square through the large plate-glass window. There was no one around. He shrugged and turned back and asked Dan for coffee, ham and eggs, buttered toast and French fries. Dan pressed his lips together and stood there indecisively for a moment, as the worried expression deepened in his eyes, but then he turned away to the grill.

Gary replied to the editor's question, "Maybe I am. No one around, though. Not like last night."

"Yeah." The older man looked bemused as he said, "There could have been a necktie party last night."

"I know. Do you think that's blown over?"

"Hard to say. People are feeling pretty ugly about you."

Dan turned partway around to say anxiously over his shoulder, "You shouldn't of come here, Gary. You don't know what it's like."

"Okay. You tell me."

"This place was jammed last night and every single person was yacking about you." He flopped a slice of ham on the grill and buttered a place for the eggs, then said, "If you'd of showed up here last night your life wouldn't of been worth a plugged nickel."

In spite of the warmth in the restaurant, Gary shuddered. "So they all think I'm the one? They've already made up their minds?"

"Well, now, you know how people are. And there's all the facts, too. You can't deny facts."

Gary snapped angrily, "What facts?" But then he sighed and said, "Aw, hell, skip it. Wait a minute, though. How about you, Dan? Do you think I actually killed that kid?"

Carson turned, too, to watch Dan's expression. Dan looked away and off into space and down at the floor and then busied himself at the grill. He had nothing to say. Carson glanced back at Gary with a cocked eyebrow. Gary rubbed his hands over his face and spun about on the stool to look out the window. He felt sick again and was thinking of walking out, but a woman passing by stared in at him and came to a sudden halt on the sidewalk. Gary turned quickly about with his back to the window as Dan placed a cup of coffee before him. He sipped at the hot liquid and decided to stay.

Carson said, "You must have walked out before Kraft got in this morning."

Gary nodded. "He wasn't there. But he isn't holding me, anyway. I'm not charged with anything. But what's with you, Mr. Carson? What are you doing out this early?"

Carson shoved his cup across the counter for a refill and said, "I guess there's no harm in telling you. Nothing was found on your property last night. Everything possible was dug up by five this morning. Bill was notified about six and he called me right after that. I went over with him to talk to the sheriff. So now the sheriff has a big posse of men heading up to Chinamen's Ridge to look over the Rigsby cabin and the surrounding country."

"Sure. That figures. But they won't find anything."

"Pretty sure of that, aren't you?"

Gary put his cup down slowly and looked into the editor's eyes. "Maybe they will find something," he said. "Maybe the killer buried the girl up there. Nothing would surprise me any more. But what I mean is that they won't find anything I put there. That's what I mean."

"I see."

"No, you don't. You don't see at all. In your mind, you're looking at a killer, a child-killer, and maybe a sexual psychotic. That's what you're looking at. So you don't really see anything."

Carson stirred some sugar into his fresh cup of coffee and was thoughtfully silent for a moment. He looked across at Dan, who was listening to everything being said, and then at Gary. "Well," he said, "you're partly right. Yesterday and last night I was positive Bill had the right man. The stuff was found in your place, Mrs. Summer's statement to the press is impressively damaging and then there was your lie about being in the Gold Nugget."

"That was no lie. That was a simple mistake. There's a difference, I hope."

"Wait'll I finish. Anyway, I've been around in this racket for more years than I like to remember and I've seen some pretty strange things. This situation of yours is about as strange as anything that has come along, but the more I think about it, and the more I think about you, the more I am inclined to reserve my judgment. I'll make up my mind when the body is found and the police close the other gaps, and not until then. Meanwhile, as far as I'm concerned, you're suspended in judgment. Is that any help to you?"

Gary gritted his teeth together and clenched his fists on the counter and said, "Yes. I'd like to ask you a favor, Mr. Carson. I'm going home from here to change clothes. How about coming along with me?"

"Why?"

"Because I have to talk to somebody who hasn't made up his mind that I'm a killer and I guess you're elected. Will you come along and listen to me?"

Carson chuckled wryly and said, "A newsman who turned down that invitation would have to be insane. You have to bear something in mind, though. I'm not on your side, Malone. If you're a guilty man, believe me, I'll lead the pack to nail your hide to the wall."

"But you still haven't made up your mind. That's all I want."

Dan placed Gary's breakfast on the counter and Gary was surprised to find that he had a ravenous appetite. He cleaned the hot plate and wiped off the egg yolk with a piece of toast. He was about to have another cup of coffee when the editor nudged him in the ribs with an elbow and jerked his head. Gary looked around over his shoulder and through the big window. A crowd was collecting in front of the place, people were hurrying down the sidewalks and automobiles were pouring in from the side streets. Gary thought, Oh God, that fool woman.

Carson jumped to his feet and threw some money on the counter and grabbed Gary's arm. "You'd better get out of here, and fast."

Gary got off the stool and was turning away when he heard Dan shout, "And don't never come back. You hear?"

Gary looked back at him, not believing that he had heard right. "What was that again?"

Dan's face was flooded with color and his eyes were narrowed to slits of hate. "You heard me," he shouted. "You killed that kid, damn you."

"Dan—"

"Go on, get out, you rat. You show your lousy face in here again and, by God, I'll use a cleaver on you."

"Dan—"

The editor shook his arm and pushed him toward the door. Gary stared once more at Dan and then went along with Carson. The moment they stepped out on the sidewalk the crowd gathered around them, but not too close, keeping their distance, as if they did not wish to become contaminated. A man mumbled, "That's him, right enough. That's the killer," and a middle-aged woman started screaming, "That's the dirty rapist. That's him. Do something, why don't you, somebody? String him up by his thumbs. Beat the dirty life out of him. Oh, God, if I was just a man right now."

A car came fast around the corner and a short length of 2x4, hurtled through the air. The chunk of wood barely missed Gary's head and sailed on to smash into Dan's plate-glass window. Someone threw a rock and fear welled up in Gary like a black flood. He started to run. Carson, however, had him by the arm and steered him through the crowd to his automobile parked at the curb. He got Gary inside and then had difficulty shoving the people aside to close the door. Gary crouched low in the seat, like an animal, his arms clasped over his head. Carson ran around to the other side of the car and got in and started the engine, but every window, except the windshield, was broken before he could get away from the curb. A hot rod, with two young men in it, tried to cut him off at the corner. Carson deliberately turned his car into them and ran the hot rod head-on into a telephone pole. He gunned the engine, careened around the corner and roared off down the street. He looked up at the rear-vision mirror and saw that no one was following and began breathing a bit easier. Gary straightened and stared out through the windshield, seeing nothing.

Carson slowed down and blew out his breath and said, "That was close. Had me scared there for a second or two." He glanced briefly at Gary and asked, "How do you feel?"

Gary said hollowly, "I feel like the caption of a cartoon that used to make me laugh, but not any more. People are no damned good."

Chapter Five

After the incident at Dan's Place, Gary was afraid to risk going home, where he might run into other crowds of people with even more serious consequences. Besides, Carson had a sudden inspiration for an editorial based on the mob action, and wanted to phone it in to his paper at once. He slowed his battered car to a crawl and tried to think of a safe place to take Gary. At last he smiled and told Gary that Jane Bestor's cottage would be perfect. Gary nodded, remembering only that she had been the stenographer who had taken his testimony at the police station.

Carson drove his car to a secluded section of Bayside and stopped in front of Miss Bestor's place, a small, white cottage far back from the road, partially screened by tall, slim pines, Scotch bloom and flowering shrubs. Carson looked about to make sure no one was around, then got out of the car. Gary helped him clean some of the broken glass out of the car, then the two walked up the gravel path to the house.

Miss Bestor showed her surprise when she opened the door and saw Gary with the editor, but she hid it quickly and asked them inside. She was wearing a practical apron over her dress, as she had just finished breakfast. Gary was more interested in the room they entered. There was a large, native-stone fireplace with a black bean pot hanging from a hook, a deep sofa before it on wall-to-wall soft carpeting, comfortable armchairs covered with flowered summer chintz, a hi-fi phonograph in a corner and a window seat piled with gaily colored cushions at the leaded front windows. Inexpensive but good oil originals were on the walls and also a grouping of family photographs. It was not a room that, as an architect, Gary would ever design for anyone, but he liked it at once; for the first time in days he relaxed.

Miss Bestor, however, glanced at his face and involuntarily gasped. Gary frowned and turned to look into a small wall mirror. There were three deep grooves in his right cheek where a woman had raked his face with her nails and blood was dripping from a gash caused by flying glass on his right temple. She led the way into a tiny bathroom, where she cleaned the wounds and applied medication and bandages. Gary explained what had happened as she worked and heard her tch-tch of sympathy, which surprised him. Who was supposed to feel sympathy for the monster, Gary Malone? He turned to appraise her, seeing her for the first time as a person, but she had finished and hurriedly left the room.

He went back into the living room and saw Carson already busy at the telephone on a small wall desk. Gary paced the floor, puffing nervously at a cigarette, but he was listening to Carson, as he dictated an editorial to the city desk of the *Sun* in Grand Point. He was greatly exercised by what had happened at Dan's Place and was delivering an emotional argument to the effect that in America a man was presumed to be innocent until proven otherwise. It was also a vituperative blast at mob rule, mob thinking, and mob action. It was a timely editorial and it did help to cool tempers somewhat in Morales County. Gary nodded with every word Carson had to say, but he was also faintly amused by the conclusion in which Carson managed to create an image of himself as modest hero and Protector of the Right.

When he had finished with his chore, Carson dropped onto the sofa before the fireplace and beckoned Gary to a place at his side. "Now," he said, "we can talk. You get in on this too, Jane. Should be interesting."

She nodded and settled herself on a leather hassock. She looked relaxed, but her wide, violet eyes were carefully watching and appraising every fleeting expression that crossed Gary's face. She was actually more interested in his expression than she was in his words.

Most of what Gary had to say she had heard before, when he had given his statement to Kraft. He went over the same ground he had covered then, explaining to Carson his every action on the fateful Friday and the day following. It was all an old story to Carson, too, but he listened attentively in the hope that something might be added, or possibly a slip made. There was but one new item:

"I brought along a twenty-two rifle with me that day. I got up to the Rigsby place maybe an hour or so before sunset and sat out on the front stoop for a while to shoot ground squirrels. I got three, I remember, and I just didn't leave them lying where they dropped. I got a spade and buried them in the garbage dump, a little hollow about a hundred feet or so away from the back of the cabin. Do you think that might mean anything?"

Carson shrugged. "The squirrels can be dug up, but all it would prove is that you did go up to the Rigsby place at some time or other, and that you did shoot squirrels. So what?"

Gary sighed and sat back in the sofa with his hands crossed behind his head.

"I see what you mean. Jees, Mr. Carson, this is awful. The police have almost a real case against me. I've damned near begun to believe them myself. The worst part of it all is the trapped feeling I have, a sort of hopeless feeling. Everything is stacking up against me and it doesn't look as if I can ever prove my innocence."

Carson glanced at him sharply and said, "You don't have to. Didn't you listen to me on the phone a few minutes ago? You don't have to prove anything. It's up to the D.A.'s office to prove you guilty."

"I know, I know. That's easy to say, but it isn't working out that way. I'm guilty as hell, is what everyone thinks. Whether or not I am ever charged with anything and brought to trial, I'm still guilty in the public mind. Somehow, some way, it's up to me to prove my own innocence. But how the devil do I go about doing that?"

"And don't try it, either. You'll just make matters worse. After all, the police have far greater facilities to get to the truth of a matter than you possess."

"I have one thing they don't have."

"What's that?"

"I know I'm innocent. They don't. So they're concentrating strictly on me. I'm the one person in the world who knows for a certainty that the killer will never be found until the search is made elsewhere."

Carson frowned at him curiously. Gary's words and attitude were so forcefully sincere. Could it be that he was the victim of freak circumstantial evidence and really was innocent, as he claimed? That was almost impossible to believe. There was too much damning evidence that had been turned up against him; the gym shoes, the rest of the Halloran girl's belongings, the testimony of the Summer woman concerning Gary's anger and his reluctance to call the police, and then the explosion of his own alibi. So much against him. And yet—

Carson got to his feet and leaned against the stone mantel, staring down into the blackened fireplace. After a minute he shrugged and sighed and turned to face Gary. "I'm afraid I don't know the answers you need," he said. "Just one. I think you should get an attorney."

"I know. I've thought of that. I guess I'll have to get one pretty soon, but not right now. I may be foolish, but hiring an attorney bears an implication of guilt in my mind. I have nothing to hide; I don't mind answering anyone's questions and I don't need anyone to cover up for me. Maybe later, if it gets too rough, but not now."

Carson again shot him a curious look and shook his head with bafflement. "Well, anyway," he said, "I don't know the answers. One other thing, though, you'd better go back to the police station. That's the only place you're safe, at least for a while."

"I guess."

"I'll run over to your house and pick up a change of clothes for you. I can bring them back to you here or down to the station."

Jane said quickly, "Bring them back here. I think he'd like to have a shower, too, and perhaps rest a little."

Gary glanced at her and said humbly, "Thanks a lot. I would like to stay here for a while."

"Of course. And I don't mind." She got to her feet, smiled at him and said, "I'll go fix you some coffee."

Carson watched her leave the room and hid a smile as he said, "Nice gal. You know something, Malone? She thinks you're innocent."

"She doesn't even know me."

"She thinks she knows you enough. I know her pretty well. She does a lot of extra work for the paper. Smart girl. If she keeps on thinking that way," he chuckled, "she may even convince me. Well, I'll be seeing you soon. Hold the fort."

He gave Gary another piercing look and shook his head, then waved casually and went out the front door. Gary hated to see him go. He had begun to like the older man and had a feeling that a certain rapport had been born between them. Perhaps if they had talked longer, if Carson had really become convinced of his innocence, then he would have a friend to stand at his side. He thought desperately of how badly he wanted a friend at that moment.

He took off his coat and draped it over the back of the sofa, loosened his collar and the knot of his tie. He was still sleepy and his eyelids started drooping as Jane returned to the room with coffee for the two of them. She placed it on a low table and sat across from him on the hassock. He rubbed his face, blinked his eyes open and watched her as she filled the cups and, at his nod, added sugar and cream. He thought that there was something different about her, then remembered that the day before she had worn her hair braided in a crown over her head. The deep brown hair was now combed out, and hung softly and gracefully about her shoulders. He noticed, too, the slight dimple in her left cheek when she looked up and smiled at him. In the weary recesses of his mind he thought that she was probably a very nice person, not as glamorous as Ellen, of course, but—well—nice.

She looked toward the windows and said softly, "The fog is burning out. Maybe we'll get some good weather now. I could use a little sun."

Gary glanced out the windows and saw streaks of sun in the pines. The fog was thinning. If it merely receded to the ocean in a great, gray bank it would be back again late that afternoon or night. When it thinned and burned away, however, it meant usually a few days of sunshine.

Jane started to say something about Gary's situation, but he shook his head. "Let's forget Gary Malone for a while," he said. "I'm getting sick and tired of yapping about myself all the time. Let's talk about you, if you don't mind. Where are you from?"

Jane told him. She clasped her hands over crossed knees and talked about herself. She had been born in Portland, Oregon, twenty-four years before, but her parents had moved to California when she was a small child. They had lived in San Francisco and then Oakland, where her father had become and still was a highly successful heavy construction engineer. Jane's life had followed a normal pattern and normal schooling, except for the years involved. She had graduated from the School of Journalism in the University of California at nineteen years of age. She had worked intermittently for various papers about the Bay Area, then had moved to Bayside for a job with the local weekly almost two years before.

"After six months," she said, "I quit. It took me that long to realize that I was not cut out for journalism at all."

"Why not?"

"I'm not tough enough. My emotions get all involved in anything I'm doing, including my work. I simply could not be sufficiently objective to be a good reporter."

Gary grinned tightly and said, "Sure, I can see that. You're strictly the subjective female."

She laughed softly and nodded. "I'm afraid you're right. I still work for the papers around here, part-time, and I do stenographic chores and things like that, but it's all really just to keep going and to remain in Bayside. I love it here."

"So did I, until recently."

"Now, don't say that. You'll love it again when this ugly mess blows over."

"Maybe. I don't know. My perspectives have all come tumbling down. Getting back to you, though. How come you never got married?"

A shadow crossed her face and her eyes clouded for a moment. "There was one man," she said. "He was the real reason I came here. He was a flyer at the Naval Air Station in Grand Point. We were very much in love."

"If you don't care to talk about it—"

"No. It's quite all right. I'm over it now. One day he went down to Los Angeles to pick up a new jet for the station. The last time he was heard from was about halfway back up the coast. He was having trouble. Whether he bailed out or not no one ever knew. The wreckage itself was never found. Apparently he crashed in the sea." She got to her feet suddenly and went to the window and said, "Mr. Carson is back. He has a suitcase with him, so I guess he has your clothes. Now, why don't you get under the shower? You'll feel a lot better."

"Thanks. I think I will."

Gary went into the small bedroom and closed the door, and a minute later was standing under a hot shower, which he gradually cut down until it was stinging cold. He was not an *aficionado* of cold showers, but he felt that that morning it would help to clear the cobwebs from his brain. He was partly correct. Fatigue remained with him, but it became easier to bear after the shower.

He peeked out into the bedroom and saw the suitcase on the floor by the bed. When he opened it and saw the clothes, he knew that Ellen had made the selections. There was a yellow tie she had given him last Christmas, but which no man in his right mind would ever deliberately put on. Gary got into a flannel suit and put on the tie he had worn with the gabardine. He could hear voices in the other room as he dressed, but when he had finished there was silence. He stored the clothes he had taken off in the suitcase and walked into the other room.

Jane was alone and talking on the telephone, but smiled at him as he came in. She finished her conversation by saying, "In about fifteen minutes, yes. I'll be there." She got up from the desk and told Gary, "That was Chief Kraft."

"How did he know I was here?"

"He doesn't know. He just called to ask me to do some more work for him. The men are there from San Francisco, you know, the ones with that lie machine."

"Yeah. That was my idea."

"And I think it was a good one. You have to convince those people that you're telling the truth."

"You think I'm telling the truth, but I didn't have to convince you."

"Remember me?" She smiled. "I'm the subjective one."

"Where's Mr. Carson?"

"He had to leave. He told me to be sure and tell you to go back to the police station. Apparently the police are searching for you everywhere and, besides, he doesn't think you're safe anywhere else. I'll drive you down, if you wish."

"Thanks." Gary asked hesitatingly, "Did he say anything about Mrs. Malone?"

"Well—"

He glanced at her sharply. "What did he say?"

"Well, he said she was rather hysterical about what has been done to your back garden. He said she is also packing to leave the house. I think he said she was going to stay with some friends."

"Here in Bayside?"

"I believe so."

"Did he tell her where I was?"

Jane nodded and looked away with embarrassment. "Yes, he did."

"I see. But she had no desire to join me here. Well, I shouldn't have hoped for that, anyway. We may as well get going."

Jane watched him as he retrieved his suitcase, then squared his shoulders and walked toward the front door. Sudden anger flooded her eyes. What kind of a wife, she wondered, was Ellen Malone?

They left the house in Jane's bright red MG and drove toward the downtown section of Bayside. The fog had left; the skies were clear and the sun beat warmly on their shoulders. The sunshine lifted Gary's spirits a bit, until they made a right turn to stop in front of the police station. The station side of the street was kept clear by a red-faced, arm-waving policeman, but across the street the sidewalk was packed solidly with a crowd of curious spectators. They were standing silently, without conversation and almost without movement, their eyes fixed intently on the police station, like a herd of cattle. They reminded Gary, however, of a pride of hungry lions waiting for the kill. He shuddered as he got out of the car and hurried into the station before many of the people recognized him.

The station was again packed with reporters and photographers and even a TV camera crew, as well as two crews from movie news services. The moment Gray stepped inside everyone went into action, though it was obvious that his sudden appearance had caught them by surprise. Gary forced his way through the crowd, with Jane at his heels, and on into the chief's office. Kraft and Welte were there, with Sam Carson and Scott Douglas, and also two strangers whom Gary assumed were the men from San Francisco. The lie detector machine was on the chief's desk. It looked rather formidable to Gary, and for a moment he doubted his wisdom of suggesting the test.

Kraft stared at Gary open-mouthed, then got to his feet and roared, "Where the hell have you been? Sam says he let you out after that mob almost got you this morning, but he wouldn't say where. We got all the state cops alerted looking for you."

Gary asked mildly, "With a warrant for my arrest?" Kraft scowled and muttered, "Not yet, but it won't be long."

"I hear you didn't have much luck with my back yard."

"Well, I never did place much faith in finding anything there. Now we got a posse searching around the Rigsby place at Chinamen's Ridge."

Scott Douglas said, "That's where she'll be found, either up there or somewhere in the valley. Look, Malone; one of Diana's schoolbooks was found on May fourteenth in front of the Gold Nugget. We know you were there that noon; that's been verified. Was it an accident you dropped the book there, or didn't you know it was in your car?"

Gary gave him a look of deep disgust and said, "You're so damned cute. I know nothing about a schoolbook."

The D.A. lifted his eyebrows with surprise and blinked innocently at Gary. "Why, it was in all the papers."

"That I know, yes. But I don't know anything about it personally. Do you have any other real cute ways of getting me to admit I'm a killer of young girls? Think of some more questions." He turned away from Douglas and glared at Kraft and said, "You people are so intelligent, aren't you? And as for you, Kraft, the F.B.I. really wasted their time on you. Two of the most important things you haven't even thought about. If I abducted that girl I would have had to use my car and there could still be some traces of her presence in that automobile. And how about the clothes I was wearing on May thirteenth? Maybe the kid put up a fight. There might even be blood on them. Have you thought of that?"

Kraft smiled lightly and said, "I looked all through your car and your clothes yesterday. I didn't find anything, but laboratory analysis would show something. I had to wait until today to get permission to send the stuff over to the laboratories at Grand Point. Your wife was kind enough to let us have the car and the clothes a little while ago. They are now being subjected to microscopic analysis. You still think we're stupid?"

Gary felt deflated, but he growled, "I sure do."

Sam Carson touched the chief's arm to get his attention and said, "You might bear in mind, Bill, that at least Malone did make the suggestion to you before he knew you had done anything."

Kraft frowned and drummed his fingers nervously on the desk. Gary was not falling into the guilt pattern at all. He had made the suggestion. He had also made other suggestions. He had cooperated all the way. He had also returned to the station of his own free will and so far there was not even the slightest chink in his personal armor. Had he really lied about that alibi, or had it been just a simple mistake? Kraft's big shoulders quivered and he shook his head violently, as if to clear out nonsensical thinking. A job had to be done, and Malone was still the only target in sight.

"Okay," he said. "I got a lot to bear in mind. Right now we got a lie test scheduled. Malone, I'd like you to meet Inspector Richtof from the San Francisco Police Department, and Dr. Thompson. The doctor is one of our eminent criminologists and also professor of psychiatry at U.C. Gentlemen, this is Mr. Gary Malone."

No one offered to shake hands, but they nodded and looked at each other in studied silence. Richtof was an amiable but shrewd-looking individual of middle age, with the beginnings of a comfortable paunch, hair combed sideways to hide a bald spot and the pinkish, well-filled jowls of a gourmet. The doctor was almost his opposite, a small, nervous man of about the same age, but with a delicate frame, a mass of iron-gray hair, piercing black eyes and the pale, sallow skin of a scholar who spent all his time indoors. He chewed constantly at a dead pipe and was in the habit of breaking stems, so carried a few spares in his pockets. He never smoked.

The D.A. smiled broadly and said, "This I gotta see. I've never watched one of these lie tests before."

Gary put an end to that idea by snapping, "And you're not watching one now. I'm not a performing seal. This is my suggestion and it's going to be done my way. Everyone can get out of here except the inspector and the doctor and—" he turned to look at Jane—"how about you, Miss Bestor? Would you mind staying?"

"Hell," Kraft snorted, "she has to stay. I want her to take notes."

"Okay. Then the rest of you can take off."

The D.A. protested loudly and even Sergeant Welte grumbled, but Kraft waved everyone out the door. Without Gary's cooperation, he knew, there was nothing in the law that could compel him to submit himself to a lie test. He could simply refuse to bear witness against himself. Kraft remained in the office himself only long enough to watch a straplike, pleated tube placed around Gary's chest and a sphygmomanometer around his arm. They were connected electrically to styli that would record changes of blood pressure and respiration on a graph. Kraft sighed and hoped for the best.

Four hours later, Gary made his way with Jane into the locker room and dropped heavily to a wooden bench. Reporters crowded around, snapping questions at him, but Gary sat with his head bowed and his arms hanging limply between his knees, too tired to raise his eyes and too worn out to answer anyone. But he was also embarrassed and deeply ashamed. My God, he thought, where did they ever dream of those questions?

Chief Kraft sat behind his desk in the closed and locked office with the inspector, the doctor, the D.A., Welte and Sam Carson. He knew without asking that something had gone wrong, but he had to ask.

Inspector Richtof shrugged philosophically and explained, "We can't always have our cake and eat it, too, gentlemen. The lie detection machine, as a piece of machinery, is about as infallible as it is possible to make it. However, the polygraph findings must be evaluated and analyzed by a human brain—my own poor equipment, in this instance—and that piece of machinery, believe me, is not infallible. The test we gave your Mr. Malone was an exhaustive one. No possible field was left unexplored. In fact, it amazes me how well the young man stood up under it. Not physically, mind you—I don't mean that—but mentally. An extrovert, such as Malone, is the first to break down and give us all the clues we need. Yet his brain never wavered at any time."

Kraft sagged lower in his swivel chair and asked, "So what did you find?"

The inspector looked apologetic and answered, "Very little, frankly. I can say only one thing with certainty, and that is that the test is inconclusive."

"Meaning what?"

"Meaning that it tells us very little as it stands, but that it could tell us a great deal if we knew a few more of the key answers ourselves. As you know, I studied the case history and all your statements on file this morning and I have also read the papers. I was able, therefore, to ask any possible question that might shed some light on Mr. Malone's guilt or innocence."

The D.A. said impatiently, "Let's skip all that. Did you learn anything at all that could be useful?"

Inspector Richtof looked at him narrowly, as one would at a curious insect, then deliberately turned his back on Douglas and continued talking to the chief. "I asked a great many questions about Diana Halloran, herself, her appearance, the clothes she wore, that sort of thing. Malone's response was mostly negative. If he ever knew the girl at all it was only slightly. If the man is guilty I would say that he was not aware of her before the very day he abducted her. Most of his reactions to any questions about her were fairly normal."

Kraft asked, "Did you question him about the stuff found in his basement?"

"Naturally. He responded with some excitement, but not necessarily guilt. Even an innocent man would be perturbed over those findings. All responses about the Rigsby place at Chinamen's Ridge were negative. If the man is guilty he is certainly not worried about anyone finding a body up there. As a matter of fact, I would be willing to bet a hundred to one that your efforts in that area are wasted."

Carson said, "I'd say that's learning something."

Kraft nodded and looked depressed. His last report from the sheriff's posse had been negative.

The inspector continued, after glancing at some notes in his hand, "He was very excited over the testimony of the Summer woman, whenever I questioned him on that point. It could be that he is a guilty man badly worried about her testimony, or it could just as easily be that he is an innocent man who is deeply angered by the defalcation of the wife of his closest friend. Nothing there. Now, about that alibi of his. That is the one thing that truly excited him, though he tried to hide it. He is badly worried about it. Unfortunately, two opposing reasons could inspire his excitement and his worry. As a guilty man, he would naturally be frightened over losing an alibi that could have saved him. On the other hand, he could also be frightened even in his innocence. I would not venture to draw a conclusion either way." He looked ruefully at his notes, tucked them away in a pocket and shrugged. "I'm sorry, but I am afraid our test will be no help to you at all—that is, from my angle. The doctor, however, learned a great deal."

Everyone in the room turned to stare at the nervous little man at the far end of the leather couch. He chewed on his pipe stem for a moment, his eyes darting from one to the other, then he smiled and said, "All is not wasted, gentlemen."

Kraft grunted, "That's welcome news. What did you learn? Is Malone a psychotic, or anything of that sort?"

Dr. Thompson held up a hand, as if to ward off the quick words. "Not so fast, please. Mr. Malone is sane, if that is what you wish to know. He is not a psychotic, or even a neurotic. He is an out-living individual, gregarious and sport-loving, with a great deal of extroverted drive. He is, indeed, almost the opposite of any sexual deviate I have ever encountered."

Kraft asked bluntly, "Is he capable of committing an assault against a young girl? Can you answer that? That is the question that has been bothering me ever since this thing broke. I'd like to have the answer."

The doctor smiled sympathetically. "It is not quite that easy. The answer is partly black and partly white. I would hesitate to say that he has committed such a crime, or that he ever would, but the possibilities are there."

"Oh? How do you mean?"

"Let me explain. Mr. Malone is suffering through a very bad sexual relationship with his wife. He is a powerful, healthy young animal and possesses an abundance of sexual drive. Mrs. Malone, however, is cold to his advances and so the young man is badly frustrated."

Kraft stared at the doctor, then burst into loud, raucous laughter. He laughed until there were tears in his eyes, then wiped them away and said, "I hate to tell you this to your face, Doctor, but you're clear off the beam. Obviously, you haven't seen Mrs. Malone. She's a beautiful gal, she has a terrific build and every move she makes is calculated to let you know just how well stacked she is. That's not just an act with her."

The doctor chewed on his pipe for a long while, until Kraft started getting nervous, then he said, "Cobbler, stick to your last. Do you wish to hear my findings, or not?"

Kraft swallowed and said humbly, "I'm sorry."

"Very well. I have not met Mrs. Malone, though I would like to, but I have seen many photographs of her. As you say, she is a beautiful woman and apparently highly desirable. Beauty, however, does not necessarily imply sexual drive, or even ability. The sexual relationship depends for success upon giving of oneself by both partners. Beautiful women are often vain, arrogant and self-centered to such a degree that it is impossible for them to give of themselves. Some of our loveliest movie stars realize that something is lacking and so leap frenziedly from husband to husband and bed to bed; but what they are seeking may be found only within themselves, and that they do not have. Mrs. Malone is such a woman."

Kraft asked suspiciously, "You got that out of Malone?"

The doctor chuckled lightly and said, "It was not easy and, besides, I learned mostly by indirection, the word between the lines, the word that was not stated, but is thereby made even more conspicuous by its absence. Yes, without meaning to, he told us a great deal about his wife. He was reluctant at first, because of the disturbing presence of the young lady taking notes, but as he tired he answered more freely and truthfully."

"So?"

"So I can tell you without the slightest reservation that Malone's sex life is very bad indeed. I doubt if his wife allows him to share her bed more than once a month. Perhaps it is even worse than that."

"Oh, no. A guy like that?"

"But yes."

"He would never put up with that."

"He does, though. You see, she has a sword of guilt dangling constantly over his head." The doctor explained what he had learned of the operation and the reasons for it, then continued, "Malone feels that it was all his fault. Mrs. Malone sees to it that he continues feeling that way. It suits her purposes very well. She is a frigid woman, she fears the sexual act—"

"But if you say her tubes are tied off she would have nothing to fear. She would certainly have no fear of pregnancy."

"That is not what she fears now. Actually—and I have a hunch she knows it—those tubes can be untied. I doubt very much if there would be any risk at this date; and she could be normal again and even a mother, if she desired it. It is not just pregnancy that frightens her. Now, mind you, I have learned most of this indirectly and without even talking with the woman herself, and I would certainly not care to go on record, but I don't mind making certain assumptions that could be a help to you. To a woman such as Mrs. Malone, the sexual act is repulsive and frightening and unclean. I rather have a hunch her mother had something to do with that attitude, but it is no more than a hunch. Anyway, we have here a woman who does not give herself and even resents being touched by her own husband. So we naturally have a young husband suffering from a guilt complex, sexually frustrated—"

Kraft interrupted sarcastically, "And you say he is not a neurotic?"

"He is not a neurotic. Man is capable of suffering many indignities without becoming neurotic. None of us, after all, lives in perfect balance. Malone's marital life is badly out of balance. He lacks satisfaction that his healthy body demands. I don't have to assume anything when I say that he undoubtedly hungers after every good-looking woman he sees. Obviously, too, he must indulge himself in sexual fancies and day dreams. Considering his condition, he couldn't do otherwise. Which now brings us to the crux of the matter. You probably lie about it to yourselves, but if you are truthful and unafraid you would have to admit that there is not a man in this room who has not at some time or other looked with hunger and desire upon a young girl just blossoming into womanhood. Think of it a moment, gentlemen."

He sat back again to chew nervously on his pipe stem and watched the others with a twinkle of amusement deep in his dark eyes. He could almost feel the wave of sudden embarrassment that swept through the room. It was almost as if it had substance, something that had been lifted out of a dark cave and exposed to the light of day. No one, at least for a moment or two, could meet his eyes.

Then he sat forward and said, "Mr. Malone may also have hungered after such a young girl. He, too, would lie about it to himself. He is, after all, a sane young man—at this moment. He also strikes me as a decent young man. But there could have been a moment when his perspective went awry, when his sexual frustrations had become too much for him to control, when he looked upon a young girl—probably encountered by accident—and found himself alone with her in that ravine. There was the opportunity and his hunger was in command and for that moment he reverted all the way to the animal that is always lurking within. We have, then, a crime." He sighed and said, "It may have happened that way. I do not pretend to know. But, considering everything, I am not reluctant in stating that it could have happened that way. Yes, Mr. Kraft, it is easily within the realm of possibility that Mr. Malone is capable of committing such a crime. Does that answer your question?"

Kraft was not sure. Anyone, after all, was capable of committing any sort of crime. He knew from experience and training that there was no such person as the criminal type and he also knew that most murders on the police blotters were committed by otherwise law-abiding citizens. Sexual deviates, too, violated patterns of behavior as well as following established patterns. The fact that the pressure of frustration may have inspired Malone to commit a crime was not satisfactory in itself. There was nothing sufficiently specific about it to cause a police officer to assume that a crime would have to be committed. As the doctor had pointed out, it was just as possible that Malone had never committed such a crime and never would.

"Well, anyway," he said, "a few things are clarified. At least, you don't say that Malone could not commit such crime."

"No. It is possible for him."

"Another thing I seem to gather from your words, if he did it it would have to be a more or less spontaneous act."

"Oh, yes. Definitely. He could never plan such a thing. If it happened at all it was on the spur of the moment, on an impulse."

"Then his story that he had never known the Halloran girl could be true—I mean before she disappeared."

"Very true. The machine also indicated that."

The inspector interrupted to add, "It also indicated that he may not have known her at all, period, now or at any other time."

"Hmmmmm. Well—" Kraft looked plainly baffled, he had expected everything to be solved by a machine, but he shook away a feeling of futility that was stealing over him and said crisply, "Thank you, gentlemen. I have made arrangements for you to spend the night at Redwood Inn. I would appreciate it very much, before you leave in the morning, if each of you will write out a summation of your findings and drop them here at the station."

The two men nodded and Kraft got up to shake hands with them. He jerked his head at Carson and the D.A., unlocked the door and walked out into the corridor. He told the editor, "I let you in on all this, Sam, on your word that you'd pass it on to the rest of the press. Don't overplay the sex angle. The issue is confused enough as it is."

Carson looked at him wisely and said, "We're thinking the same way, Bill. The guy could be innocent, so why smear him? I'll pass it on."

Kraft took Douglas by the arm and walked him around to an angle of the building where they had a certain measure of privacy. The two lit cigarettes and smoked quietly for a few minutes, each reviewing in his mind what had taken place in the office and trying to resolve it into a pattern.

The D.A. at last snorted, "Damn it all, Bill, the guy is guilty as hell and we know it. You know how those psychiatrists are, strictly yes and no boys. Everything is yes and no. You can't get a straightforward answer out of any of them. All we need to know is one thing; he did say that Malone is capable of committing such a crime."

"What crime? We don't even have a body."

"Oh, let's not go through all that again. That kid is dead and was probably assaulted first, and we know it almost as well as if it had happened before our eyes. And everything points to Malone."

"That machine didn't do much pointing."

The D.A. snapped impatiently, "Look, I'm not going to stand here arguing about it. I was talking to the foreman of the Grand Jury a couple of hours ago. He'd like to look over everything we have so far and discuss it with the other jurors."

"Curious bunch, aren't they?"

"Curious, hell! They're the ones who have to indict."

"Uh-huh. On what we have so far you can't indict anyone. All the Grand Jury wants is to get into the act, with you in the role of interlocutor. I'd like to keep it clean."

"Is that a snide remark?"

"Take it any way you like. We got a lot of police work ahead. I'd like to keep it that way. Then if we turn up with a body and if we establish a motive for Malone and if we can make a physical connection between Malone and the girl then I say you and the Grand Jury should get into the act, but not until then."

Douglas wet his lips nervously and shook his head. "It's gone too far for that, Bill. This is out of your hands. Now, are you going to cooperate and turn over the stuff I need for the Grand Jury?"

The two stared hotly into each other's eyes, anger between them. Kraft knew that the D.A. wanted all the free publicity he could get, regardless of anyone's guilt or innocence. It could interfere seriously with all the police work that had yet to be done. On the other hand, it wouldn't be wise to make an outright enemy of Scott Douglas. He wielded a tremendous amount of political power in the county and could do incalculable harm to future relations between the Bayside police and the district attorney's office.

Kraft shrugged and looked disgusted as he said, "Have it your way, Scotty. Tell Welte to give you what you need. We have copies of everything. But I'm telling you right now, don't go overboard in trying to make a case before the Grand Jury. If they get excited and think there are grounds for indictment, everything can blow up in our faces and all our work will be ruined."

"Don't tell me about the law."

"Oh, sure. Sure. You do what you want. I got work to do—and plenty of it."

Kraft walked angrily away from him and into the locker room. The reporters had all cleared out to gather around Sam Carson in the reception room and learn how the lie detector test had come out. Gary was seated alone on the wooden bench, his head still bowed and his arms hanging limply between his knees. He had not changed position since he had sat down. He looked asleep, but Kraft doubted that. Jane Bestor was in a far corner of the room, where she had placed a portable typewriter on a card table to type out the notes she had taken. One of the policemen was just leaving the room, grumbling and growling under his breath because none of them any longer had privacy in their own locker room.

Gary felt someone drop to the bench at his side and slowly his head came up and he turned his red-rimmed eyes to appraise the chief. Kraft took a pack of cigarettes from his blouse pocket and offered one to Gary, who had difficulty arousing enough energy to reach for it. The two sat back and smoked in silence, side by side, one wondering how he could send the other to the gas chamber and the other simply wondering. They finished their cigarettes before either one moved.

Gary's voice was rasping and husky from all the talking he had done, so that he was forced to whisper, "I'll tell you one thing, Kraft; I'm all through cooperating. No more. I've had it."

"Well, I can't say I blame you. It's been rough. But you have to go along with us for your own sake, if you're innocent."

Gary's eyes opened wide to stare at the chief. "I detect a note of doubt. What's wrong with the great big minion of the law? Didn't your beautiful little machine come up with the right answers?"

The chief crushed out the cigarette stub under his heel and leaned forward with his elbows on his knees to stare at the opposite wall. "Frankly," he said, "I don't know what to think any more. You're a queer guy. You know that?"

"You mean I'm a sex maniac, don't you?"

"No, I don't mean it that way. I've been learning a lot about you back in the office."

A wave of embarrassment swept through Gary and he was again ashamed. He mumbled, "Oh. Maybe I talked more than I should. That questioning was pretty damned personal and intimate. I could have told those two characters to go jump—frankly, I think that psychiatrist needs a psychiatrist himself—but I was so blamed anxious to cooperate and get this thing over with that I answered anything they asked. I'm sorry I did it. My personal life is none of their business."

"I've told you before, your personal life is now everyone's business. Have you seen any of the newspapers today?"

"No, and I don't want to."

"You're the star performer in the nation's press. The war-hero angle is being played up to the skies; practically every move you've made in your life is now in print and all the feature writers are turning out those curious little documents that read, 'Is Gary Malone hero or monster?' or, 'Is this man capable of crime?' and even, 'Read all the intimate details of the life of suspected war hero.' And, believe me, they got those intimate details. After today they'll have more. So don't tell me about your private life. It doesn't exist."

Gary crushed out his own cigarette and dug another out of his pocket, but put it between his lips without lighting it. "Anything about Luke Summer?" he asked.

"He was here while you were in the office. Did you know he's superstitious?"

"Oh, about little things, I guess. When he spills salt he always throws a pinch over his shoulder and if a black cat crosses his path he almost has a fit. He has a lot of little phobias that way."

"Uh-huh. And another is Friday the Thirteenth. He didn't work that afternoon. He says he closed his office about twelve-thirty that day and went home, where he remained."

"I suppose Betty can verify that."

"Not very well. She was in San Francisco that weekend on a buying excursion and didn't return home until Sunday."

Gary touched a light to his cigarette and tried to get his weary brain to function, then nodded and said, "I remember Ellen saying something about running into Betty at the City of Paris. I guess it was that weekend. But how about the servants? They have two, you know, a man and his wife."

"Summer says that because he was home alone he let them have that weekend off. In other words, Luke Summer was not seen by anyone from about two P.M. May thirteenth, when the servants left the house, until the following noon when he came into town for lunch at the Redwood Inn. He can verify that date and hour because he always signs chits at the Redwood. So we have a man who admits being in your basement about ten the morning of May fourteenth, but he has a blank between that time and two the afternoon before."

Gary shrugged. "Could be. Why should he lie about it?"

"He would have plenty of reason to lie if he was the one who put Diana's stuff in your basement the morning he left your reel there."

Gary blinked and looked sharply at the chief, then sat back to smoke quietly and think about it. So Luke was another who could not account for his actions on the fateful day and at the fateful hour. Assuming, then, that Luke could have committed such a crime, which was unthinkable, why would he put the evidence in the basement of his closest friend? That would indicate a deliberate frame after the act and the thinking of a hateful enemy rather than a friend.

Gary snorted, "Impossible." He explained what he had been thinking and added, "In all the time I've known Luke he and I have never had a cross word. We've been really more like brothers than just friends."

Kraft said pointedly, "I told him you were in the office, but he had no desire to wait and see you while he was here. And has he telephoned at any time to find out if you can use his help?"

"Well, there's Betty, you know—"

"Sure. But you claim this man is your friend. Maybe I'm wrong but my idea of a friend is someone who pitches in to help without being asked and stands by you when you're in trouble. Don't you expect that of your friends?"

Gary's face colored and he stammered, "Well, I—I guess—"

"Of course. So this guy is not as close a friend as you thought. Maybe, down underneath everything, he may even hate your guts. Which of you is the better golfer?"

"Oh, I am. I always spot Luke at least seven or eight strokes. Why?"

"I understand the two of you do a lot of hunting together. Who is the best shot?"

"Well, I'm not bragging, but I am. Mostly I have to help him fill out his bag."

"Uh-huh. How about fishing?"

Gary managed to smile as he replied, "Luke is all thumbs with rod and reel. He tried hard, but he's still all thumbs."

"But you're not."

"That's different. I was practically raised with a fly rod in my hand."

Kraft was beginning to smile tightly. "Then there're your wives," he said. "I've met both. Mrs. Malone looks like something out of a fashion magazine. Mrs. Summer looks like something out of a grab bag. And you tell me this guy may not have reason for hating you? Better do a little thinking, Malone."

"I still say it's impossible."

"I don't. In fact, now that I've really given it some thought, I'm going to have him back in here for some serious questioning."

Gary said quietly, but with shame, "There's one thing you're overlooking, Kraft. There's nothing wrong with Luke's sex life, that I know of. Betty may be out of a grab bag, but that gal is really romp-worthy when the lights are out. I know them well enough to know that positively." He chuckled wryly and said, "I've seen Luke some mornings when he was so pooped he couldn't make conversation with a two-year-old. Luke gets all the sex he needs and more than he can handle. So there goes your motive out the window. Let's think of someone else. How about that plumber?"

Kraft was in no hurry to drop Luke as a subject, but Gary wouldn't listen to him, so Kraft said, "Franklin checks out all the way. I had a talk with Bergstrom, the contractor. He looked up his records and pointed out where the new water heater was installed on the afternoon of May thirteenth."

"How about the grocer boy, Jerry Smith?"

"Well, he dug up another kid who remembers taking ride down the coast in Jerry's jalopy about the middle of May, but he can't remember the exact day. Jerry is probably telling the truth."

"On the other hand, maybe he isn't."

"Well, yes. I intend looking into it more."

"I've been telling the truth all along, but you haven't believed me. So why can't you disbelieve someone else, too?"

"I said I intend looking into it more. It can stand investigation. It's rare, though, for a boy that young to assault a girl and then kill her."

"It happened in San Francisco, in Dolores Park, a couple of years ago."

"Sure, it happens. I'll investigate the kid, damn it."

"How about the eight men who voted at the polls in my garage?"

"Welte checked into that. No man voted before eight-thirty that morning."

"What has the time to do with it?"

"That's the time of morning the plumber noticed the disturbed earth in your basement, so the girl's things were buried there before then. It would be sheer waste checking anyone who had access to your basement after that time." He yawned and got to his feet and stretched his powerful arms. He glanced at his watch and muttered, "Almost five. I'll bet you missed lunch."

"I couldn't have eaten it, anyway. Maybe later." He looked up at the chief and asked softly and pleadingly, "Am I still the killer in your mind?"

Kraft looked down at him with a frown and chewed at his lower lip a moment before he answered, "You're still the prime suspect."

"I know that. But what do you think? How do you feel?"

"Well, hell, I don't really know any more. If it's any consolation to you, Malone, I'm not as definite about it today as I was yesterday. That lie detector machine is quite a gadget, and Inspector Richtof is no fool. You came out of that test in pretty good shape, as far as I'm concerned."

"Thanks. I could use someone's help around here."

"Now, wait a minute. I didn't say I was going to help you. My job is to put you in a gas chamber, if I can. Don't ever get thinking I'm on your side. I'm not. On the other hand—well—by God, Malone, I do hope you're not the guy who did it."

Gary grinned as he watched the big man turn on his heel and stalk away. Thank God, he thought, Kraft's emotional jag was finally giving way to his fundamental intelligence. Perhaps, now, the police could really do some constructive work and put together a pattern that would eventually lead them to the real killer.

Gary lifted his head a bit higher and began taking an interest in his surroundings, for the first time in hours. He saw Jane still working at the typewriter and got up to join her, but was intercepted by Sergeant Welte with the information that Ellen wanted him on the phone. Gary lifted the receiver of an extension phone just aside from the locker room.

"Ellen?" he asked. "I've been wondering when you would call."

"Oh," she snapped, "you have, have you? It's a wonder you wouldn't get in touch with me."

"Where?"

"Why, at Redwood Inn, of course. You know where I'm staying."

"Now, how would I know where you're staying?"

"Well, my goodness, everyone knows. Just everyone. All the reporters are staying here, too. They've just practically taken over the whole hotel. I was lucky to get a room."

"I was told you were going to stay with some friends."

There was silence for a moment, then Ellen cried, almost hysterically,

"Friends! You and your friends. Do you think we have friends in this town? Not any more we don't. I got in touch with the Bemises and the Browns and the Carrolls and the Shephards. All of them put me off. You'd think I had the plague. Just let me tell you about the excuses they had—"

"Not now, Ellen. I don't feel up to it. But how about Betty and Luke? Maybe Betty thinks I'm a criminal, but that has nothing to do with you. Didn't you get in touch with them?"

Ellen sneered, "Our dear, dear friends, the Summers? To think of all the things I've done for that woman, the clothes I've selected for her, you know how dowdy her own tastes are, and the dinner parties and everything. And your old buddy, Luke. What a friend he is! I ran into him on the street a little while ago, on my way to Redwood Inn. I'd tried to get them on the phone, but they weren't home. When I saw Luke on the street I was never so happy to see anyone in my life. But he looked at me as if I was the criminal instead—"

Gary closed his eyes with pain and asked quietly, "Instead of me?"

"I didn't say that. Anyway, did he give me the big brush-off! My God! He just wasn't going to stand there and talk to me even one minute. And then when I got mad do you know what he said?"

"No."

"He said for me to forget we'd ever known each other. He said there was no longer any doubt in his mind that you'd killed that girl and that it just made him and Betty sick to think of how close they'd been to us and that there must be something awful queer in our marriage and that the best thing for all concerned is just to forget we ever knew each other. That's what he said." She waited a moment, then asked, "Gary? Are you listening, Gary?"

Gary had turned away from the telephone and was leaning back against the wall. He was thinking of what the chief had had to say about Luke. He was beginning to wonder,

Chapter Six

When Gary turned back to the telephone he learned the real purpose of Ellen's call. Their checking account at the bank was in his name only and she needed funds. He could have had one of the policemen take a check to her, but she also wanted to talk things over with him. Her idea of "things" might mean anything, trivial or important. He asked her to drop by the police station, but she refused, so he told her to wait at Redwood Inn and he would call her back.

He went into the lavatory and stripped down to the waist to soak his head in cold water in an endeavor to relieve the fatigue that was constantly with him. Kraft found him there, staring at himself in the mirror and rubbing the red stubble at his chin. The chief had with him the clothes Gary had worn on May thirteenth and wanted him to put them on for a few minutes.

"The press photographers," he explained, "will take some pictures of you in these clothes. They'll be run in the papers and maybe someone will recognize you by the clothes. Maybe they'll remember seeing you and where they saw you when you were wearing them."

Gary shook his head. "I told you before, I'm through cooperating."

"Look, it's for your good. You say maybe you stopped at the Gold Nugget at four o'clock on May thirteenth and then drove on after you found out it was closed. No one has been able to prove or disprove it. Okay. Maybe someone will see a picture of you in these clothes and remember seeing you exactly where you said you had been. If a thing like that should happen you'd really be out in the clear. So who are you refusing to cooperate with, the police or yourself?"

Gary sighed and got out of the clothes he was wearing and into his old hunting clothes; the short boots, the stained corduroys, the red-checked sport shirt and the old suede jacket with a leather patch at the gun shoulder. He and Kraft stepped into the locker room, where a number of photographers and a few reporters had gathered. Flashbulbs exploded and quite a number of pictures were taken from different angles.

When the session ended, one of the reporters asked Gary, "Aren't you afraid blood will be found on those clothes?"

Gary glared at him, then had to smile. "It would be damned queer if blood wasn't found on them," he said. "These are the clothes I use for hunting. These corduroys, especially, have blood on them from deer, squirrels, doves, quail and wild pigs."

"How about human blood?"

"That, too, but it's my blood. I ripped my hand open once on a jammed twelve-gauge shotgun."

The reporter asked sarcastically, "But no one else's blood?"

Kraft grabbed Gary's arm and led him, protesting, back into the lavatory. The chief went out to his own locker and returned after a minute with an electric razor. He leaned back against a wall and smoked and watched Gary shave and then change clothes again.

Gary told him about Ellen's call and said, "I have to see her some time this evening, but she won't come here. Anyway, frankly, I'd like to get the devil out of here. Do you think it would be safe for me to leave?"

"Well, after dark, maybe. I wouldn't mess around in town, though. Tempers are still pretty high, even though there has been a change."

"What sort of change?"

"Well, the way the reporters explain it to me, this case, where the public is concerned, has gone from the Big Discovery to the Big Lie and now to the Big Question. The way everything broke so fast everyone was positive you were the culprit. And when your alibi fell apart the odds were running against you a million to one. But now new factors have been added to titillate the public fancy.

We didn't find a body in your yard, which everyone was sure we would. Attention was then diverted to the Rigsby place at Chinamen's Ridge. That was the logical setting for murder; isolation, mountainous country, a lone cabin— the works. But that country has been combed all day by a posse and a couple of bloodhounds and hunting dogs and nothing has been turned up. And now, on top of all that, it comes out that the lie detector test was inconclusive. People place a hell of a lot of faith in machines, you know. So what happens? Now they're beginning to wonder about you. They're beginning to question. They still think you're guilty, but for the first time an element of doubt has crept in."

"Just like you."

The big man's face colored. "Well, yeah. Anyway, the danger of lynching has passed, but I'm not guaranteeing you wouldn't be roughed up by a mob here in town." He scratched his head, lost in thought for a moment, then said, "I'll tell you what. You know that little restaurant about twelve miles down the coast, the Blue Bird?"

"Sure. They have nice curries."

"Well, now, they should have very few customers on a Thursday night. It's strictly a weekend spot, and then mostly for tourists. Wait until maybe eight o'-clock, then pick up your wife and take her down there for dinner. Matter of fact, I'll send you down in a squad car with one of my men, just in case."

"So now you're willing to give me some protection?"

Kraft's face hardened. "Not just for your sake. You've become a valuable property. If anything happened to you now it would be my neck. But how does it sound?"

"I'll buy it. Anything to get out of here."

"I'll leave word with the boys. Right now I'm taking off for home and dinner. Do you know I haven't had more than five hours' sleep the last two nights?"

Gary looked at his own red-rimmed eyes in the mirror and said, "You're breaking my heart."

He waited until the chief had gone, then walked into the locker room. Except for Jane Bestor, the room was empty. But she had finished her work at the typewriter and was also about to leave. When she saw Gary, however, she dropped to a bench with him to have a cigarette. He was in no mood to talk, but he enjoyed her presence and let her know it with a tired smile. She gave him a glance of sympathetic understanding and was silent. When Gary's head dropped forward and he fell asleep, she took the cigarette from his fingers and tiptoed quietly out of the room.

Gary was awakened just after eight o'clock by one of the patrolmen shaking his arm. He sat up and yawned and rubbed his eyes open to stare at the officer. He was a young man new to the force by the name of Schmidt.

He was also rather excited by the idea of being in protective custody of the man making headlines in the nation's press. He explained quickly, but with an obvious touch of awe in his voice, that Mrs. Malone was waiting outside in a squad car.

Gary walked out of the police station still half asleep, and got into the back of the police car. He dropped heavily to the seat at Ellen's side and blinked at her in the fast fading twilight. She was sitting stiffly erect, staring straight ahead, her lips pressed together with anger. Gary shrugged, completely indifferent as to how she felt. He looked across the street and saw only a few curious spectators on the opposite sidewalk. The chief was right; mob feeling was slacking off. Schmidt started the engine and pulled away from the curb and Gary's head immediately fell back against the seat. He was again asleep.

Ellen let him sleep until they were out of Bayside and on the highway cut into the cliffs running south down the coast. Then she shook him awake and launched into a tirade against a certain nasty, little man. Gary came awake gradually. It was quite a while before he realized that she was talking about Doctor Thompson, the psychiatrist.

"Thompson," she said. "Of course. Haven't you been listening to me? I saw him at the hotel. I was talking to some of the reporters in the lobby, right after talking with you, and he came over and introduced himself, this doctor, I mean. Is he really a doctor?"

"He's a psychiatrist."

"I remember he said he was, but I didn't know whether to believe him or not. He was very nice at first and he sort of let me think that he was talking to me officially—you know, like I was supposed to have to listen to him?—and first thing I knew he was up in my room and I was answering all sorts of queer questions about myself and Mother and the way I was brought up and things like that. Oh, he was smooth, all right. And, like a fool, I kept right on talking to him until I suddenly realized what he was getting at and I came awfully close to slapping his silly little face for him. Now," she asked angrily, "just what did you tell that man about us?"

Gary felt about in his pockets and discovered that he was out of cigarettes. He took a fresh pack out of Ellen's purse on her lap, selected a cigarette and put the pack in his own pocket. Ellen noticed and glared at him.

He blew out a puff of smoke and said, "I guess I told him practically everything. I was taking a lie test—"

"I read all about it in the evening papers."

"Then you know the test was inconclusive. Anyway, this Thompson was there, too, and did most of the questioning. Maybe I got carried away trying to prove my innocence. I sure did a lot of talking. Sorry, baby."

"I should imagine you would be sorry. Why, the idea—He seemed to know just about everything about us, about the way you and I—I mean—well—"

"Yeah. Let's put it on the table, Ellen. We're talking about sex." He felt more awake and sat up straighter. "A funny thing about talking with him, it acted sort of like a mental cathartic. For the first time in a long while I took a good long look at myself—and at you. I didn't like what I was facing."

Ellen leaned closer to peer at him in the dark. "Why, you—you— Just what do you mean by that?"

"I mean plenty. I mean that I woke up to a few facts of life. I mean that you've been giving me a lousy time ever since that operation, and I've been a spineless fool to allow you to get away with it."

Ellen gasped and moved as far away from him as she could get. "You've lost your mind!"

"You got that backwards. I've just regained my mind. You know, baby, where sex is concerned you could really be a star performer. You don't even have pregnancy to worry about. You could let yourself go and have a hell of a good time."

"Gary!" She looked with fright toward the broad shoulders of Schmidt in the front seat and whispered huskily, "He'll hear us."

"Oh, no, he won't. But who cares, anyway? Everything about us is now public property."

She put her hands to her ears and cried, "I won't listen."

Gary turned toward her, grabbed a wrist and viciously pulled an arm down. He bit out between clenched teeth, "You'll listen, baby. For once in your life you're really going to listen to the truth. I've had an awful lot to think about lately. Practically every value I've ever known has been turned inside out. You know me, the sex maniac? Sure. You'll listen."

"I won't!"

He paid no attention to her protest and, still holding to her wrist, continued, "Like I say, my perspectives have all been destroyed but, oddly enough, I've also regained a few I lost along the line, especially like what a wife is supposed to be like. That's the big one. You're no wife. Do you know that? You're a damned mannequin I feed and clothe and keep in my house for display purposes only. Thinking of you as a wife is sheer mockery. On the other hand, I've been no husband, either. I should have slapped you around, or at least walked out on you, but I didn't. I crawled. I bought you little trinkets to keep baby happy. I paid for all your charge accounts without protest, even when it hurt. I let you run up and see that awful mother of yours whenever you pleased, knowing that every moment you spent with her she was telling you what a louse you married. But worst of all, I let you stay in your own little twin bed and tell me night after night, 'Not tonight, Gary. Not tonight.' And I would lie there in the dark staring at the ceiling and imagine ten million nude women chasing me through the night. Do you know what that did to me as a man? Man, hell! I was a eunuch."

Ellen went suddenly limp and a rasping sob of agony broke from her throat. "Oh, God," she whispered, "you make me feel unclean."

"Sure. Anything about sex makes you feel unclean. That mother of yours did that to you. I've known it all along, but it's just lately I've faced it." He sucked in his breath sharply and stared at her, then sighed and dropped her arm. "Aw, hell. I'm wasting my breath. Actually, Ellen, I feel damned sorry for you. You don't know what it's like to be a complete woman. You've never experienced that pleasure. That's a terrible pity. And such a waste, too. Forget I shot off my mouth. I can see now it's all waste."

He turned away from her and looked ahead to the rear-vision mirror above the windshield and saw Schmidt's eyes watching them. So the young policeman had overheard. So what? he thought. What was the difference?

He dropped back in the seat and would have fallen asleep again, but suddenly he felt Ellen touching him. "Gary."

"Uh-huh."

"You've never asked me why I left you the way I did yesterday morning."

"Was it only yesterday? I've lived a hundred years since then. No, I never asked. I was afraid to."

"Then you know why."

He turned his head on the seat and blinked at her in the sudden lights of a passing car. She had pulled her legs under her on the seat, her hands were clasped tightly together and she was leaning toward him with her face close to his. Her blonde hair was hanging loosely over one eye, but the other was open wide, staring at him with fascination.

"Yes," he said, "I know why. I had to face it finally. You figured I was guilty."

She nodded and wet her lips nervously with the tip of her tongue and whispered, "Yes. When I went to bed and then heard you talking to the chief of police and knew the shoes really belonged to that girl—I knew then."

Gary looked away from her and felt sick, but he managed to say, "So you ran. You were scared. Maybe the monster would kill you, too."

"No. That's where you're wrong. I wasn't frightened. I knew, but it didn't scare me. It was something else. It was something like—like you were just talking about. I was awake all night, thinking about it. I knew you had done it, but I wondered why."

"Oh, no," he groaned. "Stop it, Ellen. Please."

"But I have to tell you. I think you should know. I wondered about it all night. I wondered if perhaps I had caused you to do a horrible thing such as that. I know how you are about sex, you know. I—I can't help it if I don't feel the same way, but I know how you are. You are an animal, really. I know."

"Just a normal animal, Ellen."

"So I lay there wondering about it and I couldn't make sense out of anything. Like I say, though, I wasn't afraid. You were suddenly a stranger, like someone I might read about or see in the movies. You were no closer than that. You were in the next bed, but you were really a thousand miles away, and I wondered about you. I wondered about your—your sex life and whether you had ever had relations with another woman."

"Not since we've been married. God knows I was tempted, though."

"I know. I thought of that night at the Brewsters' party, when that Twining woman got you out in the garden. She was acting drunk and necking with you just to make her husband jealous. And when he walked out there and found the two of you and you realized what it was all about you got so violent you almost put poor Mr. Twining in the hospital. So I know about your violence, too, and I wondered about that."

"The devil with it. It all adds up to guilt in your mind. I'm surprised you feel safe with me even in a police car. The main thing is, you felt your own husband was capable of a dirty, stinking crime and you ran out. That's all that interests me." A new idea struck him and he looked at her to ask, "Do you still think I'm guilty?"

Ellen brushed her hair back from her face and looked ahead at the lights of the car skidding along the road cut into the cliffs. Below them, down the cliffs and out into space, was the black mass of the ocean, darker than the night. She felt that somehow the ride was symbolic of the past few days, a blind rushing off into space and darkness, with no signs to show the way and no destination in sight.

She said softly, "I couldn't think. I had to get away."

Gary said sarcastically, "I'm surprised you even tried to think. That's something new with you."

"I tried, but it wasn't much good. I tried to think of what I should do, as a wife. I thought of the different crimes I've read about in the papers and the wives always standing by their husbands and I thought I should be doing that and I probably would have if it had been almost any other crime. But a young girl— a girl fourteen years old—" She shook her head and again a sob broke from her throat. "I couldn't do it, Gary. No wife should have to stand by a husband who could do a thing like that. It's unthinkable."

She buried her face in her hands and Gary sat there frowning, staring at her. She, too, had become almost a stranger. He wondered if they had ever really known each other at any time. Two different living worlds that had never actually come in contact with each other.

He was silent until they had almost reached the Blue Bird, then he said, "It's strange how you could live in the same house with me for three years and then, when the thing happens, never doubt that I was the one who did it. Sam Carson, who hardly knows me at all, is beginning to doubt that I'm guilty. Even Kraft is beginning to entertain reservations. And a woman who doesn't know me at all, the one who has been taking all the testimony, is absolutely convinced that I'm innocent. But my own wife— What is it with you, Ellen? Have you been hating me all this time?"

She kept her face buried in her hands, but shook her head. "Sometimes," she said. "Sometimes, yes. Not all the time."

"Oh, brother, that's just wonderful. Not all the time, she says. I've sure been living in a fool's paradise. I thought we were supposed to be in love with each other. Isn't that why we got married? I don't remember offering you any millions and I don't remember you coming to me weighed down with a dowry. I thought it was love."

She lifted her head and forgot about Schmidt and screamed, "Nothing was the way it was supposed to be. You and all your talk of love and all you wanted to do was paw my body. Always after me. Always. You never left me alone. I thought you were good and kind and gentle and that our marriage would be something beautiful and all you had in mind was a bed and me in it and breeding children. You almost killed me. You know that. It was a miracle I didn't die on that operating table."

"On the other hand, it was a miracle it happened the way it did. You know damned well it was a freak accident."

"I don't care. You were responsible for it. I didn't want children. A woman gets big and ugly and fat and bloated and the whole idea was repulsive to me. But not you. Oh, no. All you wanted was to paw my body and you wanted children no matter what I thought about it. And you ask if I ever hated you. Yes," she screamed, "I did. Every day you came home from the office and kissed me and tried to pat my bottom I hated you. Every night you tried to get in my bed I hated you. So, you see, I knew you had raped that girl and killed her. Because I knew why. Because I know you."

Schmidt turned the car off the highway and onto a black-top parking area before the Blue Bird. He set the emergency brake carefully, switched off the engine, then turned slowly about with an arm over the back of the seat. His young face was pale as he looked long and searchingly at Ellen, then swung his hot eyes to Gary.

"Mister," he said slowly, biting off each word, "right alongside that restaurant is a cliff that drops three hundred feet straight down to the ocean. Policeman or not, by God, I'll turn my back if you'd like to kick your wife over the edge of it."

Gary was not tempted. He was too beaten. The last shreds of his world had come apart. He got out of the car and looked into the black void and was more tempted to walk off the edge of the cliff himself.

Ellen got out of the car and arranged her hair and smoothed the dress over her hips, as poised and as expressionless as if nothing had been said and nothing had happened. She had heard what Schmidt had had to say, yet she smiled at him brightly and said coyly, "I trust you won't mind waiting outside for us, Officer." She wiggled her fingers at him and started toward the entrance of the Blue Bird with the affected walk of a fashion model, one foot placed carefully and precisely before the other. Gary stared at her unbelievingly, but then shrugged and followed after her.

The Blue Bird was a small restaurant perched on the lip of a cliff overhanging the ocean. It had a spectacular view during the daytime, up and down the wild, rocky coast. The large plate-glass windows looked out on nothingness at night, which was why there were rarely any late customers, but it captured a certain feeling of intimacy that was relaxing. There was a small bar decorated with pseudo masks from the South Seas and carved outrigger models, a large fireplace in the wall opposite, candles on the tables that had been dripping varicolored waxes for months over brandy bottles, and a few fish nets and glass floats were draped over the rafters.

There was one Filipino waiter on week nights and the owner himself was behind the bar. He looked up with a bored smile as Gary and Ellen entered, but did not recognize them. There was one other couple in the place seated at a table before the large windows close by the bar. Gary steered Ellen away from them to a table at the far end of the room. They were in partial darkness, so that even the waiter could hardly see them as he took their order.

Gary had thought that he would have no appetite at all, but had no trouble putting away his dinner. His spirit was low, but as he finished dessert and sipped at a brandy-coffee he began feeling physically better. It was a relief simply to get away from the police station and the constant questioning and into a quiet, normal atmosphere.

He watched Ellen across from him and was amazed at how quickly she had switched from near-hysteria to calm poise. But then he knew that that should not have surprised him. Ellen had the facility of genius toward turning her back on reality whenever it pleased her. She merely shut off one corner of her mind and opened another. At the moment she was concerned with the car she had rented and the amount of the check Gary made out for her and some cleaning and laundry that had to be retrieved and with the room she had taken at Redwood Inn, which she did not like, and with the fact that her mother was coming down to stay with her that night and perhaps she would arrive before Ellen returned and get upset about it. The corner of her mind that had to do with murder and police and hatred and her husband had been neatly sealed off, at least temporarily.

Gary was just as happy to say nothing and sit back and nod and listen to her chatter. It gave him the first opportunity he had enjoyed in a long while to review what had happened to him, yet his mind was so numbed and frayed that the days and the hours melted together and he was incapable of constructive thinking.

Ellen said something about having to meet her mother and fumbled for her purse and gloves. Gary called the waiter over, got the check and left a tip on the table. The check, however, had to be paid at the bar. Ellen headed for the front door, but Gary went to the bar with the check and a bill in his hand. He reached there just as the other couple left their table and the man came to the bar to stand at Gary's side. Gary turned his head to smile at him and his smile became a frozen grimace.

George Halloran looked into Gary's eyes and his own opened wide, then narrowed to burning slits. The attorney's face paled, his hands trembled and tiny beads of perspiration appeared on his forehead. "You," he said, and all the hatred that one man could feel toward another was in the one word.

Gary had anticipated having to face Diana's father at some time or other in the police station, and had wondered how he would react. Now he knew. He wanted to hide, to run, to disappear, to be anywhere except facing George Halloran. Perspiration broke out on his own forehead and the palms of his hands. He even felt guilty, terribly guilty, as if he were actually the criminal who had murdered the daughter of the man before him. His mind spun dizzily and he tried to tell himself that he was reacting like a damned fool. But he still felt guilty.

He wet his lips with the tip of his tongue and said huskily, as if the other man was reading his mind, "I'm not, you know. Honest to God, Mr. Halloran. The whole thing is a ghastly mistake."

The attorney stared into his eyes and repeated, "You. To think—to think that I would ever have to face you."

Gary held up his hands, as if to stop the other man, though he had not made a move toward him. "Now, wait a minute. I'm telling you, Mr. Halloran, it's all a mistake. Even the police are beginning to see that now. That's why they're not holding me."

"You mean they don't have enough evidence against you yet."

"Believe me, Mr. Halloran, I never knew your daughter in my life. You have to believe that."

The attorney turned away from him to slam his money down on the bar, then spun on his heel and started toward the door. Gary threw his own money on the bar and ran after Halloran. He caught him just outside and grabbed his arm. "Now, wait—"

Halloran knocked his hand away and drew his arm back to slap Gary across the face. "The only thing I regret," he cried, "is that I'm not a younger man. I would enjoy tearing the flesh from your bones with my bare hands. To think— to think of a monster such as you walking around loose—"

Mrs. Halloran, who had been standing by waiting for her husband, looked around at his words and stared at Gary. She stepped closer to see him better and, though she had never met him, recognized him from his photographs in the newspapers. Her face turned chalk-white, her hand went to her throat and she tried to step back, but her legs gave way and she fainted. Gary bent over her at once and was joined by Halloran, who lifted his wife's shoulders in his arms and smoothed the hair back from her forehead.

"Quick," he said. "Get some smelling salts, or something, from the bar."

Gary brushed by Ellen, who was also bending over the woman, and hurried back into the restaurant. The owner, however, was now aware of his identity and snarled at him to get out. Gary reached across the bar and grabbed the man's shirt in his fist.

"One more word out of you," he said, "and I'll kick your teeth in. I've taken enough stupidities from all you people. Do you have some smelling salts?"

"No."

"Ammonia?"

"I—I think—"

"Get it, fast."

Gary went back into the dark with an open bottle of ammonia and some whisky in the bottom of a water glass. He found Schmidt also kneeling by Mrs. Halloran's side. They tried the ammonia, but she failed to respond. Ellen poured the whisky between her lips, but that, too, had no effect on her.

Halloran forgot for the moment who he was facing and looked anxiously at Gary. "It's her heart," he said. "I think she's had an attack."

"Do you know anything—"

"No. We'll have to get her to a hospital in a hurry."

"Maybe we can call an ambulance—"

Schmidt looked worried and shook his head. He was strictly a Bayside policeman and far out of his official territory. He had no idea what protocol would be in such a situation and was plainly not anxious to find out. He suggested, however, that he take the Hallorans back into town in the squad car with Gary following in the Hallorans' automobile. With the siren helping they could make the trip one way in half the time it would take to get an ambulance. Halloran gave his keys to Gary and the three men carried the unconscious woman to the squad car. Ellen hesitated for a moment, obviously debating whether or not to help, but when she saw the stricken expression in the attorney's haunted eyes she sighed and got into the police car to help him with his wife. Gary was mildly astonished that she should offer to help anyone.

Gary followed the police car back up the highway in the Hallorans' conservative Buick sedan. Schmidt set a fast pace, with the siren open wide. Gary concentrated on his driving, but after the first few miles he had to slow down and allow the police car to disappear ahead of him. He was much too fatigued for fast driving, his eyes would not focus properly and his coordination was so bad that he lurched and skidded on every curve. He lifted his foot on the throttle and slowed down to a speed more in keeping with his numbed condition....

As soon as he was alone on the highway he began wondering about the advisability of appearing at the Bayside Hospital. He would naturally be recognized and, considering the weird situation, there could easily be trouble. Gary was in no mood and hadn't the reserves to cope with anything more. When he reached the outskirts of Bayside he turned toward the ocean and a few moments later drove slowly by his own home. The place was dark and there were no policemen about, but curiosity seekers were driving by in a slow, steady stream and pausing to look at the house, as if it could give them the answers to the mystery. Gary drove on by. He thought of the police station, but rebelled at that idea. He thought of his many friends and agonizingly discarded all of them, afraid of what he might run into. Then he thought of Jane Bestor and knew with certainty that she would take him in.

He had only been to her house once before, however, and had difficulty finding it. He drove by the house twice before he saw a light through the pines and finally recognized the gravel driveway. He parked the Buick on the street and walked wearily up to the house. Jane's eyebrows lifted with surprise when she opened the door and saw him standing on the porch, but she also saw at once the heavy lids and the slack chin and the almost vacant stare of his bloodshot eyes. She took his arm and led him to the couch before the fireplace.

He looked slowly around the dimly lighted room and at the TV screen, on which a play was progressing, then up at Jane standing solicitously before him. She was wearing mules and a pink nylon robe and had a towel wrapped about her head.

She touched it with her fingers and smiled down at him. "I was just doing my hair. It takes hours to dry."

"If I'm interrupting anything—I know I have a hell of a nerve—"

"No, no. Please. It's quite all right. Would you like some coffee?"

"No, thanks. I've just had dinner, at the Blue Bird."

"Oh? I like their curries."

"Yeah. I went down there with my wife. We had to talk. It was the worst place I could have chosen. On our way out we ran into the Hallorans."

"Oh, no!"

She sat down abruptly on the hassock before him and he explained what had happened. When he had finished she asked, "You still have their car?"

"It's out front. I was wondering— I hate to be such a nuisance—"

"Don't worry about it. A little fresh air will do me good, anyway. Maybe," she laughed, "my hair will dry sooner. Just give me the keys. I can come back in a taxi."

Gary watched her as she started toward the bedroom to get dressed, but his lids lowered, his head fell back on an arm of the sofa and he was instantly asleep.

The sun was high and flooding through the windows of the house when Gary again opened his eyes. He lay for a long while without moving, until he realized where he was. He sat up with a groan and noticed that his shoes were off, his tie had been removed and Jane had somehow got him out of his coat. There was a pillow under his shoulders and he was covered with a light comforter. Gary swung his feet to the floor, lowered his head and scratched his fingers back and forth through his scalp. It was the first decent sleep he had had in some time, yet he had slept so hard and had dreamed so wildly during the night that he felt almost as fatigued as he had the day before. His head and shoulders were damp with perspiration and he turned and noticed that the pillow was also damp. He was momentarily alarmed, as he perspired that much only when he was ill, but then he shrugged and thought that it had probably been due to the nightmares he had suffered through.

He called, "Miss Bestor," and then, "Jane," but there was no response. He got to his feet and stretched himself and blinked at a clock on the fireplace mantel. It was just before nine. Good, he thought. He had slept at least ten hours, maybe a little more. He walked shakily into the bedroom, yawning broadly and rubbing his hands over his face, and noticed his suitcase on the floor, the one Carson had packed for him. Jane had apparently picked it up at the police station the night before. He thought, with a grin, they don't hardly make 'em that way no more, and began to feel better.

He had shaved and was out of the shower and back in his clothes when Jane returned to the house with some bundles in her arms. She smiled at him cheerily and Gary followed her into the kitchen, where she took bacon and eggs from the packages and started preparing breakfast. She also handed him the morning paper. He dropped to the tiny breakfast table by a sun-flooded window and glanced over the paper.

It was no surprise to him to read: DIANA'S MOTHER SUFFERS HEART ATTACK, and the subcaption: MRS. HALLORAN COLLAPSES AFTER ACCIDENTALLY FACING WAR-HERO SUSPECT. He read through the entire account and saw that it was fairly accurate, though highly dramatized. Other write-ups were concerned with the additional news that nothing had so far been found at Chinamen's Ridge, what the sheriff had to say about the case, what the chief of police had to say, what the district attorney had to say, what Gary himself had had to say on various occasions, what many other people had to say and, lastly, a further report from Dr. Thompson, the psychiatrist, in which it was pointed out that Gary Malone's personality make-up was not inconsistent with such a crime. Gary snorted, rolled the paper into a ball, and threw it aside.

Jane served him breakfast and sat opposite at the table to sip at a cup of coffee. As he ate, she told him, "I stayed at the hospital a little while last night after I left the Buick. What happened to Mrs. Halloran is a coronary thrombosis. I don't understand much about such things, but from the way everyone was talking the attack doesn't seem to be a fatal one."

Gary spoke through a mouthful of food, "Thank God for that."

"Yes. Mr. Halloran, of course, is a beaten man. First his daughter and now his wife. I saw him for a few minutes in the waiting room and it almost broke my heart. He looked so pitiful and so—so lost and helpless. Incidentally, I also saw your wife. She was there."

Gary looked up with mild interest. "Oh? Did you tell her where I was?"

"Yes, I did. I thought you might like her to know. She—ah—well—"

"Go ahead and say it. She didn't give a damn."

"Oh, I don't think it was that so much. She seemed pretty distraught, too."

"Sure. The police dug up her garden." He turned back to his food and mumbled, "Anything of importance on her mind?"

"She just said that you could get in touch with her at Redwood Inn. Oh, yes. She also said something about getting an attorney."

A bitter smile crept into Gary's eyes as he said, "Not for me, I'll bet."

Jane was embarrassed and looked away from him. "No," she whispered. "She was concerned with her own interests."

"That figures. Anyway, I still don't want an attorney. If it gets worse, okay, but not yet. I see you were by the police station."

"Yes. On my way home last night. Sergeant Welte was there and gave me your bag when I told him where you were. I thought the police should know, too."

He shoved his empty plate aside and asked bluntly, "Just in case they turned up a body during the night?"

Her face flushed and she said hotly, "I wasn't thinking that way at all. I was thinking they should know where you were in case you needed protection over this—this Mrs. Halloran development."

Gary blinked at her humbly and reached across the table to squeeze her hand. "I'm sorry, Jane. I'm damned sorry. Of all people—"

She withdrew her hand slowly and smiled at him. "That's all right. In your shoes, I'd be edgy, too. Let me see. Oh, yes. The chief telephoned this morning just before I went out for groceries."

"I must have really been sawing logs. I didn't hear anything. What's on his mind?"

"Well, he said it would be a good idea for you to stay right here until he calls later in the day. He's worried about Mrs. Halloran's attack. He thinks that now the people really will regard you as—these are not my words, believe me—but as some sort of monster."

"That's me, all right. Gary Malone, monster." He buried his face in his hands and mumbled, "Sure. I go around killing young girls and frightening older women into heart attacks. Oh, God, what is this all about? Just why is a thing like this happening to me?"

Jane reached over and shook his shoulders until he raised his head again and looked at her. "Don't," she whispered. "Don't give in."

"But, good Lord," he cried, "I have never willingly hurt anyone in my life. But now, all a woman has to do is look at me and—"

"Don't. Please, Gary. You have a lot more ahead. You aren't through yet. If you give in now, if you start feeling sorry for yourself—"

He bit his lip and nodded and blinked at her. "You're right. It's just—well, it gets me down every now and then."

"All the more reason you have to prove everyone wrong. You have to fight."

"Fight against what? That's the hell of it. I don't know who to fight, or where to start. We know someone abducted that girl and undoubtedly killed her. If we could find out who it was, this nightmare could come to an end. But that's strictly police work, something for which I'm not equipped at all. And, when you come right down to it, where are the police getting? Nowhere. They got me."

Jane said stubbornly, "Nevertheless, there may be something you can do."

"Amateur detective stuff? Let's not be childish. That's for the movies."

She insisted, "I don't care. Somewhere—maybe even in the back of your own mind—somewhere there is a clue. I think you should try to find it."

Gary sat back and stared at her and felt a warm glow stealing through his body. She was no more convinced than he that he would turn up anything new. She was simply worried about him and wanted to keep his mind on something constructive. But he decided to go along with her. It would be a good idea to think of something other than his own predicament, for a change.

They took the pot of coffee and some cups into the front room and reviewed the case all over again. Jane had taken down all the testimony and so knew the facts as well as anyone else. Gary explained his idea that the person who had left Diana's belongings in his basement had been merely passing by and had somehow become frightened, or perhaps had thought he was trapped on that street. Jane considered the idea from every angle and shook her head.

"No," she said. "You can't sell me that at all. He would have to know that your basement was unlocked, he would have to know that no one was at home, and— and he would just have to know too many things. Or he would have to be almost inconceivably lucky. I can't see it."

"But someone did put the stuff there."

"Yes, yes. But I think the person who did it had had prior access to your basement, or somehow knew quite a bit about it. Like that plumber, or the grocer boy, or your friend Luke Summer, or the people who voted in your garage that election day, or perhaps one of your close neighbors. I think it's somebody you know by sight and maybe by name."

Gary sighed and said, "That's a lot of people to choose from."

"We have everyone in the town of Bayside, for that matter. But I think really it's someone fairly close."

"Any sound reason for that conclusion?"

"Yes. He had to know the basement was unpaved."

Gary had not thought of that and gave Jane a pleased grin. "You're pretty good, you know. And you're right. So that leaves out the idea of a stranger. At least, that's something positive. So now where do we go?"

"How about your friend, Mr. Summer?"

Gary had been thinking quite a bit about Luke and, though it was unreasonable to believe that Luke could ever be involved in such a crime, he could not get out of his mind what the chief had had to say about him. He told Jane and they discussed the possibility of Luke from every angle. They also discussed all the others and got nowhere. At the end, just before noon, Jane suggested that they could do a little spade work on their own.

"I'll get Chief Kraft's permission to interview everyone I can, including the eight men who voted at your place that election day."

"That's a waste of time. The plumber's testimony seems to put all of them in the clear. "

Jane's stubborn streak again came to the fore. "Nevertheless, I am going to interview them. Who knows what may turn up?"

The chief saved Jane the trouble of driving by the police station by stopping at her house just as she was preparing sandwiches for lunch. He refused her offer to share the meal, explaining that Welte was waiting for him outside in a squad car. He glanced at Gary, who was watching him quizzically from the couch and shook his head.

"Nothing new," he said. "Chinamen's Ridge is negative. The sheriff is about to give up on that. Right now, though, Hank and I are going up to the Kingsley Ranch and talk to that cowboy who found the girl's book in front of the Gold Nugget."

"Why?"

Kraft shrugged his massive shoulders. "Just something to do, I guess. We never bothered with him much before."

Gary had a hunch and said, "You mean the D.A. wants something else to put in the papers, don't you?"

The chief smiled and again shrugged, without replying to the question. "When I get back," he said, "it might be a good idea for you to come down to the station again. Meanwhile, stay where you are."

"I intend staying here, for a little while, anyway, and I don't intend going down to that station again. I've had enough of that merry-go-round." Gary squinted at him for a moment, then said, "Just why have you dropped by here, anyway? You haven't had anything to say."

Kraft scratched his blond head, his eyes fixed rather sympathetically upon Gary. He seemed reluctant to speak, but finally sighed and said, "It's about your wife. I thought you should know."

Gary sat up straighter and snapped, "What about her?"

"Well, I haven't really talked to her, you know, so I dropped over to Redwood Inn a little while ago to see her. She's staying there with her mother."

"Ellen said she was coming in last night. Lovely woman. You'll be crazy about her. Only take my advice and don't ever turn your back to her."

Kraft chuckled and said, "I got that impression without your warning. Anyway, your wife's lawyer was there, too. I guess you two had a row last night, huh?"

"I did most of the talking."

"Yeah. Well, your wife is going to get a divorce, and she's got this lawyer with her to see what she can take away from you. What she has in mind, I think is everything you own, right down to your socks."

Gary sat back in the couch and closed his eyes for a moment. Ellen was acting in a great hurry, but even so, he was not surprised or even particularly interested. He had managed to wash Ellen out of his mind the night before. It was just as well that she got a divorce; it would save him the trouble later on.

He opened his eyes and looked up at the chief standing by the end of the couch. "Thanks for telling me," he said. "If you see her or her lawyer you might tell them to see me and I'm sure we can work out a settlement. I guess half of everything I have belongs to her. She's welcome to it."

Kraft looked down at him with pity and shook his head. "Half is only half enough for her. I'm not kidding, Malone, she wants it all. Figures she can get it, too. A very forthright gal, I'd say. If you don't willingly turn over to her every dollar you have, she intends going into court as a prosecution witness, if and when you're brought to trial. How do you like those apples?"

Jane studied the sudden stricken expression in Gary's eyes and cried out to the chief, "But she can't do that. She can't testify against her own husband."

"I'm afraid you don't know the law very well, Jane. A wife can refuse to testify against her husband, if she wishes, but if she wishes otherwise she can have her testimony read into the record. In this case, knowing a little of how she thinks, her testimony could be really damaging." He placed his big hands on the couch and leaned over to tell Gary, "Sorry I'm the one to bring you this news, but I thought you should know. I hate seeing a guy kicked when he's down."

Gary nodded numbly.

"Well, I just— Guess I'll be running along."

Jane walked with him to the front door and out to the porch. There she paused and explained that she wanted to interview everyone concerned, including the eight voters. Kraft figured the latter would be a waste of time, but she was so persistent that he finally told her to go ahead. He also gave his permission to make her interviews official.

He threw her a wave and walked heavily down the gravel path and to the squad car parked on the street. Sergeant Welte was at the wheel. He started the engine and pulled away as soon as the chief was seated. Kraft hunched down in the seat and stared narrowly out at the passing houses and trees without seeing them, his mind busy with the case. Discouragement was gnawing at him. So much had taken place since the discovery of the gym shoes and yet he felt that he was as far away from a solution as ever. Everywhere he turned he seemed to be running into blind alleys.

But he knew well that it could not continue that way for long. Civic pressure was already beginning to be felt. He was the chief, wasn't he? Now he had something to work on. And now he had better come up with something in a hurry— or else. Scott Douglas was already hinting publicly that perhaps a more able man could wrap things up in a hurry. The mayor, when he had talked with him that morning, had been a bit sour. Other civic fathers were looking at him askance. Even the men of his own force were not happy with him. And Welte, of course, was more or less holding his breath. He would be the logical candidate to move into the chief's shoes.

They drove up the winding valley in bright sunshine that became hotter the farther they got from the coast. When they reached Valley Center it was so hot that all the windows of the car had to be opened. Both Welte and Kraft unbuttoned their collars, loosened their ties and wiped perspiration from their foreheads. Welte continued on the main road another three miles, then turned off onto a dirt road and under a wooden arch on which was painted Kingsley Ranch, Pure-Bred Herefords. They crossed a rattling cattle guard and started up the road.

The Kingsley spread was strictly a mountain ranch, but it had good water from many springs, it was not too wooded, except for occasional giant oaks, and there were dozens of excellent dry meadows for pasture and, in the valleys, a number of flats where hay was grown. The main buildings were two miles back from the highway. The road Welte was driving was rutted and dusty and wound crookedly around spurs of hills and outcroppings of rock.

They had driven perhaps a mile when Welte heard the shrill yapping of a dog and slowed down to a snail's pace. He and the chief looked off to the left, over a meadow and up a rise beyond to a building about a quarter of a mile away. It was a small building of vertical siding about ten feet square, faded whitewash and a sagging, shingle roof. A mongrel dog was pawing furiously at the closed door and yapping excitedly. When he turned and saw the car, however, he ran away into some brush.

Kraft chuckled and said, "Spooky devil, isn't he?"

"Maybe someone kicks him around."

"Seems that way. Acts awful queer for a ranch dog. They see a strange car they usually come running at you. But let's get going. I could use some water."

"Me, too."

They drove on and after another mile dipped down into a narrow valley and drove into the ranch yards proper. Everything was whitewashed, the big house for the owner, the foreman's house, the bunkhouses, the large barns and even the corrals and fences. Kingsley, the owner, lived on a ranch in Nevada and was rarely around, so Welte stopped in front of the foreman's house, a three room cottage with a screened porch across the front. The moment the engine was switched off they could smell the odors of cooking food heavy in the air, though they could see no one around. They got out of the car, stretched their legs, then followed the food odor around the corner of the cottage. The foreman and half a dozen ranch hands were having lunch at a long wooden table under the shade of a big oak.

Welte and the chief were invited to join in, and helped themselves to heaping plates of Mexican beans and slabs of spare ribs that had been marinated in soya sauce.

They found out all they wanted to know as they ate lunch. Clarence Smith, the cowhand who had found Diana's schoolbook in front of the Gold Nugget the day after she had disappeared, told them again of the way he had found the book and then had given it to Herb at the bar, thinking a customer had lost it. As for his own activities on the day preceding that, he had an iron-clad alibi.

He had been out on the range herding calves all that afternoon. Two of the other hands at the table had been with him and verified his story. They remembered the day well because that had been branding time and some of the superstitious hands had protested about branding on Friday the thirteenth. Kraft was satisfied. He had learned just about what he had expected—another zero.

When they were leaving, the foreman walked out to the squad car with them. He was a big man with a wind-whipped and sun-reddened face, gray hair cut close to his head and the slim hips of a man who spent most of his time in the saddle. He was getting too old, however, to run a ranch and was on the verge of retirement, which was one of the reasons Kingsley had the ranch up for sale.

"Funny, isn't it?" he said. "This guy who killed that girl is the one who was gonna sell the ranch, or try to, anyway."

Kraft said, "We're not sure he killed her."

"Aw, hell, course he's the one. You found the stuff in his place, didn't you? If we had him up here, believe you me, he'd a been strung up by his thumbs a long time ago." He pried between his teeth with the blade of a knife, and said, "Seemed like kind of a nice young feller, too. You just can't tell, can you?"

"That's the one thing I know for sure." Welte was behind the wheel, so Kraft opened the right door and slid onto the seat. When he closed the door he started propping his right arm out the window, but the hot metal made him withdraw it in a hurry. "Plenty hot," he said. "A little cooler down on the coast. Well, thanks a lot for your hospitality."

"Sure. Come around any time. We like company."

"Thanks. Oh, by the way, on our way up your road we saw a dog scratching and yowling around some little building. It was off to the left of the road. Looked abandoned."

The foreman screwed his eyes tight with thought for a moment, then said, "You mean the old spring house. Used to be a nice spring down there, but it went dry three or four years ago. Nice place to store vegetables and stuff. We don't use it no more."

"Uh-huh. I was just wondering what that dog was doing there. He seemed rather excited."

The foreman chuckled and snorted, "Aw, hell, musta been one of old man Thorkelsen's mutts. We don't keep no dogs here on the ranch. You take a dog don't know its own mind too much they bother the calves. Run 'em all over hell and gone."

"I still wonder why that dog was so excited. Has me curious."

"That don't mean nothing. I noticed afore a couple dogs yapping around that shack. Seems like every time I come up the road I see a mutt over there. Took a shot at 'em a couple times. Too far away to hit, though. I guess maybe there's a coon nesting up with a passel of little ones down there under the shack. Dogs get excited over coons."

"Do you have many raccoons around here?"

"Well, now, I don't rightly know. I never seen none myself, but I guess they're up and down the valley."

"Sure. Well, we'll be running along. And thanks again."

"You bet. Any time."

Welte backed the car around, waved at the foreman, then turned onto the dirt road heading back toward the highway. Kraft kept looking out the right window of the car and when he saw the abandoned spring house again he dropped a hand on Welte's arm. "Slow down." He squinted across the meadow and up the hill and again saw the same mongrel scratching at the door. He told Welte to stop the car and sat there a moment staring across at the shack.

After a while he sighed and said, "Maybe I'm a damned fool to walk clear over there in this heat, but that dog has got me curious."

Welte looked disgusted. "You heard what the foreman said about coons."

"I don't care. I've raised dozens of dogs and I don't think that dog is acting quite right. If it's a coon he's after, why does he keep jumping up at that door? I'm going over there and find out."

Welte pointed at a faded track across the meadow and said, "Wait a minute. No sense walking in this heat if can drive over there. Let's try it."

He was able to follow some old ruts across the meadow and, though it was bumpy, he drove the car to the base of the hill. He and Kraft got out and noticed an old path going up to the shack, about another fifty yards from the meadow. Kraft started up the path and, after hesitating a second, Welte followed after him. The dog had run away again the moment the car had started across the meadow.

Welte was walking up the gradual slope with his head down, and suddenly bumped into the chief when they were still about fifteen yards from the shack. Kraft was standing still and frowning and sniffing at the hot air. The sergeant asked irritably, "What now?"

"Don't you smell anything?"

Welte cocked his head to one side and sniffed at the air and then he, too, was frowning. He looked curiously at the chief and their eyes met and widened. Each knew exactly what the smell was because there is no other like it. Welte's knees felt weak and, in spite of the heat, his face and hands were suddenly cold.

Kraft clenched his big fists tightly together and plodded on up the path. When he reached the shack the smell was so bad that he was nauseated and had difficulty examining the door. There was no lock. The door was held closed by a simple clasp. The chief pulled it open, staggered back for a moment, then stepped into the shack. Except for shelves on the walls and dust and hay on the floor, there was nothing in the room. The center of the floor, however, was fairly clean, almost as if it had been swept, or some thing dragged on it.

Kraft stared down and saw that some of the boards were loose. It was obvious that at one time, probably not long before, they had been removed and then carelessly replaced. The chief held his breath, got down on his knees and ripped the boards aside. He looked down at the form lying on the dirt under the floor, gasped and retched and shoved himself back to his feet.

He staggered outside and leaned back against the shack, shaking his head slowly from side to side and sucking in huge lungfuls of air. When he could trust himself to walk again, he took Welte's arm and hurried back down the path to the meadow. He did not stop until they reached the side of the car. There the tears came and rolled down his cheeks. Welte stared open-mouthed at the big man crying and could not believe it.

Kraft's emotions, however, were out of control only for a moment. He wiped the tears from his eyes and his features became as hard as granite. He told Welte, "It's the girl, all right: Diana Halloran. No doubt of it. You stay here and, for God's sake, keep that dog away. I'm going back to the ranch house and phone the station."

Welte cried excitedly, "Better call the sheriff, too. This is his stamping ground, not yours. He's gonna get plenty mad you made the find."

"The hell with him and everybody else. After what I've just seen—never mind. You stay here."

"Who's gonna pick up Malone?"

Kraft snarled angrily, "Why should he be picked up?"

"Well, hell's bells, man, now we got a body. Now we can charge him with murder."

Kraft stood rigidly staring off into space for a long while; then he seemed to shrink in size as he said, "I guess it has to be done and, you know, I have a hunch it's all wrong. That poor guy."

"Murderer, you mean!"

"No, Hank. I don't think so. But, God knows, he's going to get it pinned on him now for sure." He took in a deep breath of air, let it out slowly and said, "I'll pick him up myself. At least, I owe him that."

Chapter Seven

Gary was picked up that afternoon. Though the chief still refused to charge him with anything, Gary was so shocked and stunned by the finding of the body that he returned willingly to the police station. He was held at the station, subject to constant questioning, until Monday, when the Grand Jury would meet and consider an indictment.

The body was removed to the morgue in Grand Point, where it was officially identified and where it was also learned that the girl had been killed by a blow at the base of her skull from some blunt instrument. The death weapon itself was not found. Because of the time that had lapsed it could not be determined whether or not the girl had been assaulted, though no one had any doubts on that point. Pathologists learned very little more, nor did hordes of experts learn anything more at the spring house. The print of a man's shoe was found in soft earth just outside the shack, but inasmuch as it did not match anything Gary Malone wore it was not considered seriously.

Kraft's new-found public esteem soared to the skies. No one would believe his statement that the finding of the body had been simply a stroke of blind luck. Kraft was the smartest of all smart chiefs of police. Even the District Attorney, who was boiling with envy, believed that Kraft had somehow picked up a clue from Malone that had led him to the body. Kraft would bide his time until the trial and there bring out what he had learned and so become even more famous than ever. He was the hero of Bayside and there was serious talk that his salary should be increased.

The press was indeed having a field day. Quite aside from the finding of the body itself, which made headlines and sold extras all over the nation, the press suddenly found itself possessed with a wealth of headline-making statements from some of the principals involved. Foremost was the statement from Ellen Malone, which she made at a press conference held at the Redwood Inn after she learned that Gary was not going to give her freely everything he owned, and in which she was quoted as saying:

"I have always worked hard at being a good wife and a good housekeeper, but success somehow seemed to elude me. Gary was much too high-strung ever to settle down as a homebody. He was always on the go with his sports and his athletics, as if he preferred being away from home as much as possible. I rarely knew where he was except for the dinner hour, where I insisted on punctuality; but the moment that was over with he was out again like a shot, supposedly calling on clients. I didn't really mind all the time he spent at the country club and all the bars around town, but the many lonely evenings I had to spend were often quite unbearable. His temper, too—he's a redhead, you know—was really pretty unmanageable. Like the night we found that poor girl's gym shoes. He rather scared me the way he turned on me when I merely suggested that we call the police. Poor Betty Summer was so frightened of him that she and her husband left the house at once to avoid violence. I suppose some people will condemn me for starting a divorce action and not standing by him at this moment, but I think most women will know how I feel if they put themselves in my shoes and realize what it must be like to live daily facing the horrible nature of the crime that was visited upon that poor child."

Luke Summer also had his little say and was quoted:

"Yes, I knew Gary rather well and spent a lot of time in his company, but I can't honestly say I ever felt that we were friends. He was a hard man to know. When you thought you knew how he would act in a given situation, he would often turn around and act in exactly the opposite manner. Unpredictable. And he had a driving urge always to be ahead of everyone. He made himself the best golfer at the club by spending more time at the game than even a pro would allow. He had to be the best, you see. Same way in hunting, fishing, or anything else. He was always out in front, shooting at the game before anyone else, or splashing into the streams for trout before his partner could get his lines set. I guess you'd call it a psychotic urge. He was like that socially, too, always telling all the jokes at a party, making sure he danced with all the women, always the center of attention. He was an odd sort of person to know. That drive of his was really peculiar."

Mr. George Halloran, on being interviewed on what had happened the night of Mrs. Halloran's heart attack, was quoted as saying:

"He brazenly tried to face me down there in the restaurant. He even followed me outside and grabbed my arm and for a moment I was rather alarmed. I am a much older man and am quite sure I would not come off very well in a physical encounter with him. My strength has not been the best lately. I really believe it was fear that caused Mrs. Halloran's attack, when she saw the man with me, as much as anything else. He was like someone possessed."

Colonel Sebright, who had been Gary's commanding officer in Korea, was located in retirement in Virginia, and was quoted as saying:

"Gary Malone was the best-adjusted civilian in uniform and one of the finest officers and a gentleman I ever had the pleasure and the privilege to command."

The colonel's words were read, but forgotten.

Gary Malone was tried and usually convicted every morning over millions of breakfast tables and the energetic Scott Douglas was riding on Cloud Eight. He and his deputies tirelessly collected every scrap of evidence and pored over all the testimonials and put together a presentation to be made to the Grand Jury that they were confident would crush Gary Malone if only by sheer weight. The D.A.'s one worry was caused by Kraft's strange refusal to arrest Gary on a suspicion-of-murder charge. The chief maintained that, where Malone was concerned, nothing actually new had been uncovered against him and, anyway, he was remaining at the police station of his own free will. The D.A. could have acted without the chief, but he was reluctant to do so in the face of Kraft's reborn popularity.

During that entire week end Gary was able to sleep never more than thirty minutes or so at a time. In addition to the constant questioning and interviews, Gary tortured his own physical and nervous state by smoking constantly, pacing the floor hour after hour, drinking pot after pot of coffee and only nibbling at the food that was brought to him. He lost weight and became pale, so that the freckles on his face stood out like sickly blotches; his cheeks were gaunt, his lips were twisted into a thin, bitter line, his eyes were streaked badly with red and under them were dark shadows. He no longer wore a tie or coat, he had not changed his shirt in days and, because he could not stand still long enough to shave nor even care about it, the red stubble on his chin was thick and wiry. He knew he looked like a tramp and he knew that he was allowing himself to go to pieces, but he couldn't stop the process.

He had finished breakfast Monday morning and was momentarily alone in the chief's office when Theodore Baker called on him for the first time. Gary was so amazed to see his boss that he sat back on the edge of Kraft's desk and stared at him without a greeting. The older man looked nervous and uncomfortable and the shadows under his eyes revealed that he, too, had been spending some sleepless nights.

He closed the door behind him, glanced uneasily about the room, stared sharply into Gary's eyes, then sighed and dropped into a chair before the desk. His voice was hollow as he said, "I must tell you something, Gary. I am not a very brave man. Time after time I intended coming over here and seeing you, but I didn't have the courage for it. Everyone is convinced you are guilty of that—that terrible thing and I must confess that I have entertained my own doubts about you. But last night I sat up and searched my conscience, as I should have done before. I am here now to do what I can to help you."

Other than Jane, Baker was the first person Gary knew well who had come forward with an offer of help. But he was suspicious. He swallowed and cleared his throat with a cough and asked bluntly, "Why? What's in it for you? Does the firm of Baker and Allen need that kind of publicity?"

The old man closed his eyes for a moment with pain, then looked steadily into Gary's hot eyes. "Perhaps I deserve that," he said. "I should have stood with you when this thing first started. I know your character. I know what a fine person you are. But I'm only human; there was so much against you, you see. I allowed myself to be swayed by all the reports and rumors circulating about. But last night, after reading what various people had to say about you, I sat back and considered their words against what I knew to be true about you. This psychotic drive you are supposed to have is so much pure nonsense. You are simply a very much alive young man with a great deal of energy and a healthy desire to make something of yourself. You were never a great sportsman because you drove yourself to be one; with you it was simply natural ability. Contrary, too, to what Ellen had to say, I know the sort of husband you were and the father you tried to be. All the qualities about you, you see, that people so admired before, have now been twisted into something sinister and evil. I don't believe any of it. I know better." He blinked at Gary and a faint smile etched the corners of his lips as he said, flatly, "I also know that you are not the guilty man."

Gary bit his lip and turned away from him to hide an emotional dam that threatened to burst. "Thanks," he whispered. "But things are—well, they're stacking up—"

"I know. It all looks very black. I understand, though, that you have constantly refused to seek legal advice and representation."

"Yes."

"Don't you think that attitude is a bit foolish?"

Gary looked back at him with a stubborn frown. "No, I don't think so. There's nothing I have to hide, and there's actually no one who could help me, aside from the police themselves. What needs to be done is to find the real culprit. Until he is found I am going to look as guilty as hell regardless of who might represent me."

"But you need protection."

"Not yet, Ted. What is there to protect me from? I'm not even charged with anything, and getting a lawyer to get me out of here would be foolish. This is the only safe place I can stay. Maybe I'm stupid, but I've always believed a man should be able to fight his own battles, at least until he's knocked off his feet. That may happen this afternoon or tomorrow."

Baker looked puzzled. "How do you mean?"

"Well, the D.A. is taking everything to the Grand Jury this afternoon. I won't be there, because I am not guilty of anything and I flatly refuse to testify. But all the evidence is going to be presented and the D.A. is asking for an indictment. I'm waiting to see if he gets it. If I'm indicted, okay; then I'll be on my back and I'll need an attorney to fight for me, but not until then."

Baker's light smile deepened, but this time with admiration. He got to his feet. "Very well. Perhaps you're right in the way you have been handling yourself. But I have an awful feeling you're going to need that attorney."

"I know. God, I even feel it in my bones."

"A very close friend of mine, Richard Leland—"

"I've met him."

"Of course. I talked with him before coming over here. He's an excellent man, Gary, easily one of the finest trial attorneys in the business and a man of absolute integrity. He's willing to talk to you. If he believes in your innocence—but not otherwise—he'll take your case. And you don't have to worry about his fee. I'll take care of that myself. After all, Gary, I have been considering you as a sort of junior partner for some time now. I want you back in the office."

Gary could not look at him. He turned away from the hands on his shoulders and walked to the window to stare at the glazed glass. "Thanks," he mumbled.

"Take care of yourself, Gary."

"Sure."

"And if you need anything, anything at all—"

"Sure."

Gary stood where he was until he heard the door close, then he turned about and started his endless pacing of the floor. His brain was again back on the merry-go-round of wondering who the real assailant could be. During the weekend Jane had had a long interview with Luke and had spent some time questioning the grocer boy and the plumber. All the results had been negative. The plumber was positive he had seen the disturbed earth in the Malone basement on election morning. The grocer boy stuck by his story that he had been ill on the fateful Friday and had taken a ride down the coast that afternoon. The high-school records disclosed the fact that he and his friend had indeed been absent that afternoon. His friend, however, had an additional absence the day before and was still not sure whether he had been with the boy on Thursday or Friday. Luke Summer was also not able to substantiate his own whereabouts on the tragic Friday, but, on the other hand, Jane had been able to find no one who had seen him away from his home that afternoon.

She had also interviewed a number of the neighbors living in Gary's immediate neighborhood, only to learn that the Bayside police had also made a thorough canvass of the section. She learned nothing new. On that particular Monday morning she was out calling on the eight men who had voted in the Malone garage on election day. Gary doubted strongly that she would turn up with anything of interest.

Kraft came into the office with Scott Douglas in tow, and dropped heavily into his swivel chair behind the desk. He clasped his hands behind his head and leaned back to stare intently at Gary. He, too, was wondering. The D.A., though, had no doubts in his mind. He propped his buttocks against the edge of the desk and regarded Gary with great satisfaction. The D.A. was a happy man. It would have been better if he had an actual confession and it would also be a great help if there was some physical way to link Gary with the girl; but even so, he was positive that he had enough evidence to present to the Grand Jury to secure an indictment. The whole affair would then be firmly in his hands. It was easy to visualize the national publicity he would get out of the trial. And after that would quickly come into being The Hon. Scott Douglas. "And how are you today, Your Honor?" He stared at Gary and grinned broadly.

Gary had come to know the D.A. rather well and had a hunch what was on his mind. He gave him a disgusted look and turned his attention to the chief. "Have you seen Luke again?"

Kraft pursed his lips and nodded. "I talked with him an hour or so last night. Nada."

"What's that?"

"Nada. Russian, I guess, for Nothing. Strictly negative. Matter of fact, when he realized I was questioning him as a suspect he blew his top and ordered me out of the house."

The D.A. got red in the face and exploded, "Well, I shouldn't wonder. You got a hell of a nerve questioning Luke Summer as a suspect. He's one of our most prominent citizens."

"Uh-huh. And he's still a suspect in my book. Everyone is a suspect."

"Honest to God, Bill, sometimes I wonder about you. We got our man right here. I guess you're just the kind of a guy who can't see what's right under his nose."

"I know it's there when it smells."

"Meaning something personal?"

"Aw, hell, take it any way you want."

Douglas glowered at him for a moment, but he was feeling so good that when he turned to look back at Gary he was again smiling. Gary had resumed his pacing, so that when the D.A. spoke to him it was to his face one moment and his back the next. He was irritated, but nothing could smother his good spirits for long.

"Before I take off," he said, "let's go over this thing once more. You know yourself you're going to look awfully ridiculous before a jury."

Gary sighed and said wearily, "I don't have to face the Grand Jury."

"I'm not talking of that. I'll get the indictment, don't worry. I mean the trial jury you'll have to face later. Just a week ago you were all over that Kingsley Ranch, appraising and exploring every foot of it. You admit that."

"I told you before I was appraising it for a sale."

"You also had to list everything, including all the buildings. Right?"

"You know that."

"Yet you try to tell us that you were never near that spring house where the body was found. Do you really expect anyone to believe that?"

"I've told you a dozen times I had no reason to investigate that spring house. I could see from the road it was just an abandoned shack and not even worth listing."

The D.A. clasped his hands about a lifted knee to rock back and forth against the edge of the desk. He was grinning triumphantly as he said, "That's where you made a mistake, by not listing that shack. I've impounded that list of yours, by the way. The fact that that shack is not listed stands out like a sore thumb."

"Only to you, because you're so positive I'm guilty."

"Others, too, will feel the same way, including twelve jurors. There's only one reason you left that shack off your list. You're so damned guilty you can't stand even thinking about that shack, and naturally you couldn't force yourself to list it with the other buildings."

Gary paused for a second to look into his eyes then snorted, "You're so cute."

The D.A. slapped his hands on his thighs and stood up with a shrug. "Okay, so you won't help yourself. Frankly, at this point, I'd rather not have a confession from you. Maybe with a confession and a plea of guilt you might get off with life. I wouldn't like to see that happen. I'm looking forward to putting you in the gas chamber."

Gary shuddered involuntarily.

Douglas looked over his shoulder at the chief and said, "This guy really has a screw loose if he thinks he can get out of this. Just think of the timing alone. He leaves his home around three-thirty and starts out of town. The girl is seen last at four. So the time is right and he has the opportunity. He picks her up somehow and takes her up the valley. Maybe he even takes her up to that cottage on Chinamen's Ridge and keeps her there for the night, or maybe he took her straight to the shack on the Kingsley Ranch. That isn't important. We do know, by his own admission, that he had to pass the Kingsley Ranch on his way to Chinamen's Ridge and we do know he was at the Gold Nugget, where her schoolbook was found. The timing in every instance is perfect. Add all that up with his lying attempt at an alibi and the fact that her clothes were found in his own basement and the additional fact that he could not bring himself to list that shack, and you have a guy in hot water right up to his chin." He swiveled his head about to regard Gary and said, "You got guts, though. I have to admit that. You sure don't mind flirting with those gas pellets."

Gary felt suddenly sick and dropped down to the couch with his head in his hands. Kraft squinted at him narrowly, then cocked an eyebrow at the D.A. and said, "You're not getting anything out of him, Scotty. Let's let it go for now."

"May as well. I have to get over to the courthouse, anyway. You'll be there at eleven?"

"I'll be there."

"Be sure Welte is with you and Miss—ah—Benson."

"Bestor. Jane Bestor. I'll have them with me. You've taken care of all the others?"

"Of course." Douglas started to the door, but paused with his hand on the knob and looked back at Gary. "Say, Malone. One thing more. We've found every single item belonging to the girl except her brassiere. Did you leave it on the body, or take it off and hide it somewhere, or what?"

Gary lifted his head slowly and said bitterly, "Ask my wife. She'll probably tell you she's wearing it herself. Get out of here, for God's sake. Go get your indictment."

"You know I'll get it, don't you?"

"I don't know anything any more, but it wouldn't surprise me. Give me another few days and I might even confess. Meanwhile, get the hell out of here before I throw up."

The D.A.'s face got red and he screamed at Kraft, "He couldn't talk to me this way if you'd only arrest the bastard."

The chief hid his mouth behind his hand and said patiently, "Run along, Scotty. I'll see you at eleven."

Douglas glowered at Gary, but when he walked out of the office he was smiling. The door was left open, so that Gary glanced out into the reception hallway and saw the few reporters hanging around. All the others had gone over to the courthouse in Grand Point. They were not allowed in the chambers of the Grand Jury, but they would be on hand to question everyone coming out into the corridors and also to learn the verdict, if there would be one that day. The few men remaining at the Bayside police station were there simply to cover Gary's reaction to whatever happened.

Gary sat back and thought of the change that had taken place with the members of the press during the last few days. Initial excitement had worn off and had been replaced with the normal, daily, workmanlike grind. Local reporters, as well as representatives of the big wire services, were no longer as personally interested or emotionally involved in the case as they had been. To all of them it had now become merely a job. Gary had long since ceased to be a human being in most of their minds. He had been reduced to one simple word—copy. They no longer paid any attention to his presence even when he was the object of discussion.

Gary had at first been enraged by their change of attitude, then he had accepted it as at least being more peaceful for himself; but on that Monday morning, as he again considered the change, it served to deepen the chill of fear that was taking possession of him. If reporters regarded him in that fashion then so would any twelve members of a future jury. He could scream his innocence to the skies and his cries would fall on deaf ears.

His shoulders quivered with the chill that was now constantly with him and he looked across at Kraft. The chief was tilted back in his chair with his heels cocked on the desk and his eyes fixed on the ceiling. He was gently tapping a pencil against his teeth, lost in thought. Gary had a sudden ambivalent feeling of hatred and also affection for the big man. He hated him for representing what had become a grotesquerie of Law and Order, but he also knew that the chief would give his right arm to prove Gary Malone an innocent man, if it could be done. Gary thought, my nemesis and my salvation—and he is just as helpless as I.

Kraft slanted a glance at him from the corners of his eyes, then sighed and dropped his feet to the floor and stood up. "Guess I'll be shoving off."

"You have lots of time."

"I have other things to do before eleven. You've become the number-one priority over everything else, but other people still break laws and I still have a police department to run. I'll pick up Hank, but you might tell Jane to meet me at the courthouse at eleven sharp."

"Sure. She said she'd come by and see me before she went over." Gary looked embarrassed as he mumbled, "Incidentally, thanks for not booking me. I know the pressure you've been under. But it's been a help to me, at least so far, not to be actually charged with murder."

Kraft shrugged his massive shoulders and started for the door, but turned to say, "I've been acting strictly as a policeman. We have a body, but I still have no more to book you on now than I had before. As far as I'm concerned—as a policeman, mind you—all charges against you are based mostly on suspicion, conjecture and speculation. Scotty knows that, too, but with the help of a little oratory and a slight twist in the presentation he's going to make, he figures he can get an indictment."

"What do you think?"

Kraft asked coldly, "You want the truth?"

"Sure."

"You won't find an unprejudiced person in this county, where you're concerned, including the members of the Grand Jury. Scotty will get his indictment."

"But, my God, the law!"

"Laws are made, interpreted and executed by man. Look, Malone; with what has been learned so far, you are ninety-nine and nine-tenths guilty in practically anyone's mind, including legal ones. Scotty will get his indictment, you'll be charged with murder, or at the least suspicion of murder and kidnaping, and you'll be brought to trial. I can't see anything else. I wish to God this had never happened and that I could have more time for police work, but this is the way it is. One consolation for you, though—an indictment certainly doesn't mean conviction."

"I know. I know that. I also know that the evidence being presented to the Grand Jury will be the same evidence presented to a trial jury. So if the one sees fit to indict me I have a horrible feeling that the other will see fit to convict me."

Kraft had the same feeling, but there was nothing more he could say. He shook his head and went out the door.

Jane found him in the locker room when she entered the station at ten-thirty. Her hands were full of notes she had taken that morning and she, too, looked tired. She stood quietly facing Gary and read the question in his eyes and shook her head. She dropped to a bench with a little sigh and looked up at him standing before her.

"Well," she said, "I saw them all."

"The eight voters?"

"Yes. I questioned them all as to their whereabouts at four in the afternoon on Friday thirteenth. Five had been at work that day, one had been out of town, in Stockton, I think, another had been visiting a sick son in the hospital at that time and the other, an old retired gentleman, wasn't quite sure but thinks he was working in his garden that afternoon. He's out, anyway, because he doesn't drive a car and doesn't even own one. That girl, after all, was taken up the valley in a car." She looked helplessly into Gary's eyes and said, "I have a hunch all of their stories will stand up. I'll turn over my notes to Mr. Kraft, but I don't expect anything of them."

"Yeah."

She looked at one of the scraps of paper and smiled and said, "The retired gentleman is a Mr. Lew Holbein, a really sweet old man. He is very much upset over an incident that happened at your house that election day."

"Oh?"

"Yes. He doesn't have very good eyesight, you see, so when he went to your house to vote, around noontime, he thought the polling place was inside the house rather than the garage. So he just walked on in and fumbled about trying to find someone. Unfortunately, he surprised your wife in the midst of taking a shower. Very embarrassing for the two of them."

Gary chuckled and said, "I'll bet. I can just picture Ellen in a situation like that. She must have really told the old boy what for."

"I guess she did. Even months later he is still upset about it. He asked me to explain and apologize to her if I should happen to run into her."

"Forget it."

"I intend doing that. I don't think she would be interested in anyone's apology." Jane got to her feet and looked irresolutely about the room. "Well—"

"Yeah. I guess you have to get over to the courthouse."

"Mmmmm. I'd better be on my way. I hate to leave—"

"Thanks. I'll be all right. I—well, I'll be all right."

"Don't think about it too much. I know that sounds ridiculous, but do try to think of something else."

"Sure. Jane—"

"Yes?"

"Do you mind—I mean—a sort of good luck kiss—"

She blinked back sudden mist in her eyes and stepped to him to put her hands gently on his shoulders. Her lips met his softly and then she stepped back and smiled into his eyes for a moment and turned and walked away. Gary ran his hands over his face and dropped down to the bench, a shudder running through him.

Sam Carson came in shortly after two o'clock. Gary was standing at a window looking out at a damp, heavy fog sweeping in. He turned and looked at the editor and the question in his eyes was bigger than ever. Sam lit a cigarette and leaned back against the wall at Gary's side.

"Not good," he said.

"You've been to the courthouse?"

"I just left there. My men can cover that end for the rest of the day. I thought I'd come over here and see how you're getting along. You look pretty beat. Why the devil don't you shave?"

"I tried, but I can't."

"Want me to send a barber around?"

"Maybe. I don't know. How I look isn't so important any more. But how is it going with the Grand Jury?"

Carson blew out a big puff of smoke with a heavy sigh. "As I say, not good. With the exception of the chief, every witness who has testified is an adverse witness. We don't actually know what's going on inside, but the witnesses tell us as they come out, so you get a pretty good idea. The testimony of that Luke and Betty Summer is downright damaging."

"Luke, too?"

"Oh, sure. Now he goes along with his wife a hundred per cent. According to them, your actions on the night the gym shoes were found were strictly those of an angry and guilty man who wanted to cover up and get rid of the shoes in a hurry. Herb Short, too, the guy at the Gold Nugget bar, is now convinced you were deliberately trying to rig an alibi with him. And the way he explains it now it sounds exactly that way."

"Good Lord!"

"And the foreman out at Kingsley Ranch has testified that when you were appraising the ranch last week—"

"My God, was it only last week?"

"Anyway, he says he is quite sure you did leave the road one day and cross the meadow to appraise that spring house."

Gary stared open-mouthed at the editor, then shouted, "He's lying. Believe me, Mr. Carson, I never went anywhere near that damned spring house. Why in the name of common sense would a man go to all that trouble to look at something you could see from the road is just a worthless shack?"

"Don't ask me questions. I'm just telling you the testimony that's being given. Maybe the old boy thinks he's telling the truth, or maybe it's a sort of subconscious wish. But that's what he says. You can understand how that's going to look. If you had gone to that shack you could not help but know that a body of some sort was inside. The inference, of course, is that you knew it all along, so you would say nothing."

Gary shook his head and walked away to pace the floor. After a few minutes he stopped before the editor and asked, "What else? Or can it get any worse?"

"I left right after the plumber got through. What's his name? Oh, yes. Bert Franklin. He had to hurry back to a job he's doing on a new building at Third and Cypress. He was complaining bitterly about losing an hour of work while he testified, but I think he enjoyed every moment of being in the spotlight. You get lots of that type."

"Anything new with him?"

"Nope. He doesn't go in for embellishments. He was in your basement at eight-thirty election morning and again at five, when he turned the water back on. He noticed the disturbed earth in the morning and when he returned saw that it had been smoothed over. That's all. It's important testimony, though. It rules out the possibility of anyone's burying the girl's belongings down there after eight-thirty that morning."

Gary frowned and turned his glance away from the editor to stare out the window at the fog. Something had clicked in his mind, the fragment of an idea. What had been said that had brought to life a dim light of some sort? He could not think of what it might be and resumed pacing the floor.

Carson watched him closely and shrewdly, the big question still burning in his mind. There was so much against him, everything was stacking up against him, yet the editor did not believe in his heart that he was a guilty man.

He said quietly, "All is not lost, Malone. I think Scotty will get his indictment, all right, but it won't be so easy from there on when you face a trial jury with a good attorney at your elbow. There is a hell of a lot of conjecture in the testimony against you. There is also too damned much guesswork to please any judge. A lot of the stuff piling up on your shoulders will get thrown out."

Gary snorted, "Aw, hell, that doesn't mean anything. You know as well as I that you can't get an unprejudiced jury in this county. I'm convicted before I start. Tell me honestly: Do you think I have a chance before any jury in Morales County?"

Carson lowered his eyes and refused to answer. Gary smiled bitterly and continued his pacing. But something was bothering him. Something new. That dim light that had been turned on had not gone out. What had been said to cause it?

Carson left, but Gary was still in the locker room when Kraft returned to the station just before four o'clock. He looked in from the hallway and beckoned to Gary, who hurried toward him. The two stepped into the office, where Welte was standing by the window and Jane was sitting back wearily in the couch. She looked up at Gary and smiled and said, "Not yet," then turned her attention back to some notes she was studying. Gary sank to the leather couch at her side and watched Kraft take his usual place in the swivel chair. The chief looked out the upper part of the window and growled, "This damned fog is here to stay. It sure gets thick this time of year." He looked across at Gary and shrugged and teetered back in the chair. Gary waited patiently.

After a long while, the chief leaned forward and propped his elbows on the desk. "Well," he said, "the jury didn't get through all the testimony today, so they'll be convening again tomorrow. Not much left, though. They should wind it up in the morning and come through with an opinion some time tomorrow afternoon."

Jane looked around at Gary to say, "Don't get your hopes up, though. The atmosphere was strictly unfriendly."

Kraft nodded in agreement. "You could almost feel how they were thinking. And the way they asked questions, especially the foreman—well, you're a guilty character in their minds. They're not dopes, mind you. They're pretty intelligent people. Some of them jumped all over the guesswork being done and a few of them gave Scotty a bad time for trying to introduce suspicions as facts; but all in all, they really have no doubts that you are the killer. One of them expressed it very well by bringing up moral certainty. That's the key to the whole thing, actually. Quite aside from the fact that no one has yet been able to connect you physically with the girl, there is a moral certainty that you did it."

Kraft paused and looked curiously at Gary, who did not seem to be paying too much attention. In fact, Gary had leaned back in the couch and was frowning up at the ceiling.

The chief asked him, "What the hell's on your mind!"

Gary's eyes came down and he looked at Kraft with a faintly apologetic smile. "I wish I knew," he said.

"What sort of an answer is that?"

"Not much, I guess. It's just that something has been bothering me lately. Mr. Carson was here a few hours ago and told me how some of the testimony was going."

"So?"

"Well, when he told me about the testimony of the plumber, that Bert Franklin, something seemed to click in my mind. You know how I mean? Like you're looking at a picture that's been clear all along and suddenly the whole thing's out of focus."

"I don't follow you."

"I don't follow it myself. It's just that I have a queer feeling something isn't right."

"About the plumber?"

Gary thought a moment, then frowned and nodded and said, "I guess that's what started it. You were there. Did your hear him give his testimony?"

"Uh-huh. He went through again where he had been on Friday the thirteenth—"

"Wasn't he installing a hot-water heater somewhere?"

"That's right. For John Bergstrom, the contractor. Then on election day, the following Tuesday, he had this job for you. He was in your basement at eight-thirty that morning and again somewhere around five that afternoon."

"And he saw this disturbed earth when he was there the first time, but it had been smoothed over by the time he got back."

"Correct. That's about all he had to say. Anything wrong with that?"

"No, I don't think so. That seems to be all right. Funny, though, when Mr. Carson told it to me I had a very real impression that something was all haywire."

Jane was also frowning and leaned forward to say, "That's very odd. I had to be present when most of the testimony was given, you know, because I took down most of the statements." She blinked at Gary and said, "I experienced that same feeling you had when he was there on the stand. I felt, too, that something was wrong."

Gary asked the chief, "How about you?"

Kraft shook his head. "He made a straightforward statement as far as I was concerned, and he didn't deviate from his previous statements, like a lot of them did."

Welte chuckled dryly and snorted, "Maybe it's just something Malone and Miss Bestor know about. Maybe they're psychic."

Jane glared at Welte and said heatedly, "You could be right. It could be something that only we two know about."

"Then you tell us."

"I—well—" She shook her head and again leaned back in the couch, but now lost in deep thought. Welte laughed and lifted his eyebrows to the chief.

Kraft said, "Your boss, Mr. Baker, was there, too. I was talking to him later. He says he has an attorney ready to talk things over with you. Now, you listen to me, Malone. The chips are down. You call that attorney and get him over here now, or some time this evening; maybe there's something he could do before tomorrow's session. It would be a favor to me, too, you know. I'd like to stall off that Grand Jury as long as possible and get back to my spade work. Damn it all, can't you put your finger on this thing that's been bothering you?"

Gary lit a cigarette and puffed at it nervously for a while, and then said, "No, I can't."

"It started when Sam was telling you about the plumber?"

"Yes."

Welte said, "Maybe he thinks the plumber did it."

Kraft snorted, "Aw, shut up," then said to Gary, "Maybe it's important. I've had things like that happen to me before in police work. You get a hunch about something and you don't know where it came from or what it's all about and then all of a sudden you got the answer. Sometimes it's important and sometimes it means nothing. God only knows, though, you've certainly had a long time to think about every angle in this case."

Jane said, "I told him once before that the solution to the whole thing could even be in his own mind."

Kraft nodded. "If he knows anything about it, yes." He fell silent for a moment, regarding Gary through narrowed lids, then said, "It definitely started with what Sam was telling you about the plumber?"

"Yes. He was telling me about the plumber's statement of being in my basement at eight-thirty in the morning and then coming back around five when he turned on—" Gary's spine stiffened and his eyes opened wide. He sucked in a huge breath of air, let it out slowly, then said excitedly, "That's it. By God, that's it. Now I remember the whole thing." He jumped to his feet and cried, "Bill, do you have that plumber's statement here?"

"Well, I got a copy—"

"Then get it out. For God's sake, get it out."

The three of them stared at him as if he had suddenly become demented, then Kraft got to his feet and went to the files. He brought out the thick mass of papers on the case, placed them on the desk and rifled through them until he came to the plumber's statement. Gary leaned over his shoulder to study it as Welte and Jane also crowded against the desk.

Gary read quickly through the few, brief sentences, slapped his hand down on the papers and stared at the chief. "That's it," he cried. "You see where he says he didn't have the right equipment when he was in my basement that morning. He had to leave to get it. But he says he turned off the main water valve before he left."

Kraft shrugged and said, "So what?"

"So lots of things. You notice he also says he turned the water on again when he returned at five that afternoon. According to him, that house of ours had no water from eight-thirty that morning until five that afternoon."

"Don't belabor the point. I can see that."

"Sure, you can. But that's the whole thing. That's it."

Jane cried, "Oh, yes. Now I know. Now I know, too. That old man, Gary. The one I was telling you about this morning—"

"Yes, of course. If it wasn't for that we'd never know."

Kraft roared impatiently, "If you two will just shut up for a minute. What about an old man? What's this all about?"

Jane said, "Let me tell him. Please." Gary nodded, so she explained, "This morning I called on the eight men who had voted at that garage election day. One was an elderly gentleman a—a Mr. Lew Holbein. Sort of nearsighted. He doesn't see very well. Anyway, when he went to the Malone house around noontime that Tuesday he made a mistake and went into the house instead of the garage. He surprised Mrs. Malone taking a shower."

Kraft blinked at her. "Well?"

"But don't you see? That was it noontime. How could Mrs. Malone have been taking a shower if the water had been turned off earlier that morning? You see?"

Kraft nodded at them and slowly sat down in his chair. They stood there staring down at him as he drummed his fingertips on the desk and sucked his lower lip in and out. "Hmmmmm," he said. He looked up at them and repeated, "Hmmmmm. So."

Welte asked, "What does it mean?"

Kraft scratched the back of his head and replied, "I don't know, Hank. Maybe it means a lot and maybe it means nothing. Maybe Franklin was lying about what he was doing in the basement that morning, or maybe he just doesn't remember too well, like Malone with his alibi, and maybe he's simply confused about when he turned the water off and on again."

"I'd say he's just confused. Why should he lie about anything with that iron-clad alibi of his?"

"I don't know, but it's worth asking a few questions."

Chapter Eight

Gary felt like a dog that had been shoved out in the rain for piddling on the floor, but might be allowed back in the house if he behaved himself. If he had a tail he would have wagged it and his ears would have been standing expectantly high. He looked at the chief and Jane and Welte almost as if he expected one of them to pet him. He was so beaten and debased that even standing there he felt as if he were actually crawling on his belly. He straightened himself to inject some manhood into his spine, but his fate was so hopelessly in the hands

of others that his attempt to recapture some pride fell short and was rather pitiful. Jane was watching him, but bit her lip and looked away.

Kraft sat behind the desk staring off into space for a long while, but suddenly
he reached for the telephone and called the Redwood Inn, where he asked to be
connected with Mrs. Malone. She was not in her room, but she was paged and
located in the hotel's cocktail room after a few minutes.

When she answered the telephone she purred, "This is Miss Springfield
speaking. Yes?"

Kraft frowned and said, "Oh, I'm sorry. I asked to be connected to Mrs. Gary
Malone."

There was a slight pause and then her voice cooled as she said, "This is she."

"But you just said—"

"Springfield is my maiden name. To whom do I—"

But Kraft burst out laughing and it was a moment before he had himself under control and could speak again. "I'll be damned," he said. "So soon. I'll bet
you're having a ball for yourself in that cocktail lounge. Has the hotel rigged a
special spotlight for you? I'm sure one of the press services would gladly pay for
it."

Ellen snapped icily, "Now, you just look here, you—you—"

"This is Kraft, chief of police."

"Oh."

"Yeah. I have something to ask you. Do you remember the events of election
day very well? That was on May seventeenth. Your garage was used as a polling
place. It's important that you remember something that took place that day."

She was decidedly frigid as she replied, "If you will kindly give me some
idea—I remember the day well. I had been to San Francisco for the weekend.
I returned that Tuesday morning, just before noon. Maybe," she purred again,
"if you read the papers now and then you would know that."

"Uh-huh. Well, this is something that happened around noontime. There is
a certain—ah—" He glanced at Jane and she mouthed the name, so he said, "A
Mr. Lew Holbein. Mean anything to you?"

"Nothing whatever."

"He was to vote in your garage that day. He got there around noontime, but
says he made a mistake and went into the house instead of the garage, and—"

"Oh," she cried, "that horrible old man. I should say I do remember him. You
know very well that a polling place always has the flag out front and it was right
in front of the garage, so there was no earthly reason whatever for him to go in
the house, the old snooper. I should have called the police. That's what I should
have done. The lecherous old fool. Do you know what he did? He had the gall
to walk clear back into our bedroom right while I was taking a shower—"

Kraft interrupted by asking, "You are positive you were taking a shower? I
mean, you really had the water on?"

"Well, my God," she laughed, "I've never heard of anyone taking a shower without having the water on. Are you drunk, or something? Anyway, there I was in the shower and this drooling old idiot—"

Kraft cut her off by replacing the phone in its cradle. His eyebrows lifted as he looked at Gary and said, "Well, she substantiates the story. The water was definitely on at noontime. That rather clouds Franklin's testimony, doesn't it?"

"It sure does. Maybe it means something."

"And maybe it doesn't, too. That was quite a while ago. Maybe he just doesn't remember accurately when he turned the water off and on again."

Gary raised his eyes appealingly to the ceiling. "Oh, brother. Anyone else makes a statement that turns out to be false and it just becomes a mistake, but when I make a mistake it becomes a big, fat lie."

"That's because you're on the hot spot. Don't put too much stock in this, Malone."

"But it's the first damned thing that's happened—"

"I know. I know. I intend investigating it all the way. Don't worry about that. I'm just telling you not to get too excited over it. After all, there's the plumber's alibi to consider. That has been substantiated by Bergstrom, you know."

"Maybe we can look into that angle again."

"That is exactly what I intend doing. I'll get hold of him—" A knock sounded at the door and he called, "Come in."

The police clerk opened the door, stuck his head in and said, "Mr. Douglas called while you were on the phone."

"So?"

The clerk looked undecidedly at Gary, then shrugged and said, "He wants you to come over to his office in Grand Point *muy pronto*. He wants Malone here charged with suspicion of murder before the Grand Jury sits again tomorrow. That's all, Chief." He looked at Kraft's darkening scowl and was happy to back out and close the door.

Kraft got to his feet shaking his head with disgust. "What a publicity hound. He can't wait until tomorrow. He wants his name in the paper tonight. I'll have to try and talk him out of it some way."

Gary cried, "But you can't leave here now. How about talking with the contractor? How about—"

The chief shook his head. "That can wait. It's more important that I talk to Scotty before he takes action himself. He can do it, you know, even without me. But I won't be gone more than about an hour."

Gary pleaded with him to stay, but Kraft was adamant. He knew why the D.A. wanted the charge made official that day: it was something tangible to present to the Grand Jury at the next session. It meant that the police and prosecuting authorities were convinced of Gary's guilt and willing to take action on their own initiative. It was one more matter that could help to influence the decision of the jurors.

Kraft left Welte in charge of the station and hurried away, swearing bitterly under his breath. Gary got to his feet, walked around the desk and dropped into the swivel chair. Welte watched him curiously as he thumbed through the telephone book looking for the name of John Bergstrom, and moved closer to follow Gary's finger down the page. Gary found Bergstrom's office number. A secretary answered and informed him that Mr. Bergstrom was not there at that moment, but if it was urgent, he could undoubtedly be found at a new home he was building on Ninth Street between Scenic and Garcia Way.

Gary sat back to look at Jane and said, "He can't be reached by telephone. He's out on a construction job on Ninth. Do you have your car here?"

"Why, yes. It's out front."

"Good. How about driving me over to Ninth, where we can have a talk with Bergstrom and find out just how tight that plumber's alibi really is?"

She smiled and got to her feet at once. "Of course."

Gary jumped up, lifted his coat from the back of the couch and slid it on. Welte's hand immediately clamped about his arm. "You think you can just walk out of here like that?"

"Certainly. Why not?"

"Look, chum; you're going to stay right here in the office until the chief returns. You ain't going nowhere. Understand?"

Gary jerked his arm loose of Welte's grip, but the sergeant spun about and got between him and the door. Gary said softly, but dangerously, "Get out of my way, Hank. I'm telling you. Get away."

"Uh-uh. You ain't going nowhere."

Gary took a step toward him, his hands clenched into fists. "I'm telling you, Hank. You have no right to hold me here or to stop me from going out that door. Just try it and you and I are going to tangle."

Welte's hand dropped to the holster at his hip and came up with the barrel of a .38 pointed at Gary's stomach. His lips thinned to a hard line as he barked, "I say you're staying here. I'll arrest you myself," he shouted. "I don't need the chief. I'm a cop, too, you know."

Jane looked frightened and whispered, "He can do it, Gary. Please. Wait for the chief to return."

Gary shook his head, his eyes fixed unwaveringly on Welte's. "I'm going out to talk to Bergstrom right now. And I'll tell you something about that gun in your hand, Hank. You may get off the first shot, but you'll never get off a second. And, so help me, I'll take that gun and beat your brains out with it. Now, are you getting out of my way, or do I come after you?"

Tiny beads of perspiration broke out on Welte's forehead and upper lip. He was not personally afraid of Gary's threat, though he knew that the younger man was the more powerful of the two. But he saw the wild panic in Gary's eyes and knew that he was on the breaking point. No gun was going to stop him. He knew what would happen if he was forced to shoot Gary, the county's prize catch of the century. He might as well hang up his badge then and there. Kraft, he knew, would personally boot him off the force and do everything in his power to boot him out of the county, too.

He wet his dry lips with the tip of his tongue and lowered the gun barrel an inch. "Don't try nothing, Malone. Don't make a wrong move." Gary stepped toward him and he said quickly, "Okay, damn it. I'd love to put a slug in you, but you know I can't. All right. You talk with Bergstrom. But you go with me in a squad car."

Gary let out his breath and nodded. "I don't care how we go, but let's get moving."

Jane closed her eyes a moment for a silent prayer.

They went out into the damp fog and to the squad car parked at the corner. Welte saw the two of them into the back seat, then returned to the station to tell the clerk where he was going. He was back in a moment and slid behind the wheel. They made a U-turn and went down the street until they reached Ninth, where they turned left. The fog was so thick that Welte had to switch on the headlight dimmers. They crawled along slowly until they passed Garcia Way and saw a house under construction with trucks and workmen's cars parked about.

Gary was out of the car at once. He made his way through the rubble and up to the half-finished house, his glance taking in the various workmen busy about their jobs. He saw one man standing a bit apart looking over some blueprints. He was a slim, elderly man wearing short boots, corduroys and a thick flannel shirt. Gary went directly to him and asked, "Mr. Bergstrom?"

The contractor squinted at him and recognized him from the many pictures that had been in the papers. His eyes and voice were cold as he said, "That's right. Aren't you Gary Malone?"

"Yes, sir."

"I always did say we had a rotten police force in this town. How come they let you out running around?" He looked beyond Gary and saw the uniformed sergeant approaching with Jane and said, "Oh, I see. You're not alone. What the hell are you doing here?"

Gary said quickly, "Look, Mr. Bergstrom; something just came up. It may be important. You know the plumber, Bert Franklin?"

"Sure. Good man." He folded the blueprints into a roll and tucked them under his arm. He nodded at Welte as he and Jane stopped, then asked, "What about him?"

"Well, sir, I guess you know his testimony regarding his own actions on May thirteenth."

Bergstrom nodded. "Yes, I do. He put in a hot-water heater for me at the Lilly house over in the dunes. What about it?"

"Putting in that water heater is his alibi for the day. He claims he was busy on that job from about three o'clock in the afternoon until about five-thirty, when he went home for dinner."

"Let me see, now. I'm not too sure of the time he said—"

"I just looked up his statement again a few minutes ago."

"Oh. I remember now."

"Now, did you or anyone else see him install that heater at that time?"

Bergstrom scratched his head and thought a moment, then said, "If I remember correctly, I gave a statement to the police to the effect that the heater was installed at that time."

"I know. I know. I remember that, too. But I don't think you actually saw it installed."

"No, I didn't. I wasn't by the Lilly job that day, but I was by there the following Saturday. The heater was completely installed, so, naturally, I assumed that the job had been done the day before, obviously during the hours Franklin said. It takes about two and a half hours to install one. Why? What's this all about?"

Welte snorted, "He's got a bee in his bonnet about this plumber. The guy made a mistake about when he turned the water off and on at Malone's home, so now he thinks maybe he's lying about the whole business."

Bergstrom smiled lightly. "I see. Grasping at straws, eh?"

Gary persisted, "Nevertheless, you did not personally see the heater installed that Friday afternoon."

"Well, no, I didn't."

"How about some of the men working for you? They would certainly know whether or not Franklin had been there at the time he says."

Bergstrom leaned back against a workbench to light a cigarette and think things over, then said, "That's just it. None of my men were on the Lilly job that day. Except for some interior painting and the heater and a few other minor things, the job was finished."

Welte asked suspiciously, "How do you remember so well? That was over three months ago."

"It was brought back to my mind when I had to look up the records to verify Franklin's statement. I know for a fact that none of my men were there."

Jane had been following the conversation closely, so she said, "You mentioned something about some interior painting. Did you have some painters on the job?"

He smiled at her and explained, "I always let out the painting to a subcontractor, miss. I wouldn't know who was there. The painting contractor, though, was Ivan Stoddard. He would probably know if any of his men had been on the Lilly job that day. All he has to do is look up his pay slips."

"Where would we find him?"

"It happens that I know exactly where he is. Go down to the corner and turn left and you'll see a new home being painted. It's a job I just finished. Ivan is doing the painting on it. In fact, I saw him there a little while ago. He'll still be around."

Gary thanked him, but when he automatically reached out to shake hands the contractor mumbled something under his breath and turned away.

The three returned to the squad car and drove around the corner. Welte spotted the new house and pulled in alongside the paint truck. He and Jane followed closely at Gary's heels as Gary took the steps three at a time to a front porch littered with barrels and buckets and ladders. A tall, cadaverous individual in white overalls yelled at them, "Watch your step there, folks. Watch that paint." Gary saw him standing at the end of the porch swinging a paint brush up and down some vertical siding. He made his way cautiously around the barrels and asked the painter if he was Ivan Stoddard.

Stoddard recognized Gary instantly and a hint of fear crept into his eyes, until he saw Welte coming toward him with Jane. He lowered the brush and nodded and said, "That's me. Why?"

"You know who I am."

"Yeah. I thought you was locked up in the clink. What are you doing—"

"Look, Stoddard; we've just been talking with Mr. Bergstrom. He tells me you were the painting contractor on that Lilly job in the dunes back in May."

Stoddard sniffed and said, "I know when it was. Gripes, that's all you read about in the papers lately, what happened in May."

"You don't have to tell me. But I'm looking for information you may be able to supply."

"Make it fast," he growled. "I can't stand here yapping with a job on my hands."

"Okay. I notice you do some of your own painting."

Stoddard said, "I got two other men working inside. Sometimes I pitch in and help out, though."

"Sure. How about the Lilly job? Were you painting there on Friday, May thirteenth? I mean, were you there personally?"

"Well, I was by there in the morning, but not after. I had three other jobs going the same time."

"Are you positive about that?"

"Uh-huh. Like I say, that's all you read about in the papers now, that date. I got wondering once if I could figure out exactly where I was and what I was doing that day. Just for the hell of it—excuse me, miss—I looked up my records and it all come back to me. I was by the job that Friday morning, but not after."

Jane said, "However, you must have had some men working there."

"Just one, miss, on some touch-up work. Didn't need more than one man. Max Lastfogel is the man. Mighty fine painter, too." He sighed and said, "I could sure use him on this job, but he's at home with a broken leg."

Gary asked, "Was he there that afternoon?"

"Well, if he wasn't I was paying him for nothing. Sure, he was there, all day long.''

Gary turned to Jane and said, ''Then that's our man. He would know definitely if Franklin installed the heater that afternoon.''

Welte looked pained. ''You're barking up a wrong tree. Why shouldn't he of installed the heater when he said he did?''

Gary paid no attention to him. He got Lastfogel's address from Stoddard, thanked the painter and rushed Jane and Welte back to the squad car. Minutes later they were parked in front of Lastfogel's modest cottage on one of the back streets of Bayside. Welte glanced at the house and muttered dryly, ''You'd sure know a painter lived here, all right. It ain't been painted in five years.''

He got out of the car reluctantly and followed Jane and Gary up to the small porch. When Gary rang the bell a man called gruffly, ''Just a minute, for God's sake. Hold your horses.'' A moment later he was standing at the open door, leaning on a crutch, his right leg in a cast. He was a dark, powerful-looking man of middle age who was obviously vastly irritated by being incapacitated.

He looked at the three on his porch and then back at Gary, who was standing closer. His eyes opened wide and blinked rapidly. ''What the hell.''

Gary said, ''Yeah, I know. But you're safe. There's a cop with me.''

Lastfogel sneered, ''I don't need no cop around for the likes of you. Get the hell off my porch.''

Gary stuck his foot into the door before it could be closed and shoved it open. He grabbed the painter by the arm.

''I won't be here long,'' he said. ''You can sweep off the porch when I leave. All I want is some information from you.''

Welte noticed the pain in the painter's eyes and barked, ''Let go of his arm.''

''He's going to do some talking.'' He said to the painter, ''Stoddard just told us that you were painting on the Lilly job last May thirteenth. That was a Friday.''

''Hell, who doesn't know what day that was? Sure, I was there. Look, let go my arm. What are you trying to prove, anyway, that you can handle a guy with a broken leg like you handle young girls?''

Gary closed his eyes until he was sure that he had himself under control. He said slowly, ''Don't say anything like that again, mister. I haven't done any killing yet, but I'm getting closer to it every minute. Do you understand?''

Lastfogel saw Welte's hand drop back to the butt of his gun, but he was suddenly dubious of police protection. The man standing before him was out of his mind. You could see it in his eyes, the crazy lights and the wildness and in the grating tone of his voice. Maybe it would be better to string along with him.

He nodded and cleared his throat to say hoarsely, ''Sure, sure. What's on your mind?''

Gary's hold on his arm relaxed a bit. ''That's better. So you were on the job that day. All day?''

''Yeah.''

"Were you there from three in the afternoon until five-thirty?"

"Not that late. I was working overtime, but I quit at five."

"So you were there from three to five." Gary paused a minute before asking the next question. So much depended on the answer. He took a deep breath, then said, "Apparently you remember the day pretty well."

"I'll say I do. Maybe I'm not superstitious, like a lot of people, but that Friday the thirteenth always kind of gets me. Besides, that's all you read in the papers any more, what happened that day. I remember it like it was yesterday."

"Good." Gary paused again, still reluctant to ask the question, but then he blurted it out, "Were you alone all afternoon that day, or was someone else working on the same job?"

Lastfogel frowned and looked puzzled. "Someone else? Nope. I was the only painter. It was just a little finishing work—"

"I know about that. What I mean, was anyone doing any other work there?"

The painter shook his head. "Nope. Everything else was all finished. Ivan came by that morning, but he was the only one I saw all day. Why?"

Gary turned his head slowly and looked into Jane's eyes. Wild hope was gleaming in their depths as she returned his gaze. She was so nervous, however, that she was biting fiercely at her lower lip. Welte was simply looking puzzled and scratching his head.

Gary looked back at the painter and had a hard time controlling his voice as he said, "You're positive about that."

"Sure. What's this all about, anyway?"

"Look, mister; a hot-water heater was supposed to be installed that afternoon between the hours of three and five-thirty. Bert Franklin was the plumber."

"I know Bert. Funny sort of a guy."

"He says that on Friday, May thirteenth, he installed a water heater in the Lilly house between the hours of three and five-thirty. That's the same job you were on. Did you see Franklin there at that time?"

Lastfogel forgot about the pain in his arm and who was standing on his front porch. It was obvious that Malone's intensity was based on something tremendously important to him. The painter was suddenly interested and curious.

He looked away for a long while to again turn the day over in his mind, then shook his head. "Bert wasn't there that afternoon, or any time that day while I was there. The only one I saw all day was Ivan and he was by in the morning."

"Would it be possible for Franklin to be there without your knowing it?"

Lastfogel snorted brief laughter. "Hell, no. The Lilly place is just a three-bedroom house. No one could go in or out there without me knowing it. Impossible. Why? Did Bert say he was there?"

Jane pounded her fists on Gary's shoulder and cried excitedly, "He was lying, Gary. He was lying. He was lying about everything. Oh, Gary, now you have a lead on who it might be."

Gary pushed her away and dropped his hand from the painter's arm. "In other words," he said, "that hot-water heater was not installed that afternoon."

"Nope. Not while I was there. Maybe he put it in later, but not before five o'-clock." He thought of something and smiled and said, "And he wouldn't have put it in later, either. Bert never works overtime."

"Could it have been installed that evening, or that night?"

Lastfogel rubbed his arm where Gary's fingers had been biting in, and was thoughtfully silent. Then he said, "No lights. We had electricity on the job, but we always cut it off over a weekend. Kids fool around, you know."

"How about the following morning, Saturday? Mr. Bergstrom says he was by the house that Saturday and noticed that the heater was installed."

"Yeah? Well, I'll be damned! That's a queer one. I never knew Bert to work on a Saturday before, but I guess Saturday morning's when he must've put it in. I wonder why he'd do that?"

Gary said fervently, "I hope I know the answer. You've been a great help, Mr. Lastfogel. Believe me, I'll never forget you. But, incidentally, don't you ever read the papers?"

The painter stiffened and bridled. "Of course!"

"Then how come you missed Franklin's statement? It was in the papers. He said he installed that heater Friday afternoon."

"That so? Well, I don't know. Maybe I didn't read what he had to say, or maybe I didn't just pay it no mind. Anyway, I know one thing. He wasn't there when I was there, and if he says he was he's lying. You can tell him for me I said so, too."

His curiosity was becoming greater and he started asking questions, but Gary had all he wanted to know. He returned to the rear seat of the squad car with Jane, and Welte took his place behind the wheel. The sergeant started the engine, but then turned with an arm over the rear of the seat to frown at Gary. "It sure looks like Franklin was lying about something, doesn't it?"

"So you don't think it was just a simple mistake any more? Maybe he could make two mistakes in a row."

Welte scratched his chin and sucked at his teeth. "I don't know. Maybe."

"Oh, hell! We have two lies on him already. He lied about the shutoff of the water and he lied about his whereabouts during the important hours of Friday the thirteenth. By God, it has to add up to something."

"We need more. You got any other ideas?"

"Yes. The next thing in his statement is that he went home for dinner at about five-thirty. Let's go to his house and check that.... Do you know where he lives?"

"You bet."

Welte drove a few blocks to a pine-covered ridge that cut diagonally across a corner of Bayside. It could have been one of the better sections of the town, but it had started badly with fishermen's shanties and had then been developed cheaply through the years. The roads were bad and mostly unpaved, there were few yards and no gardens and a thick mat of pine needles covered everything. As Welte turned onto the plumber's street Gary noticed that the road ended at the lower edge of the ravine where the Halloran girl had disappeared. Franklin's house, in fact, was the last on the street, with a dirt back yard overhanging the ravine.

Gary pointed out this fact excitedly to Welte and the sergeant mumbled, "Yeah, that's right. Funny I never paid it any attention before. But it doesn't mean much—yet. Lots of people live along the ravine."

"Including lying witnesses, for example?"

They stopped and got out of the car and stood for a minute or so looking at the plumber's home. It was an old, two-story frame house with shingled roof and siding and tall, narrow windows. If it had ever been painted no traces of the paint were left. The small, covered porch at the front was sagging, two of the steps were missing and weeds were growing through the gaps. The front door was obviously never used.

The path from the road ran around to another small porch at the side of the house and a door opening into the kitchen. There was a broken teeter-totter in the yard, a rope swing was hanging from one of the trees and at one side was a large sand box for youngsters. Three very small, towheaded children were playing in the box. Beyond was a tool shed in fairly good repair and two rusting jalopies resting on their axles.

Gary and Jane and Welte started down the path to the side porch. The children stopped their playing and stared at the intruders, but with little expression. Gary reached the porch first and rapped on the door with his knuckles. He could hear someone stirring inside, but there was no immediate answer. He rapped again, harder. The door opened slowly and a young girl about fifteen years old looked sullenly at Gary. She was a plain, thin girl with blonde hair tied in two braids. She was wearing old tennis shoes and a cheap cotton dress.

She looked suspiciously at the three on the porch and said, "Just a minute." Then she turned and cried piercingly over her shoulder, "Ma. Oh, Ma. Someone here." She walked back into the kitchen and dropped into a wooden chair at the side of a table.

Gary looked through the open door and across the kitchen to another door that apparently opened into the living room. An enormously fat woman carrying a baby at her hip waddled slowly through the door and cautiously across the floor toward Gary. She, too, had blonde hair, but it was untidy and matted and hung in thick strings about her shoulders. The skin of her face was as milky and smooth as a baby's, her eyes and mouth were small and her nose was a mere button, but her jowls hung level with her three chins. A dirty blouse was stretched to the breaking point over her bosom, the quilted skirt she was wearing was smeared with milk, and on her amazingly tiny feet she was wearing men's carpet slippers. The baby at her hip, wearing diapers only, sucked at its thumb and stared owlishly at Gary.

Her face was completely without expression, but there was cold, naked fear in her eyes as she looked furtively at the three guests. Her glance dwelt longer on Welte's uniform, then swung slowly back to Gary.

"Mrs. Franklin?" he asked.

She shifted the baby slightly and her eyes almost disappeared into the deep rolls of fat. When she spoke her voice was so low that it could hardly be heard. "I don't know nothing," she said.

Welte looked startled and said, "Hey, better let me handle this."

Gary ignored him. He looked beyond at the girl at the kitchen table, then back to the woman. "Do you know who I am, Mrs. Franklin? My name is Gary Malone."

Still in a whisper, she said, "I been expectin' you. I knew you'd come. I kept tellin' him you'd come one of these days. But he just gets mad and don't listen."

Gary tensed and his own eyes were also narrowed. "I see. I know what you mean, Mrs. Franklin. But I'd like to ask you something. It won't take a minute."

"I don't know nothing."

"I think perhaps you might remember a certain Friday, last May thirteenth. That was the day the Halloran girl disappeared, right at the edge of that ravine behind your house." He paused, then spoke as if to a child, "Now, you remember that, don't you?"

"Yes."

"Good. Your husband has made a statement that on that day he was installing a water heater in a new home being built in the Dunes, the Lilly home. He says that he quit work there about five-thirty and came directly home to dinner. I'd like to know about that, Mrs. Franklin. We know already that your husband was not where he said he was on that afternoon. I don't think he was home for dinner that day, either. Isn't that so, Mrs. Franklin? Isn't that true that he did not come home at all that afternoon, or that evening?"

A shudder ran through the heavy rolls of fat and her voice lifted to a whining, querulous pitch: "I told him you'd come. I told him all along. And it's just like I said; I told him the police'd be with you, too. I told him that all along, but he just gets mad and won't listen."

"Mrs. Franklin, about the dinner hour on that particular day—"

She shook her head and the blonde hair danced grotesquely about her jowls. "I can't tell you nothin'. He says he'd kill me, and he does like he says. You don't know him. He's strong for his size and sometimes, like when we got married, he's real nice, but he can be mean, too, and if he says he'll kill me I know he'll do it, one way or another."

Gary gritted his teeth together and pressed his lips into a thin, white line. He said reassuringly, "No one is going to kill you, Mrs. Franklin. If you tell me what you know, the police will pick him up instantly and he will never be able to harm you, or anyone else. Believe me, Mrs. Franklin, I know what these police can do. There is no danger for you. I give you my word."

She was silent for a long while and two tears pressed out between the slits where her eyes were hidden. She shuddered again and then her shoulders sagged and she almost dropped the baby. The child, in spite of its tender age, felt sudden fear and began to whimper. In a moment it was howling lustily.

Mrs. Franklin didn't seem to notice as she sighed deeply and said, "I guess there's no use. I told him all along it would come out this way. Just yesterday he slapped me for sayin' it again. But I can't help sayin' it. It preys on a body's mind, a thing like that. Like a couple years ago he done a big job up in Oakland. We was there seven months. But there was a couple girls livin' next door and at nights he got to stealin' their panties and things off the washlines. I found out and told him the girls'd get wise and they did like I said they would and he had to quit that job and we come back here to Bayside. But you can't tell him nothin' that way."

"Suppose you tell us about that Friday. That's really all we're interested in. He didn't come home for dinner, did he?"

Her eyes opened a fraction to stare at Gary as she said simply, "No."

Gary clenched his fists to control the wild emotions sweeping through him and said, "I have a hunch he didn't come home at all that night."

"Oh, he come home, all right, but it was maybe around two or three in the mornin'. That was just a couple months after the baby here was born and he still had a feedin' at two in the mornin'. I was feedin' him when Bert come home."

"I see. So you know the time pretty well. How was he acting?"

She shrugged her massive shoulders. "Like always, when I gotta feed the baby, he was mad. He went to sleep on the couch in the livin' room. But he took the alarm in with him to get up at five cause he said he had a job to do before somebody noticed he didn't get it done the day before. I know what the job was. I read what he said in the papers."

"You mean the water heater. So he got up at five to install the heater early that Saturday morning and then claimed he had done the job the day before."

"I guess that's the way he done it. I read it in the papers."

"One thing more, Mrs. Franklin. Has he ever told you that he is the one who killed the Halloran girl?"

An odd smile tugged at the tiny lips and opened them and there was a momentary gleam of perfect, tiny, white teeth.

"No," she said, "he never told me nothin' like that. But I knew without him tellin' me."

Gary said grimly, "That isn't quite enough, Mrs. Franklin. My wife thought she knew, too. Do you have anything more definite than a woman's intuition?"

Her eyes opened a bit wider, she looked off into space and her voice again dropped to a whisper. "Under the seat of his truck there's a little paper bag. That's where he keeps the girl's bra."

Gary turned away from her and staggered blindly down the porch steps. Jane ran after him and caught his arm to help him along the path. Shock was biting into his brain so deeply that he was almost blind and could barely see. Jane had to open the door of the car and help him into the back seat. He sat there stiffly, staring ahead, seeing nothing, but hearing the woman's words over and over again in his mind.

Welte returned to the car after a few minutes and got behind the wheel. He, too, sat there silently for a long while. Never, since the night the gym shoes had been discovered, had he ever doubted Gary's guilt. Kraft's change of attitude had never made sense to him. Now he had to admit that the chief had been right all along. He was so embarrassed that for a moment he wondered if he should leave the force, but he put that out of his mind at once.

He swiveled his head about to stare at Gary and said, "I guess that just about wraps it up."

Gary nodded and whispered hoarsely, "Looks that way. That poor woman—and all those kids."

"Yeah. I used her phone for a second to call the station. Some of the men will be up in a couple minutes to stake out the house, just in case Franklin returns before we get him."

"Do you know where he is?"

"Sure. She told me. He's on a construction job at Third and Cypress." He glanced at his watch and whistled under his breath. "Hell, it's four-thirty. That's when he quits. We'd better get going."

Welte started the engine in a hurry, spun the car about and started down the dirt road. He had the headlights on and could see ahead well enough, but the heavy fog was so dense he was afraid someone might pile into them from a side road, so he switched on the siren. When they arrived at Surf Avenue they tore down the main street with the siren screaming and took the corner onto Third almost on two wheels. Welte had suddenly realized what it would mean if he, Welte, brought the real criminal to justice. He stepped on the gas and ripped into the fog and had passed Cypress before he was aware of it. He slammed on the brakes and backed up to lumber and other building materials piled at the side of the street, where he quickly pulled on the emergency and jumped out of the car. Jane was worried and remained in the car, but Gary went along with Welte.

The building under construction was three stories high, designed to hold offices for dentists and physicians. All of the framing was in place, the roof was on and the lower floor was boarded over, but otherwise the building was still a skeleton. Welte loosened his gun and hurried into the building itself. Workmen getting into their cars came to a pause and lifted their eyebrows to stare after the policeman. Gary came to a halt and looked off to his right, where a small pickup truck was parked near a pile of building materials. There was no writing on the truck, but the vises and other equipment attached to it were obviously those of a plumber. Then Gary saw Franklin standing at the tail end of the truck putting away some pipes and tools. He, too, had paused to stare curiously after Welte.

Gary walked slowly toward him, taking in the dirty workmen's boots and the leather jacket and the knitted stocking cap on his head and the sturdy torso that should have belonged to a bigger man with longer arms and legs. Franklin started to put away a heavy Stillson wrench, but then turned his head and saw Gary and froze where he was, his teeth snapping together with an audible click. He knew at once why Gary was there. It was in the stiffness of his back and the slow way he walked and the way his arms were tensed for action, and it was also in his eyes and the pinpoint lights in their depths. The plumber turned slowly to face him, his fingers tightening on the heavy wrench.

Gary came to a stop directly before him. He looked into the man's little eyes and his senses reeled and for a moment he felt sick and faint. He was not thinking at that instant of what the plumber had done to the girl; he was thinking of what the man had done to him. He was thinking of the agonies he had suffered and his friends turning on him and decent people regarding him with contempt and loathing and of what the mobs would have liked doing to him and of the sleepless nights and of the heart attack Mrs. Halloran had suffered merely by looking upon him and of the moment when even he had begun to wonder about his own sanity. All of it spun through his mind in a crazy kaleidoscope of depraved patterns and in the vortex of it all, causing it all, was the man before him. Gary had a single, wild desire—to kill the man with his own bare hands.

But before moving, he cleared his throat and asked one question, "Why did you try to pin it on me?"

Franklin thought of a dozen different protestations of innocence and knew that none of them would be any good. Perspiration broke out on his forehead and he looked desperately about for a place to run, but the truck was in the way, Gary was before him and at his back was a pile of lumber. He screamed shrilly, "You don't know what you're talking about. You're out of your mind." He wet his lips and his eyes darted about and he saw Welte coming out of the building and there was still no avenue of escape. He felt the wrench in his hand and his muscles contracted and he swung the tool with all his might at Gary's head. Gary ducked, but his reflexes were not good and he was not quite in time. The wrench crashed into his shoulder and from there grazed the side of his head just above the left ear. Gary was spun completely about by the force of the blow, and crashed onto his back in a small pyramid of gravel.

The plumber ran for the side of the truck and ripped the left door open, but at that moment Welte reached him and grabbed him by the collar of the leather coat. He pulled back with all his strength. The plumber was jerked from the truck and twisted about, but he managed to swing again and smashed the wrench into Welte's arm. Welte let go with a shout of pain. Franklin hit him on the side of the neck with the wrench and Welte pitched forward full-length on the ground. Franklin looked wildly about at the workmen, immobile, staring at him, their mouths hanging open, and then he started to run.

He made the mistake of running down the open street. Welte rolled to his side, jerked the gun from its holster and propped his elbow on the ground. He squinted along the sights high on Franklin's pounding legs and squeezed the trigger. The .38 barked and jumped in his hand. The plumber doubled over and hit the street rolling and then lay squirming and wriggling on the ground, screaming his pain into the fog.

Gary was not clearly aware of the events following. His head was spinning from the blow he had received, and he seemed to lack simple initiative in thought or action. Jane helped him to his feet and he stared blankly at the plumber lying in the street and Welte bending over him. Later he was aware of sirens and the police and crowds running and of being taken to the hospital in an ambulance, where four stitches were taken in the scalp above his ear. He noticed the friendly smiles of the nurses and the resident surgeon and noticed also that they seemed ashamed in his presence. He was so numbed that he could not understand why.

The doctors urged him to remain at the hospital overnight, but his mind was focused on one desire, to go home. When he went into the corridor he heard someone else screaming and cursing and crying and pleading and was informed that a bullet was about to be removed from Franklin's back. Welte's shot had traveled a bit higher than he wanted. He saw Kraft in the corridor, too, but the chief paused only a second to squeeze his arm, then hurried on. The last thing he remembered was arriving at his own home with Jane, and falling down on his bed.

It was very quiet when he awakened, and the bedroom was dark. His head was throbbing badly. His mouth was dry and his left shoulder felt as if it had been crushed. He rolled to his back with a groan and from the corners of his eyes, near the windows, saw the glow of a cigarette. He had difficulty clearing his throat to ask, "Who's there?"

The answer came back, quietly reassuring, "Sam. Sam Carson. Want me to turn on the lights?"

Gary propped himself on an elbow and squinted in his direction, but could see nothing in the dark. "No," he said. "Leave them off for a little while. What time is it?"

"A little after nine. How do you feel?"

"Awful."

"Yeah. Jane figured that. She stayed here with you until I dropped by about an hour ago." There was silence for a moment, then the editor said, "I may as well tell you now, Gary; playing nursemaid to you is not simple altruism on my part. I want your story, when you feel well enough to give it. And I want it exclusively, if that's all right with you."

"Hell, you don't have to ask. You got it."

Carson coughed and said gruffly, "Thanks. I don't know why the hell you should feel so friendly toward me—"

Gary shoved himself to a sitting position on the bed and fireworks jumped before his eyes. When the display ended and his head stopped spinning he said, "I owe you something. You wanted to believe I was innocent. You did your best to believe it. Maybe you didn't succeed, but it's what you wanted, that means something to me. You can have any story you want. By the way, what about the plumber? Was the girl's bra found in the truck?"

"Yeah. Right under the front seat. Plenty has happened since then. Thirty minutes after he was in the hospital he signed a full confession. He seemed even eager to confess everything. He knew the girl, by the way. She went to school with his older daughter, Doris. He used to pick her up sometimes in his truck and drive her home. He knew that short cut she took. He knew plenty about her."

"That figures. I never did go for the idea that a stranger would be responsible. So he picked her up in the ravine that day?"

"No. She had gone through the ravine and was on the other side on her way home when she ran into Franklin in his truck. He was on his way to install that heater in the Lilly house. He stopped to talk with her. He got ideas. He told her he had just seen her father up the valley, on the Kingsley Ranch. How kids can be so trusting I don't know, but when he said he was going back to the ranch and she could go along with him, she thought it would be a lark to surprise her father. He knew about that abandoned shack." There was a pause for a long while, then the editor continued, "What the hell, you know the rest of it. When she got terrified he got scared, too, and killed her. He used a wrench, maybe the same one he swung on you. That's all being investigated now. On his way back home that night he stopped for a couple of quick ones to steady his nerves at the Gold Nugget. That's where he accidentally kicked the schoolbook out of the truck."

"How about that alibi of his? Didn't he know there would be a painter working on the Lilly job that day?"

"No. He never knew that. He had been talking to Stoddard only the day before and the contractor had informed him that he was all through with the Lilly job. He forgot to mention that there was a little finishing up to be done. So Franklin installed the heater early Saturday morning and figured nobody would know the difference when he said he had put it in the day before."

"I'll be damned."

Gary turned about on the bed and dropped his feet to the floor. His eyes were adjusting to the dark and he could dimly make out Carson's shape in a chair by the windows. "But why," he said, "did he try to pin it on me? I don't remember ever crossing the guy in my life."

Carson said, "Oddly enough, he wasn't trying to pin anything on you, at first. He was in your basement at eight-thirty election morning, like he said, but he didn't have the stuff with him to complete the job. He still thinks he turned off the water, by the way, but that's where his memory slipped, you see."

"Thank God for that."

"You can say that again. So he went back later to complete the job. That's when he got scared out of his wits. Except for the bra under the front seat, which he intended keeping—those sex deviates are that way, you know—he had all the rest of the girl's stuff in a tool box on the truck bed. He came out to get a length of pipe, or something, and found a couple of kids playing in his truck. They were even opening the tool box. He chased them away and grabbed the box and lugged it into your basement. He was scared, and it suddenly dawned on him that your basement was as good a place as any to hide the stuff. So he got it out of the box, dug a deep hole and buried it, and then smoothed it over."

"But the shoes! The gym shoes!"

"Uh-huh. That was a mistake. He meant to put them on a cardboard carton until he finished digging, but apparently they fell down between two of the boxes and when he buried the rest of the stuff he didn't see them and didn't miss them. That's how it happened. All he was trying to do was get rid of the incriminating evidence. Then, of course, when it all broke in the papers he did a little fast thinking and came up with the story about seeing the disturbed earth. It wasn't a very bright story, but it was the best he could do and you have to admit that it worked. Doesn't it all seem so simple now, when you look back on it?"

"Yeah." Gary stood up and mumbled, "Let's go in the other room."

He switched on a hall light and Carson followed him into the living room, where Gary turned on one lamp in a corner. His eyes hurt and he did not want much light. He opened two bottles of beer in the kitchen and came back to the living room to hand one to Carson. The two dropped onto the couch and sipped at their beer.

After a while, Carson said, "Your boss phoned while you were asleep."

"Ted?"

"Mr. Baker, yes. He was so damned happy for you he was all choked up. He said to tell you to knock off for a few weeks and get out of town and wash this thing out of your system."

Gary said bitterly, "Some things don't wash."

He heard a car stop outside and someone coming up the walk and then the doorbell ringing. He had a hunch the door was unlocked, so called, "Come in."

He turned to look over his shoulder as Dan walked slowly through the doorway and stopped by the end of the couch. Gary's mind jumped to the last time he had seen Dan behind his restaurant counter, cursing at him; and then the mob outside and the sickness he had felt when they closed in on him. Looking at Dan, he felt the same sickness all over again.

Dan stood there twisting his hat in his big hands and chewing at his lower lip and looking humbly down at Gary. He blurted out finally, "I couldn't wait, Gary. I had to come as soon as I heard. I had to see you right now. I'm a lousy friend, all right. I'm stupid, that's all. So I'm a damned moron and a hell of a jerk to call a friend and I'm the one who knows it. Gary, if you could only forget—"

Gary squinted up at him and said coldly, "Get out."

"Sure, Gary, sure. I know it's a lot to ask and I know what a heel I was, but if you could just think of me as a stupid jerk who meant no harm—"

Gary lifted himself slightly and shouted, "Get out!"

Dan sighed and shuffled his feet and looked imploringly at Gary, but turned and walked out of the house.

Carson tilted the bottle to his lips, his eyes on Gary, then lowered it and said, "That took a lot of guts."

Gary said fiercely, "You were with me that morning. Do you think I should welcome him with open arms?"

"Well, I don't know how I'd act in your shoes. It's hard to say. But it took a pretty big man to come here the way he did."

"The last time I saw him he threatened to use a cleaver on me."

"I know. You have a lot of adjustments to make, but so has everyone else in this town, you know. You were a rather loathsome object. Now, suddenly, the hated man is somewhat of a hero. The embarrassed citizens are undergoing a powerful purgative right now. I doubt if one person in a hundred will be able to look you straight in the eyes for a long, long while."

Gary jumped to his feet and started pacing back and forth before the fireplace. "Sure," he said, "and the hell of it is I feel the same way. So much of that filth rubbed off on me that I still feel depraved. I can't look anyone in the eyes. I'm scared. I'm afraid I'll see in their eyes what I was reading in the papers, the sort of person I am—the twisted psychotic, the creature capable of assaulting a young girl. How do you like that? Isn't that one for the books? I can't look into a person's eyes any more than they can look into mine. You know what? We're all scared. And for what, for God's sake?"

"I'm afraid I don't know the answer."

The telephone rang and without losing a stride in his pacing Gary swung into the hallway and picked up the instrument. "Malone speaking."

"Gary? Hey, that's wonderful. I was hoping I would catch you at home."

Gary frowned and said, "I'm sorry, but I don't—"

The voice cried happily, "Luke. This is Luke. I just heard the good news. Naturally, I had to call at once. By God, Gary, this is the happiest day in my life. You know I was pulling for you all along. Man, the misery Betty and I have gone through, trying to convince people, arguing with them, pleading with them just to hold their judgment—"

Gary lowered the receiver from his ear, stared at it with a grimace of bitter distaste and dropped it into the cradle. He went back into the living room and told Carson, "Luke Summer. He just wanted me to know how he was in back of me all along."

Carson shrugged and said mildly, "That son-of-a-bitch. That's one you can scratch off the list."

"And a few thousand others. I'm scratching the whole town off my list. They can all go to hell. I won't even begin to feel clean until I get a thousand miles away."

The editor cocked an eyebrow at him and asked, "You got some place in mind where there are no people? We're all the same, Gary, wherever you go. We're all suspicious and we're mighty fast with our judgments and quick to condemn and, in fact, so are you. You made your own fast judgment of that plumber without benefit of jury. From what Jane tells me, if he hadn't hit you with that wrench you would probably have choked him to death."

"That's what I had in mind, all right."

Gary paused and leaned back against the fireplace bricks to think about it. He heard a car stop out front and tensed himself for another bad encounter, but it was Chief Kraft who came through the door, and with him was Jane Bestor. Gary smiled for the first time in a long while and was surprised that he was smiling. It was not alone for Jane and her own smile and the warmth she brought with her when she walked to him and touched his arm. It was also for the big blond Viking in police uniform who teetered back and forth on the balls of his feet before Gary, looking as happy as a small child. The chief held out his big hand and Gary gripped it hard.

Kraft chuckled and said, "This is a real pleasure. How are you feeling, boy?"

"Oh, a little woozy, but otherwise okay."

The chief put a hand on Gary's chin to turn his head and frowned at the bandage above the ear. "Four stitches, I hear. He must have really walloped you one."

"My shoulder took most of it, or he would have split my skull open. How's he doing, by the way?"

"Franklin? Hmmmm." He turned away and dropped heavily to the sofa and looked back at Gary. "He won't be doing much of anything until they put him in the gas chamber. That slug of Hank's hit him in the spine. He's paralyzed."

"Fine. That's fine. And even that's too good for him."

The chief said softly, "That's what they were saying about you. Remember?" He saw fear creeping back into Gary's eyes and said quickly, "You know who's the big shot now? Hank. Man, is he strutting around. But maybe a thing like this will make a good cop out of him. One thing for sure," he sighed, "I'll have to promote him to lieutenant." Then he laughed.

Jane smiled into Gary's eyes and said, "We just dropped by for a minute to see how you were doing. I'm surprised to find you awake."

Carson said, "He woke up a few minutes ago. We've been doing a little talking. Gary, understandably, is a pretty bitter man. He wants to wash himself clean of the town and everyone in it. Yet it's the same town and the same people he loved so much before. I think he should stay here and sweat it out. There will be a lot of embarrassment on all sides for quite a while, but it will wear off in time."

Gary shook his head. "No dice. The way my friends turned on me—"

Jane stated quietly, "You've made new friends, Gary."

He looked at her and at Carson and Kraft and nodded. "That's true. I feel closer to the guy who tried to crucify me in his paper and the guy who tried to put me in the gas chamber than anyone else in this town, except Mr. Baker, of course. He was a real prince."

"Not everyone turned on you."

"Well, even that isn't all of it. Everything has been so useless, no point to anything, no direction—"

Kraft said, "Oh, now, wait a minute. Hold on. You can't say that."

"The hell I can't. I'm not about to drown in self-pity, but after all—"

"Sure, sure. I think I know how you feel." Kraft leaned forward and said earnestly, "So you've done a lot of suffering and you've gone through the tortures of the damned, but it wasn't in vain, Gary. If it hadn't been for you a killer would be roaming loose in society today, and maybe he would kill again and again."

"Hell's bells, I never solved the thing."

"I'm not saying you did. A number of circumstances were responsible for it. But you were the instrument used by justice."

"Now, please—"

"I mean it, Gary. I've seen justice work in some very peculiar ways at times, and this is certainly one of them. Just give it a little thought. The shoes were found in the basement of a man of good character. That started the ball rolling. Then the other stuff was found and your alibi fell apart and it certainly looked as if you were the one. But I believed it only for a short while, and Sam here believed it only for a short while. You stood up too well.

"We began to have our doubts. I could have thrown the book at you at once, but it was your character that got in the way and stopped me. Because of you and only because of you, court action was held back just long enough. Jane went to work in your behalf, because of your character. And because of her interest in you and only because of that she turned up with the seemingly trivial piece of information that blew the whole thing open and led inevitably to a dangerous killer being dropped in the street. Now do you see what I mean? You suffered, yes—God alone knows the agonies you went through—but without you a killer would still be at large today to prey upon others. You were the instrument of justice. Is that small pay for your suffering?"

Gary whispered, "No," and turned away from them. He could not face their kindness and the obvious fact that with all their hearts they wanted him to stay with them, his friends, so that they could help ease his way back to normalcy and decent living. He walked to the front window and looked out at the dark street and the fog sitting like a vast gray nest in the trees. It would not be easy remaining in Bayside. People would point him out on the streets and they would talk about him and the "case" for a long time to come. It would be even more difficult facing the friends and acquaintances who had been so quick to condemn him. Yet, he thought, I wasn't so different, either. I was just as ready to condemn and even kill with only a few facts to go on.

He saw a car stop on the street before the house and the blinking light of a taxi on the roof above the windshield and a door open and a pair of slender legs stepping into the light. He spun away from the window, jerked the front door open and hurried down the walk to the taxi. Ellen was opening her purse to pay the driver, but she paused to smile lightly at Gary.

"Hello, darling. My goodness, I was afraid you might be in bed. There was such a little light on in the house. Be with you in a minute."

Gary dropped a hand to her arm and turned her about to face him. "What is it you want, Ellen?"

"Well, gracious," she laughed, "this is no place to talk. Just wait till I pay the driver—"

"No. You tell me now."

She smiled and patted his cheek. "Now, Gary, you're being obtuse. Isn't it quite obvious? Getting a divorce was a stupid idea in the first place, and only today I told off the lawyers trying to force me into it. I told them to go their own way and just please leave me alone. I never really had any serious intentions— Honest." She stood up on her toes to press her cheek against his and continued, "We can just forget the dreadful past, darling. I'll help you to forget it. Honest I will. We can just go right back the way we were before with everything nice and smooth and living our own lives without all sorts of horrible people interfering—"

"Ellen!" he shouted.

She stepped back with a little pout and blinked at him. "Really, Gary, I can hear you."

"Fine. Then listen closely. You're getting back into that taxi and you're going to get the devil out of here before I knock every single one of your teeth down that lovely throat. You're going through with the divorce and, so help me, I hope I never see you or your mother again the rest of my life."

"Why, of all things—"

Gary turned her around and shoved her into the taxi. He lifted his right arm as high as it would go and brought the open palm down with all his might with a resounding and stinging slap across the skirt stretched tightly about her bottom. She pitched forward with a scream and collapsed on the seat.

Gary told the astounded driver, "Take her back into town, or anywhere. Just get her out of here. I'm a violent man, chum. I may lose my temper."

"Yes—yes, sir."

Gary stood for a moment watching the taxi disappear, then walked slowly back into the house. Carson turned away quickly to hide a smile. Kraft had his own laughter stifled behind a huge paw, and Jane looked uncomfortable and embarrassed, but also trying to keep from smiling. So, he thought, they had all witnessed the little scene out front. He started walking toward Jane, looking a trifle shamefaced, but as he walked he could not contain himself and when he reached her side and took her arm he suddenly burst out laughing.

Jane looked over at the chief and said simply, "He'll stay."

THE END

Killer in Silk

H. Vernor Dixon

Chapter One

Morgan O'Keefe used the few dollars he could borrow to buy a Greyhound bus ticket from Los Angeles to San Francisco. He had sent an airmail letter to his New York agent a few days before, telling him where he was going. When he arrived at the Riverton Hotel a Western Union money order for $360, his latest royalty, minus commission, was waiting for him. He checked into the hotel, enjoyed a steak dinner, and dropped into a bar on Sutter Street for a couple of cold beers. There he got into an argument with an ex-Infantry officer and switched to bourbon highballs. Within an hour he was drinking the whisky straight and was well on his way.

Five days later he was broke. He pawned his only possessions, a suitcaseful of clothes and personal effects and a portable typewriter. He had no difficulty locating San Francisco's Skid Row on Howard Street and patronized the saloons there, drinking cheap sherry and muscatel. On the tenth night of his drunk he was picked up sleeping in a doorway and wound up in the drunk tank with a dozen derelicts. He had no record in San Francisco and it was also obvious to the judge, in court the following morning, that Morgan was neither a vagrant nor a derelict. The judge let him go with the admonition that he stay away from Howard Street. "Your kind doesn't belong there." Morgan felt like laughing, but he controlled the impulse.

He made his way outside and came to a halt in the thin fog blanketing Kearny Street, wondering what to do. A uniformed policeman who had been in the courtroom followed him outside and leaned against the stone wall to watch him. The cop was curious. He had seen all kinds picked up on Howard Street, but never anyone quite like Morgan. He puffed lazily at a cigarette and appraised the other man.

Morgan was a tall man with good shoulders, but the frame of his body was so thin and wiry that he seemed almost weightless, in spite of his height. His straight brown hair, cut short and parted to the left of center, appeared to be graying at the temples. The effect, however, was caused not by gray hairs but by light yellow streaks acquired in the sun on the blazing white beaches of Southern California. His blue eyes were set deeply in a bony, angular face; the prominent, eaglelike ridge of his nose was sharply thin and skin was stretched tightly about the slight suggestion of a cleft in his chin. There were a few freckles high on his cheekbones. He seemed to be in his late thirties, but his eyes and mouth were tired and the lines etched deeply in his face were those of a man far beyond his years.

He was wearing a lightweight sport shirt open at the throat, a suede jacket that had been obviously and expensively tailored for him, beige gabardine slacks and Weejun moccasins stained dark cordovan. The jacket now was ripped at one shoulder. There was a rip in the left knee of his slacks, and the buttons had been ripped from the back pockets. His clothes were so soiled and wrinkled that he looked and smelled as if he had been crawling through a sewer.

The cop flipped his cigarette into the street, approached Morgan and tapped him on the shoulder. "Got any place to go, Mac?"

Morgan looked at him out of bloodshot eyes. At first he thought it was another arrest, but then noticed the cop's open, even friendly, expression. He shook his head. "No, I haven't."

"I figured that. How long you been in town?"

"Ten days."

"How long you been drunk?"

"Ten days."

"Uh-huh. No dough?"

"No."

"No dough and no place to go. And right now you need a place to go real bad or you're gonna wind up screaming your brains out in a psycho ward. Is that the picture?"

"I can feel it coming on."

"You look it, too. I know. I had a brother like you."

Morgan said in a low voice, "If you know of anything—"

The cop rubbed his chin and said slowly, "Well, now, maybe I do. There are a couple of clinics for drunks, but all they'll give you is a sedative shot and shove you along. Maybe you could get into the county hospital, but all you'll get there're the same sedatives and in a couple days you'll be outside facing the screaming meemies and maybe on your way back to the tank. If that judge sees you again so soon you'll get the full treatment—ninety days."

"If you know—"

"Yeah. I'm telling you. There's a gal here in town named Irene Wilson. Every once in a while she takes in a stray drunk and puts him back on his feet."

Morgan's lips twisted into a sour grimace. "A Bible thumper?"

The cop was amused. He chuckled and said, "Far from it, Mac. Don't ask me why she does it. I don't know. The main thing is, she does it and if you're real lucky maybe she'll take you in. It's worth trying. Now, you go up here a couple blocks and catch the forty-one bus going west. Get off at Fillmore and Union and transfer to the twenty-two. That'll take you to the top of the hill. That whole section in there is called Pacific Heights. Very ritzy. So you walk east down Pacific Street a block and a half. Her place is between Green and Buchanan. I don't know the number, but it's a big stone place set back from the sidewalk with a curved driveway in front and fancy white pillars at the entrance. Think you can find it?"

Morgan nodded. "I can try. Irene Wilson?"

"That's right. You got bus fare?" Morgan shook his head. The cop sighed and handed him fifteen cents. "Okay. Better be on your way before you go to pieces. And good luck."

The cop slapped him on the shoulder and walked away. Morgan stood indecisively a moment longer; then he started walking toward the bus line. There was a great scream within him, bubbling to burst forth into maniacal howls of despair. He kept the scream contained by walking stiffly, his elbows pressed tightly against his ribs. If he relaxed even the slightest degree he knew he would wind up in a strait-jacket.

He found the bus stop and boarded the first forty-one that came along. He sat far in the rear. Other passengers wrinkled their noses, stared at him with distaste and moved forward. He had the rear of the bus to himself. He missed the transfer point and had to walk back three blocks to Fillmore. It was then he realized that he had also forgotten to get a transfer. He looked up at the towering ridge of Pacific Heights. Some of the steepest streets in San Francisco climbed to its crest. The sidewalks angled up so sharply that they were made of concrete steps. Morgan's heart sank. He doubted that he had the strength to make the climb. But it had to be attempted. His will to keep going was hanging by a last shred. Anything could snap it.

He started up the Fillmore Street hill, pacing himself by looking down and counting steps, afraid to look up, afraid that if he did he would never make it. He walked slowly, holding himself in tightly, perspiration heavy on his forehead and upper lip. His mouth and throat were so dry that his breath rattled in his lungs.

When he reached the top finally he had to lean against a telephone pole to keep from collapsing. Even that was dangerous. Too much rest and his eyes would close and he would sink down. He shoved himself away from the pole, staggered, caught his balance and shuffled down Pacific Street.

He found the house the cop had described and he bared his teeth in sudden rage. It was a trap, a goddam trap. The cop was a lousy sadist having a little sport with a helpless drunk. No one living in a house like that would even speak to a drunk. It was a broad, gray mansion of granite that looked as if it had grown on the side of the hill. It looked more like a public library than anyone's home. He looked around and saw only other mansions and expensive new apartment buildings. Pacific Heights was undoubtedly one of the wealthiest districts in the city, obviously because of the spectacular view embracing the Golden Gate, San Francisco Bay, the Marin hills to the north and most of the East Bay shore.

Morgan's shoulders sagged. If he could make it back downtown—walking—he might get a collect call through to his agent in New York for enough money to buy his way into a private sanitarium. It was the only alternative, but two things were vitally wrong with it. He was too exhausted to walk another block. And even if he did make it to a telephone, he knew it would be hopeless. Earl was a good man and even sympathetic, but he had had enough of Morgan's binges and would no longer advance him a dollar unless drawn against definite royalties. There were no more royalties due at the moment, or in the near future.

He looked again at the mansion, teetering back and forth on his heels. It was a trap, he knew that, he was positive of it. But maybe— Anyway, there was nothing else to try, and he could go no farther. The boys in the white jackets could pick him up here as well as elsewhere. What difference would it make?

He shuffled up the half-dozen granite steps of the square portico and punched the bell by the side of a huge oak door edged with bronze. Perhaps half a minute passed and then the door swung ponderously, smoothly, silently open. A butler in dark trousers, black bow tie and white linen jacket, faced him without expression. He was a short, stocky, rather powerful looking man with iron-gray hair, mild blue eyes and the smooth skin of a Scandinavian. He was not at all surprised by Morgan's appearance.

He said simply, "It is Mrs. Wilson you want?"

A faint hope crept back into Morgan's weary mind.

He nodded. "Yes. A cop downtown—he told me—if I came up here— maybe—"

"Come in, please. And wait."

The door closed behind him as Morgan stepped into a long hallway. The butler disappeared through an open doorway straight ahead. Morgan was not especially conscious of his surroundings. He was only just aware of an atmosphere of wealth and good taste. He told himself over and over again that he had to hold on—just a little longer.

When the woman came into the hallway he noticed first the cobwebby sandals she was wearing. Then his eyes raised slowly to take in the white linen dress, the black bolero jacket draped over her shoulders, and the tiny white straw hat on the back of her head. Apparently she had just come in, or was just going out. She was not at all what he had imagined. She had good, slim legs with long thighs, a narrow waist and breasts that were either naturally full or well padded—it was always difficult to be sure—narrow hands with long, tapered fingers, a smooth throat and a face that gave the impression of being full and round and yet, oddly enough, was not. There was a certain hollowness about her cheeks and a thinness along the line of her jaws that seemed not to belong there. He noticed, too, the faint shadows under her eyes, that were either dark brown or black, and the tiny, bitter lines at her mouth.

Her thick, glossy hair was coal-black and caught loosely in a bun at the nape of her neck, and either she was deeply tanned or her complexion was naturally olive, or perhaps both. Somewhere in her early thirties, he guessed, and probably lousy in bed. Too reserved, too cool, too much the lady to be the giving kind.

She glanced at the butler standing a few paces behind and to her side, then swung her eyes levelly to Morgan. "A policeman told you to come here?" she asked.

He swallowed and nodded. "Downtown. I was in the tank last night. The judge let me go this morning. This cop told me you might be willing to help."

"How long—"

"Ten days. I'd just come up from Lotus Land, Los Angeles. I had some money, but after a ten-day binge I'm clean and I have no place to go."

"Do you know what shape you're in?"

"I'm afraid I know only too well. It's bad."

She chewed at her lower lip for a moment, staring at him, appraising him. Then she said, "I could give you a little money—"

He sucked in air sharply, let it out and shook his head. "That wouldn't do any good. I'd just use it to get drunk. Right now I'm sick, damned sick. I know what I'm facing. Tonight I'll have the d.t.'s. I've had them before, you see. I know what I can take and what I can't take. I need someone to help me get through it." He paused. "Maybe if you're so goddam big-hearted you could send me to a sanitarium."

She ignored the sarcasm and again appraised him silently. He was certainly different from any other alcoholic she had ever known. He was also better dressed, in spite of the wear and tear of his binge. And his language was not that of Skid Row.

She hesitated a moment longer, then sighed and said, "I'll help you get through it. There is an apartment you can occupy here on the ground floor. Carl will take care of you and you'll also get the best medical attention."

He tilted his head on one side, squinted at her and said bluntly, "Why?"

She ignored him again and told the butler, "Show him to the apartment, Carl. See that he has a bath and gets shaved and put him to bed. I'll call Dr. Rigsby."

She glanced at Morgan as if to say something, thought better of it, and walked away. But at the door leading into what Morgan guessed was the study, she paused and looked back at him. Morgan thought he must be wrong, but her expression was obviously one of resentment. A do-gooder resenting the helpless target of her goodness? What goes on here? he wondered.

Carl jerked his head and Morgan turned to the right to follow the butler to the end of the hallway. Carl opened a door and led the way inside. The apartment was a large corner room that at one time must have been the library. The walls were paneled and covered with shelves stacked with books. There was a large fireplace at one side, an enormous flat desk and a deep leather sofa and chair. In one corner, by the tall windows, was an oversize studio couch. There were other chairs and hassocks and small end tables and a wide variety of lamps, good paintings on the walls, current magazines in a rack and an enormous Oriental rug on the parquet floor. A small but complete Pullman-type kitchen had been built into the end wall and alongside was a door leading into a large dressing room and a bathroom with walls and floor of Italian tiles. Morgan managed a smile, in spite of his condition. It was the sort of apartment he had dreamed of designing for himself one day.

Carl helped him off with his clothes and assisted him into the bathroom. Morgan was able to take a shower. He was beginning to realize that he was safe, and relaxation crept in, and along with it the shakes. He was not able to hold a razor in his hand, let alone use it. Carl sat him on the edge of the tub, steadied him with a hand on his bare shoulder and shaved him. Carl also found and helped him into a pair of pajamas, turned back the sheets of the studio couch and tucked Morgan in.

Morgan was now beginning to shake violently and said to Carl through chattering teeth, "I need—a drink. Stiff one. Plenty stiff."

Carl nodded, still without expression. "I know."

"Good. You know everything. A stiff one, then."

The butler gathered Morgan's clothes from the floor and left the room. He returned with a double shot of straight bourbon, which he poured carefully down Morgan's throat. He got some logs and kindling and built a fire in the fireplace. It was just starting to blaze when the door opened and Irene Wilson came into the room followed by a middle-aged, amiable looking man with a small paunch, thin hair graying at the temples, a healthy flush, and piercing eyes that missed nothing.

"So," he said, "another of your pet patients. I don't know why you do this, Irene. You just ask for trouble and you don't do them any good, anyway. Give them a month or two to forget the last one and they're right back at it again."

Mrs. Wilson seemed angry and snapped at him, "If you'll kindly dispense with the lecture, Dr. Rigsby—"

"Okay," he laughed. "Let's see if this one has something besides alcohol in his system."

The doctor placed his bag on the floor and sat on the bed at Morgan's side. He examined his eyes and tongue, listened to his heart, checked his pulse and took a reading of his blood pressure. He sat back and looked down at Morgan, shaking his head.

"You're in very bad shape, young man. You're suffering from malnutrition, among other things. If you had been deliberately trying to commit suicide I'd say the job is about ninety per cent accomplished."

The double shot he had consumed had slowed Morgan's shaking, so that he was able to speak lucidly. "Isn't that what all drunks are after?" he asked. "The death wish is at the bottom of alcoholism."

Dr. Rigsby's eyebrows raised in surprise. "That's an interesting idea. But I suppose now you would rather live. Well, we'll see what we can do about that. I'll give you some vitamin shots, sedatives—"

Morgan interrupted with a shake of his head. "Vitamin shots, yes, but not sedatives. I'd rather fight this out on my own."

"You're joking."

"I'm serious. All I need is rest, vitamins and food." He looked in Carl's direction and said, "Bring me another shot of whisky in an hour, another in two hours, another in three and so on until I'm off completely. Don't leave a bottle in here and each time you leave the room lock the door." His eyes swung back to the doctor's astonished expression. "I've done it this way before, Doc. Maybe I like to torture myself. Maybe I like to pay myself back for being such a jackass. Whatever it is, this is the way I prefer doing it."

"But you can't do it, man. You must have sedatives. You're not too far from delirium tremens right now."

"I know. I'll sweat it out."

"But with the help of a mild sedative—"

Morgan lost his patience and shouted, "Look, I know more about myself than you do! Do it my way, or get the hell out of here!"

The doctor shrugged. He gave Morgan two vitamin shots, then wrote out a prescription for Carl and a diet list for the next few days. "Not that he'll be able to hold much of it down," he said, "but some of it will stay with him. Give him a few days and he can tackle solid foods. Meanwhile, occasional vitamin shots will be his greatest help."

He walked out to the hallway with Irene Wilson, closed the door and stood there for a moment lost in thought. At last he sighed and said, "That's quite an unusual man in there. The first demand of any alcoholic is a sedative to slow him down and quiet his nerves. But this man prefers doing it the hard way."

"Do you think he can manage to sweat it out, as he says?"

"Well, if he does he's the damnedest alcoholic I've ever run into. Sweating it out will take almost fantastic will power, which poses a peculiar question. If he has will that strong, why is he an alcoholic? Or maybe we have another question to face. Is he really an alcoholic?"

"He claims he is."

"Well, time will tell just what he is, if anything. But there's one statement I can make right now. I have never been in agreement with your urge to help alcoholics. All you are doing is feeding fuel to the fires of your own guilt complex. It isn't good for you and you really do little or no good for the drunks. But this one time I think is an exception. I have a hunch that that man is worth all the help you can give him."

She turned and looked at the closed door and the odd resentment that had been in her eyes gave way to curiosity. During the ten long years she had been helping occasional drunks, she had never thought of any one of them as a human being. But this man had impressed her at first sight, which, she now realized, was why she had been reluctant to help him. Now, because of the doctor's words, he had also acquired human stature and even a personality. A slight, rueful smile tugged at her lips. She didn't even know his name.

The doctor left, saying as he went, "Give me a ring when the d.t.'s hit him. Regardless of what he thinks of his own powers, he'll need my help."

Morgan came down with delirium tremens late that afternoon, sooner than he had expected. It started with a chill, was followed by fever and an itching, prickling sensation and then by one feeling that he was covered with slime. An hour later he could feel thousands of caterpillars and centipedes squirming and wriggling all over his body. He began to scream. The violence of his delirium became so great that the butler was forced to tie him to the bed to prevent him from digging his nails into his own flesh.

The doctor returned that night and grimly prepared a sedative. Morgan fought wildly against the needle, cursing the doctor with every breath with the most loathsome expressions he could find, but the doctor jabbed him with the needle, anyway. Morgan subsided.

Later he dreamed of the great books he was going to write and the great murals he was going to paint and the giant statues he was going to carve from cold marble. He dreamed of women, their nude bodies pressing upon him, hundreds of women of every shape and color, and he could smell their perfumes and scents and could feel the softness of their flesh. He dreamed of cities floating in the clouds and of roaring jets and ships at sea and then he dreamed of dank, dark alleys and garbage cans and rotting humanity and of snakes and weird animals and of sewer rats chewing on his knuckles and he awoke screaming, the sheets soaked, his body bathed with perspiration and spume at his lips.

For two days and three nights he fought the damage that had been visited upon his mind and wasted body, and eventually the poison wore off. The twice-daily injections of vitamins took hold and the soups and Jello and gruel that Carl spooned between his lips began to stay down. The bindings were removed from his wrists and ankles and for the first time he slept the deep sleep of exhaustion.

He awoke in midafternoon and lay quietly on his back staring up at the paneled ceiling. After a long while he realized where he was and disgust was deep in his bloodshot eyes. So he had done it again. An intelligent man, even talented, once more a beggar and an object of charity. And this time it had been a woman who had helped him. A damned eunuch, he thought. Reduced finally to a eunuch.

He turned his head and saw her seated alongside the couch. She had been reading a book, but she lowered it to her lap and watched him. Dr. Rigsby had told her the night before that their patient would probably snap out of it that day, so she was not surprised by the look of reason in his eyes. She handed him a glass of milk from a table at her elbow. He sat up weakly and drank it, savoring every drop of the delicious coolness as it trickled down his throat. He leaned forward to rest his elbows on his knees, his shoulders hunched forward and his head bent, but tilted to one side so that he could watch her from the corners of his eyes.

"Thanks," he said weakly. "You've been very kind."

She said primly, "I feel that people in my position have a duty—"

He interrupted with a grunt and said sourly, "Oh, stuff it, for God's sake.

Duty is always a cover-up for something else. People like you appall me. They're always asking to be shot or stabbed by less friendly souls."

"Are you the less friendly type?"

"Not exactly. I haven't shot anyone yet."

She caught her breath sharply, color ebbed from her face and her lips thinned out. Morgan wondered what he had said that had inspired such a reaction in her. Before he could ask, her expression was again coolly passive. She touched a lighter to two cigarettes and handed one to him. He inhaled deeply, feeling a little dizzy as he blew out the smoke.

He asked her curiously, "Do you make a practice of taking in drunken bums this way?"

"You don't impress me as—as—"

"A bum?" He smiled. "We come in all shapes and sizes. Bums don't go around any more in cast-off clothes and patched pockets. There's my kind, you see. When we're in the chips we patronize the most exclusive shops, live in apartments built around kidney-shaped swimming pools, drive foreign sports cars, lunch at Romanoff's and dine at the Beverly-Hilton. But we're still bums. Because there's always that black day of reckoning when a check doesn't arrive when you think it should and your credit runs out and you try to ignore it all and hide in a bottle and you always wind up in the same place, the drunk tank. That's when the tramp that is always in our nature comes out and I find myself precisely right here."

Irene Wilson looked at him with interest. "You're unusually frank about your level in life. But are you sure you aren't ribbing me about yourself?"

"God, no! I only needle stupid, helpless people. You look as if you could fight back."

She smiled and said, "Perhaps." She poured him another glass of milk from a chilled pitcher on the table. "But this level of yours—I don't quite understand it. You must have some sort of skill, or trade?"

Morgan debated whether or not to tell her the truth. He saw his suitcase and portable typewriter on the floor near the dressing room. He assumed that the pawn tickets had been found in his pockets. Probably the butler had redeemed his stuff. Apparently, though, the suitcase had not been opened and his hostess had no inkling of his identity. Maybe it would be better to leave it that way. Quite often, with strangers, he would create entirely new lives for himself, lives with exotic backgrounds—test pilot, deep sea-diver, smuggler, bookie, or, one of his favorites, long-term criminal just out of prison and now determined to go straight. He dominated his audience, he played upon their sympathies, he stretched credulity to the breaking point. He had a wonderful time doing it and he always learned something that added grist to his mill. He had such a tremendous fund of spotty knowledge in so many fields that he never failed to make himself convincing. But he decided, on this occasion, to tell the truth. He was too weak and exhausted to play games for any length of time.

So he said, "My name is Morgan O'Keefe. Does that mean anything to you?"

She frowned and thought for a moment. "No-o-o, I can't say that it does. I saw M. J. O'Keefe on your pawn tickets, but it didn't mean anything to me. Should it?"

"Not necessarily. If it meant something to everybody I asked I'd be famous and I wouldn't be here accepting your charity. I'm a writer, you see. I write dreary little books about dreary little people that sell in the dreary hundreds instead of the thousands. My publishers should have stopped printing my stuff years ago—God knows they barely break even—but they keep on with me in the wildly insane hope that some day I may click."

"If you could mention a few titles—"

"Forget it. You wouldn't know my stuff. You belong to some book-of-the-month club and a local rental library and whenever you buy anything else you consult the bestseller lists. You won't find Morgan O'Keefe in that company."

She was slightly annoyed, principally because he was right. "Well, after all, I do try to read the best."

"Of course you do. So, naturally, you haven't read anything of mine."

She stared at him and then burst out laughing. She stopped suddenly, obviously startled by her own outburst. Morgan wondered about it. Mrs. Wilson was evidently a woman who did not laugh easily, or often.

"Is that what you were doing down south, writing?"

"How did you know where I came from?"

"You told me when I first met you."

"Oh." He thought of what he had been doing down south and looked as if he might be sick. "Well," he said, "the answer to that is yes and no. I wasn't writing for the movies, if that's what you're thinking. I wanted to. I beat my brains out trying to get in, but they didn't want me. I had exactly one chance all the years I was there. My Hollywood agent got me a deal with MGM at seven-fifty a week and an office in writers' row. I thought I was set. Then the powers-that-be gave me some other author's book to adapt for the screen. That was okay, too, except for one thing. The story was about the war and the main character was an officer who was a goddam lily-white hero." He shook his head, clenched his fists until the knuckles were white, and closed his eyes.

Mrs. Wilson said curiously, "What was wrong with that?"

He kept his eyes closed. "It was the worst thing they could have handed me. I wound up in fifty-two in an army psycho ward, where I damned well belonged. I despise anyone in uniform and anything even remotely suggesting Army makes me deathly ill. I tried, but I couldn't do it. I couldn't even force myself to read halfway through the book. So, naturally, I got drunk and I stayed that way. That ended my association with MGM, or any other studio."

She said simply, "I'm sorry."

He clasped his thin arms about his knees and looked away from her toward the sun streaming in through the windows. Mrs. Wilson was watching him closely. Her curiosity had given way to enthralled attention and she wanted something more of the man than simply a fragmentary picture. She wanted something she could use at the cocktail party that night.

"I don't really mean to pry," she said, "but is that why you left the south, when you lost that job? If I'm getting too personal—"

He looked back at her with a twisted smile. "Of course you're prying and you're getting too personal, but I have to repay you somehow or other. Don't I? No, that is not why I left the south. Would you really like to know why I left?"

"Well—"

"I'll tell you. I suppose you've guessed, or the doctor must have told you, that I'm an alcoholic. When something bothers me too much I go for the bottle. But I don't drink like ordinary people. I drink to drown myself. I go on and on, day after day. I start with the best and when I run out of money I pawn everything the hock shops will take and switch to cheap sherry and muscatel and keep going until I finally drop from sheer exhaustion and wind up in a drunk tank and sometimes the county hospital. In Los Angeles I made the tank nine times. Nine times in three years."

She dropped a solicitous hand to his arm, her dark eyes brimming with compassion. "Please. If you don't care—"

"Hell," he laughed, "I don't mind. Maybe I even get some sort of perverse pleasure out of my little purges. Anyway, the last time I was in the L.A. tank was once too much. I was brought into night court. The judge remembered me and looked up my record. He gave me a long lecture and in the end he let me go, but he also gave me a warning. He said that if I was picked up once more I would get the full ninety-day treatment behind bars, which is par for the habitual. Ninety days behind bars, or even nine, would be the end of me. But I knew the threat wouldn't stop me from another binge the next time I blew my stack. So I did the only thing possible. I ran. I figured I'd be safe here in San Francisco, where the police don't know me." He paused, and then added tiredly, "Now I'm on record already."

Mrs. Wilson looked away from him. His words had evoked an image in her mind of Jay Wilson on one of his little binges. But Jay, even at his worst, had never been like this man. Sometimes, when he had gone out drinking, he had failed to come home until dawn, and then in a pretty sodden condition. But, still, he had always come home and for at least a day even the sight of a bottle of whisky could make him ill. Jay had been a heavy drinker, but not an alcoholic. Once again, as had happened so often during the past ten years, she was proven wrong. Oh, God, she wondered, how many more times must I be faced with my own stupidity?

She glanced slyly and curiously at Morgan, who had dropped to his back on the bed and was again staring at the ceiling. He didn't look like an alcoholic, nor was he her idea of what a writer should look like. If he had said that he was in the advertising business, or sold used automobiles, or was perhaps a clerk in a department store, she would have believed him without question. But a writer— that seemed hardly to fit his highly strung nature and the glib way he talked about himself. He was probably lying to pass the time and because they were strangers. But then she noticed the sensitive mouth and the sharp alertness of his penetrating eyes, even in a weakened condition, and she had a feeling that, regardless of what his background might be, he was a man of unusual—and provocative—intelligence.

The discovery bothered her. For ten years she had been carefully avoiding unusual people, ruling out anyone who might be able to crash through the many barriers she had erected. Her days were planned, her life was serene, and she wanted nothing to alter the condition she had chosen. But give this man a little more time to get well and strong and he would probably enjoy punching holes in her defenses.

She got quickly to her feet and told him, "I must go and help Anna."

"Anna?"

"Carl's wife. She's the housekeeper. I'm having a few friends in tonight for cocktails."

He stretched his arms and rubbed his eyes and asked, "Incidentally, is there a Mr. Wilson somewhere in this establishment?"

"Not any more. I am a widow."

"Oh. Sorry."

"It's quite all right. It happened ten years ago."

He swung his head on the pillow and watched her as she left the room and closed the door. Ten years? But she couldn't be over thirty-two. That would mean her husband had died when she was only twenty-two. But a woman that young and that attractive and obviously possessing considerable wealth would certainly have married again. What the devil was the matter with her?

His imagination was titillated and he forgot his own problems and lay there thinking about her. When the door opened again he thought she was returning, but it was a stranger, a dark, little man with frog eyes who was carrying Morgan's jacket and slacks. He grinned at Morgan and held up the clothes for him to see.

"These belong to you?"

Morgan nodded. Whoever had worked them over had done a very good job.

The cleaner noticed his look of approval and his smile deepened. "Fortunate for you," he said, "we got a good tailor in the joint and there's a guy here in the city that specializes in suede. When I first seen the stuff I threw up my hands. I told Mrs. Wilson to chuck 'em in the garbage can. But now look at 'em. It's a miracle, believe me."

"And cost plenty?"

The cleaner chuckled slyly and winked at him. "No worry for you. Mrs. Wilson paid. I know what goes on here, chum. You're the third guy I seen in this apartment the past couple years." He walked to the other end of the room, put the clothes in the dressing room, and started toward the door.

Morgan called after him, "Wait a minute. Have you been doing business here very long?"

"Twelve years."

"Good. Then maybe you can satisfy my curiosity. Was the man Mrs. Wilson was married to a very old man?"

"Naw. Jay Wilson was a young squirt, maybe three-four years older'n his wife."

"Really? But to die so young—"

"He didn't die, chum. He was killed, right here in this house." The little man paused, enjoying the moment to the utmost. Then he said, "It was Mrs. Wilson who shot him to death."

Chapter Two

As soon as the cleaner had gone, Morgan got out of bed and stood unsteadily on the floor until he felt some strength in his legs. He went to his suitcase, opened it and saw that the contents were undisturbed. He got out a pair of yellow slippers and slid his arms into a light pongee robe. He found a bowl of fruit in the kitchen and selected a red apple to munch on. The slight exercise of moving about tired him, so he dropped into a leather chair by one of the windows.

He thought of what the cleaner had told him about Mrs. Wilson. Murder was dramatic and suspenseful and highly entertaining—especially when a woman such as Mrs. Wilson had played the leading role on the spotlighted stage of death.

Morgan chuckled and leaned back in the chair with his eyes half closed. His writer's imagination began immediately to hatch plots and counterplots. Because he knew virtually nothing about the principals involved, he was able to do as he pleased with what he was already calling the Wilson affair. His mind raced with all sorts of conjectures and theories. He was having a splendid time and thoroughly enjoying himself.

Morgan had the capacity to entertain himself without moving a muscle. He could lose himself in a daydream for hours on end, complete with dialogue, Technicolor, three dimensions and a story line on which he was able to hang fantastic situations and incidents and characters. Sometimes his dreaming took on such a sharpness and clarity that he was forced to drop the pose of dreamer and become a writer and critically assess the idea for book material. A large percentage of his stories was derived in such a manner. His dreams, however, were not for that purpose alone. He enjoyed them also for the passing pleasure they afforded him.

His life was composed as much of dreams as it was of solid substance. Rarely did he ever know where one left off and the other began. Though never having played the game himself, he had once written a story about a great tennis star. For the purpose of information and factual background, he had haunted tennis courts, studied rules and regulations and interviewed hundreds of players. In the end, he knew more about the game than most of the champions and so began using bits and pieces of tennis lore in dinner-table and barroom conversations. Ultimately, it was he, himself, who had been the great tennis star and could have been a champion except for an unfortunate fracture of the right ankle just before he was to play at Wimbledon. Whenever his audience was unusually sympathetic he felt such a twinge in his right ankle that he actually limped.

As a child he had learned to lie so plausibly that he was rarely challenged. He had always been the biggest liar in whatever school he attended, and during recess and lunch hours never failed to be surrounded by a gaping audience. Quite often his junior audience knew he was lying and he knew that they knew, but their pleasure in his tales was not lessened because of the fact.

The transition from free and easy amateur lying into professional writing had been so easy that he was hardly aware of having made a change. The great difference was principally in the larger audience. He was forced to become more critical and selective in the tales he put together. He was also forced to broaden his understanding of human nature, and had a better idea of what made people tick than a conference of psychiatrists. The ability to analyze, appraise and judge became instinctive with him. It was a talent that was never at rest and was always at work during his every waking moment.

Ordinarily, when he was convalescing from one of his binges, he suffered a state of depression so low that he walked on the brink of suicide. He had never made the attempt, he had never held a gun to his temple and he had never stood on the edge of a cliff, but mentally he had been so close so often that a grain of sand could have tilted the scales into the abyss.

On this occasion, however, a new element was introduced into his convalescence that shoved the old problem of self into the background. His creative faculties wrested depression from his shoulders and settled excitedly on the questions posed by Irene Wilson. It was undoubtedly the best medicine that could have been given to him.

When Dr. Rigsby arrived, just before the dinner hour, he was amazed to find his patient in far better spirits than he had anticipated. He suspected that Morgan had started drinking again, but found that not to be true and was more puzzled than ever.

He gave Morgan a hasty examination and said, "You've snapped out of it all right, but there's a lot of damage to be repaired. You need sleep—"

"I need sleep like I need a hole in the head. Rest, yes, but all I've been doing is sleeping."

"But not quite the sort of sleep you need. The main thing is food. You can eat solids from now on. Also drink a lot of milk and fruit juices between meals. I'll tell Carl what to prepare for you." He snapped his bag closed, studied Morgan, and said, "Mrs. Wilson tells me your name is O'Keefe and that you're a writer."

"That's right."

"I don't believe I've ever heard of you."

"Don't get snobbish about it. You're only one small unit of the largest organization in the world, the hundreds of millions who have never heard of O'-Keefe."

The doctor chuckled and said, "I see you have a sense of humor."

"Don't kid yourself, my friend. What passes for humor has its source in my bile. But I'll bet you're quite a card when it comes to flipping butter pats around at the Rotary luncheons."

The doctor's amiability vanished. He remembered having flipped butter pats at a Rotary luncheon and his face reddened. "Well," he grumbled, "you're getting along. A few more days and you'll be out of here."

"I'll hate to leave. This place has such an intriguing atmosphere. For the past hour or so I've been enjoying myself by wondering where she killed him: here in this room, in the hallway, on the stairs, in the study? No, not the study. I don't know why it is, but in fiction the corpse is always found in the study. Never in real life. When a gal scrags a man she doesn't give a damn where she is and she certainly wouldn't do it in the study, or even be found dead there herself. The latter is a rather dubious pun, my eminent physician."

The doctor chewed at his lower lip and his scowl deepened. "Carl wouldn't have told you."

"No. The cleaner was here a little while ago."

"He told you the whole story?"

Morgan shook his head. "All he said was that my benefactress had shot her husband to death here in this very house. He seemed quite elated about it. At least one of his customers has distinguished herself in the realm of higher dramatics. You can't say that about everyone. But tell me, Doctor, were you in on the Wilson affair?"

The doctor said stiffly, "No. I was the family physician, but I was not in on the affair, as you put it. It was an accident, you know."

"No, I didn't know. An accident, you say? Now you're ruining everything. How did it happen?"

The doctor glanced at his watch and sighed. "Sorry, but I don't have the time. However, you can read all about it right here. Mrs. Wilson has a leather-bound scrapbook filled with newspaper clippings of the tragedy. She keeps it in the study. Ask Carl to bring it to you."

Morgan squinted narrowly at the doctor, not quite sure he had heard right. "You mean to tell me she keeps a scrapbook about her accidental killing of her own husband?"

"That is correct. I have tried for years to get her to destroy it. She refuses. Frankly, Mr. O'Keefe, I have known Irene since she was a child, but I must admit I don't understand her. But then," he sighed, "none of us ever really understands another person."

Morgan said, "I do. I'm beginning to understand you only too well. I think you're strictly a society doctor and you can probably guess what that means in my dictionary."

Dr. Rigsby gasped, and then roared, "By God, but you're impertinent!"

Morgan laughed. "Not impertinent, Doctor. Impertinence implies a lack of due respect of the humble toward his superior. Of the two of us, therefore, only you could be the impertinent one."

The doctor gasped again, spun about on his heel and slammed the door as he went out. Morgan scratched his head and wondered, Now, why did I do that? The doctor was probably a nice old slob. He shrugged and forgot the incident.

Carl came into the room with his first full-course meal, and Morgan devoured it with a ravenous appetite. After having eaten he knew that he would sleep well, so decided against asking Carl for the scrapbook that night. And as long as he still knew little or nothing about what had taken place, he could make up all sorts of dreams and fantasies that would help him to sleep and stave off the depression that was normally his at that point.

He remained by the windows until it was dark, and then, as his lids began to droop, he got into bed. He heard the door open softly and turned his head to see Irene Wilson standing in the shaft of light at the doorway. She asked softly, "Are you awake, Mr. O'Keefe?"

"I just got into bed."

"Oh. I'm sorry—"

"It's okay. What's on your mind?"

"Well, nothing important, really. I just wanted to see how you were doing. Carl said that you were in such good spirits—"

He chuckled softly and said, "Forget it. Would you like to kiss me good night, Mrs. Wilson?"

"I'm afraid I don't—"

"On the other hand, maybe you'd better not. That gown you're wearing may inspire the rise of something loftier than my mind."

She gasped and slammed the door. Morgan rolled over on his side and went to sleep.

Irene started angrily down the hallway, but as she came opposite a gilt-framed full-length mirror she stopped for a moment to stare at her reflection. Contrary to what most men thought of all women, Irene did not clothe herself simply to attract men. Prior to Jay Wilson's death, she had made some effort to buy the things he liked and that were attractive to him and to other men, but since the tragedy she had had no desire to attract any man, and so bought her clothes only with an eye to what was currently fashionable. She frowned and pivoted before the mirror and for the first time realized that the cocktail gown she was wearing, though simple, was indeed cut so well and fitted her so perfectly that it revealed every line and curve of a very good figure. She was annoyed and thought of changing to something else, but there wasn't time. As she walked away from the mirror, though, she looked back once and the ghost of a smile appeared in her dark eyes.

She passed the darkened living room, which was rarely used because of its size, and went on to the softly lighted study to arrange the vases of flowers a florist had delivered that afternoon. The study was a large, outsized room that had once been the formal dining room. It was long and narrow, with a massive wall of plate glass at one end that looked north over the necklace lights of the Golden Gate Bridge. A fairly large bar, complete with sink and hidden refrigerator, had been built into one wall and elaborately stocked. There was also a large desk in a corner, book shelves, a tall, glass-faced cabinet for filing purposes and a grouping of chairs that had come from the original library. Otherwise the room looked not at all like a study and was decorated and furnished as a living room.

The upstairs, where the master bedrooms and guest rooms were located, had been left intact, but since the deaths of her parents and her subsequent marriage to Jay Wilson, Irene had made a number of changes on the main floor. Thomas Tinsley, Irene's father, a man who had enjoyed living in the grand manner, had built the house for large-scale entertainment as well as for gracious living. The kitchen wing, in fact, was equipped to handle anything from a pair of boiled eggs to a banquet for two hundred. During his life it had often been pressed to its utmost capacity and beyond.

Irene sighed as she thought of how those days had been. She had been an only child and had arrived late in the lives of her parents, so that she knew them only as middle-aged and then as elderly people. It was almost as if she had been raised by her grandparents. She had been a spoiled, arrogant, domineering child. She had been shielded so carefully that she was almost in her teens before she realized there were other people in the world who did not sit down to a formal dinner with fifty or sixty guests at least once a week.

Her world was the world of wealth and fashion and the great people who wined and dined at the Tinsley mansion. Opera stars and senators and state governors occupied the guest rooms. There were winter weeks at Palm Springs and golf events at Pebble Beach and every summer quick flights to Europe and leisurely returns on the plush liners. It came to an end in 1941 when the Tinsley yacht went off course in a heavy Pacific fog, struck a reef and went down off Point Sur. Irene's parents were lost, along with her father's partner, Jeb Wilson, and Wilson's wife. The following year Irene married Jay, the younger of the two Wilson sons, and for the first time in her life had to cope with reality.

Now she bit her lower lip and walked over to the windows to look out at the lights of the great bridge. She had failed, she knew; it was not Jay who had failed. He had tried to understand her unreasonable demands and her snobbish arrogance and he had tried to exercise patience with her, but he had been young, too, and his tolerance was limited. In the end, he had begun drinking heavily and staying out late at night and then rowing with Irene every following morning. If Jay had not been killed that summer they would have been divorced anyway, before the year ended.

She heard the door chimes, but knew that Carl would be on hand and remained where she was. When Frank and Glenna Wilson entered they had to walk the full length of the room to be greeted by Irene. Glenna's amber-green eyes narrowed and the hatred that was never far from the surface danced into view. She was positive that Irene had deliberately made them walk that far. But she touched a cheek to Irene's, forced a smile and stepped aside as Irene shook hands with Frank.

They were an oddly matched couple. Frank had just reached his fiftieth year and looked it. The fringe of hair around his bald head was white, his big frame had become heavy with flesh, his large nose and cheeks were mottled with blue veins and the constant flush of his face was caused by high blood pressure. He had once dressed as gaily as had his much younger brother, Jay, but he had become extremely conservative, and even dowdy, with the passing years. One glance at him and anyone knew instinctively his position in life, president of a bank, chairman of the board and long-time member of the Stock Exchange.

Glenna Wilson was forty-eight, and she looked almost young enough to be her husband's daughter. She was the envy and despair of all her friends and the constant amorous target of their middle-aged husbands. Her waist was still twenty-two inches, her breasts were firm and high, her hips were slim and her legs were as gracefully curved as they had ever been. Men half her age turned to smile at her on the street and tried to pick her up in cocktail lounges. Yet, except for a light henna rinse applied to her dark blonde hair—that was always worn in a full page boy—and carefully applied make-up, Glenna did absolutely nothing to keep her figure trim, her eyes clear and her skin smooth. She ate and drank whatever she pleased, she lived as hard as she pleased and she simply did not age. She was not, however, a contented woman. Her twenty-year-old daughter, Sue, was running with a fast, Bohemian crowd and Tommy, her twenty-four-year-old son, was about to make her a grandmother. But the main source of her discontent was the rapid aging of her husband and their friends. She still felt as young as she looked and she hated being constantly in the company of what she had begun referring to as "the old crowd."

Perhaps because they disliked each other so intensely, Irene was always aware of her sister-in-law's attitudes and so knew more about her than anyone else. She was the only one in the family who seemed to realize that it would not take much for Glenna to walk out on her husband and children and take off for Reno. She also knew that when and if it happened she, too, would be partially responsible, though innocently so.

Irene asked Frank to act as host, so he moved heavily to the bar as other guests began to arrive. The party was small, comprising only a dozen couples, and represented the social residue of the chipping away and wearing down of ten years. Most of Irene's friends had deserted her immediately after the tragedy. Others she had cut adrift herself when she realized that the loyalty of so many of them was based on the color of the Tinsley-Wilson millions. There were also large social groupings in the city wherein Irene was no longer welcome or acceptable. The people at the party were those who believed in Irene's innocence and, if they did not, kept it to themselves and liked her, anyway.

Irene gave her cocktail parties every other Friday night. The pattern was so well established that no one was any longer invited. They simply arrived at the proper time. The parties were never very gay and they never lasted more than a few hours. A few drinks, some hors d'oeuvres, a little chatter and the guests began drifting away to late dinners and other, more lively affairs.

This Friday night, however, was enlivened by the introduction of Morgan O'Keefe's name. Irene was standing by the fireplace, talking over business of the bank with Frank, when Nicky and Tina van Ostrand wandered over to join them. Irene smiled at her two closest friends, relieved to break off the boring conversation with Frank. Nicky was tall, slim, blond and handsome and at one time had been the target of most of the city's debutantes. It was still a surprise to everyone, even after eleven years, that he had married Tina. She was small, she was chubby, her lipstick was always the wrong shade, the best hairdressers could never do anything with her mouse-brown hair, and she made expensive gowns look like cheap hand-me-downs. Tina, however, was more of a woman than any woman had a right to be, a fact of which Nicky was happily aware. She had a vast love for humanity that encompassed almost everyone, she adored her husband and children and she had a talent for savoring every moment of living that was sheer genius. She would not have traded places with any woman in the world and Nicky, though he still had a roving eye and occasionally had to be reminded where the home pasture was located, felt exactly the same way. They were the only two people with whom Irene had absolutely no reservations.

Nicky sipped at his highball, winked at her and said, "I saw Doc Rigsby today, the old quack. He tells me you're competing with the Salvation Army again."

Frank groaned, "Oh, no. Irene, do you have another of those drunken bums in the apartment?" She nodded and he sighed, "God knows why you do it. Jay was never an alcoholic, you know."

"I've known that for years."

"Then why do you persist? If you feel you must help them, just give them some money and send them on their way. One of these days you're going to have trouble, bringing bums like that into your own home."

She arched her eyebrows and said quietly, "I have learned a great deal about alcoholics. When they reach that last step where they must have someone else's help they are in no condition to be trouble to anyone."

"But don't you allow them to convalesce here for a few days?"

"Of course."

"In which case, they get back on their feet and—"

She interrupted. "They aren't like ordinary sick people. I've never known one yet who wasn't humble and grateful and—" She paused and thought of Morgan and of the remark he had made while she was standing in his doorway, and suddenly the incongruous humor in his words struck her and she giggled.

Tina stared at her. She had heard Irene laugh a few times during the past years, but never giggle. A giggle was something new.

Intuitively she said, "This new bum doesn't fit what you were about to tell us."

Irene shook her head. "No, he doesn't. And he's not a bum. He's not like the others in any way, except for his binges. All the others have been middle-aged or old, strictly Howard Street characters. Mr. O'Keefe is something quite different. He is about in his mid-thirties, I think; he's rather handsome in a hawk-like way, and there's nothing humble about him. In fact, he's decidedly sarcastic and sometimes downright insulting, even to me."

Nicky gulped at his drink and looked at her with surprise. "You're taking him in and putting him on his feet and he still has the temerity to insult you?"

"He certainly has. I think O'Keefe's a man who would much rather have your hatred than your love. Then he knows where he stands and he doesn't have to become involved."

Tina protested, "Now, Irene—"

Nicky chuckled and said, "You'll never get Tina to believe there's anyone in the world like that."

Irene noticed that other guests were drifting over to listen, as she said, "Well, this man is that way. And the things he says about himself— One moment he seems to be the supreme egoist and the next moment he destroys himself as casually as if he were talking about a stranger. And I have a quite definite impression that he enjoys lying about himself. As I said before, he's far from being a bum, so I suppose he doesn't want me to know who he really is." She smiled. "He claims to be a writer. He says he writes dreary little books about dreary little people. Imagine."

Everyone smiled except Nicky and Tina. They stared at each other with the same thought in mind. Nicky finished his drink in one gulp and swung his eyes back to Irene. "I know this is impossible," he said, "but could this O'Keefe's first name be Morgan?"

Irene stared. "Why—why, yes. How did you—"

Nicky snorted and said, "Oh, no. This is crazy. Morgan O'Keefe?"

Tina cried, "But it has to be! That description, Nicky!"

Irene said excitedly, "My goodness, do you know the man?"

Nicky shook his head, amazed and baffled. "No. We've never met him. It's just that he happens to be my favorite writer. Tina can't stand his work. He hits too hard and too low for her tastes, but I've always been crazy about him. Morgan O'Keefe, here in this house! My God, that's hard to believe. And a drunk at that. That's even harder to swallow. But it must be the same guy. Last I heard, though, he was living in Los Angeles."

Irene said, "That's right. He came up from there only recently, about two weeks ago." All the guests had crowded around her so Irene explained why Morgan had left Los Angeles and what had happened to him in San Francisco. She felt a little guilty, as if she were exploiting a confidence, but she went on anyway, pleased by the reaction of her guests. She told them what little else she knew about Morgan and ended by saying, "So he wasn't lying, after all. I had no idea I was taking care of a celebrity."

Nicky corrected her, "Not a celebrity, Irene. I doubt if very many people have ever heard of him. He's not a popular writer. People who read him either go crazy over his work or hate the guy. I'm afraid it's mostly the latter. He has one glaring deficiency, a total lack of sympathy for the ordinary guy, or what's known as the common man. If he ever corrected that fault he could become a literary giant overnight. But to think of him here in this house, a broken-down alcoholic—God!"

Tina said, "But you must have read him, Irene."

"No, darling. The name doesn't register with me at all."

"But don't you remember? About three or four years ago I gave you a book of his. I said at the time that I couldn't understand why Nicky liked him so much, so I wanted to see what you thought."

"I guess I've forgotten all about it. Did I return the book?"

"No. It was a gift."

"In that case, I must still have it. Maybe it's here in the study."

All of them turned to the book shelves. Nicky picked it out at once. "The Long Day's End," he read aloud, "by Morgan O'Keefe." He handed the book to Irene. "There you are. Now you'll have to read it. And, believe me, I'll give ten to one you don't like it."

Irene turned the book over and looked at the author's photograph on the back of the jacket. Though his face was a bit fuller, there was no doubting that he was the man in her apartment. She felt suddenly as if a secret door had opened somewhere and a chill wind was blowing on her back.

The guests examined the book and passed it around. Nicky held forth at great length concerning the man and his works and the party did not break up until an hour or so later than usual. All of them were vastly intrigued by Irene's guest. They demanded that Irene produce him for inspection before she turned him loose, and finally she said she would let them all know as soon as he was back on his feet. Perhaps a little dinner party, or a luncheon, or a Sunday brunch, where they could all meet him.

Even Glenna Wilson was intrigued. She and Frank were the last to leave, as usual. Glenna always went directly out and down to the car, anxious to quit the house as quickly as possible. But this time she paused at the door. She was afraid that she would not be included in the group that would meet O'Keefe.

She hated to ask a favor, but she drawled, "Don't forget to include me, Irene. And Frank, too, of course. We'd like to meet this oddity of yours, too."

Frank said musingly, "He does sound interesting. You will call us, Irene?"

If it had been Glenna alone, Irene would have ignored the request. But she could not refuse Frank, and so promised to call them. As she closed the door, though, she wondered suddenly what Morgan O'Keefe would have to say about meeting her friends.

She took his book with her to bed that night, intending to read for half an hour or so. But she found that she could not put it down until she had finished it, at four in the morning. Her mind was unsettled as she fell asleep and when she awoke in the clear light of morning she was even more disturbed. No book she had ever read had had such an impact on her emotions. It was almost as if he had directed every word at her and had carved each word into her brain with hammer and chisel. The man, as a writer, took perverse pleasure in punching holes in illusions, he seemed to have pity for no one, there was humor in his tragedy and cynicism in his love and he attacked his characters as a surgeon would with a scalpel. But he did breathe amazing life into his people and made them walk and talk as human beings rather than as carefully polished fictional characters.

Irene could understand why he was not popular, but she also realized, as did Nicky, that it would take very little to make him famous. The slightest injection of sympathy into the book she had read and it would have been a great work of art. It seemed to her, from what she had read, that he had been on the verge of sympathy a number of times, but had deliberately forced himself to write away from it. Obviously he regarded any trace of sympathy as weakness. Perhaps if he changed his attitude ...

After breakfast she went into the study, where a pile of papers had been stacked for her to sign. Inasmuch as she owned three-quarters of the Tinsley-Wilson financial empire, she had certain duties that could not be relegated to anyone else. She had faith and confidence in Frank and allowed him to run the business without interference from her, and she had also given him power of attorney in some of her affairs, but some decisions she had to make herself. Saturday mornings were put aside for such matters.

She was about halfway through the papers when the butler came into the study and waited quietly at her elbow. She affixed her signature to a paper, put it aside and looked up. "Yes, Carl?"

His expression was bland as he said, "The gentleman would like to look through your scrapbook."

There was no need to ask which scrapbook he meant. It was lying before her on the desk. It was always on the desk and had been there for ten years, another form of torture in which she indulged herself. It was there for anyone to read, but she was reluctant to let Morgan O'Keefe look through it.

She put her reluctance away and nodded toward the scrapbook. "Very well. Take it to him. How is he feeling, by the way?"

"Much improved, ma'am. He says he slept well last night, and he had an excellent breakfast this morning. Shall I inform him that you think he is well enough to leave this afternoon, or perhaps this evening?"

Irene turned and stared sharply at the butler. He had never before been anxious to get rid of one of their patients. Carl not only liked helping others, but his wages were also doubled when the apartment was occupied.

"Why?" she asked.

"I guess you haven't seen this morning's paper, ma'am." He took the *San Francisco Examiner* from under his arm, folded it over to Herb Caen's column and placed it on the desk. He pointed about halfway down the column and Irene read the item, "Morgan O'Keefe, erudite but little-understood author, is currently the house guest of Mrs. Got-Rocks herself, Irene Tinsley-Wilson. Seeing as how the fabulous heiress is the very soul of charity and whereas O'Keefe is a man of exotic and numerous hates, we wonder what cooks on the front burners."

Irene was furious, but she restrained her anger. She tapped a pencil against her teeth and thought it over, then said, "Say nothing to him now. I shall tell him myself, but later."

Chapter Three

Morgan was wearing slippers, slacks and a sweatshirt when Carl came into the apartment with the scrapbook. He took the huge, leather-bound volume from the butler, thanked him and then waved him impatiently out the door.

He dropped the scrapbook onto the couch and resumed pacing the floor, puffing nervously at cigarettes which he lit one from the other. The red streaks were beginning to clear from his eyes, some color was creeping back into his hollow cheeks and his hands were steady and no longer shaking. He was still weak and had to stop pacing every once in a while to rest, but he was well on his way back to normalcy.

He knew that within another day or so he would be ready to leave, but that was the problem. Where was there to go? He was flat broke and he knew of nothing that would alter that situation within the near future.

There was only one reasonably certain way to get money, but even that would take time. The last book he had written, *Cry of The Eagle*, had run into the usual objections from his publishers, Norwood and Buttle. It was the same old complaint—that every character in the book was completely unsympathetic. Always, he thought, the same scream of anguish. Simpatico. Simpatico. A man beat his brains out to create a picture of a perfect heel and then his publishers wanted him to inject sympathy into the bastard. They had accepted the book, however, and had paid him the usual advance of $2,000, which he had managed to spend over the bars in Los Angeles a month or so before. But this particular book apparently had excited them more than his previous works, so Norwood and Buttle had offered to advance him an additional $2,000 against royalties if he would follow their suggestions for revision and rewrite to inject some sympathy into the three major characters. He had been given sufficient time to think it over.

His immediate reaction had been Nuts to that, but now he had to consider the offer. He knew he could make the changes the publishers wanted with little or no difficulty and could complete the job in a matter of three or possibly four weeks. That would be his closest approach to the smell of new money. But how was he to live during that month? It was a problem that seemed to be insoluble.

He decided finally to let it lie for the moment and dropped into the deep leather chair by the couch. He picked up the scrapbook and flipped open the cover. He stared down at the first page of a San Francisco newspaper with the screaming black headline: TINSLEY-WILSON HEIRESS KILLS PLAY-BOY HUSBAND.

Morgan frowned and looked up. Tinsley-Wilson. Why, that was one of California's great financial empires. They were in banks and lumber and land and shipping and oil and about everything else big and profitable in the state. The Irene Wilson of the vast Tinsley-Wilson enterprises! So that's who she was! Cripes, he thought, that little brunette bundle of inhibitions and frustrations is loaded to the teeth. He turned back to the scrapbook with heightened interest.

As he went through all the columns and clippings and headlines his memory stirred and he had a vague recollection of having read about the case ten years before, though then he had had a war on his hands. The tragedy had taken place after Germany had folded in Europe and the big move was on to shift all power to the Pacific to crush Japan, and the nation had been preoccupied. It had made a big splash only in the local sheets. At any other time the affair would have been nationally prominent. Morgan thought that Irene Wilson had been lucky, in a way.

He studied photographs of her and of Jay Wilson in the papers, of Frank Wilson and other members of the family, of the mansion and one of "... the fatal doorway." The latter was simply the upper hall doorway of Irene's bedroom, showing part of a bureau with a suitcase underneath it. There were also sketches of the upper floor plan with a large X where the body of Jay Wilson was found in the hallway, and sketches of the stairs and the lower hallway where the prowler was captured by Frank Wilson.

Morgan settled back and read through all the accounts of the killing, his own problems forgotten. It was not a complicated affair, in the beginning. A vicious prowler by the name of Joe Scapini had been operating in the Pacific Heights area for a number of months without being caught. He broke into mansions late at night and stole whatever he could find and carry away, which was normal operating procedure for a second-story worker. He differed from others, however, in the fact that he minded not at all being accosted by his victims. Whenever a sleepy homeowner investigated a strange noise, the prowler seemed to take grim delight in pistol-whipping the victim. He had put three men in hospitals and had also beaten a helpless woman almost to the point of death. The citizens of Pacific Heights, therefore, were understandably terrorized.

Most of them began keeping guns by their bedsides, as did the Wilsons. Jay Wilson bought a .38 revolver for his wife, told her how to use it and to keep it lying on the night stand by the side of her bed. It developed later that she had never before fired any pistol, including the one Jay Wilson had purchased for her.

On the fatal night, Jay Wilson had been downtown drinking with some friends at a hotel cocktail lounge, but had gone home earlier than usual, just before midnight. Mrs. Wilson claimed later that she had not heard her husband return and did not know he was at home. She had been in bed and asleep for perhaps an hour when she was awakened suddenly by a noise and, as she described it, a feeling that someone was standing by the side of her bed. The bedroom door was open, though she had closed it earlier, and she could see the glow of a tiny night light burning in the hallway. But it was dark within the bedroom and as she awakened with a start she saw the form of a man in the doorway. She was still mostly asleep and thought at the moment that the man was fully dressed and also that he was much shorter than her husband. She thought instantly of the prowler and, believing she was home alone—the servants had been fired two days before—she was frightened out of her wits. She was not sure whether she screamed, but she remembered grabbing for the pistol and holding it in both hands as she turned it in the direction of the doorway and pulled the trigger. She thought she fired twice, but on examination it was learned that only one cartridge had been fired.

The form disappeared and she heard someone fall and groan in the hallway. She heard also the sound of running footsteps. It was a minute or two before she could summon enough courage to get out of the bed and investigate. When she stepped into the hallway it was her husband she saw on the floor. He had apparently taken a few steps before falling. He was in his pajamas, lying in a pool of blood. He was already quite dead.

Mrs. Wilson was not at all sure of what followed. She was never able to re-member, but the subsequent events were easily put together. She had gone in-stantly to the telephone and called her husband's older brother, Frank. Then she had returned to the hallway, where the shock of what had happened swept over her and she became hysterical and collapsed on the floor by her husband.

Frank Wilson had been at his home, a block away, at the time and had not yet gone to bed. When the call came from his sister-in-law and he grasped what had happened his first thought was of his brother, rather than of calling the police. He ran the block to his brother's home and let himself in with a key he had to the front door. He flicked on the lights of the lower hall and made for the stair-way, only to come to an astonished halt. Joe Scapini, the prowler, had obviously been on the upper floor, had heard the shot and had tried to get away. But in leaping down the stairs he had tripped and fallen, and was lying in the lower hallway with a broken leg when Frank Wilson arrived. Fortunately for Wilson, for the first time in the prowler's career he was unarmed.

Frank Wilson saw that the man couldn't move, so he ran on up the stairs. The shock of what he found there unnerved him so much that it was minutes before he was able to take action. He called the police department and reported what had happened. At the same time he called a hospital to send an ambulance for his sister-in-law, knowing that when she came around she was going to need medical attention. The hospital was only a few blocks away, so the ambulance arrived immediately and Mrs. Wilson was gone a moment or two before the po-lice reached the house. The lieutenant from Homicide was understandably an-gered by Mrs. Wilson's quick removal, and instantly dispatched two officers to the hospital to interview her. Mrs. Wilson was already under sedatives and it was three days before the shock wore off sufficiently so that she could talk co-herently.

A coroner's jury later ruled that the killing was an accidental homicide.

Frank Wilson was enraged by the finding of the coroner's jury. He was con-vinced that Mrs. Wilson had deliberately murdered her husband and had the whole case rammed through to the attention of the Grand Jury, where he sought an indictment for murder. It was his contention, and he was not alone in his belief, that Mrs. Wilson had simply seized upon a provident opportunity to do away with her husband. He claimed that she had not been asleep and that she had known her husband was in his own bedroom. It was probably Jay who had opened her bedroom door to tell her he was home before going to his own room. Later she had heard the prowler in the house and had seen and identi-fied her husband standing in her doorway, who had also undoubtedly heard the prowler and had come out of his room to investigate. The situation was made to order for her, and she acted upon it. She killed her husband deliberately, knowing that under the circumstances the odds were all in her favor that the killing would appear to be accidental.

A number of factors could have inspired her to commit the deed. Witnesses testified before the Grand Jury that the Jay Wilsons were on the verge of divorce. It was brought out in court that, although Jay Wilson was merely a social drinker, his wife accused him of being an alcoholic. She nagged at him constantly because of his drinking; she accused him of running around with other women—which was determined not to be true—and during the weeks prior to his death had had many explosive scenes with him while others were present. It was also easily determined that she was a badly spoiled and arrogant young woman who enjoyed the power of the Tinsley-Wilson empire.

That, to Morgan, seemed to be the crux of the whole matter. He learned from the clippings that the elder Messrs. Tinsley and Wilson had each owned fifty per cent of their organization. Upon their deaths, therefore, the two Wilson sons inherited half of the vast empire and Irene Tinsley inherited the other half. When she married Jay he had his will made out to her as sole beneficiary. Upon his death she came into an additional twenty-five per cent of the financial barony, giving her a total of three-quarters, or major control. Frank Wilson contended that the killing had been deliberate to secure that control.

The Grand Jury, however, thought otherwise. It did not seem likely to them that anyone could have so acted on the spur of the moment. Furthermore, there actually had been a prowler in the house who had been apprehended and was in custody. But the clincher lay in the fact that no one could disprove Mrs. Wilson's statement that she had never before fired that particular pistol or any other. It was highly unlikely that she would have chosen a weapon with which she was totally unfamiliar, and even more unlikely that she would have actually managed to hit anyone with it, except, of course, through sheer accident. The Grand Jury refused to indict and the case was dropped.

There was one final clipping, a year later, to the effect that Joe Scapini had been killed by another convict in a knife fight in San Quentin.

Morgan put the scrapbook aside and got up to resume pacing the floor. He thought better on his feet. As he paced he thought of all he had read and fitted the details together in his mind. He considered it from two angles, that of the unfortunate woman who had killed her husband accidentally, and of the other, the more interesting angle, of the woman who had deliberately killed her husband at a propitious moment. The latter was not at all unlikely. Many people had, many times before, killed others with weapons with which they were totally unfamiliar. Women, especially, seemed to have a wonderful talent in that direction. Normally they couldn't hit a barn at ten paces, but when it came to aiming at a lover or a husband they seemed to suddenly acquire the deadly accuracy of a sharpshooter. And they didn't mind trying.

What if she had fired and missed? Her claim would merely remain the same, that she had thought she was firing at a prowler. She had nothing to lose either way. It was easy to see, however, why the Grand Jury had refused to indict. There was really no evidence that could be used against her. Frank Wilson, therefore, could have had good cause for his suspicions and accusations. Morgan wondered what subsequently had happened to him.

He was still thinking about it at the noon hour when the butler came to ask him if he would like to lunch with Mrs. Wilson on the terrace. Morgan accepted enthusiastically. He followed the butler through the study and out to the sun-flooded terrace.

Where the mansion was built, on the north side of Pacific Street, the ridge fell off steeply toward the Marina district below. The structure, therefore, was built out over the slope on a level higher than the roofs of the buildings on the lower street. There was an unobstructed and breathtaking view of all of the north bay, the Golden Gate, Marin, Mount Tamalpais, Alcatraz, Angel Island and, on the north side, the yachting centers of Belvedere and Tiburon. Morgan had seen most of the great panoramas of the world, but knew of nothing to exceed the view before him.

Irene watched him standing there for a long moment, and then said, "Beautiful, isn't it? I've lived here all my life, but I never tire of it."

Morgan filled his lungs deeply with the salt air and turned to look at her. She was seated at a wrought iron, glass-topped table covered with bowls of fruit, glassware and luncheon service. She was wearing a simple cotton frock and sandals, and she seemed to be at ease. But it was a forced ease; he noticed the nervous play of her fingers on the table. *Already she regrets inviting me to join her,* he thought.

He walked to the edge of the terrace to look down at a tennis court and noticed the missing net and the faded white lines. Apparently it had not been used in years. He glanced over a formal garden beyond the court, then turned to drop into a chair facing his hostess at the table.

"You're a lucky woman," he said. "A person could just sit here and soak in this view and tell the rest of the world to go to hell. Now I can understand why you've remained in this house. And I suppose it's also your way of telling the world to go to hell, as well."

Carl brought out two bowls of fresh strawberries and placed them on the table. She waited for him to leave before replying. "You've read through the scrapbook?"

"How did you know I was reading it?"

"I was in the study when Carl picked it up."

He shook his head. "You're a strange woman. Anyone else would never want anything around to remind them of that tragedy, yet you keep a public scrapbook of the whole affair. Why?"

She said stiffly, "It's a personal reason."

He had to chuckle. "Well, naturally. What else would it be? All you really have to say is that it's none of my damned business. But you can't stop me from guessing. I know a character down in Hollywood who once did some time in prison. He's a big man now, one of the fat-cat producers in the business, and probably no one would ever know he had a record. But on the wall of his office is a framed release signed by the warden of the prison. It's a constant reminder to anyone who looks at it that the big man had once been a bum, and even a thief. One day he told me why it was there. He's afraid that if he tried to hide his past someone else would be sure to drag it out in the open and, because he's such a big target now, the whole thing would be exaggerated. So he beats the world to the punch with that scrap of paper on the wall and, by so doing, he doesn't have to worry about it. Are you beating the world to the punch?"

Her eyes dropped away from his and she began to eat. He shrugged and turned his attention to his own dish. He thought she wasn't going to reply, but she sat back suddenly and said, "It's not quite the same. Perhaps, in a way, I am beating the world to the punch, but it goes beyond that, too, just as I think it does with your friend. You see, Mr. O'Keefe, there are many people in this city who do not believe my husband's death was an accident."

"I figured as much."

"Yes. I had literally hundreds of friends and acquaintances who were convinced that I—that I was a deliberate killer. They still feel that way. You are apparently a man of imagination. What was your opinion after going through the clippings?"

He grinned. "You want my honest opinion?"

Her face colored. She nodded and whispered, "Yes."

"The hell you do, but I'll give it to you, anyway. Maybe it was an accident. I wouldn't know. The point is, though, that it could have been deliberate. The motive was strong, the weapon was at hand and the situation was perfect. It's far more interesting to me, as a writer, to think—"

He broke off as Carl came out with a plate of cold cuts, salads and relishes. As soon as he had gone, Irene said, "That's what I mean. Too many people considered what they called motives, rather than the person behind them. Merely because my husband and I weren't getting along and because, upon his death, I would inherit his share of the estate to add to my own, I was supposed to be capable of murder." She paused for a moment, her dark eyes flaming with suppressed fury. "The fact that it would have been a simple solution to divorce my husband seems not to have entered their minds. Murder is easier. And the additional fact that I already possessed a fortune far in excess of anything I could possibly use also didn't count. I had to be greedy and want more, and murder was the way to achieve it. Even after all these years it's impossible for me to understand that kind of thinking."

"Nevertheless," he said pointedly, "you have an odd feeling of guilt."

She glanced across at him, and the anger she felt was turned in his direction. He started to say something, noticed her expression and thought better of it. She was no longer in a mood to pursue the conversation.

Morgan ate and waited patiently. Sooner or later, he knew, she would return to the subject, and he was not at all surprised when she did so over coffee. Irene, however, was the surprised one. During the ten years following the tragedy Irene had never explained herself to anyone. Arrogance had been responsible at first, and then hurt, and then pride. Her reasons for keeping the scrapbook she had always kept to herself. Her reasons for helping alcoholics she kept to herself. Her reasons for doing anything she kept to herself and, she told herself repeatedly during the meal, she certainly had no intention of explaining herself to this man, this alcoholic, this object of charity, this perfect stranger.

Yet, she thought, the man was a writer and, from what she had learned from his one book, he had a certain amount of insight. It was possible—highly probable—that his judgments were warped and perverted, but even so they would be interesting. The compulsion to explain grew in her so strongly that, by the end of the meal, she was no longer able to control it.

She crossed her slim legs and sat back in the chair. "You speak of a feeling of guilt," she said. "Exactly what sort of guilt did you have in mind?"

Morgan took a sip of his coffee. "As I said before, I don't know if you scragged your husband or not—"

She blinked at him. "Scragged?"

"Erased. Murdered. Got rid of. A slang expression."

She snapped at him, "If I had thought this subject was humorous to you—"

"Now, now. Don't get in a pet. Maybe I do see humor in what was sheer tragedy to you. Why shouldn't I? I'm grateful to you for your helping hand, but that doesn't mean I have any sympathy for you, or even liking, and it certainly doesn't mean my heart is bleeding for you."

"Well," she gasped, "of all things—"

"Does honesty always shock you that way? Anyway, let's get back to this guilt idea. If you scragged your husband—incidentally, I'm using that word deliberately now—but if you did, then naturally you would have a feeling of guilt and there's nothing more to be said about it. But if it was an accident, your feeling of guilt—as displayed in keeping the scrapbook and helping characters such as yours truly—has its birth in another source. From what I read, I gather that you thought your husband was an alcoholic and nagged him about it rather constantly. So?"

Irene was momentarily confused, and didn't know what to say. The conversation had taken a turn she had not anticipated and control had passed from her hands to his.

She said haltingly, "I—well, I was rather young at the time—my attitude toward drinking was established by my father, who never drank unless he was with guests and—Well, yes, I was very much wrong about Jay." She sighed and said, "To be perfectly honest with you, Mr. O'Keefe, I did nag at him for something of which he was not at all guilty. I've known for a long time now that I was wrong, and I have been paying for it ever since."

Morgan smiled and spread his hands. "You see how easy it is? There we have it. You feel guilty and you're doing penance by helping characters who really are alcoholics. By the way, do you do this very often?"

"No. Not really. You're only the second this year."

He laughed abruptly and scratched his hawklike nose. "In other words, you wear sackcloth and ashes only when the mood moves you. It's a lot more convenient that way, isn't it?"

She moved angrily, but she bit back her words, and then she could not restrain a smile. "I suppose you're right. I'm not really a do-gooder." She paused to wonder why she was actually enjoying this conversation. She supposed it was even stimulating to talk with someone who was completely objective where she was concerned. That was so rare that she doubted if she had ever experienced it before.

Her attitude of ease was no longer forced and she was relaxed as she said thoughtfully, "I made such a ghastly error with my husband about his drinking that it ruined our marriage. So I have been paying for that error by occasionally helping others who really need help. My conscience doesn't trouble me too much, however, because I get bored and turn away many more than I help. I came very close to turning you away. I wonder what would have happened to you if I had?"

Morgan knew what would have happened and shuddered. He did not want to dwell upon it or return to his own problems. He said quickly, "All right, we've resolved that. But the scrapbook is a different matter. How do you explain that?"

"That," she said, no longer surprised by her confessions. "I don't really know the answer. Perhaps it lies in many reasons rather than in just one. I didn't start it in the first place, you see. At no time did I ever save a clipping from the newspapers, or even think of doing so. One day, quite by accident, I learned that my brother-in-law, Frank Wilson, had put such a scrapbook together. That is the one you read. I had never read many of the news reports myself, so I borrowed the scrapbook from Frank. Maybe I wanted to torture myself. I don't know. Anyway, I borrowed it and then I asked to keep it and it wound up in the study. I guess I began to feel that if anyone had any twisted ideas on the subject—well, there was the factual report to look through and set them straight."

"Which all comes back to what I said before; you're beating the world to the punch." He looked about the terrace and up at the granite façade of the house. "And so you continue living here, where it happened. It's amazing."

She drank the last of her coffee, shoved the cup aside and shook her head. "Not really. I went away for a while—seven or eight months. When I came back I meant to close or sell the house and live elsewhere. But that was when I first learned that so many people thought I was guilty of shooting my husband deliberately. It was a shock, a terrible shock. Except for a very few people, I hadn't thought that anyone doubted my story. But then, to my horror, I learned that doors were closed to me everywhere, various clubs and organizations dropped me from membership lists and people I had thought were close friends cut me dead on the street." She bit her lower lip, reliving the agony of those days. "At first I was so appalled I wanted to run and hide, anywhere, it didn't matter where. But when the initial shock wore off I became angry—"

"And," he interrupted, "you decided to show the world."

"Yes. Something like that. I felt that by running I would be confirming the opinions of those who thought I was guilty. So I did the reverse. I not only remained in the city, but also moved back into my own home. I'm glad now that I did."

Morgan leaned back in his chair and stretched and yawned. "You're a remarkably stupid woman. I thought you might have some intelligence, but I see that I was wrong."

She gasped. "Why, you—you—"

"Don't say it. You'll hate yourself later. How else could I think of you? All right, I admit that it took courage to move back into this house and that you were being a brave girl and perhaps even sensible to snarl back at the pointers-with-scorn. I admire a fighter, sometimes. But a year or so in this hotel would have achieved all you wished. Longer than that is nonsense. What you've done to yourself since then can be classed only as stupidity. Instead of making some attempt to wipe out the past and start a new life, you've forced yourself to live with a corpse. You could have rediscovered sex, you could have married again, and could have had children, you could have lived a full life. But by remaining in this house as long as you have you drape the mantle of the past about your shoulders, you're reminded constantly of the tragedy, all of your friends are reminded of it, and anyone new who comes along is almost immediately made aware of it. You've mummified what would otherwise be an attractive and desirable body and you buried yourself with your husband. I ask you seriously how stupid can a woman get?"

Irene shoved back her chair and got angrily to her feet. "You arrogant tramp!" she cried. "You accept the shelter of this house, my charity, my food—"

He laughed. "Send me a bill, lady."

"Common courtesy, decency—"

"Throw in gratitude and forget the others. I'm grateful, but I'm rarely courteous, and decency I sometimes wonder about. All of it doesn't mean that I'm blind."

She started to turn away.

He said, "Wait a minute," and curiosity brought her to a halt. "I'll tell you something else, Mrs. Wilson. You're very neatly put together. Normally, now that I'm getting my manhood back, I'd be making a terrific play for you at this point. Maybe you're no good in bed—I have a hunch that's probably true—but I'd certainly be interested enough to find out." She flushed. He smiled as he continued, "That would be normal. But there's this house to consider and the scrapbook and the smell of death in the air. Normal reactions go out the window. You see what I mean? The stage setting is all wrong. That's why I say you're not really very bright. With another setting, another background, you and I might have a ball for ourselves. But when you deliberately bury yourself in a tomb—"

He broke off as she whirled and left the terrace. He got up and smoked a cigarette as he looked out over the broad panorama. His mind turned away from Irene as completely as if she no longer existed. When he left the terrace the view he had been looking at was still in his mind, and his hostess was forgotten. He saw her in the study and came to a halt and for a moment looked at her absently. She was standing stiffly by the desk staring at him. He wondered why she was blinking back hot tears.

He asked mildly, "Something wrong?"

"You!" she snapped. "Never in my life has anyone dared speak to me the way you have."

He remembered their conversation. He smiled and said, "You have a talent for choosing the right word. Dared is exactly it. You're loaded with that beautiful green stuff and obviously you have a lot of power in your particular world. But I have nothing to sell you and you have nothing to sell me, so in me you're looking at someone who doesn't give a damn about holding your hand and patting you on the head and telling you how sweet you are."

"That's obvious enough."

"Then why not accept the fact and perhaps even profit from it? You may learn something that might do you some good. Who knows?"

She said sarcastically, "I suppose you writers consider yourselves psychiatric geniuses as well?"

He walked toward her and sat on the edge of the desk, dangling one thin leg. He looked amused. "You have a point there. I think most writers instinctively know more about human nature than psychiatrists are ever able to learn. One thing we know, you see, is never to trust the word."

She looked perplexed. "The word?"

"Yes. Any word. After you have been dealing with words for a certain length of time and twisting them about to suit whatever purpose you have in mind you inevitably become deeply distrustful of them. You begin to know the limitations of the written and spoken word and you learn that feeling is to be trusted far more than the word. Psychiatrists don't know that. At least the ones I've known don't know it."

"I don't follow—"

"It's simple enough. Psychiatrists tag you with a word. You're a paranoiac, or a schizophrenic, or a simple neurotic, or something else that labels you. The only way the psychiatrist can get at you, you see, is to pin you with a word or a combination of words and so catalogue you neatly in his files."

Her anger was dissipated and she was again interested in Morgan. "But if a person really is, let us say, a paranoiac—"

"Now, there, you see, is where you and the psychiatrists turn down the wrong road. No one is a paranoiac—not even a paranoiac. You are a collection of cells and blood and bone and of so many years of living and so many years of thinking and so many thousands of ideas and fancies and dreams and bits of reality and so you, as you, are absolutely unique. There is no other you anywhere in the universe, and regardless of certain psychotic tendencies you may have that appear to be similar to the tendencies of others, you are nevertheless different and there is nothing about you that can be labeled by a single word or by any combination of words. Which is why I maintain that any creative writer would have a feeling about the sort of person you are that would be a hell of a lot closer to the real you than anything a psychiatrist could put into words."

She frowned and looked away from him. "But still, you would also have to put that feeling into words, wouldn't you?"

He burst out laughing and got to his feet. "There you have me. Yes, I would also have to put that feeling into words, and I would run into the same limitations the psychiatrist faces. However, I do have one advantage. I would be distrustful of my own words and I would not be inclined to label you." He was not inclined to pursue the subject any farther. He walked by her, then turned. "If you don't mind, I have a few problems of my own to face. Maybe you can help by telling me when you intend turning me out into the cold, cruel world."

She was slow to return to reality. "Well, I don't know. I was thinking— You're feeling better, aren't you?"

"Sure. My appetite has returned, food stays where it belongs, I'm able to sleep and, as you can see, I'm ambulatory."

"You look a little weak, though."

"Naturally enough. After the beating I've given myself it will take at least a month to really get back on my feet. All in due time."

She thought of the item in the newspaper and she knew that if he remained longer rumors could really begin to fly. She also considered that he aroused her easily to anger, that he was arrogant and insulting and that in spite of his protestations of gratitude he probably felt that any help he received was his just due. He was thoroughly despicable and under no circumstances should he be allowed to stay in the house even one night more.

She started to tell him so, but when she looked into the mocking eyes she bit her lip and said, "Suppose we wait until Monday. We can discuss it then."

Chapter Four

Morgan got the address of the house from the butler, who was in the hallway, and went on to his own apartment. He closed the door, lifted the telephone at the desk and called Western Union. He dictated a wire to Earl Bester, his agent in New York, reading: "Will rewrite book as suggested by Norwood and Buttle stressing simpatico all the way. Meanwhile, am flat and need any advance possible. Wire money order immediately to accompanying address. Love and kisses. Morgan." He charged the cost of the wire to Irene Wilson without giving it a second thought. Earl would not get the wire at his office until Monday, but at least he knew that he had that much grace. On the other hand, he didn't really expect the wire to achieve anything. It was better than doing nothing at all and—who knew—maybe a miracle would happen.

He was feeling tired again, so he stretched out on the bed and slept for a few hours. Later he paced the floor, had dinner alone, read the newspapers Carl brought to him and finally undressed and went to bed. He awakened at dawn, and knew that it would be at least a few hours before the butler would put in an appearance with breakfast. He got the carbon of *Cry of The Eagle* out of his suitcase and settled back in a chair to read it through.

The publishers wanted sympathy and sympathy they would get. It was his only chance to get back on his feet, but he hated the task he was facing. Because of his experiences, bitter acid had seeped into his brain, and he had taught himself to believe that sympathy and pity were synonymous with weakness and ignorance. The taste of his writing, therefore, was too harsh for the average palate and created more enemies than friends. He knew it well, and he didn't care.

It took him only two hours to scan through the manuscript and refresh his memory of what he had written. At the end he knew precisely what had to be done to meet the publishers' request, but it made him almost physically ill to think of it. He wanted to get out of the apartment and away from the manuscript, so when Carl came for the breakfast dishes, Morgan asked where Mrs. Wilson might be.

Carl glanced at the warm sun streaming through the windows and replied, "I believe she is taking the sun on the roof deck, sir. She usually does on a morning like this."

"Not a bad idea. How do you get to the roof deck?"

"Up to the second floor, sir, and at the west end of the hallway you'll see a narrow stairway going up to the roof." He hesitated. "But if I were you, sir—I don't know—Mrs. Wilson may not wish to be disturbed."

"Well, I'll think about it."

He thought about it for ten or fifteen minutes after the butler had gone and decided to ignore the warning. He felt like talking with her and that was all that counted. To hell with her privacy. She should be grateful that he would bother himself to seek out her company.

He put on slacks and sweatshirt, went up to the second floor and had no difficulty finding the narrow stairway. When he stepped out onto the roof he saw that half of the broad expanse had been floored with tile. Flowers and tubbed bushes were scattered about and there were beach chairs, iron tables topped with huge umbrellas and the kind of flat couches found about barbecue patios. The view from the roof was spectacular and unobstructed in all directions, yet privacy was complete.

At first he did not see Irene and walked across the deck toward the far edge. He saw her then lying on a large mattress of sponge rubber that was covered with a Mexican blanket. She was on her back, with an arm crossed over her eyes. Except for a towel around her hair, she was nude.

Morgan came to a halt and caught his breath as his eyes swept over the clean lines and curves of her body. She was completely tanned, without any areas of white flesh. He was startled to see his book, *The Long Day's End*, propped against the side of the mattress. He had no way of knowing that she was reading it through a second time.

He started to turn, intending to go quietly away when her arm lowered from her eyes. Her lids were pressed tightly closed, her dark brows were drawn together, and her lips were parted either in rapture or in agony. She had been crying. For a moment, Morgan almost pitied her.

She opened her eyes and blinked into the sun without seeing anything. But then she turned on her side, looked up and saw him standing a few feet away. She stared, and then gasped. She sat up with a jerk and reached frantically for the beach robe at her side. She pulled it quickly over her smooth shoulders and tried to drape it about her body. She did not succeed in covering a great deal.

Morgan smiled and said, "I'm sorry, Mrs. Wilson. I had no idea of surprising you this way and I was just about to leave—"

She flushed deeply and hot anger glowed in her eyes. "You had no right to come up here."

"The butler told me—"

"He certainly could not have said that I'd welcome you up here. Didn't he tell you—"

"Well, I must admit, he didn't think you'd want to be disturbed. But I felt like talking to you and, as I say, I didn't realize—"

She pulled at the robe and glared at him. "You are a man of uncommon nerve, Mr. O'Keefe. For anyone to have the unmitigated gall—"

Morgan burst out laughing. "Oh, shut up, for God's sake. I didn't come up here to rape you. So what if I did catch you in the nude? Yours isn't the first body I've gazed upon and I doubt if it will be the last. If you want I'll strip down, too, and then we'll be on even terms. Maybe we could start a nudist colony up here. At least, it would be a damned sight more entertaining for you than lying here alone and crying."

She caught her breath and brushed the back of her hand quickly across her eyes. The robe fell away from her body and again she snatched at it and pulled it across her. She turned away from him and whispered huskily, "You—you saw me crying?"

"Not exactly. But the puddles were there." He stepped across her legs and dropped into a low beach chair facing her. She frowned at him, still unhappy about his presence, but he no longer cared. He leaned forward with his elbows on his knees and his bony chin resting on his fists. "Do you cry that way very often?"

"Not often," she whispered.

"What prompted you this time—self-pity?"

She tugged at the robe angrily. "Are you really such a cynic, or is that a pose?"

"A little of each, probably. I have all sorts of poses. But don't we all? You have a rather bedraggled pose yourself, that of the long-suffering tragedienne."

"You honestly think I'm posing?"

He shrugged. "Partly, I think. Quite by accident you killed a man and the man was your husband. Incidentally, I have made up my mind that it was an accident."

She said coldly, "Thank you so much."

"Think nothing of it. Anyway, what happened to you was a terrible thing to happen to anyone. In the beginning you must have suffered badly. But to keep at it all these years required conscious effort on your part, and that's where posing creeps in."

"You know, you have the most amazing misconceptions of what people are really like. I'm surprised you've been able to get anything published."

"I could have written that statement for you. People always say that when they don't like what I have to say about them." He nodded at his novel. "Like the book?"

She twisted about to get her arms into the sleeves of the robe and bared her firm breasts for a moment. She sighed with embarrassment and anger.

"I don't know," she said. "I read it the other night. Now I'm going through it again."

"You flatter me."

"I just can't make up my mind about it. You have such a horrible way of drawing your characters; yet they're rather fascinating, too."

"I lie about everything else, Mrs. Wilson, but never about my characters. I put them down exactly as I see them."

"The way you see them, though, is so distorted. I suppose that's why you're an alcoholic. Your attitude toward everything is distorted."

He clasped his hands behind his head and leaned back in the chair, watching her from under narrowed lids. "At one time," he said, "I was a normal, social drinker. Then the Army got hold of me. I've been an alcoholic ever since."

She wanted to hurt him. "What an adolescent, schoolboy attitude that is! The Army got hold of millions of men, but it didn't make alcoholics out of them."

"It did to the ones with imagination, or it damaged them in other ways. It wasn't so bad in the big war. Those years I had a rifle in my hands and there was the comradeship of the frightened men and boys at my side. There was also the knowledge that we were doing something big. I hated being in uniform and I hated the Army, but even so I felt that what we were doing was right and I came out of it undamaged. I was one of the lucky ones."

"But you said—"

"That happened in the Korean fracas. I was recalled to duty in nineteen-fifty. Meanwhile, I had become a professional writer, a man of imagination, the worst sort of man ever to put into uniform. I don't think I could have made the grade again even if I had been sent into combat and even if I had believed again that I was part of something big. But I never saw combat and I was sick and disgusted with a stinking war being waged by politicians. I didn't even get out of this country, by the way."

Irene leaned forward with interest. "But then you must have had it very easy. Think of the men who did go into combat and were killed or wounded."

"That," he said dryly, "I would have preferred. That would have been easy— maybe. I don't know. In fact, I don't know why I'm telling you this, except for the ecstatic pleasure I get out of hearing my own voice. You would have to know the Army to understand. I was a second lieutenant; I started with that rank in forty-two and I ended with that rank in fifty-two. I was probably the oldest second lieutenant in the Army, and rightly so. I should never have been more than a buck private."

She said intuitively, "You dislike officers."

"That's an understatement. I was one of the privileged class and I thoroughly despised them. If I had been an enlisted man I might have come out of it all right. But I was an officer and so I was trapped."

"I'm afraid I don't understand."

"And I don't think you ever will. When I was recalled to duty it was learned that I had become a writer, that I had some sort of audience scattered about the country, and that I had access to publishers, editors and so on. There was a certain colonel who decided to use me to benefit himself personally. He was in Purchasing in Los Angeles and had me put on his staff. I was never able to get away. I squirmed and I screamed to be transferred and all he had to do to damn me was to stamp 'Satisfactory' on my record, which is the lowest dirty name you can call an officer, and there I stayed. An enlisted man could have managed to get loose, but not an officer."

"You say he wanted to use you? How?"

"Very simple. He was bucking for a brigadier's star. A little publicity goes a long way in the Army, you know. So I became this jerk's personal writer. For two long years I sat at a lousy desk in Los Angeles and did all this bastard's writing for him. Army writing. Speeches, orders about how to shine shoes and buttons, bits of the colonel's battle wisdom for Army periodicals, the colonel's cheerful letters to parents concerning their darlings, menus for the day—"

"Oh, no."

"Really. I even wrote a piece about the fascinating problems of Purchasing, supposedly written by the colonel, of course, that managed to find publication in a national magazine. That was the one that got him his star. But by that time

I had cracked. The dreariness of the life, the snobbery surrounding me, fighting a battle not for the sake of my country but merely to pin a star on a heel, the fact that I was trapped, that there was no way out short of a court-martial—it all got to be too much. I went to pieces. I blew my stack. The day the jerk got his star I got drunk. That night I staggered into his quarters and beat the living hell out of him. He wasn't my size, so I can't brag about that, but I am proud of smearing his blood all over his damned, ignorant face.

"All hell broke loose. I suppose I would have been shot or something, but there was a little matter that saved my life. This moron had at least sense enough to know that he wasn't capable of writing the piece that got his star for him and that I would certainly bring out that fact if I ever had to face a court-martial." He paused and grinned tightly. "He interceded on my behalf, cut everything off before it could get started, and had me tucked away neatly in a psycho ward where I could do no damage to anyone."

Irene cried, "How perfectly ghastly!"

"No, not exactly. By that time I really was a psycho. It was pretty rough taking the crap the pink-cheeked Army psychiatrists were dishing out to me, but I kept giving them the answers they wanted and in five months I was discharged. So it worked out rather well. However, I'm still psychotic about anything concerning the Army. When something goes badly for me I get the same feeling I had the day I blew my stack, a sort of overpowering sickness, and so I go for the bottle and try to drink it out."

"But if you know what it is, as long as you realize—"

He shook his head. "I still get sick. As a matter of fact, even talking about it now, I don't feel too good. Let's drop it."

She persisted, "But being able to talk about it this way—"

His face colored. "God damn it, I said to drop it. I know when I've gone far enough. What the hell do you know about it?"

She was surprised to hear herself saying humbly, "I—I'm sorry."

He was surprised, too, and blinked. "I'm sorry, too. I'll tell you one thing more before we drop the alcoholic soul of Morgan O'Keefe back where it belongs, in the gutter. I don't drink because I like the taste of alcohol. In fact, I don't even taste it any more. I drink strictly for the sting in my throat and what it does to me. Sometimes I've wondered what would happen if I just tried to drink normally again. Maybe if I tried a little drinking between these terrible compulsive binges—you know?" She nodded and he said, "But I'm afraid. I'm afraid now that alcohol is associated with that sick feeling and any attempt to try it normally would simply lead into another binge. So I can't try. I just don't dare. Now then, let's drop the whole dreary subject."

She asked him then what his plans were for the future. He told her about the new manuscript and what the publishers wanted and what had to be done. "The job will take anywhere from three weeks to a month. I know exactly what they want; they've always wanted the same thing, so there's no problem there.

However," he sighed, "there is the economic difficulty of living for that month."

"You have no resources of any kind?"

"None. Maybe that's why I wanted to talk to you this morning. Maybe my subconscious was prodding me into putting the bite on you. It wouldn't take a great deal to keep me going, and once the job is finished I could repay your loan."

Whenever one of her alcoholic patients departed the house, Irene had always handed out a twenty-dollar bill. She had never budged from that twenty-dollar rule. What Morgan was asking would amount to considerably more than that. There was also the suspicion in her mind that if she advanced him a loan sufficient to carry him for a month he would simply go off on another binge and then be back on her hands again.

"I don't know," she said. "Maybe. I'll have to think it over."

Morgan was embarrassed and said, "Sure," and got to his feet.

She stood up with him, the robe fully wrapped about her body now. "This noon," she told him, "my brother-in-law and his wife and some friends are dropping by for brunch. It should be beautiful on the terrace. Why don't you join us, Mr. O'Keefe?"

He smiled and shook his head. "Thanks, but no. You say your brother-in-law? Would that be the Frank Wilson who tried to get you indicted?"

"Yes."

"Now I'm the one who doesn't understand."

"Well," she said, "let's say he had a change of heart. At first he was absolutely positive that I had deliberately murdered his brother. When the Grand Jury refused to indict me, he almost went wild. I was even afraid, for a while, that he might try to exact vengeance upon me himself. That was one of the reasons why I left the city. But when I returned he had changed completely and was the first person to call on me."

Morgan asked bluntly, "Why?"

"Well, for one thing, he had known me all his life. We all grew up together, you see, though he was much the older one. So when his grief lessened and he was able to think rationally he knew that I was incapable of committing such a crime. He begged my forgiveness and after a while I was able to understand what had prompted him. Ever since I believe he has suffered even more than I. He has aged terribly because of it."

"A man with a conscience."

"Yes. You—ah—I believe you would enjoy meeting him."

"No, thanks."

He started to turn away, but she called to him, "Just a minute," and he looked back at her with his eyebrows arched. She frowned, wondering what to do. She had arranged the brunch and invited her friends that morning for the sole purpose of meeting Morgan. It was too late to cancel the invitations. But if the guests arrived and Morgan was not present, the brunch would certainly die with a dull thud.

She said, "There will only be about a dozen couples and I'm quite sure you'll enjoy yourself."

He saw the desperate look in her eyes and was instantly suspicious. "But I'm not so sure. I don't feel up to meeting a lot of strangers. Besides which, a lot of them would guess why I am here. Or maybe that's the reason—" Her eyes slid away and he knew that he had guessed correctly. "So you've asked a gang here in order to exhibit your alcoholic object of charity. I've been wondering when I would have to pay for your kindly, helping hand."

"No!" she cried. "Honestly, Mr. O'Keefe. A friend of mine found one of your books in the study, he happens to be one of your fans, he asked to meet you—"

"Forget the alibi. I do owe you something. I told you, before I'm grateful. Okay. My gratitude is boundless. I'll be at your damned, stinking little brunch. You can depend on it."

He was so angry that he almost tripped when he turned away from her and disappeared into the stair well. She stared after him with the sudden conviction that it would probably be a lot better for all concerned, including herself, if Morgan did not appear. But he had said that she could depend on him. She knew he would be there.

Chapter Five

Morgan was furious by the time he reached his apartment. He paced the floor, swearing under his breath, but there was still his empty wallet to be considered. He wouldn't walk out now. He needed that loan. Irene might decide in his favor, in which case all his worries would be resolved, he would be able to finish the book, and there would then be the additional advance from the publishers. He would be back on his feet again and maybe, this time, he could stay there.

He was trapped.

Just before one o'clock the butler looked into the apartment to tell Morgan that Mrs. Wilson was expecting him on the terrace. He had already shaved and showered, but was walking around in a robe. He put on slacks, a light sport shirt and the repaired suede jacket. When he was dressed, however, he deliberately waited another half-hour, like a petulant child.

All the people from the Friday night party were scattered about the terrace, chatting together in small groups and drinking Ramos fizzes, when Morgan appeared. Every eye was turned curiously upon him, and conversation died to a murmur. Irene, in red hostess slacks and a silk blouse, was at the far end of the terrace. She started toward Morgan at once.

Nicky van Ostrand, however, reached him first with a broad grin. He held out his hand. "This is quite a pleasure," he said. "You're Morgan O'Keefe, of course. I'm Nicky van Ostrand."

Morgan squinted at him narrowly, shook hands limply and mumbled, "Glad to know you. Are you the one who's supposed to be a fan of mine?"

"Irene told you? Yes, that's right. I've read everything you've had published. You could have knocked me over with a feather when I learned you were here." At that moment Irene reached his side. For the next half-hour he was too busy meeting people and sorting out his impressions of them to do much talking. All of them were obviously people of great wealth and the assurance that went with it. They were expensively but casually groomed and, except for the Wilsons, they were all about his own age. Some of the men, he noticed, resented him at once, which rather pleased him. All of the women were surprised and pleased by his appearance. They, too, had apparently expected to meet some creature from the gutter. He was feeling better already.

Frank and Glenna Wilson intrigued him, partly because of the little he knew of the man's history, but mostly because of the disparity in their appearance. He was amazed to learn from one of the other guests that Glenna Wilson was forty-eight years old. He had thought that she was a considerably younger woman who had married her husband for his money. He was also curious about the unusually warm smile she turned upon him and the obvious excitement and interest in her eyes.

He was greatly surprised to realize that Nicky, and also his wife Tina, to a lesser measure, were sincerely interested in talking to him and hadn't the slightest intention of patronizing him. The others, however, patronized him openly, and made no attempt whatever to accept him on their level. To them he was a case history. Morgan had difficulty keeping his temper in control. It burned slowly and dangerously.

Nicky cornered him as they were eating the elaborate brunch and discussed certain details of the O'Keefe books he had read. Morgan was at first blunt and noncommittal, but then he actually began to like the other man and he chuckled finally and told him, "You're not flattering me, you know. Talking over books I've written is a damned boring business I can easily do without."

"But I thought—"

"You're wrong. Writing a book is one form of giving birth, and it takes a hell of a lot out of a man. On the other hand, it differs from childbirth inasmuch as once the baby learns to walk you get sick and tired of the little bastard and would just as soon forget him. Your love is directed solely toward the new baby in conception. As a matter of face, Mr. van Ostrand—"

"Nicky."

"Nicky. As I was saying, about a year after a book has been published I have a terrible time remembering what it was all about. I get titles all mixed up. I identify my own characters with the wrong books and the story line of one becomes the story line of another. Undoubtedly you know more about my books than

I do."

"That's amazing."

"No. Not very. In writing, you don't look back. You can't. Once a writer does that he commits creative suicide. What you've written you put out of your mind and make room for the next book to come. Your concentration is always on the one in the works and the next to follow." He paused for a moment and smiled. "To tell you the truth, Nicky, a writer is never satisfied with what's been done. The enthusiasm you feel while writing turns to distrust and dislike once the job is done. And after the book's been printed, you're quite sure only a moron would buy it. So when you praise a past book of mine I wonder what kind of fool you are to find something good in what I'm convinced is a stinker. The only good book is the one in the works."

Nicky had no literary pretensions, but he read a great deal and he often wondered about the people who wrote the books that pleased him. Morgan's work had always impressed him more than any others, so he was more than a little thrilled to find himself in the man's company. He realized, however, that there was considerable sophistry in what Morgan was saying and that in the event of adverse criticism the writer would probably defend his past works as fiercely as a mother protecting her young. It was quite all right for him to call his own books stinkers, but Nicky had a hunch that if anyone else dared use the same term Morgan would swarm all over them.

Nicky asked him if he were doing any writing at the present. The subject was beginning to bore Morgan and he was more interested in watching the other guests, but his liking for Nicky was growing and he did not wish to offend the other man. Reluctantly, he explained about his latest book and what the publishers wanted and what he intended doing about it. Nicky could hardly contain his excitement. His sole criticism of Morgan's writing was the deliberate withdrawal of sympathy in his characterizations. So if the man were going to correct that fault in his new book, Nicky was convinced that it would be a literary bombshell—and said so.

Morgan wrinkled his thin nose and made a sour face. When Nicky left his side for a moment to speak to his wife, Morgan turned to watch Irene chatting with a group of guests. He wondered why she was eying him so anxiously and then he saw her reason for alarm. Directly at his elbow was a glass table on which Carl had placed a silver serving tray loaded with Ramos fizzes. So, he thought, she was afraid he might be tempted. That she should even consider the idea angered him and deliberately he reached for a white, frothy glass. He raised it to his lips in a mocking salute and smiled at her. She frowned and snapped her eyes away. Morgan chuckled and lowered the glass without drinking.

He left his chair and, taking the fizz with him, strolled away to sit on the stone balustrade at the edge of the terrace. Glenna Wilson left her husband and crossed the terrace to sit on the stone at Morgan's side, her hands clasped about a slim knee. He looked over the trim lines of her figure and the amazing smoothness of her skin and the young-girl poise and suppleness and wondered, What cooks with this blonde queen? Learning the answer might be interesting.

She cocked her head to one side and looked into his eyes. "I understand you haven't been in San Francisco very long."

"That depends on what's considered long or short in a nightmare. I've been here a few weeks."

"Like it?"

"What I've seen." He looked out over the bay. "That, of course, is terrific. That's the most staggering view I've seen anywhere." He pointed with his chin to the north and said, "That piece of land jutting out over there across the water, the one with the trees and houses on it, is that Belvedere?"

She twisted about to look over her shoulder. "Yes. It's really an island, though you can't tell from here. That little collection of buildings just over to the right of Belvedere is Tiburon. The cove in between is Tiburon Cove. That's where I keep my boat."

"Do you sail?"

"No. It's a fifty-foot cruiser, twin screw. We used to sail, but Frank lost interest in any sort of yachting some years ago."

He asked sharply, "Ten years ago?"

She looked again into his eyes and smiled and ignored his question. "I'm the only one who goes out cruising now. That's where I would have been today, if—" She paused, then asked brightly, "Do you enjoy yachting, Mr. O'Keefe?"

"I don't know. I've never tried it, but I doubt it. A boat, to me, is just something you have to use to cross water. But then I feel the same way about everything else, horses, bicycles, automobiles, trains and so on. They're something you have to use to get from A to B. You may have a wonderful boat over there, but to waste all that beautiful machinery and all the intelligence that went into building it just to go cruising around in circles is ridiculous."

She burst out laughing and cried, "But think of the sport involved!"

"You think of it. I'm no sportsman. People waste too damned much time on what they call sport. They run back and forth on football fields trying to gouge each other's eyes out, they plod around golf courses lying to each other every step of the way, they try to break each other's legs on polo ponies and each other's skulls with hockey sticks, they stand and cheer at fighters beating each other's brains out— No, thank you. Sport is not my idea of a way to pass time."

"And what is your idea?"

"Contemplation, my dear woman. Either contemplation or conversation." He noticed that she had placed her empty glass on the balustrade between them, so slyly he switched glasses with her. He continued, "There's a horrible lack of both today. People think they must keep running and running or they'll somehow miss something. The ability to contemplate is lost entirely and the silly chatter that passes for social conversation is enough to make me vomit. So what have we? Minds filled to the brim with push-button knowledge and no intelligence whatever."

"I suppose this is all very instructive—Tell me, Mr. O'Keefe, are you married?"

He chuckled at the quick switch. "No. I haven't found a woman yet who's good at both bed and board."

"Haven't you ever fallen in love?"

"My dear woman, I have been in love practically ever since I was eleven years old. Almost any reasonably attractive woman with all her organs in the right place can inspire me to such heights of ecstasy that I wish to get in bed with her."

She barely managed to smother a titter. "That isn't what I meant at all."

"Of course not. We use different dictionaries. But have you ever been in love?"

She glanced over at her husband's tired bulk and back at Morgan and frowned. "Yes. Once."

"Pleasantly?"

"It—it was fun while it lasted."

"And you're looking for it again."

She said heatedly, "I should resent that."

"You won't, though. You're playing a little game of pattycake with me right now that could lead into something more serious than footsie. You know it and I know it. Shall I give it a name?"

Her eyes flamed with interest, but she shook her blonde head and looked away from him, out over the bay, smiling.

Morgan sat back and appraised her. He was already aware of a number of facts concerning Glenna Wilson. She was restless and dissatisfied. She was definitely on the prowl for some excitement. Morgan decided that she would be relatively easy to get into a strange bed and wondered if he should afford himself the pleasure. And it could prove to be entertaining. He promised himself to give the idea some thought.

Meanwhile, he was curious about her attitude toward her sister-in-law. There was obviously no love lost between them.

He tried to question her about it, but she was evasive until he finally said flatly, "Look; it's pretty apparent to me that you dislike her or even hate her." He fired a shot into the dark. "I assume it has something to do with the killing of her husband?"

She raised one thinly arched brow. "Oh, you know about that?"

"I read the whole thing in that scrapbook she keeps."

"And what was your opinion?"

"Hmmmmm? Oh, yes. I see what you mean." He had made up his mind that Irene had been innocent in intent, but he had a strong hunch that Glenna had decided otherwise, so he lied as he said, "Well, it would have been a damned convenient way to get rid of the erring spouse and pick up some extra lettuce to boot."

She leaned toward him and whispered huskily, "Naturally. The only reason that jury didn't indict was because of her money and her background."

"Your husband certainly tried hard enough to get the job done. How come he did such an about-face later on?"

"Money," she snapped. "We have a son, Tommy. He's the only one in his generation of the male Tinsleys or Wilsons. Irene, in her peculiar way, has always been fond of him. Shortly after she left town, right after the killing, Frank learned that her will was made out to our son. Except for a few charitable bequests, Tommy is to be the sole beneficiary. So, naturally, Frank changed his tune and came running back to Irene, bowing and scraping."

He asked dryly, "And you, too?"

"I'm here, aren't I? But I've never changed my mind about that woman."

She darted a venomous glance toward Irene, but as her eyes came back to Morgan she realized what she had been saying and regretted the whole matter. That she had been so foolishly frank with a perfect stranger, however, made her even more curious about him and heightened her interest. But she changed the subject.

Nicky rejoined Morgan and gave him his address and telephone number and asked Morgan to call when convenient. Frank Wilson also wandered over, principally to discover what was holding his wife's attention so long. When he saw the lights of excitement in her eyes, his jaws hardened and he looked at Morgan with obvious hostility. Inwardly he groaned, and wondered wearily where it was all going to end. He was afraid he knew the answer. Twenty-seven years of love and respect and admiration, and it was all going down the drain because God was unkind and had given Glenna a face and figure that seemed impervious to age.

The butler passed about a new round of fizzes and Morgan found himself temporarily alone with the banker. He said casually, "You're a lucky man to have such a beautiful wife, Mr. Wilson."

Frank stared at him coldly and said bluntly, "Sometimes I wonder."

Morgan's head snapped up and his teeth gleamed whitely in the sun. "Oh? So beauty is not always an unmixed blessing?"

"Not always. How would you feel, Mr. O'Keefe, if strangers persisted in mistaking your wife for your daughter?"

"I don't know. That's a hard one to answer. But I see what you mean."

"Even in her late thirties she was often refused service in bars and cocktail lounges. Naturally she didn't mind at all, and at that time it even amused me. But it goes on and on." He wanted to kill any interest that might have been aroused in Morgan, so he added, "She's forty-eight, you know."

"So I've been told. Remarkable."

Frank looked sharply into Morgan's eyes. "It sometimes gets a bit tiring fending off the younger men."

"And," Morgan suggested, "cutting them down to size?"

"At times. The Tinsley-Wilson field of influence is pretty wide." He smiled thinly. "We have connections even in your business."

"I'm not in any business."

"In your profession, then. Many of the Hollywood studios are indebted to us for various loans; we control some of the distribution channels of Eastern publishers and we also have interest in numerous newspapers, which of course, have book-review columns. You see what I mean?"

"Perfectly." Morgan flushed darkly. "I detect a warning in your words. Doesn't it make you feel a little silly for a man in your position to be forced to threaten a bankrupt alcoholic?"

Frank's own anger flared and he was about to retort hotly, but the others returned and he choked off what he was going to say. Irene also chose that moment to join them, and most of the other guests crossed the terrace with her. Morgan found himself surrounded by the crowd. He made a great display of exchanging his empty glass for another filled to the brim and again raised it toward Irene in a mock salute.

She looked worried, but she said, "You seemed to be having such an interesting conversation over here that I just had to break in. What were you all talking about?"

Morgan glanced at Frank and back at his hostess. "Plots," he said. "Plots and counterplots. The air is full of them. There's enough material on this terrace for at least a dozen books."

"Oh, really?"

"Of course. The difficulty would be getting them by the censors."

Jimmy Brockway, a brown little man with brown hair and eyes, brown suit and brown tie, snorted and burst into a laugh. "I say, that's very good. But speaking of books, I suppose I must have read some of yours. I do like a good book, you know—but for the life of me I just can't seem to place your name."

Morgan looked astonished and said, "What an amazing coincidence. I can't place your name, either."

Brockway looked puzzled. "That isn't what I meant at all, old man. Authors are supposed to be in the limelight. Their names are generally known."

"Only a few, my friend. The vast body of truly good literature is written by hundreds of professional journeymen you have never heard about."

"Oh, I don't know. I read most of the better ones."

"You continue to amaze me. I didn't know you could read."

"I beg your pardon!"

"Granted."

Morgan looked about at the crowd and saw that the moment had truly arrived. They had all eaten and drank well, they had chatted together long enough to be relaxed. Now they wanted their sport. Very well, he thought, his anger now burning on a short fuse, they shall have it.

Mrs. Rockway, a thin blonde with a laugh that always ended in a nervous giggle, was bursting to get into the act. She told Morgan in a high-pitched voice, "Writing must be a terribly fascinating occupation. I've thought of writing a book myself, but I simply don't have the time."

Morgan said dryly, "I imagine you have all the qualifications, though. A clean sheet of paper and a dirty mind? But tell me, what sort of book would you write—that is, if you had the time?"

She fluttered her hands in a helpless gesture. "Oh, you know. There's so much to write about. My own life, for example."

"What a shame you don't have the time. I know the confessions magazine that would be interested."

Jimmy Brockway growled, "I say, old boy, aren't you being a bit insulting?"

Morgan looked surprised. "I? What a thing to say! Why should I be insulting to someone who has just paid me the supreme compliment of implying that any giddy housewife could write as well as I if only she had the time?"

Mrs. Brockway gasped, "Giddy housewife, indeed!"

Irene said quickly, "I'm sure she didn't mean it that way, Mr. O'Keefe. Most people do think they can write, you know."

"I know. And when they get a good look at one who really can, they figure that if that dope can do it, anyone can."

Norman deKalb, a young trader on the Exchange floor, said patronizingly, "There is perhaps something basic in that idea, O'Keefe. Any literate person is, after all, a writer of sorts. Take myself, for example. I studied a bit of journalism at college and since then, in the evenings, I dabble about now and then with short-story ideas. In fact, I came up with a beauty the other day, a really terrific idea. Pressure of business, though—I simply can't get it on paper. But I'd be glad to pass it on to you, even for nothing."

"That," said Morgan, "is exactly what it's worth. Any story idea out of the brain of a layman is completely worthless. Before Sinclair Lewis started doing his own writing he used to peddle story ideas among writers in New York I think the highest he ever got for one was fifteen dollars, and then he was probably being overpaid. So thanks again for your unbounded generosity. But, for God's sake, keep the story to yourself."

Mrs. deKalb, a lush redhead with a brain that outraced the racy lines of her body, was annoyed because she could see that her husband was annoyed. And whenever Norman became annoyed he had to take it out on someone, especially his wife. She had more than one bruise on her body bearing silent witness to his irritations.

She looked at Morgan with a dangerous glint in her eyes, but smiled warmly as she said, "You fail to appreciate the fact, Mr. O'Keefe, that Norman was simply trying to be helpful. He thought you might be able to use the money you could get for his little story."

Morgan looked at her with simulated admiration. "Ah, that's very neat. Puts me right in my place, doesn't it? The drunken writer, flat on his back, grasp-

ing eagerly at any handout. Maybe you'll even allow me to pass the hat around."
He looked about at the secret smiles in most of their eyes, then back at Mrs.
deKalb. "But that isn't why he made the offer, my dear. He knows I can do the
job. He can't. But, through me, he could possibly find his brainchild in print.
Then he might even have guts enough to try it himself. I'm afraid, however, that
it takes more guts, more ability, and considerably more talent than your husband possesses."

Mrs. deKalb sneered, "You certainly think a lot of yourself, don't you?"

"When I leave here, my dear woman, you'll be slumming."

"Well," she cried, "if you're so good what are you doing here?"

"I can tell you why I'm here on this terrace. My charming hostess wishes me
to repay my indebtedness to her."

Irene said, "Please—"

"So I'm obliging. I place myself freely before a pack of hyenas so that you may
have something to laugh about while clipping your coupons." He got to his feet
then and smiled benignly upon them all. "Is there anything else you care to
question me about? My sex life should be interesting. You see, I don't follow the
pattern of the average red-blooded American male. Most Americans submit
dutifully to the sexual whims of their women, which means as little sex as possible and no romance whatever; then they run off to the nearest whore house
for their real kicks. Or they play footsies with their friends' wives and gratify
their lust in hot-sheet motels. My pattern is different. I believe that a man owes
it to a woman to study her closely enough to bring out her latent talents, and
then to dominate her completely. In no other way can true sexual gratification
be achieved."

He paused for a moment, but before anyone else could say anything he continued, "Or perhaps my powers of perception may astonish and entertain you
more. In this little group, I know already of one marriage on the rocks and can
make a good guess at two or three others. If you like, I'll dust off the crystal
ball—"

Norman deKalb interrupted with a snarl: "You're sure going out of your way
to make a spectacle of yourself."

"Not at all. I am a spectacle."

"And a damned conceited one, as well."

"But naturally. You are gazing upon the most monumental conceit you have
ever known."

Nicky tried to alter the atmosphere by smiling and observing, "I think you
mean that all writers are more or less conceited."

"More or less, hell. We possess towering conceits. You can't work without it.
Consider the fact that we expect thousands of people to read and be entertained
and sometimes instructed by what we write. That requires conceit of an epic nature."

Nicky said, "You're being a sophist. I think you really mean confidence rather than conceit."

Morgan laughed and said, "Keep the secret to yourself. No one else will ever discover it. Incidentally, how come you're so perceptive?"

Tina said simply, "Nicky just happens to like people."

"Really? What can he possibly find to like in the most destructive animal on earth?"

Frank Wilson snorted, "Destructive! What a nonsensical idea. How can you look at the great dams we build, and our cities, and our vast railroad systems—"

"Oh, for God's sake, Mr. Wilson, leave us not be naïve. Man builds for himself alone. He contributes nothing to nature. We take, but we never give. We level the forests and change the courses of rivers and ruin quiet scenery with obscene concrete and steel and eventually the natural lines of the horizon become excrescences of spire and dome. I must admit one thing, though. We have managed to excel the beasts in the field in one department. We have finally learned how to kill each other more efficiently than was ever done with tooth and claw, or even with stone, arrow, bullet and dynamite. We have now reached the penultimate of our glory. Now, in one raging ball of fire, we can not only destroy ourselves but everything we have built as well. Nature may get another chance, after all."

Mrs. deKalb asked, "Are you trying to tell us you're strictly a Nature Boy?"

"Not at all. I am nature's crowning insult. I search the soul of her enemy and even immortalize him. I may not participate in the general rape physically, but I certainly help to write the book of instructions. Nature should spit on me and, as a matter of fact, does quite often—whenever I look too dearly upon the grape and the grain."

Mrs. deKalb purred, "Are you really an alcoholic, Mr. O'Keefe?"

He looked deeply into her eyes for a moment, and then said, "There's certainly nothing objective about you. But you have me curious. What are you afraid of? It can't be me." He glanced at the glowering Norman. "Perhaps your husband?"

He was pleased to see the color recede from her thin skin. He was tempted to pursue the interesting discovery further, but he noticed Norman's lips thin and his fingers begin to twitch. The man was obviously in a mood to slug him, and he looked a little too big to handle.

Morgan was also getting bored with his own act and was tiring fast. He said, "If you don't mind, gentle people, I'll bow out. We alcoholics must get our rest, or that ole debbil bottle whips us again."

He shook hands with a few of the guests close to him, then turned to face Irene. She sighed deeply and managed to smile at him, obviously relieved that he was quitting the group. But the smile and the reason for it enraged him, and all of his still burning anger was focused upon her. She was the one responsible for the exhibition.

The scene on the roof that morning returned to his mind and Morgan had difficulty keeping himself from laughing outright. He leaned toward Irene and whispered in her ear, a whisper husky enough to be heard by the guests surrounding them: "You know, I've been wondering about something. Why don't you have that little mole removed from your left hip? It bothers me."

Glenna Wilson gasped, and Tina van Ostrand was startled, then shocked. It was obvious that at least two people knew that Irene actually did possess such a mole on her left hip. Morgan smiled and squeezed Irene's arm and waved at the others, then disappeared through the study doors, happy in the knowledge that he had evened the score.

Irene was dumfounded. A flush reddened her skin as she faced her guests. Glenna made no attempt to hide a vicious smile of triumph and even broke into a giggle. Tina continued to stare at her friend in amazement and disbelief. The others were not quite sure what had happened, but it was obvious that something had happened.

Irene was unable to say anything. She then worsened matters by ushering her guests from the terrace as quickly as possible and using every strategy to dispatch them from the house. Only Nicky and Tina remained. Irene joined them in the study and paced back and forth before them, a thoroughly outraged woman.

"That maniac!" she cried. "But I should have known. God knows, I should have known."

Nicky said, "Just what was that remark all about, anyway?" and Tina inquired curiously, "How on earth did he know, Irene?"

They were seated together on a sofa. Irene paused to face them, her hands angrily on her hips. "This morning," she explained, "I was taking a sun bath on the roof, in the altogether, if you must know. Suddenly I looked up and there was O'Keefe. I don't believe he had been aware of what he was going to run into and he was rather apologetic about it, but there he was and he didn't leave. I got into a robe, naturally—"

Tina said, "Naturally."

"—and he sat down and we had a little chat. But apparently he noticed that little mole before I could get the robe on."

Tina was more puzzled than ever. "But his implication—"

"Can't you see? He's been angry ever since I told him about the brunch. It was his way of getting even with me for putting him on exhibition, as he believed. You know, that man's really a monster."

Nicky slapped his hands on his thighs and burst out laughing. "By God, that's really funny."

Irene snapped, "I fail to see any humor in it."

"But he's such a child, you see. Exhibition. Yes, I can understand that. I'm surprised he didn't thumb his nose at all of us before he left."

Irene sighed deeply and looked down at Tina. "I wouldn't have minded so much your hearing the remark, but for Glenna to be there, too—" She shuddered at the thought of what Glenna would do with such a choice morsel for gossip. "You know exactly what she'll be saying. But there's some consolation. He'll be leaving tomorrow."

Nicky asked, "Do you know where he's going?"

Irene shrugged. "No, and I don't care. He thinks he might get a loan from me so he can do what he calls a rewrite job on his new book."

Nicky said enthusiastically, "He told me all about that. It should be tremendous. You're going to give him the loan, aren't you?"

Irene frowned. "I don't dare. He is an alcoholic, after all. I'm afraid that if I give him a sum substantial enough to keep him going for a month or so he'll simply go off on another binge. As a matter of fact," she added heatedly, "after what he did to me I don't even know why I'm talking about it. I'll give him the usual twenty, and that's it."

Nicky leaned back and chewed at his lower lip. "I think you're probably right about giving him money. He may just throw it away. But here's something all of us should consider. The guy's a genius."

Tina protested, "Now, Nicky, don't go overboard."

"But I'm not, really. O'Keefe is definitely a genius. He may be an alcoholic and an arrogant, insulting son of a bitch, but under all that is terrific talent. He's mad at the world about something, and he's bitter, and it comes out in the cold-blooded way he handles his characters. That's been his one weakness. But if he does what he says he's going to do in this new book, it'll be a literary bombshell. That book has got to get finished and maybe it's up to us to see that the job is done."

Tina laughed. "How you carry on."

He grinned wryly and looked embarrassed for a moment. "Well, maybe I do. But I feel pretty strongly about this sort of thing. We're all of us really just merchants. We keep the world's goods moving and we get pretty fat doing it. A man like O'Keefe, though, is in a different world. He deals in the nature of man. So I say we owe him something."

Irene was aghast. "He's the object of our charity, and yet you say we're the ones who owe him something?"

"Certainly. Without him and the others like him there'd be no culture whatever in this world."

She said reluctantly, "Well, there's something in what you say—"

"But what's to be done? Give him money and he may go off on another bender. He has to be supervised, sort of."

Tina burst out laughing and leaned over to kiss Nicky's cheek. "My goodness, next thing you'll be wanting to move him in with us while he dashes off this great epic."

Nicky nodded. "Don't think I haven't been considering the idea. There's that extra guest room—"

"Oh, no! The children, Nicky."

"I know. That's what stops it." He squinted into Irene's eyes and said, "Well? How about you?"

"You mean—you mean let him stay on in the apartment?"

"Sure. Why not? It's a perfect setup. He has his own place away from the traffic of the house, your privacy is not invaded, he isn't likely to go off on a binge and, anyway, he won't have the money for it—"

"Nicky!" she cried. "No! You don't know what you're asking. Tact is a dirty word in his vocabulary, he says the most horrible things, he delights in irritating people—you saw how he was on the terrace—in no time at all he would simply take over the whole house."

"No, Irene, I don't think so. The man's worried, and I'll bet he's frightened, too. If you gave him the opportunity to get his job done he'd probably be so grateful you'd never know he was around. Think it over, Irene." He got up and put an arm about her shoulders. "All these alcoholics you've been helping—you know you haven't really done any of them any good. They just go right back to the bottle, first chance they get. But this time, just this once, you have a chance to do something really good and maybe even great. So think it over. But if you do decide to turn him out, let me know first. I may think of something else. Okay?"

"I'll let you know."

She had no intention whatever of thinking it over, but for hours after her friends had gone she couldn't get the idea out of her mind. It kept her awake for a long while that night and it was the first thing she thought of as she awoke in the morning. She made her decision at the breakfast table and then called on Morgan.

He was standing before a mirror knotting a tie and, at her knock, called for her to come in. He watched her in the mirror, without turning around, approving of the light cotton dress that accented the good lines of her figure. He thought wistfully that if he had known her earlier, perhaps ten or twelve years earlier— Then he shrugged and finished knotting the tie.

He turned as she said, "Good morning." His suitcase was packed, but lying open on the floor. He squatted to close the cover and secure the straps.

"If it's any consolation," he said, "I feel pretty lousy about that crack I made. Under the same circumstances I would undoubtedly do it all over again, but I'm not in love with myself because of it. You have to live with those characters. I don't. So—well—I'm sorry."

"It was a nasty thing to say. My sister-in-law, especially, will make the most of it."

"I knew that when I said it. She hates your guts." He looked up then with a broad grin. "Incidentally, why don't you get that mole removed?"

Irene stared at him incredulously, then suddenly burst into laughter. She laughed until there were tears in her eyes and she was so weak she had to sit on the edge of the bed. "Honestly," she gasped, "you really are an incorrigible."

He squatted there on his heels and chuckled with her. "And you have a better sense of humor than I had imagined."

"Does it surprise you so much?"

"More than a little. I didn't think there was room for it under those widow's weeds you wear over your eyes." He got to his feet and nudged the suitcase with his toe. "That does it. Thank you again for your kindness. I will leave by the front door, if you don't mind."

She was no longer laughing as she said, hesitantly, "I've been thinking—you have that work to do on your book—"

"So?"

"Well, it's just that there's this apartment—" She straightened with an unnecessary show of defiance. "I have been thinking over your situation, Mr. O'-Keefe. I shall be perfectly honest with you. I'm afraid that if I advance you any sort of loan you'll simply throw it away."

He shook his head. "I never drink when I'm working on something."

"You were drinking fizzes yesterday. I saw you."

He grinned again. "I was being an adolescent thumbing my nose at you. Actually, I drank nothing and kept switching glasses with empties. Believe me, if I had poured any of those fizzes down my throat I'd still be plastered today and well on my way."

She said dubiously, "Well, I don't know. Anyway, I have a proposal. Nicky suggested it and I've been thinking it over. Mr. O'Keefe, I'm willing to let you stay on in this apartment, if you wish, until you finish your book and secure the advance you mentioned. Frankly, it will be an inconvenience for me, but—well—"

He stared at her through narrowed lids for a long while. Then he crossed the floor and sat down on the bed at her side. "This is pretty hard for me to understand, Mrs. Wilson. And it doesn't make sense. Yet there has to be a reason for it."

"I told you it was Nicky's suggestion—"

"All right, but you're the one making the offer. Why? Why are you going out of your way to help me out? Tell me."

She looked beyond him, her eyes desolate and her lips drawn back in a grimace of pain. She whispered so softly that he could hardly hear, "There has been a horrible idea in me that for ten long years has almost driven me out of my mind. I go to sleep with it at night and I wake with it in the morning and no matter what I do it never leaves me. You see, Mr. O'Keefe, it is possible that I did kill my husband deliberately. Maybe I did know it was Jay standing there in the doorway and maybe I did have a subconscious urge to kill him and maybe I really did know what I was doing and—and—" Her head lowered and her hands came up slowly to cover her face. "I've told myself a thousand times that such an idea could never have been in my mind and that such an act was beyond me.

But what of my subconscious, Mr. O'Keefe? You know about such things. I know you know."

Morgan stared at her, and for the first time he really pitied her. He realized finally what the years had meant to her and why she had pursued her semi-cloistered course through life since the killing. But what was there to say? Only she would know if such an urge had been in her subconscious mind. Only she would know if it had been strong enough to drive her to the act. No one else was capable of knowing or explaining. There was nothing to say.

He realized also why she was willing to help him. He cleared his throat and said huskily, "That's a damned rough thing to live with, Mrs. Wilson. And you think I know about such things. You think that if I'm around for a while some of it may rub off on you. That's what finally decided you to make your generous offer. Already I've jarred some of your misconceptions loose, and now you think I may really be able to help you." He placed a hand gently on her shoulder. "Maybe you're right. Who knows?"

Chapter Six

Irene's revelation forced Morgan to re-evaluate and alter drastically his attitude toward her. He could no longer consider her a stupid woman glorying in her martyrdom. He had now to face the fact that she was a woman of some intelligence and undoubted imagination. Before she left the apartment he appraised with new interest the glossy blackness of her thick hair, the dark, brooding eyes, the smooth skin and the slimly curved lines of her figure. Probably, he thought, if she were not a haunted woman she would again come fully alive and regain her former beauty. He wondered if he could help. He doubted it very much. They were not the types ever to have much in common. Shortly after she had gone, the butler brought him a notice from Western Union that a money order was waiting for him at the Van Ness Avenue office. Morgan could hardly believe it. He borrowed a dollar from Carl and took a bus down to Van Ness, where he received a check for one hundred dollars—which he cashed—and the accompanying message: "Best I can do. Hope you are sincere about rewrite job. Good luck. Earl."

It was a minor miracle, and Morgan felt so much better with a little money in his pocket that he decided to walk back to the Wilson house. He tired after a few blocks, but he stayed with it and enjoyed the crisp air and the bustle of the traffic and the sights and sounds and smells that were strictly San Francisco. He dropped into a bar on the way and ordered a Coke. He asked the bored bartender, "Been around here long?"

The man shrugged. "Eighteen-nineteen years. Not at this one spot, though."

"Then maybe you'll remember a killing that took place here about ten years ago. I wasn't here myself, but I've gotten interested in it. The Wilson affair?" The bartender frowned and shook his head. Morgan said, "This Irene Wilson shot her husband in their own home. Claimed she had mistaken him for a prowler. Very wealthy people."

Another customer said excitedly, "Hey, I remember that. I was driving a truck for the *Chronicle* then. Made a big splash in all the sheets. That was some case. They never did bring her to trial, though."

"So I understand."

"Yeah. Shows what big dough can do."

"Then you think she should have been tried?"

"Hell, man, that babe was as guilty as they come. Her husband was a big guy and he was wearing pajamas. I remember all the details. Had to read 'em every day. But this prowler was kind of a little guy and he sure as hell didn't look like her husband. And there was even some kind of light in the hallway."

The bartender's face lit up. "I remember it, too. And you're right, by God. She couldn't possibly mistake her husband for that prowler."

Morgan said, "Well, she had awakened from a sound sleep—"

"That's for the birds, Mac. That babe knew what she was doing." He turned to the other customer and said, "You know what decided me, Pete? Her brother-in-law. Didn't he try to get her—whaddaya call it?"

Morgan suggested, "Indicted?"

"Uh-huh. Indicted. He done his best, didn't he? She had more dough, though. But that was the clincher, far's I'm concerned. That guy knew. Know what I mean? He knew."

Pete nodded. "You're goddam right he knew. He knew, all right. Who'd be in a better position to know? Her husband's own brother. Yeah, that was some case. But it just goes to show, when you got the loot you can commit murder and get away with it."

Morgan asked mildly, "Like Loeb and Leopold?"

Pete and the bartender frowned at him without understanding. Pete said, "I don't know about them guys, but I sure remember that Wilson case. She knew what she was doing with the old Roscoe. And you can't tell me she was any amachure with that gat. One bang, that was all it took. Remember, Al? By God, I remember the whole thing. Then there was that Dillon case—remember that babe shoved a shiv in her old man when he was in the shower? That was a hot one, too. Why, I remember the time—"

Morgan finished his Coke and walked out of the bar. He frowned thoughtfully during the balance of his walk home. The case had certainly made a definite impression on San Franciscans. Even ten years later two men in a bar could remember most of the details, and the more pertinent fact that they had considered Irene guilty. Probably, he thought, most people still thought she was guilty and that she had escaped trial only because of her wealth. What a thing to have to face every day, year after year. His sympathy for her was deepening.

When he reached the house, however, he put Irene out of his mind at once and concentrated on his work. He fell immediately into a pattern of living. Every morning he got up at five and paced the floor for an hour or so, arranging his thoughts. Then, after a quick breakfast, he went to work at the typewriter. He worked without moving from the machine until at least one o'clock, or until he started making subconscious typographical errors, always a sure sign that he was exhausted. It was an hour or so before he could eat lunch. It took that long for his nerves to relax and his stomach to accept food.

He got a front-door key from Carl, so that he could go in and out at will, and in the afternoons he took long walks. During those hours his mind became a terrier and shook the story to pieces and put it back together again and resolved what was to be done the following day. Even in his sleep the creative process was at work. He dreamed of the story every night and knew that he was dreaming and tried to exercise some control over his dreams, yet always failed. The story took on different shapes in his dreams and, though there were always some minor similarities, it was without rhyme or reason and went off at wild tangents and never was there any part of it that could be used.

Irene was at first aware of his industry only while he was at his typewriter. It astonished her to discover that he arose so early in the morning and maintained such a rigid schedule without allowance for even the slightest deviation. She had assumed that writers worked mostly by inspiration and only as the mood moved them. It took time for her to realize that the creative process was not a product of mood or fancy, and that self-discipline played such a rigorous role in its use. It took even longer for her to understand that his brain was always at work, regardless of where he might be. Often in the afternoons, if she happened to encounter him in the house and tried to engage him in conversation, he simply stared beyond her into space, or walked away from her in the middle of what she was saying. When she understood that he was not really present she left him alone.

Morgan had breakfast and lunch in his own apartment, but he had his dinners with Irene in a small room just off the terrace that contained so much glass it was almost a solarium. Carl did the serving, but Morgan also met his wife, Anna, who was housekeeper and cook. She was a small, round woman with graying blonde hair crossed in braids over her head. There was also an outside maid who did the nominal cleaning five days a week, a man and wife team that did the vacuuming every Tuesday, and a window washer who took care of the view windows twice a month and the others once a month. The establishment ran very smoothly.

Morgan relaxed at the dinner table and, though a part of his mind remained with the book, he was more aware of his surroundings and enjoyed talking. Irene proved to be a good listener. She had become more curious about Morgan than about anyone she had ever known, and she had a feeling that somewhere in his fund of odd bits and pieces of knowledge might be a key that would unlock the question that had been so long torturing her. She listened closely to everything he had to say.

She almost rebelled at his presence in the house, however, toward the end of the first week. Tina telephoned in great excitement and asked her to read a certain column in one of the newspapers. Irene secured the paper and found the item that had aroused Tina. It read: "One of our most famed widows was put on the well-known spot last Sunday at her Pacific Heights home. Seems that her house guest, a young author now down on his luck, mentioned a certain little mole she possessed in a certain intimate location. It was the faux pas of the season. Excitement prevailed."

"Trash," she snorted and threw the paper away, but it worried her. She could well imagine the gossip that was currently enlivening cocktail parties. And as long as Morgan remained, that gossip would undoubtedly increase in volume. She knew of the hundred dollars Morgan had received and was tempted to add to it and request that he do his writing elsewhere, but she could not force herself to such action. She had committed herself to a certain course and stubbornly she intended to stay with it.

Nicky van Ostrand also helped to worsen matters. Twice he telephoned inviting Morgan to his own house of an evening, but Morgan had no desire to become socially involved with anyone until his work was finished, and refused the invitations. So Nicky did the next best thing and dropped by alone one evening to call on Morgan. They sat in the study and talked until a late hour and Nicky enjoyed himself so much that he made a habit after that of dropping by almost every evening.

Irene was annoyed. She tried joining them at first, but it was obvious that she was not wanted in their far-ranging discussions and that she was the intruder in her own study. So whenever she saw Nicky with Morgan she set her lips thinly and stalked off to her own bedroom. Morgan knew what was bothering her and chuckled quietly to himself, but said nothing. Nor did he bother to take Nicky to his apartment. He went out of his way deliberately to use the study.

During his second week Morgan ran into Glenna one afternoon coming out of her own home, a block from Irene's. She was thrilled to see him and asked immediately if he worked on Sundays. He said that, no, even the Lord had to rest one day a week. Glenna then asked him to join her for a cruise on the bay that coming Sunday. She would pick him up. Morgan was turning a writing problem over in his mind and was hardly aware of what she was talking about. He mumbled absent-mindedly that it would be nice, and walked on. A moment later he had forgotten the encounter.

Sunday morning, however, Glenna was at the house in her station wagon before anyone was out of bed. The butler informed Morgan, who cursed long and heartily. He would have preferred staying in bed for the morning and taking it easy that afternoon. He got out of bed and showered and dressed in slacks and a sweatshirt, but he felt that he had been tricked somehow and was in an unpleasant mood when he joined Glenna outside.

But the sight of Glenna in sneakers, faded blue denim slacks, a formfitting horizontally striped sweater and a yachting cap perched on the back of her blonde head changed his mood in a hurry. She was also in such high spirits that his mood soon matched hers and he settled back in the seat in the happy anticipation of what might be an adventurous day.

They crossed the Golden Gate Bridge and left the freeway to go down into Sausalito, where they had breakfast. Then they traveled on north again, with Glenna chatting away every mile about matters of absolutely no consequence. Morgan was more interested in the scenery, which differed so radically from what he was used to in Southern California. Again they left the freeway to take the winding road to Belvedere and Tiburon, skirting the mud flats and the edges of the bay. Morgan caught his breath and shook his head in wonder every time he had an opportunity to look south over the water at the thrilling sight of San Francisco, which seemed to be floating on the waves, anchored only by the thin ribbon of the great bridge.

Tiburon proved to be a small village with a cluster of minor business establishments, bars, and eating places, and a number of wharves and piers and repair shops over the water for small boats. Glenna parked the car at the end of the single business street and led Morgan to the yacht club, a short distance away. It was a beautiful, warm day, with not a cloud in the sky. A slight breeze rippled the otherwise calm waters of the bay. There was intense activity at the club. Small craft of all kinds were being put into the water and the larger ones at anchor were being readied for cruising. Farther out, the water was already dotted with dozens of sails and ribboned with the curving wakes of power cruisers.

Glenna laughed and said, "Heavenly, isn't it?"

"I don't know. I have my fingers crossed. Can you get seasick on a day like this?"

"Well, some people do. Do you?"

He shrugged. "I've never been on anything smaller than a liner or an army transport."

"Did you get sick then?"

"No. I was always positive it would happen, but it never did."

"Then stop worrying. You'll be all right." She waved toward a nearby pier and said, "There's my boat, the *Teal*. Come on."

She led the way down the pier and aboard by way of the after cockpit and took him on a quick inspection tour of the *Teal*. Morgan was pleasantly surprised. There was a broad flying bridge above the superstructure containing all the controls, deck chairs, a long leather settee and ample space for lying on deck. Under that was the deckhouse, mostly of glass, with chairs, tables, a broad lounge that could convert into an extra berth, a radio, and most of the fixtures of a small living room. Aft and down a few steps was the owner's stateroom with single and double berths and a decent bathroom, complete with shower. Forward of the deckhouse and also down a few steps was a well-equipped galley and roomy dinette, and forward of that, in the bow, was the guest stateroom containing two berths. The hull and superstructure were mahogany, the decks were of teak and everywhere was the gleam of finely polished copper and mirrorlike surfaces of varnish. Underneath the floor of the deckhouse were the two powerful engines. It took no knowledge whatever of yachts for Morgan to realize that he was aboard one of the best.

He realized also that the cruiser was kept in tip-top shape by a highly competent crew, though there was no one around. He questioned Glenna about it when they went up to the flying bridge and she got the engines started. "Seems to me," he said, "that you need at least a couple of men to run this thing."

She looked away from him. "I can handle it alone. I've done it before."

She went up to the bow to cast the lines loose, then hurried back to the stern to throw off the lines there. When she came back to the bridge Morgan persisted, "But you do have a crew?"

"Oh, yes. Two men. Their job mainly is maintenance. They live ashore." She said brightly, "Yesterday they stocked the galley for us. I thought maybe we'd cruise over toward the city, and—"

He grinned and said, "In other words, you gave your crew today off."

She slanted a glance at him and nodded. "Yes. Do you mind?"

"Not at all. A splendid idea. But as long as that's the case, we may as well start the day off right."

He turned her away from the wheel and took her into his arms and crushed his lips fiercely against hers. Her fingers clasped the back of his head and held him tightly to her. Then she pushed him away with a short laugh. She looked nervously toward the club and saw that no one was watching them; then her eyes came slowly back to Morgan. She laughed again and patted his cheek, but gave her attention to the controls. She backed the *Teal* skillfully away from the pier and out into the anchorage, changed gears smoothly, eased the throttles open and turned the bow away from the club and toward San Francisco. Morgan lit a cigarette, watching her closely. When she looked at him again he saw the promise in her eyes and returned her warm smile. Maybe, he thought, there's something to this yachting business, after all.

Morgan had put on a little weight; the hollows in his cheeks had filled out, his eyes were sharp and clear and there was a healthy flush in his skin. He stripped down to the waist and revealed a tan left from the Southern California beaches. Glenna appraised him from the corners of her eyes and noticed the sharply etched cage of his ribs, but saw also—with relief—the long, tight muscles, the hard, flat stomach and the squareness of his shoulders. She was pleased to discover that alcohol had not yet ravaged his physical structure.

As they headed across the straits toward San Francisco she asked him, "Where were you Friday night?"

"Friday?"

"Yes. We were all at Irene's, the same crowd you met before. Irene has a cocktail party every other Friday night, you know, regular as clockwork."

"I didn't know. Anyway, she didn't say anything to me. I went out to the movies."

"The movies! I thought all you people abhorred the slick Hollywood product."

Morgan blinked at her with surprise. "Why should we? Some of the best entertainment I've ever had was in a movie theater. Also some of the worst. But that's true of all forms. You can't always expect the best. The best is too rare, no matter what art it may be."

"But the slick way they do it in Hollywood—"

"Oh, some of it, yes. But I like their technical perfection and their camera work a hell of a lot better than in any foreign movies I've seen."

She laughed. "Well, you surprise me. Anyway, getting back to the party—Irene didn't invite you?"

"She didn't say anything."

"I guess she was afraid you'd let loose with another blast."

Morgan lit a cigarette and leaned back against the mahogany. "She had no reason to invite me, you know. Simply because she's been kind enough to let me use the apartment is no reason why she should also make me one of the family."

Glenna frowned with annoyance. "You seem to be defending her."

"My God, woman, why shouldn't I? She gave me a hand when I needed it desperately and now she's giving me breathing room to finish my work. You have no idea how grateful I am."

Her irritation was growing. She snapped, "You didn't act like it at that silly brunch."

He chuckled. "I was angry. She was defenseless, so I took it out on her. A man of great courage, you see."

"She's a bitch."

"Oh, now—"

"You don't know her. I do. I've known her all her life. Even in her teens, she was the most arrogant, spoiled brat I've ever known."

He said quietly, "She's intimated that herself. It's easy to understand, though, with her background. Incidentally, what was your early background like?"

"About the same."

"Oh?"

"Oh, yes. I was raised about the same way Irene was, but there was quite a difference in our inheritances. Mine were considerably smaller."

"But still ample?"

"Much more than that. Once a year, at tax time, I'm told what I'm worth and that's about it. Otherwise, I don't give it much thought. I don't have to."

"Marvelous. What a way to live!"

"Irene's situation is a little different. Because she owns most of the business she has to take an interest in it. She has a lot of papers to sign and that sort of thing. She's a pretty shrewd character, anyway. She likes power."

Morgan looked amused. "I doubt that. Being around the house, I've learned a few things about her. All of her business and the paper work she has to do takes exactly one morning of the week. Ninety-nine per cent of the business authority she has delegated to your husband. That doesn't fit the picture of someone who likes power. Your trouble is that you hate her and you blind yourself to everything about her."

"You'd hate her, too," she cried, "if you ever knew Jay. He was one of the most easygoing and nicest guys I've ever known. And she murdered him."

"You're positive of that."

"Oh, good Lord! Of course she murdered him. You yourself, a stranger to the affair, said it was a convenient way to get rid of him."

"Murder is hardly ever convenient. But do you have any reason for your opinion more compelling than what I've read in the papers?"

She hesitated a moment, then said, "Yes. There's one thing that never did get in the papers. This pistol she used to kill Jay wasn't the one he'd bought for her. Jay always bought the best. This pistol was a cheap one, and even the serial numbers had been filed and burned off."

"Well, I'll be damned."

"You see? The police never did find out where, but they figured it had been bought in a pawn shop. I don't think Jay had ever been in a pawn shop in his life. Irene bought that gun herself, somewhere."

"Now, wait a minute. Was it actually the weapon that killed Jay?"

"Oh, yes. The police had a test—what do they call it?"

"A ballistics test?"

"Yes. The bullet came from that gun. It was there on the floor, in the hallway, with Irene's fingerprints all over it."

"Very queer."

"Of course. The police had a theory that maybe Jay happened to be walking by a pawn shop while he was thinking about the prowler and he just happened to see the pistol in the window, so he went in and bought it. A spur of the moment thing. But I know better and you would too, if you knew Jay. Seeing a pistol in a window might give him the idea, but he would never have bought it there. He would have gone out of his way to get the most expensive pistol possible in the most exclusive shop possible. Jay was that way."

"I see. So what's your theory?"

"As I say, Irene bought that pistol herself. She bought it to use—on Jay. Then, after using it, I suppose she intended to get rid of it. And if it was found it couldn't be traced to her. But before her plan could be put into effect, whatever plan she had in mind, this prowler happened to break into their house. It was the perfect opportunity for Irene and she seized upon it to kill Jay."

Morgan flipped his cigarette overboard and scratched his head. "Was this particular pistol presented to the Grand Jury?"

"Naturally."

"Did Irene identify it as the one her husband had bought for her?"

"Well, she just said that she knew so little about pistols she wouldn't know. They all looked alike to her." She paused, then asked, "Now do you understand?"

"Frankly, no. But it's something to think about."

They had crossed the straits and were approaching the St. Francis Yacht Club. Glenna spun the wheel and turned the bow of the cruiser east into the channel. Morgan went below to the galley and returned to the bridge with cold beer for Glenna and Coke for himself. They relaxed in the warm sun as they cruised along the Embarcadero, crossed under the bay bridge and then turned again to round Treasure Island and head north up the main body of the bay. It was shortly after noon when Glenna again approached the Marin shore far north of their starting point, and nosed the cruiser slowly into a small, isolated cove. She explained to Morgan how it was done and he managed to drop the anchor without difficulty. Glenna cut off the engines and in a moment the boat was swinging at the end of the chain and rocking gently in the light swell.

They went below to the master stateroom, where Glenna found some swimming trunks that would fit Morgan. He got into them in the forward stateroom, then went up on deck to the after cockpit. The water looked so inviting that he dived in without waiting for Glenna and blew and snorted and splashed about and swam a few yards away from the boat. He heard the splash Glenna made and turned to face her at his side. She wore a white bathing cap over her blonde hair.

She smiled and called, "Race you around the boat."

Apparently she had thought she could win, but Morgan was an excellent swimmer, in spite of his still weakened condition. He won the race by a good many lengths, got into the after cockpit, then reached down to lift Glenna up. She landed on her feet at his side and whipped off the cap to shake out her hair. Morgan appraised her dripping figure and his eyes narrowed slightly, hungrily. She was wearing a peach-colored two-piece suit that consisted of a halter so narrow that it merely made a suggestion of hiding her firm breasts, and panties that were snug and brief. Knowing her age, Morgan was more amazed than ever. Her lightly tanned skin was smooth and unblemished, her stomach was flat and the slim lines of her excellent figure were those of a twenty-five-year-old girl.

Morgan put his hands on her bare waist and looked down into her eyes, shaking his head. "It's unbelievable," he said. "You're another Madame Pompadour, du Barry, Cleopatra, Helen of Troy—"

She laughed at him and wriggled free. "Well, thank you, kind sir."

"Don't thank me. Thank God. I have a question, though. Were you even more beautiful when you were a young girl?"

"Oh, no. About the same. But do you really think I'm beautiful?"

"Don't be an ass. A woman such as you gets born about once every few hundred years. Kings lose their crowns, cities get sacked, women are raped and heads roll in the gutters. How come you haven't set the world on fire?"

She snorted one word, "Frank," and ran from him up to the bridge. She got two inflatable mattresses out of the locker under the bridge settee and Morgan pumped air into them and placed them side by side on the deck. She stretched out on her back and Morgan sat on the other mattress, facing her, his arms clasped about his knees.

"So," he said, "it's Frank who's the anchor about that lovely neck of yours. Ever since you were married, or just recently?"

She closed her eyes against the sun and sighed. "I don't know why I shouldn't tell you. I'm going to have to tell someone, or I'll burst."

"I remember a remark you made at that silly brunch, as you insist on calling it. You said that you had been in love once and that it was fun while it lasted. I assumed you were talking about your husband."

She nodded. "Frank, yes. I fell madly in love with him when I was sixteen and married him when I was twenty-one. The boys used to follow me about like hounds after a bitch in heat, but I was in love and was hardly aware of them. I had a brief affair before I married Frank. That doesn't shock you, does it?"

"You'll have to try harder than that."

"But it was only to satisfy my curiosity. It was always Frank I loved, and when I married him I was truly in heaven. He was very handsome then—you wouldn't believe it—and tall and straight and slim and almost as much fun to be around as Jay. He was more sober than Jay, he had his eye on business and power and things like that, but, even so, he knew how to relax and enjoy himself and we led a wonderful life."

Morgan commented dryly, "With all that loot and all your beauty, how could you miss?"

"Yes." Her features hardened as she continued, "It all changed when Jay was killed. Oh, that bitch! What she's done to us! Frank seemed to age practically overnight. One day he was the nicest husband in the world and the next day he was old and tired and lifeless and boring. He was crazy about Jay. He was so much older, you see, that his fondness for Jay was more that of a father toward a son and, naturally, Jay's death completely unhinged him. That I expected—but he never got over his grief. Time just made him older and older, that's all." She paused a moment, turning a thought over in her mind, then said, "Worst of all, though, he began hating himself for trying to get Irene indicted."

"I thought you told me that it was money that caused his change of heart.

Wasn't it something about your sister-in-law's will?"

She admitted reluctantly, "Well, yes, I did say that and maybe it was true at first, but it wasn't long before he believed completely in her innocence. And now he goes around like a sick cat and when he isn't working, which is rarely, he tries to think of something nice to do for Irene. I've never in my life seen such a change in a man. It's as if he's carrying the whole world on his shoulders. I've argued and argued with him and I get nowhere. Every summer for the past five or six years I've been going off somewhere by myself for three or four months, but even that doesn't get through to him. He won't change. He won't snap out of it."

"He has quite a problem with you, you know."

"He's fully aware of that. We haven't discussed it yet, or anything like that, but he knows I'm going to leave him. Or he should know."

"You've made up your mind?"

"Very much so. I can't tolerate the situation any longer. That's why I've remained at home this summer. I have a few personal matters to straighten out and then I'm leaving for good." She opened her eyes again to look at Morgan and shielded them from the sun with her hand. "Can you blame me?"

Morgan shrugged. "I don't know enough about the situation to say. Anyway, you've made up your own mind. You're leaving him."

"But definitely. It's not easy to do. I don't think anyone can lightly rip twenty-seven years out of their life and just casually throw them away. Then there are the children, too, you know, even though they're adults now—and all our friends. I would have to leave the city, and that will be very difficult to do."

"Why leave?"

"Well, I don't want to embarrass Frank by staying here. After all, we'd be bound to run into each other constantly and it would be awkward for our friends and—you know." She pursed her lips, then said, "I shall probably travel a great deal. If I settle down at all I think it will be in Paris. I've always loved it there."

"My heart bleeds for you."

She said sharply, "Why the sarcasm?"

"Instead of searching your soul for the evil that has destroyed twenty-seven years you're reading travel brochures."

"Don't you think I've suffered enough?" she cried.

"I don't know. What interests me is the suffering your husband has obviously been going through for the past ten years."

She said heatedly, "I'm no longer interested. He can continue wallowing in self-pity if he pleases, but I've had enough of it. Besides, I think I've exercised more patience than most women would in the same position."

"Perhaps you have. Yes, I imagine you have."

"I'm glad you think so."

"Why?"

She stretched her arms lazily and arched her body and said, "I seem to want your good opinion. Even at the brunch I was on your side. But I held my breath. I was afraid you might turn on me, too."

"You were safe. You didn't say anything."

She stretched out on her back again, clasped her arms behind her head, so that her body was drawn into provocative lines, and squinted at Morgan through the sun. She said huskily, "Do you like to travel, Morgan?"

So, he thought, she writes all the cues, and this is where it starts. His eyes drank in the lines of her body and he wondered if he should feel some revulsion because of her age. He couldn't feel it. The thirteen years that separated them had been voided by nature. She was as desirable—perhaps even more so—as a woman half her age. He thought briefly of her husband and possible future complications and dismissed them.

He leaned over her, his arms on either side of her body. His mouth met hers and he felt her hands caressing his shoulders, the long nails digging lightly into his skin. She held to him tightly and pressed her body fiercely against his and whispered her ecstasy upon his lips. She had been made a desert upon which no rain had fallen and he could feel the wild surge of life under him. He hastened to relieve the terrible, mounting pressure.

But when they were naked she moaned and her lids opened and her eyes stared fearfully into his and she whispered, as if she were being tortured, "No."

"What—"

"No, Morgan. I can't. God knows I want to, but I can't."

"But—"

"No. I asked for it. I wanted you and I let you know I wanted you. But I can't." She started laughing, almost hysterically. "Crazy, isn't it? But I find I can't commit adultery. And I wanted to so badly and I still want to and I can't."

"Now, look. This is the damnedest situation—"

"I know, and it's all of my creating and I—I'm sorry. I planned it all and of course you knew it and I can't think of anything more gratifying than to fulfill that plan. But I can't. I have never committed adultery. I even think it's a rather silly word and something no civilized person should worry about, and yet it stops me. Can you understand?"

He frowned down at her, beginning to get angry. "I'm afraid not. You've made up your mind to leave your husband; you—"

"But I haven't left him yet and suddenly I know that until I do I shall have to wait. I said before that you just don't throw twenty-seven years away casually and now they're in my way. The least I can do, darling, is to end it—decently. I must do it that way, no matter how badly I want you."

"Or," he snapped, "any other man?"

She pulled his head down until her cheek was pressed against his and whispered, "Please don't be angry. We won't have to wait too long. I promise."

Morgan shoved himself away and glowered sulkily at her body. Suddenly he snickered and then he started laughing.

"Okay," he said. "I'll dig up some accommodating whore, meanwhile, to keep me occupied while waiting. And the answer is yes, I do like to travel."

Chapter Seven

Glenna prepared a midafternoon luncheon in the galley of the *Teal*, which they ate out on deck, in the sun. They had gotten dressed. Glenna's skin had begun turning too pink. The sun had also lost its strength and a slightly cool breeze was rippling across the water, cooled by a large fog bank moving in from the ocean. Another yacht had moved into their cove and the other people were on the beach drinking beer and getting a barbecue ready.

Morgan watched Glenna's every move and was amused by her chatter. She assumed, without question, that he was more than willing to be her lover and would follow whatever program she had in mind. She wanted three or four weeks to arrange matters with her attorneys, have it out with her husband, and then she and Morgan could leave for Reno, where she would establish residence and get a divorce.

She asked him, "Do you like Reno?"

"I don't know. I've never been there."

"You'll like it."

That seemed to take care of Reno. After the necessary six weeks it would take to secure the divorce they could start traveling. "Just anywhere," she cried. "No itinerary of any kind. We'll stay where we please and leave when we please and go where we please. And as far as finances are concerned, you won't have to worry about a thing."

He suggested dryly, "Maybe I can pay my way by doing your washing."

She laughed delightedly. "You'll pay your way. Don't worry."

"Incidentally, why am I, especially, being so honored?"

"Now, don't be sarcastic," she pouted. "The first time I saw you I knew that living with you would be exactly the tonic I need. I made up my mind then— well, maybe not quite then—but I did make up my mind about you and I know I'm right. Besides," she said seriously, "I think I can do you a lot of good. Nicky says that it would take very little to make you famous. I would like that. I would love to help. It would give me a feeling of—well—of accomplishment."

Morgan thought, lying lazy and relaxed in the sun, that it could be quite entertaining, for a while, anyway. There was no doubt that she would be a satisfying woman to live with and to travel with. Perhaps he could even get a new book out of her. It had happened that way before, and it could again.

Living on her bounty, however, was another matter entirely. Morgan had been obligated to so many people on so many different occasions that his sense of obligation had become atrophied. But being obligated to Glenna, he knew, would not do at all. He would resent her, then despise her and ultimately would come to hate her. That was not a sensible foundation on which to base an affair.

He would pay his own way and she could spend as she pleased. He smiled as he thought of what a comfortable arrangement it could be. Coming to San Francisco had been providential, after all—the immediate future was neatly wrapped up in a scented package and tied with an ermine bow.

Glenna became worried about the fog, which was swirling about Mount Tamalpais and creeping in like a gray ghost through the narrow slot of the Golden Gate. She started the engines and rode forward on the chain and Morgan got the anchor up on deck. Fog was also lying in Raccoon Straits, between Angel Island and the mainland, and when they nosed into it the world was blotted out. Glenna slowed the cruiser and tensed at the wheel and cocked her blonde head to one side to listen to the moaning horns.

Morgan was treated to a cool display of objective reasoning and mathematical calculation he had never known existed in a woman. Glenna kept her head cocked to the horns, her eyes darting from a stop watch, to a chart, to the compass. There was a pencil lying on the chart, but she never used it. All calculations as to direction and distance of the horns were made in her own mind as she took the cruiser though the straits, into the crowded anchorage at Tiburon and safely on to its berth at the club pier.

Morgan could have applauded her, but he was also wondering if her brain worked in the same manner when it came to romance. After all, she had been able to shove him away and say "no" at a moment that had nothing whatever to do with objective reasoning.

It was after six o'clock when they got into Glenna's station wagon. Morgan was hungry again, but Glenna had a dinner engagement with her son and his wife that could not be missed. She drove through the fog at a speed far above safety, but she made it into the city without incident. Morgan had her drop him off on Chestnut, the business street of the Marina district. She dug her fingers into his shoulders, kissed him fiercely and whispered in his ear, "It will only be a little while. Wait for me, darling. Wait."

"Sure. I'm not going anywhere."

He stood on the curb and waved to her as she pulled away, then walked down the street until he found a large Italian restaurant. He dined on minestrone, salad, antipasto and fresh tagliatelli covered with sauce and spicy meat balls. When he stood again on the foggy street he felt heavy and uncomfortable and decided against taking a taxi the seven or eight blocks to Pacific Heights. He had eaten too much. The walk would do him good.

He made his way slowly up Fillmore as the street lights came on, enjoying the damp feel of the fog and the slight suggestion of ocean salt in his nostrils. But when he reached Union Street he was thirsty and paused on a corner to stare at a bar called the New Rainbow. He could almost taste the cold beer in his throat and decided that a bottle or two would be safe enough. He had yet to go on a binge while working, and never had his alcoholic adventures been inspired by weak California beer. He turned into the bar.

It was a fairly large room with a bar in the shape of a figure eight cut in half. There were divans, couches and small tables in the section away from the bar, and a grand piano in one corner. A Negro woman was at the piano singing popular tunes in an excellent voice. Morgan stood just inside the door for a moment listening to her and liking her and looking about at the few dozen other customers. Then he moved to the bar and to an empty leather stool at the service end and squinted at the name on the bartender's white jacket.

"I'll have a bottle of beer, Nat. Cold. Make it Olympia."

Nat was an amiable Italian with thinning hair, shrewd eyes and the build of a middleweight stevedore. When he brought the cold bottle and the glass to Morgan he watched him pour and drink deeply, then said, "I don't think I've seen you around before."

Morgan sighed with satisfaction, poured more beer into the glass and shook his head. "I'm a stranger in town. Morgan O'Keefe is the name, by the way." He reached across the bar to shake hands and smiled. "I always introduce myself to bartenders, if I like the place. Then, at least, they know who I am and where to send the body."

Nat laughed. "Good idea. Where do you get your body sent?"

Morgan told him Irene's Pacific Street address and Nat frowned thoughtfully for a moment, then said, "Yeah. That's between Buchanan and Webster. About a block from Frank Wilson's home. What a man! Do you know Mr. Wilson?"

Morgan was about to reply that he did and thought better of it and lied, "No, I haven't had the pleasure. Heard of him, though. Why do you say, 'What a man'?"

Nat laughed at some secret joke and said, "No reason," and walked away to wait on someone farther down the bar.

A little man with a bald head and far gone in his cups was sitting next to Morgan. He nudged Morgan with his elbow and tittered and said, "Nat don't talk about his customers. Says it ain't good business. I seen this guy Wilson, though, lotsa times. Big guy and a big shot, too. A real wheel downtown. They don't come much bigger'n this guy Wilson, believe me." He eyed Morgan's sweatshirt and figured he wasn't so much, so he said, "But he's a real good guy, too. Regular. Know what I mean? Almost like you'n me. Buys me a drink every time I see him. Been doing' it for years." Something struck him funny and he tittered again and subsided into silence, staring into his glass.

Morgan said quickly, "You say he comes in here quite often?"

The little man bobbed his head. "Regular's clockwork. Let's see—" Then he looked down the bar and bawled at Nat, "Hey, Nat. How often's that Wilson guy come in?"

The bartender slanted a suspicious glance in their direction and growled, "None of your business. Why don't you shut up, Johnny?"

Johnny shut up for perhaps a long minute, then forgot about Nat and snickered. "I remember now. Once a month he comes in. Him and another guy. Regular's clockwork. Been doin' it for years and years. This Mr. Wilson has a couple highballs and sets 'em up whoever's at the bar and then he just takes off. Never hangs around. But Casey always stays and gets himself rip-roarin' plastered and then he takes off too for the whore houses over the hill."

"Casey, you say?"

"Yeah." He glared at Morgan and said accusingly, "Hell, chum, you know Casey. Casey, the carpenter?"

"I—ah—I'm afraid I don't know the gentleman."

"Cripes, he's in here practically every night. Husky old Irishman maybe in his sixties? Red face. Big blue nose. But he ain't no carpenter no more, though. Uh-uh. Been retired for—let's see—well, for years and years. Uh-huh. Fell into some dough somewheres. Lives off the fat a the land."

"And this carpenter is a friend of Mr. Wilson?"

Johnny stared at him with his mouth open, then burst out laughing. When the laughter subsided into a coughing fit and then that ended he said, "Friends, my ass! Way it looks to me, they hate each other's guts. I never could figure it out. No, sir, and I'm tellin' you the truth, it's got me. You know how Casey is."

"Sure."

"Kind of a slob, y' know. Always braggin' 'n' blowin'."

"Only man I ever seen should wipe his mouth with toilet paper. Jeez what a foul ball that bastard is. But you know Casey."

"Sure." Morgan called Nat over and bought another beer for himself and a double highball for Johnny, who regarded him suspiciously for a moment until he made up his mind that Morgan was not a fairy on the make.

Morgan said, "This is all pretty interesting. Men like Wilson and Casey. You don't see opposite types like that together very often."

"Every month, pal. You know how Casey is, he's here alla time, but once a month, regular as clockwork, he comes in with Mr. Wilson. It beats me, by hell. I never could figure that out. And this Wilson's such a regular guy, too. Big wheel, but regular."

That was all Morgan was able to learn. He sipped slowly at his second beer and plied the little man with another double highball and kept him talking, but he was simply repeating himself. Morgan left the bar while Johnny was bellowing across the room at the singer, "Hey, Inez, how 'bout a little good ol' rock 'n roll?"

Morgan's curiosity was aroused to the point where he had to know more. That Frank Wilson should patronize a neighborhood bar was strange enough, but that it should be a habit that had extended over many years and always in the company of a man such as Johnny had described was a mystery that cried out for solution. Possibly, he thought, the answer was something very simple, such as Casey being an old retainer, but it hardly seemed likely. Morgan felt instinctively that there was something secretive about the monthly meeting, and secrets maddened him. He had to know more. He promised himself that he would make a habit of dropping into the New Rainbow from then on.

He went up the steep Fillmore Street hill in far better shape than when he had walked it originally and turned down Pacific to Irene's house. He let himself in and started down the lighted hallway toward his apartment, but paused at the open door of the study. Irene was seated at a desk looking through the scrapbook. She was turned partly away from him, in a pool of light from a single lamp. He could see her profile and the agony etched in the lines about her eyes and mouth.

When Morgan walked into the room she started guiltily and quickly closed the scrapbook. She was in slippers, nightgown and a robe, her heavy black hair pulled back and tied with a pink ribbon. She had apparently gone to bed, then had got up, for some reason, to look through the clippings.

Morgan dropped into a leather chair away from the light, shook a cigarette loose from a pack in his pocket and touched a match to it. He blew out a puff of smoke. "Sorry I missed dinner. Have anything special?"

She was looking down at her hands, which were placed flatly on the desk, as if she did not wish to meet his eyes. She said softly, "It was a very nice roast, the kind Anna says you like. She's very fond of you, you know."

"That's a compliment. She's a wonderful woman. Sorry I wasn't here."

"If you wish to go back to the kitchen—"

"Thanks, but I ate a little while ago." He nodded toward the scrapbook. "I see you're indulging in a little self-torture again. Do you think possibly you may have a masochistic streak in you?"

Her lips thinned. "If you don't mind—"

"But I do. I have also become rather fond of you." He leaned forward with his elbows on his knees and said earnestly, "Look, Irene. Have you ever taken your problem to a psychiatrist? I like to rib those characters, and most of them have a hell of a lot less knowledge than they need, but I have respect for a few of them."

She was silent for a moment, still looking at her hands, then her eyes swung around to meet his. "A few years back," she said, "I went to a psychiatrist for perhaps a dozen visits."

"And?"

"It was no use."

He said angrily, "For God's sake, Irene, you can't go on living this way, torturing yourself and wondering and wondering year after year. That's easy to say, I know, but, damn it all, you do have to make an effort to believe in yourself."

She leaned back in her chair and said wearily, "I do believe in myself, most of the time. I know positively I could never have done such a thing. But then—then—Oh, God, I don't know. The doubt is always there. It never really leaves, even when I'm positive."

"So you're never positive." He puffed at the cigarette and blew smoke to the ceiling. "I learned something new today. I was out with Glenna on her cruiser—"

"I know."

He glanced at her sharply. "How did you know?"

"Frank called."

"Oh."

"He knew. He's quite upset and more than a little angry. He doesn't trust your kind very far, as he put it, and I guess at this point he doesn't trust Glenna at all. He asked me to send you on your way at once. In fact, he demanded it. He offered to send over some money for you and an airplane ticket for wherever you wished to go. The farther the better." She paused, then added, "He could make it well worth your while to leave."

"I see. And what did you say?"

"I said that I would tell you about it."

"I mean other than that."

She looked down at her hands again and after a moment her eyes came slowly around to his. Morgan saw pain in their depths. She said, "I said that I would tell you and pass on his offer. However, you don't have to leave because of his demand. You're free to stay and finish your work."

"Looks like I'll be causing trouble between the two of you."

"Do you prefer to accept his offer?"

He chuckled. "No. I'm staying right here. Anyway, as far as he's concerned, the bird has already flown. She's definitely going to leave him, and there's nothing he can do to stop it. I don't suppose that's what he had in mind, though. Probably what ails him is his fear that she's in the mood for an affair and I happen to be conveniently handy and unattached. As well," he laughed, "as being a red-blooded American boy. He can stop fretting about that. Glenna seems to be allergic to adultery, surprising as it may sound. I know, because I was in there pitching."

Irene stiffened. "You can say the most awful things about people. Why are you so deliberately common?"

"I was born that way and since then I've logged some real hours working on it."

"You're a guest in my home. If you had an affair with Glenna I'd feel responsible for it."

"Don't be so damned prim and proper. If I had an affair with Glenna it would be because the two of us wanted it and responsibility begins and ends right there. Where do you get off trying to get into the act? You're certainly not pimping for me."

She buried her face in her hands and moaned, "Oh, my God. The garbage in your mind—"

"Good God, why don't you take off those blinders you wear? As far as that goes, why don't you take off those clothes and let's roll on the floor together? I've been frustrated once today. That's enough. Once more and I'll be a eunuch."

Her head snapped up and she was about to reply hotly, but he had leaned into the edge of light and she saw the laughter dancing in his eyes. "Sometimes—" she said, and let it go unfinished.

"Forget it," he said. "I was kidding, even though it is a splendid idea. Getting back to what I learned, though: Glenna was telling me something interesting. She says that the pistol you used to scrag your husband—" he saw her stiffen again, but continued— "was a cheap model that was probably bought in a hock shop. She says also that your husband would never have dreamed of purchasing anything but the best, and that you were probably the one who bought it somewhere. I'm curious. How about that?"

"Glenna would say that."

"Oh, sure. But how about it?"

"I guess it was a cheap model. So I was told. I don't know anything about guns."

"But was it the gun your husband bought for you?"

She frowned and chewed at her lip as she thought for a moment. "It had to be. It was on the night stand beside the bed. I picked it up and—and fired it."

"Then you're positive it was the gun he bought for you."

"Well, no. I didn't say that, exactly. But I guess it had to be."

"You guess it had to be."

"Yes. As I say, I don't know one gun from another, but it was there and that was the one I used and the police made some tests and they said it was the right gun."

"Uh-huh." He sat back, not quite knowing what he was after, but feeling that he was on the edge of something solid and substantial. "I see. On the other hand, though, the gun your husband bought for you originally could have been substituted by another and you would never have known the difference."

She looked puzzled, but nodded. "I guess so. But what would be the purpose of such a substitution?"

He crushed his cigarette out in a tray and slapped his hands on his thighs. "I'm damned if I know. But I do think Glenna knew what she was talking about in one particular. She said flatly that even if Jay had seen such a gun in a pawn shop window he would nevertheless have gone far out of his way to buy the best. Was he that way or not?"

"Oh, yes. Very much so. Jay was a snob in some ways—I guess we all are—and he would never settle for anything less than the best. Even during the war he drove a Rolls-Royce convertible, which was a decidedly unfashionable thing to do at the time. But that's the way he was. Always the best."

Morgan smiled wryly. "Then that would definitely seem to indicate that you were the one who bought the gun to fulfill some criminal design of your own. Can you blame Glenna for thinking the way she does?"

"Yes, I do," she cried. "I never bought a gun in my life, neither that nor any other. Never!"

"Okay. I believe you. I believe you even more than you believe yourself. So you never bought the gun. But someone had to buy it. The only other person is your husband, and he wasn't the type to buy that kind of gun. Where does that leave us?" He sat up suddenly and cried excitedly, "Hey, wait a minute. The prowler who was captured here. What was his name?"

"Scapini."

"Yeah." He stared at her and shook his head and sank back into the chair. "No, that couldn't be it. He was unarmed. Besides, he was a desperate character, and if he had had a gun he would never have allowed Frank to take him. He would have found some way out, even with a broken leg. No, that's out. You know, by God, that gun has my head spinning. There's something important about it. I know it."

She got to her feet and looked down at him and said gently, "You're trying to make something else out of this tragedy, Morgan. But it's all simple enough, really, too terribly simple. Apparently, for one of the few times in his life, Jay did not go out of his way to buy the best. Probably somebody he knew told him that I should have a gun in the house and sold that one to him, or gave it to him, for all I know. I don't think there's any great mystery about it. Perhaps I'd like to, but the facts indicate otherwise."

"I don't know."

"Well, I do. Good night, Morgan. I think I'll go back to bed."

She walked to the doorway and he inhaled the perfume in the air and watched the graceful swing of her body. She paused and looked back at him. "By the way, how's the book going?"

"Very well. About another week, I think." He got to his feet and joined her in the doorway. "Funny thing about this rewrite job. When I started it I was damned resentful at being forced to do it. But not any longer. Lately I've noticed that I've become more than a little interested and perhaps even excited over changing those characters of mine. Odd, isn't it?"

"I guess so. I'm glad it's going well."

He looked down into her dark eyes. "Or perhaps it's not so odd, after all."

Her eyes slid away. "Why do you say that?"

"Because I think you're responsible. For the first time in a long while I've felt deeply sorry for someone. I couldn't live in this house and be around you as I have without feeling it."

She whispered, "I don't want anyone's sympathy."

"Whether you want it or not has nothing to do with it. You have it. Allow me to enjoy the luxury of sympathy, please. It doesn't happen to me often. And somehow or other it has crept into my writing."

"That's a good thing."

"A few weeks ago I would have given you an argument on that. But now—maybe you're right. Last night I lay awake for quite a while thinking things over. Perhaps I've been tilting at windmills and punching at empty air long enough. Suddenly it seemed that way."

"Truly?"

"I think so. I've always assumed there was direction in my work, but when I tried to pin it down last night I found that it didn't exist. I've been writing simply because I have to write. It's a compulsion that cannot be denied. But there must be direction. There has to be."

She moved slightly away from him. "I should imagine so."

"Of course." He reached out and touched her shoulder gently. "It's pretty queer, but watching you has unlocked something inside of me."

"I—I'm glad—"

"Are you, really?"

She tried to look into his eyes but could not. He noticed then that her body was trembling slightly at his touch and when his fingers tightened on her shoulder she jerked convulsively and pulled away. She whispered something inaudible under her breath, turned, paused with indecision, then hurried away from him and down the hallway and up the broad staircase.

Chapter Eight

Morgan worked hard the following day, took a long walk in the afternoon, and that evening had dinner with Irene. She was quiet and withdrawn and had little to say, so he did most of the talking. Nicky dropped by shortly after nine o'-clock and he and Morgan went into the study to talk. Though they were opposites in temperament and character, in the short time they had known each other they had become fast friends.

Their conversation ranged through literature and politics and the weather and the good restaurants San Francisco had to offer, but after an hour or so Morgan pinned it down to something more specific. He wanted to know more about Frank Wilson.

Nicky sat back lazily in his chair opposite Morgan and frowned. "He's a hard man to fathom. I thought I knew him pretty well, at one time, but not any more. He's changed so tremendously."

"I understand it's all happened since his brother was killed."

"Oh, sure. It had a terrible effect on him. Possibly some feeling of guilt is involved in it, too."

"You mean because of his attempt to have Irene prosecuted?"

"That's part of it, but that isn't what I mean. It had to do with his brother. They'd always been crazy about each other, but at that particular time they weren't getting along at all."

Morgan's eyebrows jumped. He said sharply, "I'd never heard that before."

Nicky chuckled. "I suppose there's a lot you haven't heard. No one is anxious to dig up old ghosts. Besides, I don't think too many people knew about it. I knew, because Jay and I were very good friends and he was a guy who liked to blow off steam with someone, so I was the one who had to listen to him. I don't think even Irene and Glenna were very much aware of what had happened between the two brothers."

"What had happened?"

Nicky reached for a cigarette and took his time lighting it. "Well, old Frank has always resented the distribution of the Tinsley-Wilson estates. Can't say that I blame him, as a matter of fact. Of course, you can't blame old Mr. Tinsley for leaving everything to Irene, his only child, but it did make it rough on the Wilsons. Frank winds up with a mere twenty-five per cent, yet he's the one who's always had to run the whole damned works ever since the three of them inherited."

"I imagine he takes a nice fat salary for that, doesn't he?"

"Naturally. But that isn't a drop in the bucket compared to the dividends and bonuses and odd profits that come pouring in. So he does all the work, and his brother Jay got almost as much out of it as Frank, and Irene collected as much as the two of them put together. Hardly seems equitable. Wouldn't you say?"

"Depends on how many millions you need to scrape along on after you have the first one."

Nicky laughed. "Maybe so. But it really isn't an equitable arrangement and Frank was plenty peeved about it. Then Jay and Irene had their troubles and Jay started living pretty fast. He had always been a reckless driver, but then he started driving more recklessly than ever, especially when he had a few snorts under his belt, which was most of the time. About two months before he was killed he wrecked a car down the Peninsula doing pretty close to a hundred miles an hour. The car was totaled out—completely. How in God's name he ever got out of that alive I don't know, but he walked away from it with little more than a few scratches and bruises."

"Sounds like his guardian angel was riding on his shoulder."

"Must have been. Anyway, Frank expected the accident to slow him down, but Jay's foot was just as heavy on that pedal as ever. Then Frank got scared and raised hell with him. It got him nowhere. Jay lived as he damned well pleased, and even Frank couldn't slow him down. So, a couple of weeks before the shooting, Frank told Jay that if he kept on the way he was going he would undoubtedly kill himself. Frank asked him to put all his affairs in order and to make out a will. Jay told him that he had already made out his will the year before, leaving everything to Irene. Frank hadn't known that before, and literally blew his stack." He smiled and said, "I wasn't there, but the way Jay described it to me later it must have been quite a scene."

"I'm beginning to see a light dimly."

"Uh-huh. If anything happened to Jay, then Irene would own three-quarters of the whole works, which, of course, is the way it did happen. Frank couldn't buy that at all. He pleaded with Jay to change the will, either with himself as beneficiary, or his son and daughter, or all three."

"Wait a minute. Did Frank have some specific dislike for Irene?"

"None whatever. He was very fond of her. That's not the idea. With him it was strictly business. In case something happened, he didn't want control passing into anyone else's hands. Not just Irene—anyone. He ran the business and he wanted no interference. Of course since then Irene never has interfered. But how was he to know that at the time? So he wanted that will changed and he and Jay had a hell of a row over it and were hardly speaking to each other when the end came—" he snapped his fingers—"like that."

Morgan sat back and thought it over. "Seems to me Jay would have been amenable to changing his will, the way he was getting along with Irene."

"That none of us will ever know. I think that Jay felt that Irene would eventually snap out of her prissy attitude and that everything would work out all right between them. He was really very much in love with her. On the other hand, if it had come to divorce, Jay would naturally have changed the will. Anyway, that was the bone of contention between Frank and Jay."

"I see. Maybe there's something else you can tell me. The way it all adds up, Irene was the one responsible for the trouble between her and her husband. Is that true?"

Nicky glanced at his watch and stood up to leave. "Yes, I'm afraid so. Irene is a wonderful person, and Tina and I are damned fond of her, but at that time she was a little difficult to get along with."

"Spoiled?"

"God, yes! She was so used to having everything her own way that when she married Jay she expected him to jump every time she snapped her fingers. But Jay wasn't the jumping kind. And every time he failed to jump she got mad and they had a row and things went from bad to worse and—well, Jay just started going his own way."

"It's hard for me to think of her as that kind of person."

"Sure. Because she's so different now." Nicky smiled and said, "I've been wondering about when you finish your book. Do you intend staying on here in San Francisco?"

Morgan thought of Glenna and her plans. "I don't know. Why?"

"Well, there's a friend of ours a few blocks from where we live who has a beautiful studio apartment over the garage. He has no need and no desire to rent it to anyone, but I've told him about you and I'm pretty sure I can get it for you. It would be terrific having you so close to us."

Morgan looked at him warmly. "Thanks, Nicky. I'll let you know."
"Sure. Well, I gotta run. Be seeing you."

Morgan was interested in what Nicky had had to say about the two brothers, but he was considerably more interested in Casey. The following night, immediately after dinner, he walked down the Fillmore hill and into the New Rainbow bar. Nat recognized him and grinned and started after a bottle of beer in the cold locker, but Morgan asked for a Coke.

A few couples were at the tables and half a dozen people were seated on the stools at the bar. Morgan spotted a stocky Irishman with a beet-red face and a bulbous nose. He dropped onto the stool at his side. The Irishman was wearing corduroys, heavy brogans, a loud flannel shirt, a leather jacket and a heavy knitted stocking cap. He had a barrel chest and his shoulders were heavy from a lifetime of labor, but his big hands had gone soft. He was talking loudly and belligerently with Johnny, the little man Morgan had met before, who was seated on the stool at the Irishman's other side. Johnny said, "Aw, you're nuts, Casey." Morgan relaxed. He had the right man.

He listened quietly to their conversation for a long while without attempting to cut in, and he realized that Johnny had understated the case when he had said that Casey had a foul mouth and was a braggart. Morgan had once known a sergeant exactly like him and figured that Casey had the same weakness, a terrible hunger for flattery.

Johnny got angry finally and stalked away from the bar. Morgan turned to Casey and said, "That was quite a discussion you two were having. Frankly, I agree with you."

Casey turned his head slowly on a bull neck and growled, "What the hell's it to you?"

Morgan said patiently, "Nothing, really. I was just interested in what you two were saying."

"Yeah? Say, look; you go around alla time stickin' yer nose in other people's business? I ain't never seen you before."

"O'Keefe's the name. Morgan O'Keefe."

"Sounds like an Irishman," he sneered, "but you sure's hell don't look like one. You look like one a them dudes from the Presidio in civvies. That what you are, a second looie, or somethin'?"

"Not at all." Morgan thought quickly and said desperately, "I'm a carpenter."

Casey stared at him for a moment, then reached suddenly for Morgan's hands and turned them over. "By hell," he bawled, "you sure's hell ain't no carpenter, but you're one, big son-of-a-bitchin' liar. What's the con act for, you silly lookin' butinsky?"

Nat hurried down the bar and leaned over to look steadily into Morgan's eyes. "Better break it off, mister. I don't want any fights in here."

"But I'm not doing anything. It's this stupid jerk who's popping off. I was merely being polite—"

"Break it off, mister. I don't want any fights. Casey, here, is one of my best customers. In case of a row you figure out which one I'll ask to leave."

There was no longer any point in trying to ingratiate himself with the Irishman. Morgan shrugged and walked out of the bar, but he knew he would try again. His curiosity was now so acute that it had to be satisfied, even at risk of getting into a fight with the burly Irishman....

He was back at the bar the following night. There were more people—the place was almost filled—but he found a stool at the service end of the bar. The moment he sat down the bartender placed a bottle of beer before him and, looking down toward the other end of the bar, said, "This is on Casey." Morgan followed the direction of his eyes and saw Casey smiling and nodding. Morgan returned the nod and wondered what miracle had happened.

Casey picked up his own drink and came down the bar to join Morgan, and it was soon apparent what had taken place. Nat had obviously told Casey that he had tangled with a "gentleman" who lived on Pacific Street and Casey was duly impressed.

"I only know one guy up there," he said. "You know Frank Wilson?"

"I've heard of him."

"Nat says you live between Webster and Buchanan. You know Irene Wilson? That's where she lives."

"I know. I'm right next door to her."

"Oh. Nice gal?"

"Seems to be."

"Yeah. I figured that." He looked at his own image in the backbar mirror and burst into loud laughter at some joke, then turned his sharp little pig eyes back to Morgan. "What was all that crap you was handin' out last night 'bout bein' a carpenter? That's what I was and you sure's hell ain't."

Morgan smiled. "I thought it was more in keeping with the place. I guess I was wrong."

"You sure was. Lotsa swells come in here."

"I suppose the two of us just got off on the wrong foot."

"Yeah. You seem like a good joe. What's yer line, anyways?"

Morgan told him the truth and Casey was more impressed than ever. He mentioned a few newspaper reporters he had known in the old days, but Morgan was the first book writer he had ever met. In no time at all Casey was completely at ease with his new-found buddy and began talking volubly of the old days. After an hour or more, with Casey doing most of the talking and all the heavy drinking, Morgan again brought the conversation casually around to the Wilsons. "I've been thinking a lot about that case," he said. "I imagine you remember it well. Don't you?"

Casey snorted, "Ha!" and chuckled quietly as he stared down into his glass.

Morgan said, "It's so interesting that I went down to the library and read through all the old newspaper reports. I have a hunch there's a good story in that case."

"How d'ya mean?"

"I mean fiction."

"Is that the way you get books?"

"Sometimes. Of course, when you take something from life, such as the Wilson case, you have to alter it considerably to avoid libel. But it would be altered, anyway. Things that happen in real life rarely make good fiction. It's important, though, that the writer does have all the facts at hand. I imagine you remember the case quite well?"

"Yeah." Casey grinned at himself in the mirror and said, "I'll say I remember it." He burst into laughter again and took a long time subsiding. "Jeez, do I remember it! I could tell you things, mister—" But then he caught Morgan's eyes in the mirror and stopped smiling. His own eyes narrowed suspiciously. "Hey, look," he asked, "what's the pitch? What's goin' on here?"

Morgan said innocently, "I'm afraid I don't understand."

Casey turned on the stool and stuck his nose forward a few inches from Morgan's face. He said dangerously, "Casey ain't no fool, mister. Alla time I been talkin' you been nice and polite and you listen real good. But the only time you talk yourself it's about the Wilson case."

He twisted about and yelled at Nat and when the bartender stood before them Casey asked him, "What's that address this guy told you he lives at?"

Nat's eyes jumped from one to the other and he said, "I don't remember."

"Don't gimme that crap. I know you. You got a memory like an elephant. What's that address he told you?"

Nat scratched his head, as if trying to think, then told him the address. Casey left the stool and walked into the telephone booth, where Morgan could hear him rustling through the leaves of the telephone book. Morgan had a hunch what he was looking for and got up to leave quickly, but Casey was back and standing before him.

He sneered at Morgan, "Next door, says you. You don't live any next door. You live right smack in Irene Wilson's place. I remember now. You're the guy what was mentioned in Caen's column. Say, what's the pitch?"

Morgan was taller than Casey and considerably younger, but the gray-haired Irishman still had a lot of tough muscle on his frame and Morgan had an idea he would be an expert in rough fighting. His mind raced for alternatives to a brawl and he came up with one that was a stab in the dark, but might work.

He got to his feet and smiled thinly, but wisely, at the Irishman. "Maybe," he said, "you'd better ask Frank Wilson. And maybe, if you do, you'll have to start working as a carpenter again. Now do we understand each other?"

All the fight was drained out of Casey as fast as if he had been hit with a baseball bat. His mouth went slack, his jowls sagged and he stared fearfully at Morgan. He was incapable of speech. He turned slowly away from Morgan and walked through the swinging glass doors and out of the bar like a sleepwalker.

The bartender blinked. "I don't get it."

Morgan sucked in a huge breath of air and let it out in a sigh. "Neither do I—yet. But I will."

He went home and thought about it for hours that night in bed. All that he knew about Casey was that he was a retired carpenter who seemed to have sufficient funds to drink as he pleased; he had been meeting Frank Wilson at the New Rainbow once a month for many years, and yet, according to Johnny, Wilson and Casey had no liking whatever for each other. The situation was a minor mystery, yet there was really nothing in it to inspire the remark he had made, the remark that had frightened the carpenter.

Yet he had made the remark, and somewhere, perhaps on the very edge of conscious thought, was a reason for the inspired statement. But he couldn't force it into the open that night, and the following day he was again hard at work and had put it entirely out of his mind.

That evening, Glenna telephoned and wanted to meet him secretly in some theater. "Frank," she said, "knows about our spending Sunday together. I think he pays one of the crew to let him know about everyone who goes aboard the *Teal*."

"Are you worried?"

"Well, no, not especially. We've already had a scene about it." She laughed throatily and said, "He thinks I should be more select in my choice of friends. Anyway, I would like to see you for a few minutes—"

"Sorry," he lied, "I'm doing some polishing on the book. Besides, I can't see myself necking with you in some theater balcony. Now, if you had only suggested a motel—"

"You fool," she laughed. "Can't you wait until I go to Reno?"

"It isn't easy. And it's going to get a lot tougher when I finish my work, in a few days."

"Why?"

"Because then I won't have anything on my mind except you. And that little scene on the deck of your cruiser is going to raise hell with my imagination."

She promised breathlessly, "It won't be long, darling, believe me."

"When are you telling your husband?"

"As soon as my attorneys tell me that everything is in order. Just a few weeks. But look; I do have to see you again. The cruiser is out. I don't want another row with Frank before the big blowup. Why don't I meet you somewhere Sunday morning and we'll go for a long ride?"

"I don't like long rides."

"Morgan, are you being deliberately difficult?"

He laughed at his own foolishness and said, "I guess I am. I'm sorry. I have the book on my mind and I have to get rid of that before I can think straight.

Give me a call some time Saturday and we can arrange a place to meet.''

Morgan was feeling restless, after the call, and the idea of seeing a movie suddenly appealed to him. He went into the study, where Irene was reading a magazine, and looked through the movie page of one of the newspapers. There was a double feature at the Metro a few blocks away. One of the films had been written by an acquaintance of his in Hollywood and might be interesting.

And if not he would at least enjoy himself tearing the other writer's work apart.

He turned to Irene, who was watching him curiously, and asked, "How about you? Would you like to see a movie with me?"

She stared at him as if he had lost his mind. She said, "But I—I haven't been to a theater—"

"Sure, I know. You haven't been to a movie in ten years. You haven't done anything in ten years. Look. A movie would do you good. The Metro is just down on Union Street, so we can walk. Put on your bonnet and we'll take off in ten minutes."

He went back to his apartment and put on a white shirt and tie and jacket. He didn't think that Irene would go with him, but when he stepped into the hallway she was waiting for him at the main door. She had perched a little hat on the back of her head and a mink stole was draped about her shoulders.

She took his arm as they went out the door and laughed. "This is kind of an adventure for me."

"You bet. Out in the big, wide world."

"Don't make fun of me, please."

He patted her hand and smiled at her in the dark. "Sorry."

They went down Webster, dark and steep, to the well lighted Union Street and into the loge section of the Metro. In a very short time, Morgan was more interested in Irene than he was in what transpired on the big, curved screen. It had been so long since she had seen a movie that her reactions were almost those of a child. She laughed softly at anything even remotely suggesting humor, she stiffened with tension during moments of suspense, her features were soft and her eyes gentle during the love scenes, and at the tragic ending of the first film her eyes were filled with tears. When the lights came on for intermission she borrowed a handkerchief from Morgan.

The second film was a good Western with the sort of action Morgan enjoyed—lots of horses and gunplay and chase scenes and the climactic showdown at the old corral. But he enjoyed Irene even more. She watched the unfolding of the story with all the wide-eyed naiveté of a young girl. Whenever the action became furious she grabbed Morgan's arm and dug her fingers in until they hurt. And at the end she looked at Morgan and nodded seriously as if to say, "I'm glad that villain got his."

When they were outside and had started up the dark hill, Morgan said, "You really had a time for yourself, didn't you?"

She had to laugh at herself. "It's been so long," she said. "I guess I did everything but shout, 'They went thataway.'"

"You weren't far from it."

"I remember the first movie I ever saw. I was four years old. I couldn't have been any worse then. The hero in that one died and I was almost hysterical that night. It took days for my father to convince me that the man was just an actor and that he wasn't really dead. Even then I wasn't really convinced until he took me to another theater where the same actor was playing and that time he was alive at the ending."

"Do you feel everything so deeply?"

"I—I guess so. When I'm on guard I can hide my emotions rather well, perhaps better than most people, but tonight, well—" she laughed—"I was just off guard, that's all. I had forgotten the impact movies can have on people."

The hill they were climbing was one of the steepest in San Francisco, and at the end of two blocks Irene was winded. They paused to rest, then continued on. Morgan put his arm about her waist to help her along, and at once felt her body tense. She did not protest, but he had to put his hand back to her elbow before she was able to relax again. For weeks he had been assuming that she was a frigid woman, but now he was beginning to realize that her reactions were those of sexual awareness.

He looked down at her, at the sharp rise of her breasts and the intensely feminine sway of her rounded hips, and his mouth was suddenly dry. She glanced up at him with a smile and caught his eyes and the smile faded. She looked quickly away and walked faster, even though she was breathing hard.

They were thirsty when they arrived at the house, so Morgan got some cold beer from the kitchen and brought it into the study. They drank standing up by the large windows, looking out over the lights of the Marina District below.

Morgan asked Irene, "By the way, did you ever know anyone by the name of Casey?"

"Casey?" Irene frowned and shook her head. "I don't think so."

"He's an Irishman in his sixties, a retired carpenter."

"No, I don't think I know him. Some carpenters made a number of changes in the house some years back, but as I remember they were all rather young. Anyway, the name isn't familiar."

"He seems to be a friend of Frank Wilson. I met him down at a neighborhood bar recently. From what I understand, this carpenter and your brother-in-law meet at the bar exactly once a month. They've been doing it for years. They don't especially care for each other, either. It struck me as being pretty queer."

"Very strange. But why do you ask about it?"

"You just gave the reason yourself: very strange. I got curious. I thought you might know. So the name doesn't ring a bell?"

"No."

"Then let's skip it."

She sipped at her glass, then said, "Morgan—"

"Hmmmmm?"

"You're almost through with the book?"

"Just about."

"What are your plans then, I mean, for the future?"

He shrugged. "Nothing definite. Why?"

Her voice wavered faintly as she said, "I've been wondering if—if Glenna entered into your plans somehow. I know she's going to leave Frank; it's been coming to a head for some time. She's a beautiful woman and she has a natural hunger for glamour and excitement and—and love, too, I suppose."

"She's built for it."

"I—I guess so. And I can't really say that I blame her for feeling as she does. Frank has withdrawn into a shell; he concentrates on business only, and he makes no attempt whatever to see that Glenna has a more satisfactory life. I know he loves her—"

"How do you know that?"

She looked surprised. "Why, he always has. He still does—it's quite obvious, just the way he looks at her."

"Then I'd say he's a damned odd bird. Here he has a beautiful wife he's supposed to be in love with and yet he's allowing her to slip through his fingers with no attempt to meet her halfway and save the marriage. How do you account for that?"

"It is preposterous, isn't it? I don't know how to account for it, except to say that there's something badly wrong with him. There's something eating away inside of him, something he fears."

Morgan said sharply, "It isn't simply that guilt feeling over trying to indict you?"

"No," she said slowly, "I don't think that's all of it. Not any more. There's something that goes deeper than that."

Morgan smiled thinly. "Sure. You know what? Your perspective is changing. You're beginning to think. Of course there's something deeper gnawing away inside the man. So he made a mistake about you and he regretted it, but, believe me, it is not human nature for a man to suffer over something of that sort for ten long years."

"Well, there was his brother's death too—"

"Not that, either. Perhaps a man leading a sedentary sort of life would grieve longer than anyone else, but he's a damned active man, at least in his business."

"He changed at that time."

"Uh-huh. But something else did it."

She walked away from him to put her empty glass on a table, then returned to stand at his side. Her shoulder brushed his accidentally and she jerked away. Morgan looked at her curiously. The idea that had suddenly come to his mind must be wrong. It had to be. The lady and the drunk? Never.

She said, "I think you're right. Lately, since you've been working here, I've been reliving that terrible ordeal all over again. What it's done to me is understandable, but I can no longer accept the surface reasons for Frank's attitude. He's not carrying the burden of his brother's death on his shoulders. Nor does he have to look into the eyes of people who are convinced that he's a cold-blooded killer."

"Yet he's been suffering as long as you have."

"I know. And I no longer understand it." She looked deeply into Morgan's eyes and asked breathlessly, "Do you?"

"I don't know, Irene. There's something nagging away at the edge of my brain, a light seen dimly in the distance. I have the same feeling when a new plot begins creeping into my mind and I know it's there and I can feel it, but it still lacks shape and identity and I can't name it."

Her shoulders sagged and she whispered, "I had hoped, with your imagination, your awareness—"

"It may come into the light yet."

"But not soon enough to help."

"To help whom?"

"Glenna and Frank. Someone has to help them, or everything's going to come apart."

"I'll be damned." He burst out laughing for a moment. "A few minutes ago you seemed to think Glenna was part of my plans for the future—"

She said stubbornly, "I still think so. You're exactly the kind of man who would fascinate her."

"And in your next breath you seem to think I could be the savior of their marriage."

"I think that, too."

He put his hands on her shoulders and spun her about to face him. "Look, Irene; I'm not interested in their marriage and I don't really give a damn about either of them. I am interested in you, though. You pose a challenge." She tried to squirm free, but his fingers tightened on her shoulders. "A tragedy has cut your life off and buried you in this granite tomb. But I have a feeling about you that might breathe life into you again, a feeling that something's haywire and that there's a terribly big key piece missing in the pattern of your situation. I'd give my right arm to know what that key might be. You see," he said softly, "you wish to be loved, too—even more so than Glenna. But to be loved again you have to live again."

Tears came into her eyes and she leaned into his arms and clung to him fiercely. But then she broke from his arms and turned and ran from the room.

Morgan remained standing where he was for a long while, staring at the door through which she had disappeared. Rage was burning within him. He walked to the study bar and poured a tall glass half full of bourbon, but when he raised the glass to his lips he knew what would happen. One drink was too much and a thousand drinks were never enough. He poured the whisky carefully back into the bottle. But he still wanted to strike out at someone, almost anyone. Someone else had to be hurt to the same extent Irene had been hurt.

Chapter Nine

The next time Morgan saw Irene she was as cool and distant as ever, as if she had never been crying in his arms. He was tempted to stir her emotions again, but put it aside to lose himself in his work.

The rewrite job was completed at midafternoon of a Friday. He pulled the last page from the typewriter, stacked it with the others and separated the carbon copies from the original. He had slightly over a hundred pages of inserts, which he placed in a manila envelope with a brief letter to his agent. He walked down the hill to Union Street and airmailed the envelope; with any sort of luck, Earl would be able to wire him the additional advance from the publishers within a week. It wasn't necessary for his agent to actually secure the check from Norwood and Buttle. As long as he had their confirmation he would be willing, Morgan knew, to send the money from his own funds. And then, he wondered—Reno?

He went outside the post office and stood on the sidewalk looking across the street at the New Rainbow bar. He was thirsty for a beer or two, but he was also afraid. If he stayed with beer he'd be all right, but the dangerous period with him was always the time immediately following a hard job of writing, when he felt empty and drained. He decided against taking any sort of chance, even with beer.

He lit a cigarette and leaned back against a market window and thought of Irene and Glenna. Suddenly he was thinking again of what Glenna had told him about the pistol Irene had used to shoot her husband. The more he thought of it the greater grew his curiosity, and finally he had to laugh at himself, knowing his curiosity must be satisfied.

He got into a taxi at the corner and told the driver to take him to police headquarters. Going voluntarily to the police about anything was something new, and it amused him. He was not so amused when he found himself back at the gray building whence he had been discharged at the end of his binge. He shrugged and went inside, located the Central offices and was directed to Homicide. He ran into complete indifference from the men on duty until he mentioned the Wilson name. He was directed down a hallway and shortly found himself in the cubbyhole office of Lieutenant Scanlon. The officer nodded at him from behind a desk littered with papers and waved him to a hard chair.

Scanlon was a big, bulky man of middle age, with thinning gray hair and the wise, tired eyes of one who has seen too much of the wrong side of life. He listened patiently as Morgan explained his interest in the Wilson case, and became alert when he learned that Morgan was a novelist.

"Well," he said, "it's all good stuff for a story, all right. And you say you're a guest at Irene Wilson's home?"

"Yes."

"Does she know you're down here?"

"No. She's told me a great deal about the case, though, and also made available to me all the old newspaper clippings."

"I'll be damned. I'd imagine she'd be trying to forget it. A terrible thing to happen to anyone. I was in charge of that one and I don't think I'll ever forget it."

"You remember it well?"

Scanlon grinned. "Every detail. That was my first big case and I was anxious to pin a murder rap on someone. But it blew up in my face."

"You sound as if you, too, were convinced that the killing was deliberate. Were you?"

"Now, Mr. O'Keefe, do you honestly expect me to answer that question?"

Morgan shook his head. "I suppose not. However, what I am interested in more than anything else is the gun that was used."

Scanlon sat up straight in his chair, leaned forward with his elbows on the desk and looked into Morgan's eyes. "Just what is it about that pistol that interests you?"

"Virtually everything about it. From what I've learned, it was not the sort of gun Jay Wilson would have bought, no matter how available it may have been. His widow seems to think he may have got it from a friend—"

Scanlon interrupted by shaking his head. "We had to buy that idea, too, but I still don't believe it. Also, Jay Wilson did buy a thirty-eight revolver just prior to the killing. It was on record right here. He bought the gun at Roos Brothers' Market Street. It was the most expensive Smith and Wesson in the place—and it wasn't the gun that Mrs. Wilson had in her possession that night."

Morgan sat back and stared at the lieutenant. "No?"

"No. And that particular gun never has turned up."

"But—but—that sounds like the one he would have bought for his wife."

"That's right."

"Then how do you account—"

"I don't. Frankly. I've never been satisfied with the outcome of that case. I've always felt there was more to it." He smiled sheepishly. "Matter of fact, I get the files out every once in a while and study them again. But I never learn any more than I knew at the time."

"You know more than I, though. Mind if I ask a few questions?"

"Fire away."

"Okay. Did you ever learn where the death weapon did come from?"

Scanlon sucked at his teeth, looked off into space, then shook his head. "No. I'll tell you about that pistol. It was a cheap make of Colt and one that had been around a long time. It'd seen lots of service. It was exactly the sort of pistol a criminal like Scapini would have in his possession. He was the prowler we took that night, you know."

"I know."

"The serial numbers were gone. Usually that doesn't bother us. We have ray machines that can tell us the serial numbers no matter how well they've been filed off. But this one stumped us. The numbers had been altered first before they were filed, which makes it rough because the machine comes up with the wrong numbers; then intense heat had been applied to the steel, probably a welding torch. A real professional job. Only a pro would have a gun like that."

Morgan caught his breath and said, "Scapini."

"Exactly."

"He was unarmed that night. Why?"

"I used to ask myself that same question, over and over again. I asked him plenty of times, too. He was the kind who would never operate without a weapon; we knew he had always packed one before. But he claimed he'd lost it a few days before. He didn't know where. That was as far as we ever got with him."

When he paused and drummed his fingers on the desk, Morgan said sharply, "There's more to it."

"Uh-huh. Two things more. The only fingerprints found on the Colt were Mrs. Wilson's. That didn't make sense to me at the time and still doesn't. If her husband gave her that gun he must have handled it and his prints would be on it. They weren't. Except for her prints, it was clean as a whistle. I asked her if she had wiped it clean. Someone had, obviously. She didn't know. She couldn't remember. In fact, the only time she could ever remember handling it was when her husband gave it to her, showed her how to handle it, then loaded it and placed it on the stand by her bed. That was it, period. She wasn't even too damned sure whether or not it was the same gun her husband had given her."

"I know that. What do you believe?"

Scanlon chuckled. "That's another one I don't think I'll answer."

"You said something about two points—"

"Yeah. Wilson was hit by a straight shot coming from directly before him. That meant that he had to be standing in the doorway of his wife's bedroom and looking inside the room as she fired at him over the foot of her bed. But here's something to consider: the impact of a thirty-eight slug at that short distance is something terrific. It should have slammed him back against the wall on the other side of the hallway before he went down. His body, however, was found a bit farther down the hallway. All right. So maybe he staggered a couple of steps and then went down. I guess it could happen that way."

"But you don't think so."

"I didn't say. I just said it's something to consider, that's all."

"Okay. Now, just for a minute, let's assume that the gun wasn't the same one Wilson had given his wife, and—"

Scanlon placed his hands flat on the desk and shoved himself to his feet. He smiled, but shook his head. "Oh, no, you don't. I'm not assuming anything. I may have my own opinions about that case, but—" he pointed a thumb at his head—"they're staying right in here. I'm not about to tangle with that Tinsley-Wilson dough just because of an opinion. I'll bet you've got things to think about, though."

Morgan got to his feet and shook hands with the lieutenant. "Thanks a lot. You've been very kind."

"It was a pleasure. By the way, Mr. O'Keefe. Do me a favor. Let me know if and when you come up with an idea."

"It's a promise. And thanks again."

Morgan left the office, questions spinning through his head. It was a long walk from Kearny Street to Pacific Heights, but he could always think better on his feet.

It was obvious to him that Scanlon didn't believe the shooting had been accidental. His attitude had been evident in every word he had spoken. But what did he believe? That was not so easily determined. Could he be thinking the same as Glenna, that Irene herself had secured the murder weapon somewhere for same plan of her own, and then had used it at a more opportune moment? Morgan doubted that. Even with all her wealth it would not be easy to secure a weapon like the one used. For one thing, she would have had to have some contact with underworld characters, which was a ridiculous thing to consider. Or perhaps she could have paid someone who did have such contacts to get the gun for her, a very weak and unsatisfactory idea because then the someone else would know all about it. It was highly doubtful, therefore, that Irene had ever seen that gun before in her life.

Yet her prints had been found on it and the slug taken from Jay Wilson's body had definitely been fired from it and Irene had admitted doing the shooting. Didn't make sense.

What did make sense, though, was Scanlon's insistence on the fact that only a professional criminal would have such a gun—and especially Scapini. Morgan followed that line of reasoning and assumed, for the moment, that the gun had indeed belonged to the prowler. But that would mean that either Scapini had given the gun to Irene, which was a pretty weird theory to consider, or that it had been taken from him. Even the latter was unlikely. How could Irene, or anyone else, take a gun away from a character as desperate as Scapini without shooting him first?

Morgan was cutting through the Italian section of North Beach and came to a sudden halt as an idea struck him with considerable force. He continued walking again, thinking even harder. Maybe the gun could have been taken away from Scapini, after all. The man had been running down the stairs from the upper floor, he had tripped and fallen into the lower hallway and he had broken his leg. It was possible, even probable, that during such a fall he had also dropped his weapon. Someone else, then, could have picked up the gun while the prowler had been helpless and in pain.

Morgan smiled thinly, satisfied that he knew what was in Lieutenant Scanlon's mind, or was at least close to it.

He continued with the same line of reasoning. Irene could have heard the man fall, had gone downstairs to investigate and so had come in possession of his weapon. On returning to her own room, possibly to call the police, she had encountered her husband in the upper hallway and had seized the propitious moment to shoot him, using the prowler's pistol.

But a situation of that sort was senseless, and gave Irene no credit for any intelligence whatever. The only reason for doing it that way would be to pin the murder on the prowler. But even a woman such as Irene would know about fingerprints. To clean her own prints from the gun she had handled would also mean cleaning away Scapini's prints. No policeman would have any trouble figuring out what had really happened if he were faced with a gun with no prints on it at all. Morgan dropped that idea.

Jay Wilson? he wondered. But if he had taken the gun from the prowler he would then have had to wipe it clean and turn it over to Irene so that she could kill him with it. Morgan wasted no time on that theory.

He came, then, to the one person he had had in the back of his mind all along. Irene had apparently called Frank Wilson immediately after the shooting. Wilson had run the few hundred yards from his home to Irene's home. He was undoubtedly in the lower hallway within a very few minutes after the time of the killing. It was he who had found Scapini lying on the floor. It could also have been he who had seen the prowler's gun somewhere on the floor and had taken possession of it. Then he could have run up the stairs to come upon his brother's body and the hysterical Irene also lying on the floor.

Morgan started breathing harder. The pattern was coming into focus. There could have been two guns involved, the prowler's and the one Jay Wilson had bought for his wife. Frank had taken the expensive Smith and Wesson from Irene, who at that time was undoubtedly in no condition to know what was going on, and had placed the gun in his pocket to dispose of later. He had then wiped the prowler's gun clean and had pressed it into Irene's hand to get her prints on it. After which, he had probably taken it from her with a handkerchief and placed it on the floor for the police to find.

Frank also had a strong motive for such an act. If Irene had been convicted of a deliberate killing she wouldn't have inherited her husband's estate, regardless of the will. That would then have been murder for profit and the will would have been voided. In which case, Frank would have come into his brother's estate and would have owned at least half of the business. That could have been the reason why he had fought so hard to get Irene indicted.

Morgan felt confident that he was getting closer to the pattern, but the theory concerning Frank had one glaring weakness. Frank would have had to know that it had been Scapini's weapon that had killed Jay Wilson rather than Irene's. If only one weapon had been fired, it would have been easy to determine which one by sniffing at the barrel. But Irene claimed that she had fired the pistol and even thought she had fired it twice. Regardless of the fact that she had been frightened and probably still half asleep, she would certainly have known if she had not fired a gun. So there was probably no doubt that the two guns had been fired.

Yet how would Frank know or determine which one was the death weapon? It was, after all, impossible for him to know which slug was in the body of his brother. Morgan sighed. It was such a beautiful theory, but it all fell apart on that one point.

Morgan intended talking over what he had learned with Irene, but when he reached the house the butler informed him that Mrs. Wilson was confined to her bedroom with a severe headache. Morgan saw her in the study the following morning, shortly before noon. There were faint circles under her eyes, but otherwise she was looking well and explained that she had lost the headache during the night.

"Do you have them often?" he asked.

"Now and then, yes."

"You spend too much time alone brooding."

She nodded and walked away from him to the front windows. "I—I suppose you're right."

"Do you do much shopping downtown?"

She was silent for a long while, then replied, "Never."

Morgan stared at her back, then crossed the room to stand at her side. "You're kidding. No woman could give up shopping. That I refuse to believe."

She said softly, "I did, though. My photographs always look exactly like me. Apparently I'm easily recognized. The first few times I went downtown after the accident I was virtually mobbed and—and even roughed up a bit. I stayed out of all public places for two years. Then one day I went down to the City of Paris to purchase something or other. I was standing at a counter with other women, whom I was sure had not paid a bit of attention to me. Yet when I handed a twenty-dollar bill to the salesgirl a middle-aged woman at my side glared at me and asked loudly, 'Is that part of your blood money?' Then she said something vile and I turned and started away. But I hadn't gone more than a few feet when the shock of what she had said hit me and I fainted. I have never gone shopping again."

"Which, of course, is just what you should do. But skip it." He looked out over the bay and up at the clear skies. "Nice day to take a ride and look the city over. How about you?"

She looked back over her shoulder at papers piled on the desk and frowned.

"I hadn't quite finished the morning's work—"

"Forget it, for once. Do it tomorrow."

"I always do it Saturday mornings—"

"Sure, sure, I know. Maybe I can rent a jalopy somewhere."

Her frown deepened as she stared at the papers on the desk, then suddenly her eyes jumped to his with lights of excitement in their depths. "All right," she said, "I will forget it. I'll tell Carl to get out the limousine—"

Morgan exploded, "Get out the what!"

"The limousine, of course. Carl is also my chauffeur."

"No dice. Don't you have another car?"

"Well, there's the one the servants use, a Ford station wagon."

"Does it run?"

"Naturally."

"Then that's the one we'll use. Put on something simple and we'll mingle with the peasantry. How about slacks and an old sweater?"

She put a thumb to her lips and thought a moment, then said hesitantly, "There are some levis I used to wear in the country when—a long time ago. I wonder if they would still fit?"

"Try them. Anyway, make it simple."

"Half an hour?"

"Good enough."

Morgan was waiting for her when she came downstairs to the main hallway. He smiled wryly and shook his head, telling himself that he should have known better. She was wearing faded blue levis, but they had obviously been altered to mold every curve from her waist to her ankles. The short walking boots were also western and custom-made. The blouse was white Chinese silk open at the throat and over her shoulders she had draped a light suede bolero jacket. Her black hair had been pulled back and tied with a bow. She was smiling shyly, rather pleased with herself in what she thought was a rough and rugged costume. Morgan hadn't the heart to say anything. Besides, he liked the outfit and what it did to her figure. She looked younger than he had ever seen her look and even seemed to have recaptured her former beauty. She got the station wagon keys from Carl and Morgan backed it out of the garage to pick her up at the curb. He was laughing silently to himself as she got in and he pulled away. Even the station wagon was a deluxe model with special leather upholstering, green rubber tires to match the custom paint job, a chrome baggage rack on top and every expensive gadget possible. It had probably cost more than a Cadillac and looked it. Morgan decided that, what with one thing and another, it would not be advisable to mingle with the peasants, after all.

Morgan knew little or nothing of San Francisco, so Irene directed him to the points of interest. They had a look at the St. Francis Yacht Club, drove through the Presidio to the beach, and had a few beers at the redwood bar in the Cliff House. Down at the Strand, Morgan picked up hot dogs and little Mexican enchiladas on paper plates, which they ate as they drove slowly through Golden Gate Park. They went up to Twin Peaks for a spectacular view of the city, then on out to the new western additions and up to Skyline Boulevard. They followed the curving road on the high ridge for mile after mile of breath-taking scenery and turned off late in the afternoon to cut down through a canyon to El Camino Real. They started back north toward the city through San Mateo and Burlingame and all the Peninsula places that had once been small, distinct villages, but were now growing and merging into a large city of its own, Suburbia, America.

Morgan was partially preoccupied with what he had learned the day before and had little to say during the long drive. Irene seemed content simply to be out in the open and riding and also had little to say. It was a lazy, peaceful drive, and the two were content and relaxed as they again came into the outskirts of the city just at dusk.

Irene pulled her legs up and turned sideways with an arm over the back of the seat to face Morgan. She sighed and said, "This is the first time I've taken this tour in a long, long while. It's been nice."

"Sure has. I'm not much of a sightseer, but I've enjoyed it, too. Now, how about a place for dinner?"

"In these clothes?" she gasped. "Oh, no!"

Morgan glanced at her briefly and laughed. "Actually, you're too well-dressed for what I had in mind. But maybe a drive-in?"

She pursed her lips and thought of it, then shook her head. "Let's not spoil the day. Do you know what I would like to do?"

"You name it."

"You're going to think I'm pretty childish."

"No," he chuckled. "Name it."

"Very well. Morgan, I adore Chinese food and there's a place here in the city that cooks it beautifully and delivers it piping hot to your home—"

"Chinese food delivered?"

"Absolutely."

"Must be a mess when it arrives."

"Not at all. It's delicious."

"Okay, if that's what you want."

Irene telephoned the order as soon as they arrived at the house. When the food was delivered Carl and Anna took command and served it in the dining room. The food was good, but with the candelabra, the linen and all the silverware on the table, the fun had gone out of it for Morgan. He was amused only by Irene's antics with ivory chop sticks. She couldn't use them very well, but she tried hard and refused to use a fork. Morgan had finished and was replete when she was still halfway through the meal.

He sat back and watched her somewhat sadly. She did not really know how to relax and enjoy herself, and probably never had. The same food served in the exotic atmosphere of a Grant Avenue restaurant would have been far more enjoyable. He doubted that she had ever been in such a restaurant. When he asked her she replied that whenever her parents had wanted Chinese food they hired cooks to prepare it in the Tinsley kitchens. Morgan wasn't surprised. Wealth had apparently been more of a burden to her than a blessing. She had been too well insulated from the outside world and had known little or nothing of simple pleasures.

He wondered what it would be like being married to such a woman. She had suffered during the past years; she had learned much and her character had obviously undergone a great change, probably for the better. Yet she had become even more insulated and apart than she had been as a girl and a young woman. She hadn't the remotest idea of how to mingle with ordinary people, she had little or no understanding of the realities of life and her vast wealth would forever keep her on a special, untouchable level.

Yet she did present a challenge that was intriguing. It had become increasingly apparent during the past few weeks that another change was taking place. Morgan knew that his presence had opened her eyes somewhat and that she was at last questioning the life she had been leading. Her soberness had given way to spontaneous laughter on more than one occasion, she had willingly disrupted her hard-and-fast schedule at least a few times, and she had attempted to enjoy herself doing simple things with Morgan. She wanted change. It was also apparent that she wanted to be loved.

Morgan slouched in his chair and watched her from under lowered lids. She glanced across at him with a faint smile, then her eyes fell and she concentrated on the manipulation of the chop sticks. He studied her body and wondered what she would be like in bed. Shy, perhaps, and maybe a bit cool and even frightened at first, but then she would respond normally. But he could be entirely wrong. It could be that her passions had been held in check for so long that when the dam burst she would respond with wild and complete abandon. His breath quickened and he shook his head to clear it of alluring imagery.

Marriage to her could be quite an adventure and perhaps even a lasting one. Then he yawned and wondered why he was bothering his mind with such idle and ridiculous thoughts. The lady and the drunk?

She pushed her plate aside finally and touched a silver table lighter to a cigarette. She blew out a puff of smoke and smiled contentedly across the table at Morgan. "That was good," she said. "Did you enjoy it?"

"Sure."

Her smile faded a bit. "Not too much, though?"

"Well, I was just thinking—it isn't important." He shoved his chair back and got to his feet. "Let's go into the study. I've had something on my mind all day I've wanted to talk over with you."

She followed him into the dimly lighted study, where logs were burning in the fireplace. Morgan stood with an arm draped on the mantel, looking down into the fire, and Irene dropped into a chair facing him. She was watching the flickering of the flames across his thin face.

He cocked an eyebrow and glanced at her and she looked away. "Irene—"

"Yes?"

"I've told you before I felt I was on the edge of something, but couldn't quite put my finger on it. The nagging idea, whatever it may be—"

"Wait," she interrupted. "Don't go on, Morgan. It's been such a lovely day. Must we ruin it now?"

"I think this is important."

"No. I know what you've been thinking. You just cannot accept the idea that I'm the one who shot my husband. Isn't that it?"

"Well—"

"Of course. I felt for a while that you might be helpful and in many ways you have been, but I'm afraid you're also allowing your sympathies to get in the way of logic and fact. I did shoot Jay and there's no eluding that fact. No one else could have done it and we know exactly how it was done. What we don't know is the motive behind the act. I thought you might help to resolve that in my mind. But you've gone off on another tangent that's sheer waste—even though," she added gently, "I do appreciate your reasons for it. So, if you don't mind, I would prefer not to discuss it."

Morgan snapped at her, "I do prefer to discuss it, though, so consider your day ruined."

She sighed and sat back in her chair. "Very well," she whispered, "if you must."

Morgan was suddenly angry. "Oh, for God's sake, let's not be big about it. Being the martyr just as often as not means playing the damned fool."

"Let's not have words."

"Oh, brother." He shoved himself away from the fireplace and started pacing the floor. "I've been doing a little investigating," he said. "I've learned that your husband actually did buy an expensive thirty-eight just prior to the killing."

She said patiently, "That's right. But did you also learn that Jay had quite a large collection of guns and was in the habit of buying a new one every now and then?"

He paused to blink at her. "Well, no."

"That's what I thought. Jay did a great deal of hunting. He owned dozens and dozens of guns."

"I've never heard of hunting game with a thirty-eight revolver."

"Nevertheless, Jay did collect guns."

Morgan paused to frown at her. "This particular thirty-eight has never been found."

"I know. I gave the police permission to search for it. It was never located. But that really means little. He could have lost it somewhere, or he could have given it away to one of his hunting friends, or it could even still be around in a place where no one has thought to search. The gun I fired that night is undoubtedly the gun Jay gave to me."

Morgan almost shouted, "You don't know that absolutely."

"I don't know anything about that night that is absolute."

"Isn't it possible that the gun could have been Scapini's?"

She smiled faintly and shook her head. "The gun had my fingerprints on it, and no others. But I think I know what's in your mind. You think there were two guns involved—"

"I've never heard you express this thought before."

"I gave it up years ago. There was an Officer Scanlon from the police who questioned me at great length and explored that whole field. We got nowhere. Mr. Scanlon, you see, entertained the idea that the weapon could have belonged to the prowler and that, somehow or other, someone else had effected a switch of guns. But that would have meant that the prowler had fired a shot as well as the shot I fired."

"So?"

She sighed. "It just wasn't so. The only bullet found was the one in—in Jay's body. There was no other. Nothing upstairs was touched and the police took photographs of everything and made a thorough search for a possible bullet hole. There was nothing to be found."

"Oh." Morgan dropped heavily into a chair facing her. "I hadn't thought of that."

"Mr. Scanlon did. So, you see, there was only the one gun involved and the one bullet, and no other. If another gun had been fired the bullet would have to go somewhere and leave a mark easily found—"

Morgan waved a hand to silence her. "I understand. And I suppose the police were thorough—"

"Very."

"The hole couldn't have been plugged before they arrived?"

"The police would have noticed. They went over every inch of the area where a bullet could have lodged and they allowed no one upstairs. No one could touch anything for four or five days. There was no other bullet, for the simple reason that there was no other gun."

Morgan sat back and rubbed his chin, feeling deflated. "Yet," he said, "Scanlon is still not satisfied."

"Oh? You've seen him?"

"Yes. He told me flatly that he's never been satisfied with the outcome of the case."

Pain appeared in Irene's eyes and her shoulders sagged. "That," she said, "is because he's another who thinks I killed Jay with deliberate intent."

"I'm not so sure about that."

"Oh, but I am," she cried. "Every policeman on the case thought the same way. And maybe they're right," she gasped. "Oh, God, maybe they're right."

She buried her face in her hands and Morgan swore softly to himself. There was no doubt about ruining her day. He had done a thorough job of it. He got to his feet and stood over her and touched her shoulder. "Sorry," he said. But she shook her head and wouldn't look up at him. He felt a little sick and turned and walked slowly out of the room.

He went into his apartment without turning on the lights and sat on the edge of the studio couch with his head down and his arms dangling between his knees. The creative mind, he thought. How oddly it was able to twist simple facts into wild fantasies. An unfortunate accident had occurred and that was all there was to it. But he couldn't be happy with something so simple. He had tried to rearrange what had actually occurred into something more dramatic and more satisfying to his imagination. And all he had actually accomplished was to disturb further a person who needed someone to understand, rather than a detective.

There was a knock at the door. Irene called softly, "Morgan?"

He raised his head. "Come in."

The door opened and closed slowly. His eyes had accustomed themselves to the dark, but she could not see and asked, "Where are you?"

"Over here, on the couch."

"Oh, I'm sorry. I didn't think you had gone to bed."

"I haven't. I'm just sitting here calling myself a thousand different kinds of fool."

He watched her dim figure crossing the floor. Her legs bumped his and she stopped and looked down at him. She said gently, "Don't feel sorry, Morgan."

"I should have kept my big fat mouth shut. You had such a good time today. But, no, I have to keep poking around in the ashes."

"But I understand why. Really."

"I don't think you do. I'm just a slob with a hyperthyroid imagination—"

"That isn't it and you know it. Your sympathy has been awakened and you felt sorry for me. You wanted to help. I—I think you even like me—"

"That's for sure."

She caught her breath. "So, because of your sympathy and because of your liking, you can't accept what's happened. You would rather make something else out of it." She laughed oddly, a catch in it. "Really, Morgan, all you've been trying to do is place me in a better light. Isn't that about it?"

"I guess so, partly."

"You don't like to think of me as an infamous sort of woman who shot her own husband—"

"Oh, for God's sake, stuff that silly idea. I wouldn't give a damn if you were Annie Oakley herself." He placed his hands on the rough texture of the levis, but could feel the softness of her thighs under the cloth. "Matter of fact," he chuckled, "you're wearing the right costume. Shall we go gunning together?"

He felt her quiver slightly as she said, "Don't joke, please."

"Why not? Even tragedy has its moments of laughter. Otherwise, we would all be stark, raving maniacs."

"Maybe," she whispered, "that's what's wrong with me."

His hands tightened and he looked up at her face, faintly luminous in the dark. "Now, wait a minute. There isn't anything very much wrong with you other than what's happened to you."

"Do you really believe that?"

He was again exasperated. "Of course I do. It would take so little to make you a normal woman again. It's a crime, really, how little it would take. You're highly desirable, you're not at all as cold as I thought you were, you're dying to be loved and you certainly have all it takes—"

He paused and looked up at her standing so close before him and slowly his hands traveled up her thighs to her hips and to her waist and he turned her gently and drew her down to the couch at his side. She did not resist as he pressed her down and into his arms and her lips met his softly at first and then hungrily. She held to him tightly, but drew her lips away and pressed a cheek against his. She whispered huskily and so low that he could barely hear, "I think I'm falling in love."

Morgan was physically aroused, but he was also confused. The scent of her hair and the perfumes she used and the softness of her body in his arms and the obvious yielding dictated a course for passion to follow. A few weeks before, there would have been no question as to his next move. Sexual gratification would have been dominant and no other thought would have stood in the way. But Irene was not Glenna. Irene was not thinking with her body, nor was she using it as an instrument of purpose. Furthermore, he was not too sure of himself. The situation had come about so suddenly that his mind had not yet had time to accommodate itself toward what had happened.

He kissed the hollow of her throat and said, "That's a pretty big statement to make."

"I know. And I'm not really sure. But I feel it, Morgan. I've been feeling it for some time."

He rubbed his lips into the thick mass of her hair and said huskily, "Maybe you confuse it with something else. You wish to be loved. That I know. You have a deep hunger to be loved, but I think rather in the abstract."

"No."

"I think so, though. Remember me: Morgan O'Keefe, the arrogant, conceited drunk, the object of your charity? No, I don't think it's possible that way."

"I think it's happening." Her lips met his for a brief moment, then she was whispering, "I never believed it would happen again."

"Look, Irene; I'm flattered. Believe me. But you're the antithesis of everything I stand for. With us—no. It's not possible for you to fall in love with me. I think it's simply that your feeling and your capacities for love have been awakened from a deep sleep and I happen to be conveniently handy."

She bit the lobe of his ear gently and he thought he detected faint laughter deep in her throat. "Oh, Morgan, you're so wrong. I have never ceased wanting to be loved. It's always been there, inside, but repressed. It took you to bring it to life. Don't you understand?" Again he thought he heard laughter as she said, "Please credit me with knowing my own mind. I'm not the sort of person who could ever dream of love in the abstract."

"You're feeling good, aren't you?"

"I feel happy. I'm crying a little and I guess I'm laughing a little, too. It's all mixed up."

He brushed a finger across a long eyelash and felt dampness. "You are crying a little."

"Yes."

"How else do you feel?"

"Warm."

"That's putting it mildly, where I'm concerned."

"I—I'm sorry. I didn't mean—"

"I know. But love with me is something different. Little white cottages with roses over the door leave me cold. And the touch of a hand and that secret, domestic smile leave a hell of a lot to be desired. My romantic inclinations are on a different level. When it comes to love, my dear, I am virtually all physical and all animal."

He heard her laughter then and felt the shake of her head against his. "You don't know yourself at all, Morgan. Of course you're intensely physical, but I think, too, you're highly romantic. That's something *you've* been repressing."

"That's strictly female talk. Already you're trying to change me. And I don't think you know what you're talking about. You're in the arms of the wrong man."

"No."

"But you are. In my own way, in time, perhaps I would be in love with you, too. Maybe I am right now, a little. It's possible. No other woman has ever affected me the way you have."

She pressed her lips against his cheek. "What way, Morgan?"

"Well, I'm a rather nasty character most of the time, and deliberately so. I have a dread of being too involved with anyone, especially a woman. Yet, with you, without really wishing it that way, I've gone far out of my way to involve myself with you and your affairs. Helping you to adjust yourself to your tragedy has become of primary importance to me, even more so than the fate of my last work. That's never happened before. And it can't be called simply gratitude."

"I'm glad."

She crushed her lips to his and when she pulled away, even in the dark, he could see her smile. He swallowed and said huskily, "My hunger is not the same as yours. I feel your clothed body in my arms, but in my mind's eye you are naked and I see you that way and that's where my hunger lies. I'm being honest with you, Irene, and even that is unusual with me. Talking with you here in the dark is pleasant, to kiss your lips is wonderful and holding you is pretty close to ecstasy, but it's not enough for me. It's never enough for me."

She brushed her lips across the thin bridge of his nose and his eyelids and whispered, "I'm not a virgin, Morgan. I don't think my passions are any different from yours. Curbing those passions all these years has been my most difficult task. At times I thought I would go out of my mind entirely. Do you remember the day you surprised me taking a sunbath on the roof?"

"I'm not likely to forget it."

"Well, at that moment, I was thinking of Jay and our first months together. I was a virgin when I married and it took me a while to adjust to what I considered physical crudities and absurdities and indignities. But when I had become adjusted I astonished myself as well as Jay. I was so eager, in fact, that I was often rather ashamed of myself and thought that I must be a pretty common sort, after all."

"Oh, now, wait a minute. If your sex life was so damned good you would never have had so much trouble with your husband."

"Now you make me feel ashamed again, but I must tell you. It was a one-sided eagerness. Jay did not have the sexual drive that had been aroused in me. Though he was a big man, he was very gentle and tender. He was not at all aggressive and I think he preferred looking at me and enjoying my company more than he did possessing me. He was not sexless, I don't mean that, but it took a great deal to arouse him and he was satisfied with very little. But I had been aroused and I was demanding and—and that really started it all."

Morgan felt a sudden chill up his spine that cooled the ardor pulsing in his veins. He said quietly, "I see."

She kissed the tip of his nose and squirmed more comfortably in his arms and continued, "That's when I started nagging him and that's when he started drinking, because of my unreasonable demands. I shall never forgive myself. I was so spoiled, and all that I wanted I thought should be mine merely because I wanted it and everything was ruined." She paused for a moment, then lifted her face to look into Morgan's eyes. She whispered softly, "I have never lost that drive. I buried it because I had to and because I hated myself for it and what it did to me, but I have never lost it. I'm only human, too."

"I've been finding that out."

"I've thought of you in that—in that regard. I've lain awake at nights, wondering, imagining— Even now I want you, too, terribly—but I don't know. I don't regard myself as a whole and complete person. I would like you to possess me, but I'm afraid it would only be my body and nothing else." She was silent for a long moment before she added, with pain tugging at her voice, "There are so many barriers. So many."

Morgan raised himself and lifted her to a sitting position. "It's no good," he said. "You're not capable of giving yourself."

"But if you think—"

"Don't talk yourself into something you'll regret. Body and soul are one with you. That's why you've suffered more than anyone else would in the same situation. You can't give one without the other. If you tried you would eventually despise yourself."

She clung to him tightly and cried, "Oh, God, Morgan, what am I to do? Tell me what to do."

"I don't know," he said. "I just don't know."

Chapter Ten

Morgan was awakened in the morning by Glenna on the telephone. "I tried to call you all day yesterday," she complained.

He yawned and said, "Sorry, I was out. Anything important?"

"But—but you asked me to call you on Saturday."

"I did?"

There was a heavy silence. Then she said, "We were to go out somewhere today. Remember?"

He sat up in bed and stretched. "Sorry, Glenna, I was half asleep. Sure, I remember. What do you have in mind?"

"Well, I can't make it for the whole day, as I thought I could. Tommy and his wife are spending the week end with us and Sue is being difficult, as usual, and—and—but I do have to see you and I think it's rather urgent."

"Whatever you say. There should be a matinee somewhere. Maybe I won't mind necking in the balcony, after all."

"No, no. I can get away only for a few minutes. There's a little bar near you on the corner of Fillmore and Union—"

"The New Rainbow. I know the place."

"Oh, you do? Good. I'm not likely to be recognized there—"

"On a certain day of each month you could be."

"What was that? I don't understand."

"Skip it."

"You're being mysterious. I don't know if I like it. Anyway, I shall be there at two o'clock sharp."

"Good enough."

"You're sure you'll be there?"

"I know of no reason why I shouldn't be. Bring your travel folders."

"Oh, you fool," she laughed. "Be seeing you at two, then."

Morgan was at the bar a few minutes before two, after a long, leisurely stroll through Pacific Heights and the Marina District. A few men were at the bar, an argumentative group was clustered about the juke box picking out selections, and a man and woman were playing the pinball machine near the door. Morgan got a beer and carried it to a table in a dark corner of the room. He had hardly seated himself when Glenna came in and all heads swiveled to take in her blonde beauty and the mink jacket she had draped over one shoulder. She was wearing a tiny hat with a veil that covered her eyes and the ridge of her nose. Glenna's idea of disguise. When she joined him she said she wanted a silver fizz, so Morgan got it at the bar and brought it back to the table.

He was again astounded at the disparity between age and appearance, and again wondered if it should repel him. But the years had no true meaning as he gazed at her. He told himself that she was really half her age, she was beautiful and she wanted him. That was enough.

She squeezed his hand nervously and started chatting about her daughter Sue. He sat back and half listened and amused himself by reviewing their history together. She had spent exactly one day in his company, yet was looking forward to deserting home and family and running away with him. Morgan would never have dared to use the same situation in one of his books. It was too thin.

But he was also well aware of the roots and causes behind her designs. He knew he didn't enter personally into any of the reasons prompting her departure for Reno. That she intended to do whether or not he had ever existed. Her interest in him was based on the facts that he had an acceptable appearance, his profession intrigued her and she could exert the age-old feminine prerogative of trying to change him and make him a success. That alone would keep her occupied and happy, at least for a while. There was also no doubt that she had a sexual drive that was frustrated and demanded satisfaction. Morgan could minister to her desires. There was nothing else any deeper, or of any great importance.

It could be pleasant, he thought. Neither was likely to become overly involved emotionally with the other and they could go their separate ways, when the time came, without pain or a backward glance. Morgan couldn't think of a situation more ideal and more to his liking. Yet, for a reason he was unable to fathom, he felt no great enthusiasm for it.

He was suddenly conscious that Glenna had not had anything to say for some time. He looked at her guiltily. She sipped at her drink, eying him. "I don't think you heard a word I said."

He shrugged. "How do you expect me to be interested in someone I haven't even met?"

"I'm sorry, darling. I'm nervous today. I've even forgotten to ask about your book."

"All finished. I sent it off to my agent Friday. Now I have to start thinking of the next one."

"So soon?"

"There's always an idea or two simmering on the back burners. But what's all this urgent business you hinted about?"

"Well—" She looked away from him with a frown and bit her lower lip. Then her eyes came back to his with anxiety in their depths. "Things aren't going to be as simple as I'd assumed and as my attorneys had led me to believe. Frank is going to fight the divorce."

"Oh? Then he knows about it."

"Yes. I had it out with him yesterday. I simply couldn't put it off any longer, so I told him of my plans yesterday. There was something else, too. I felt I owed it to him to warn him. Isn't that ridiculous? So now he says he's going to fight the divorce."

"Why should he? I imagine he's known for some time that you'd eventually leave him."

"I suppose he has, but he refuses to accept it. He maintains that I'm too much a part of his life and that he can't face the future without me. He even told Tommy and Sue what I intended doing and now they're angry with me. It's really terrible at home. A constant row. If only," she sighed, "I'd kept my mouth shut."

"Sounds like shreds of loyalty to me."

"No. It was just downright foolishness," she snapped. "Anyway, he's going to put up a fight and it may get a little rough. It doesn't alter my plans, though, except for one thing. I'm going to leave for Reno a little sooner than I'd expected. At the end of this week." She smiled for the first time and again squeezed his hand. "To tell you the truth, darling, I can hardly wait."

He sat back and scratched his chin. "Seven days from now? Hmmmmm. I may have to meet you up there later. I'm waiting for a check that may not be here so soon."

Her smile gave way to a grim expression and she shook her head slowly. She said pointedly, "It would be advisable for you to leave at once, tomorrow at the latest."

Morgan leaned across the table to stare into her eyes. "So now we arrive at the position of urgency. What happened?"

"Well, I—I don't really understand it all myself. But a few nights ago—I guess it was early in the week—an odd sort of individual called on Frank. He looked like a rather elderly Irishman and he had a decidedly Irish brogue. I was just coming home at the time and happened to enter the house with him. Frank was very upset and didn't bother to introduce us and at once took the man into the library. That door doesn't close very well, however, and sometimes springs open again. It was open a bit when I walked by later and I heard Frank and this other man arguing violently. I heard your name mentioned."

"Did you hear the other man's name mentioned? Was it Casey?"

"Well, no—Wait a minute. Yes. Frank called him Casey at the door. How did you know?"

"Go on. Keep going. What else?"

"It's all so peculiar. Anyway, I didn't hear much, really. They were arguing about money and Frank wanted to pay five hundred dollars for something for which this Irishman was demanding a thousand. I don't know how it was resolved. But at the end, just as the door started to open and I ran, I heard Frank say, 'Understand, now, put the fear of God into him. You don't get paid the other half until he leaves town.'"

She paused and Morgan asked, "That was all?"

"Yes. That was all. I thought about it after that, but it just didn't make sense. Last night, though, after our big row, I was alone in the living room with Tommy. He was arguing with me about my plans and trying to talk me out of the divorce. All of a sudden he brought up your name and I got the surprise of my life. His father had told him that I was leaving because of you. Turning him against me, you see. And Sue, too. I tried to explain what I had been going through all these years and that you had nothing to do with my decision, but he simply refused to understand. I got a little angry, too, and started to walk away. That's when Tommy called after me, 'You're not going to get that two-timing writer all in one piece. You may as well forget about him.' Then I could see everything and—and—"

Morgan smiled thinly and nodded. "I see it a little better than you. Your husband is a man of determination."

She closed her fingers tightly about his wrist. "I think it's going to be dangerous for you to stay here. I can't quite understand Frank's attitude toward you—"

"I do. And don't flatter yourself. It's not just because you're leaving, or because he thinks I may be going with you. There's more to it. I've been feeling it all along. I'm almost positive about it. Tell me something, Glenna."

"Of course."

"Was Jay Wilson a homosexual?"

She blinked at him without understanding. Then she sat back and gasped and stared at him as if he had lost his mind. "Of all things—Jay—of all things—"

"Well, was he?"

"You're not serious."

"I am, though. I've never been more serious. Was he?"

"Jay? Good Lord, no! Jay was many things, but—but—no! He was a gentle person in many ways."

"So I understand."

"But not a homo. After all, he did marry Irene—"

"Many of them get married at some time or other, usually as a matter of protective coloration. Anyway, you don't think he was a homosexual."

"Positively not. Whatever inspired such an idea?" She paused, then said angrily, "Irene, of course."

"Let it go, Glenna. I was just curious."

"It has to be Irene."

"Oh, let it go, for God's sake. It was my own idea. So I was wrong—maybe. Let's drop it."

She glanced at her watch and sighed and got to her feet. "I have to run, darling. Now, look; I'm worried about you. Why don't you go up to Reno tonight or tomorrow morning and I'll meet you there at the end of the week. Check into the Riverside, so I'll know where you are."

He stood up, too, and shook his head. "No can do. I have to wait for my check."

She smiled and patted his cheek. "I've thought of that. Here." She took a sealed envelope from her purse and handed it to him. "Be seeing you, sweet." She kissed his cheek and turned to hurry away. "'Bye."

He watched her disappear through the door, then opened the envelope and counted ten $100 bills. He laughed at first, then swore under his breath and put the bills and the envelope into the inside pocket of his jacket. Beggars, he thought, could be choosers, after all. But not when you were about to be worked over by a person or persons unknown with a single mission, "... put the fear of God into him." Pride was then worth exactly one thousand dollars. He patted the envelope in his pocket, reassuring himself that it was really there.

He walked out of the bar, turning the matter over in his mind, the beginning of fear in the pit of his stomach. He doubted that Casey would make such an attempt himself. The old Irishman was a rugged character and could probably make a good accounting of himself in any sort of brawl, but Morgan was considerably younger and even the egotistical Irishman would entertain some element of doubt as to the outcome. There was also the possibility of recognition. Casey would play it cagier than that. He would know characters who would do the job for him, probably for less than he had been paid, and that was undoubtedly the way he would go about it. A person or persons unknown.

Morgan turned the corner and started walking up the lower and less steep part of the Fillmore grade. From the corners of his eyes he saw a shabby jalopy tear around the corner, but paid little attention to it. He had almost reached Green Street when the jalopy veered suddenly across the street and pulled in to the curb opposite Morgan. Two young men jumped out of the car, one angling in ahead of Morgan and the other to his rear. Morgan came to a frozen halt.

The two men, one tall and the other shorter and stockier, were wearing what had become a standard costume for the marijuana and rock 'n' roll fringe of the motorcycle set: short, black field boots, tight-fitting black levis and short black leather jackets with belts in back and overwide shoulders. They wore their hair long, brushed carefully and painstakingly to the rear to form Drake's tails, and unusually long sideburns. The stockier one had bad acne scars on his face and neck. The taller one had a razor-thin, black mustache. Neither could have been over twenty years old.

The tall one moved in with a forearm under Morgan's chin and the other grabbed the collar of his coat and pulled it down to Morgan's elbows, rendering him helpless. Virtually in the same action, he was shoved back into a deep doorway, more or less out of sight from the street.

When the tall one spoke he was definitely aping Marlon Brando. "We got a message for ya," he snarled, trying hard not to move his lips. "Ya gotta get outa town. Unnerstan'? Ya gotta get the lead out 'n' get movin'. See? It ain't that we got anything against ya, pal. We're just passin' on the word. Unnerstan'? Just blow outa town 'n' we'll love ya like a brother. Hang aroun' 'n' your own mother ain't gonna know ya. That's all, pal."

He lowered his arm, then slammed his fist suddenly into the pit of Morgan's stomach. The heel of the other man's palm came down viciously on the back of his neck at the same moment. Morgan's legs gave way and he sank down to the concrete. He tried to steel himself for what was to come, expecting to be booted in the head and the ribs, but nothing happened. He heard the jalopy roar, and shoved himself up on his elbows and lifted his head as the car spun around the corner onto Green Street. He saw Casey sitting between the two punks, looking back at him, grinning. Then they were gone.

Morgan managed to sit up on the broad step of the doorway. He could hardly turn his head and his stomach felt as if it were on fire. It was quite a few minutes before he was able to breathe normally, and longer before he could force himself to stand. But soon he was able to proceed on up the hill.

Morgan was not an especially brave man and the encounter had frightened him badly. The greater fear, of course, was based on what would happen if he did not leave town. Yet he was puzzled too and more than a little surprised. He had not been worked over at all and he had not really been hurt. Why had it not been worse? The street had been empty of anyone else at the time and the two punks could have booted him unmercifully. But he had been left relatively undamaged. He could only conclude that Frank Wilson, or perhaps Casey, had not wanted to take a chance on hurting him seriously, believing that the single warning would be sufficient to get him out of town.

He bathed the back of his neck when he got home and rested on the couch for a few hours. He fell asleep for a while and when he awakened he felt considerably better.

That evening he called Nicky and asked him to drop by the house for a few minutes. When Nicky arrived and started for the study, Morgan beckoned to him and led him into his apartment, where he closed the door. He waved Nicky to a chair and started pacing back and forth before him.

"I'm going to ask you a question," he said, "and I want an honest answer. You were Jay Wilson's closest friend. You probably knew him better than anyone else."

Nicky nodded. "Probably. Why?"

"Did you know anything about his sex life?"

Nicky had started to light a cigarette. He lowered the lighter slowly and stared at Morgan for a long while, then raised the flame and touched it to the cigarette. He was deliberately slow about putting the lighter away and puffing at the cigarette before replying, "A little, I guess."

"Did you go around with him before he was married?"

"We went to school together."

"Uh-huh." Morgan paused and faced Nicky. "Then tell me something. Do you know whether or not Jay was a homosexual?"

Nicky's eyes slid away. "That's a rather difficult question to answer."

"I don't hear you denying it."

"I don't enjoy raking through old ashes."

"This is important, Nicky, believe me, or I wouldn't bother you about it. Was he or was he not a homosexual?"

Nicky leaned wearily back in his chair and pressed his hands to his eyes. When he dropped his hands he looked at Morgan squarely. "Well," he said, "you've stumbled across something, I guess."

"A hunch, more than anything else. Now, how about it?"

Nicky was silent for a while and blew smoke to the ceiling. Then he said, "I didn't really notice anything different about Jay until we were in high school. He disliked basketball and football, but he was quite an athlete otherwise, especially at track, tennis, golf and so on. You know, the kind of sports where the individual counts most and there's no body contact. Jay really excelled. But in our senior year the coach finally talked Jay into trying out for football. Jay was in exactly one scrimmage. He wasn't hurt, you understand, but he was physically ill for days after and, needless to say, he never again had anything to do with football. I was naturally surprised by his reaction and tried to question him about it. The only thing I could ever get out of him was that football was strictly for animals. Then, when we went to college, I noticed that in the gym locker rooms Jay always rushed through his shower, dressed and got out as quickly as possible. He kept his back turned, he wanted no one to look at him and he tried to blind himself to the bodies of the men around him.

"Then there was the night before he married Irene. A bunch of us threw a stag for him and some character brought along a camera with a pornographic movie. You know the kind; two girls and a man and every position possible."

"Sure."

"Jay lasted until about the middle of the thing, but that was all he could take. He rushed out of the room and into the lavatory and was sicker than I've ever seen him. I had to take him home, to an apartment he was living in at the time. He tried to commit suicide by jumping out the window. I managed to grab him just in time. He broke down and cried like a baby and kept telling me over and over again that he didn't deserve to live, that he wasn't normal."

"Did he say any more than that?"

"No. Not then. But some time after he was married, after he and Irene started having trouble, he came to me and put his cards on the table and explained everything. By the time Jay was born his father was too busy to pay much attention to his youngest son. So Jay was literally raised by his mother, who doted on him, unwisely and too well.

"And then Jay transferred the love he should have had for his father to his older brother and Frank became the father-symbol. But that, too, developed into an unhealthy affection and when Jay became old enough to understand he realized that he had all the tendencies of a homosexual."

"So he did understand. He knew what he was when he married Irene."

Nicky bit his lip. "I don't like the way you say that, Morgan. Jay never gave way to those tendencies. I'm positive about that. He idolized Irene, he did his best to be a good husband—"

"Yet he failed. That's why he turned to you. Just what did he want from you?"

"Damn it, Morgan, it makes me sick to have to think of it again. All the poor guy wanted to know was how a normal man went about leading a normal sex life with a normal woman. That's all. Just that. But all so damned important to him, you see."

"And still he failed."

"I'm not so sure—"

"I am. He failed. I've never really been able to understand just what happened between those two. Now it's perfectly clear." Morgan started pacing again and said angrily, "Think of Irene. For ten solid years she's believed implicitly that she was the one solely responsible for their troubles, because she was spoiled, conceited, arrogant and so on. She believes it still. A guilt complex gnaws away in her like a cancer. And she's plagued, too, with the horrifying idea that perhaps she did know it was Jay standing in her doorway that night and that her subconscious mind, poisoned with hatred and frustration, prompted her to fire at him."

Nicky was startled. "Oh, no. Not Irene. She could never believe a thing like that about herself."

"She does, though. She's told me so. That's why she buries herself in this mausoleum. She simply cannot rid her mind of the idea that she was to blame for everything that happened and that she may have fired deliberately at her husband. In other words, she holds herself solely responsible for his death. And then she has to face people who are positive that she murdered her husband deliberately, it's impossible for her to move freely in her own society, she faces restrictive barriers and condemnation everywhere she turns and even in her own mind she's harassed by a terrible question that's impossible for her to resolve…" He paused, and then said quietly, "I wonder if it would ever have entered her mind if she had really known about her husband? I doubt it very much. But now—well, the damage is done."

"You don't think it would be wise to tell her at this late date?"

"There would be no profit in it." Morgan sighed and dropped into a chair facing Nicky. "Telling her now could even have an undesirable result. At least, her memories of her husband are those of a man. Having to reconsider him as a person with homosexual tendencies could be so repulsive to a woman of her morals that it could cause serious emotional damage."

"That's one thing I can verify. She does have unusually high moral standards for our screwy set."

"Glenna, too."

Nicky blinked at him. "Beg pardon?"

"I was just thinking out loud."

"But you said, 'Glenna, too.' Were you implying that she's a moral person, too?"

"Well, isn't she?"

Nicky stared at him, then burst out laughing. "Don't be an ass, old boy. That blonde has really been playing catch-as-catch-can in the extramarital field lately."

"Well, flirtatiously—"

"I mean all the way. I know personally of two motel romances she was carrying on last year. I've heard gossip about others."

"You're not kidding?"

"Hell, no." He shoved himself to his feet and said, "I have to get back home. One thing I'm glad about, that you aren't passing this information I've given you on to Irene. Jay was a damned good friend of mine and really a very nice guy. You would have liked him. So, all right, he had a sexual weakness and his emotional perspective was haywire. I don't condemn him for it; he did have strength enough not to give way to it."

"Which is why you've never said anything to Irene about it?"

"Exactly. Why destroy the dead?" He smiled and held out his hand. "See you later, Morgan. Let me know when that check arrives and we'll see about a place for you to live."

"Sure. So long."

When Nicky went out the door Morgan started chuckling to himself, then burst out laughing. He was remembering the little scene on the deck of Glenna's yacht. So she was incapable of adultery, was she? But if she had been playing around before, then why the big stall? He thought he knew the answer to that. The whole situation had been a deliberate tease to arouse his passions and keep him panting at her heels until they arrived in Reno. She was cleverer than he had realized. And quite an actress, too.

He was still smiling when he went to bed, but the back of his neck hurt as he lay down and he thought again of the two thugs. That warning to get out of town had not been made in jest. They would probably follow through with a real going over the next time they ran into him. He wondered if he should really start running, but he had a headache now and he decided to think about it in the morning.

In the morning he had a high fever and was not able to get out of bed. Irene became alarmed and called Dr. Rigsby. The doctor arrived and examined Morgan and told him, "Just the common flu bug. Have you been out in the open very much?"

"I've been doing a lot of walking."

"And probably without adequate clothing. This sunny San Francisco weather fools you. It's not as warm as it seems. And you aren't entirely recovered yet from your bout with the bottle. Your resistance is low. Nothing to be excited about, though. A week in bed and you'll be back on your feet again better than ever."

"That's me all right; always getting better than ever."

"What other way is there for you to go?"

Morgan sniffled and had to smile. "Not bad, Doc. But suppose you go peddle your pills somewhere else."

"I'll be glad to. When you need me again I hope it's for something far more serious."

"Thanks, Doc. And the same to you."

Morgan did not mind at all his short confinement to bed. He did a great deal of reading, and Carl moved in a TV set so that he could watch the evening programs. But he especially enjoyed Irene's company. She had all her meals in the apartment and also spent an hour or so with him just before retiring. She chatted with him about anything that came to her mind and he lay back and watched the lively play of her expressions and listened with pleasure. Only now and then did a shadow cross her eyes and she would fall silent and stare hollowly into space. The shadow was never very far away, even when she was most animated. Morgan was always aware of its presence.

The subject of love had evidently become taboo, as she never mentioned it. Either, he thought, she had reconciled herself to the fact that she could never again give herself completely to any man, or she had discovered that she was not in love, after all. Better still, she had probably come to the conclusion that Morgan was hardly a fit object for her affections. That, he thought, was probably it.

Glenna telephoned the third evening he was in bed. She had heard that he was ill and was worried, but was reassured when he explained that it was simply a flu bug. She was even more reassured when he said that he would be able to leave for Reno as soon as he got on his feet. "Splendid," she said. "I don't think it would be wise for you to stay around town." With which cheery note she hung up.

Morgan refused to stay in bed for a full week. On the fourth day he lounged around the apartment in pajamas and robe and on the fifth day felt fully recovered.

It was Friday and Irene was again looking forward to her every-other-week cocktail party. Over the breakfast table that morning, Morgan invited himself to the affair. Irene thought that he should rest a few days longer, yet she was obviously pleased that he would be present.

As soon as she left the apartment, Morgan decided to try a short walk, and got dressed. It was a sunny day, but he heeded the doctor's words, and slipped a sweater on under his coat. He was about to leave the room when Carl knocked and opened the door to inform him that he was wanted on the telephone.

Morgan picked up the telephone, learned that New York was calling, identified himself and in a moment heard the voice of his literary representative:

"Morgan? Earl. How are you?"

"Fine, Earl. But how did you know where to call me?"

"You had the phone number on the letter you sent with the manuscript."

"Oh, did I? I'm getting absent-minded."

"You always were. Look, Morgan: I'll make it short. I got the insert pages Monday morning and checked them through with the original. By God," he exclaimed, "it was wonderful! You did a superb job."

"Well, thanks—"

"Absolutely staggered me. Not only the best thing you ever did, but worth all your other books put together. Incidentally, I put my personal check for seventeen hundred in the mail this morning. You should have it tomorrow. Now, here's the rundown. I turned the script over to your publishers Monday afternoon. Norwood telephoned yesterday to tell me how pleased they were and Buttle dropped by the office a little while ago. He just left. To put it lightly, they're thrilled. We all are. You know damned well all you ever needed was to stop getting so rough with your characters and treat them with a little sympathetic understanding. So, all right, you've done that in *The Eagle*. But here's something else. I don't know if you know it or not, but the Guild has been interested in your work for some years. Their only objection has been your rough treatment in characterizations. That objection is now removed, so Norwood and Buttle have turned the manuscript over to the Guild. I'll give ten to one that they take it. Do you know what that will mean?"

Morgan grinned. "I have an idea."

"Well, for one thing, it will mean a guarantee of at least thirty-five thousand dollars." He said dryly, "Can use? I'll bet you can. And you know, too, with Guild prestige you'll undoubtedly get a nice, fat movie sale as well. Sound good?"

"Keep talking, sweetheart. I'm falling in love with you all over again."

His agent laughed. "Well, that's about it. All tentative, you understand, but I have a hunch it's going to work out for you all the way. I think this is it, Morgan." He paused for a moment, then said, "One thing, though. For God's sake, promise me you'll keep your nose clean."

"Sure."

"I know those promises. This time you have a chance to be great, but if you hit the booze again you'll ruin everything."

"I give you my word, Earl."

"I hope you mean what you're saying. I'll let you know what pops. And if I ask for confirmation on anything wire it to me, will you?"

"Okay."

"Good. You should be hearing from me in a few weeks. And watch that booze, now. You hear?"

"Sure, Earl. Thanks for calling. Thanks for everything."

Morgan looked for Irene in the study, but Carl told him that she had gone up to her room. He took the stairs two at a time to the upper floor. He had never been in Irene's room, however, and was not sure which it was of the many doors opening onto the upper hallway. He rapped on a door in the middle and received no answer, so tried the next one toward the end. He heard Irene's muffled voice, opened the door and stepped inside.

It was a large, very feminine room on the view side of the house with enormous windows looking out over the panorama of mountains, sea and sky. The floor had deep, wall-to-wall beige carpeting, the walls were tinted a light peach shade deepening in tone toward the high ceiling, the chests and drawers were hand-rubbed natural wood of Chinese modern design, and the oversize bed, on a slightly raised platform, was covered with eggshell pink silk of a heavy weave. There were a few oil paintings and water colors on the walls and over the main dresser a collection of family photographs. In the air were the mingled scents of many lotions and perfumes. Through an open door to one side Morgan saw a large room, and a bath beyond.

Irene had just come from the dressing room. Morgan told her his news, and Irene was just as thrilled and excited as he knew she would be and exclaimed that now they would really have something to celebrate at the cocktail party.

"Nicky will be terribly pleased, too," she said. "He admires you so much."

Morgan laughed and said, "He has a talent for choosing the wrong idols. Anyway, I feel pretty good about the whole business. I guess I'd better go out and take a long walk to cool off. I'll be home in a few hours." His smile faded. "Funny, I keep calling this place home. It won't be any longer, now."

She asked quickly, "Why do you say that?"

"Well, my check will be here tomorrow. I have no reason to presume on your generosity any longer. I can probably clear out—"

"You don't have to hurry," she interrupted. "A few more days—"

"We'll see."

He turned away and as he did so he happened to look down and noticed an odd piece of wood lying on the carpet near the door. He picked it up and asked Irene over his shoulder, "What's this?"

"Oh, that's just an old knot. There's a hole down there in the baseboard where it belongs. I've had it glued a dozen times, but it keeps falling out. I guess the slam of the door loosens it after a while. Will you put it back, please? Carl can glue it in later."

He squatted on his heels and examined the hole in the baseboard, about four inches in diameter. He slipped the knot into the hole, where it fitted perfectly, then stood up again. He winked at Irene, threw her a wave and left the room. But as he went down the stairs he felt something tugging at his mind and paused in the lower hallway to wonder what it could be.

He walked slowly on, and then paused again. He remembered replacing the knot in the baseboard. Nothing important about that. The room came again into his mind's eye and he could see the baseboard, of natural oak with a light, cloth-rubbed stain, the beautiful grain of the wood accented and plainly visible. Nothing important about that, either. But the knot. There was something about the knot. He scratched his head and thought of it and got nowhere.

Morgan left the house in a happy frame of mind. During all the years of their association, Morgan had never known his agent to arouse false hopes. He never truly believed in the sale of anything until the check was actually on his desk. If he was willing to bet that the Guild would take *Cry of The Eagle* as one of their book-of-the-month selections it meant that he had other and more important information on which to base his optimism.

Quite aside from the money involved, which was considerably more than Morgan had ever made, Guild approval was also worth a small fortune publicity-wise. It could easily be the springboard toward national prominence, which could be established and solidified if he forced himself to be equally careful in future books. For the first time, Morgan admitted to himself that most of his publishers' criticism had been justified all along, and that his own attitude toward his characters had been that of a petulant child wanting to hurt someone. He could not hurt the living people he associated with, so he had been taking it out on the creatures of his mind.

He was so bemused by what had happened that he found himself turning into the New Rainbow without being conscious of having taken steps in that direction. There was no other customer in the place. The bartender, too, was a stranger to Morgan. The man's name was Egisto and he was Nat's partner. Morgan started to order a Coke, but changed his mind. Some sort of celebration seemed to be in order, so he asked for champagne. That would be harmless enough. He couldn't ever remember starting a binge with wine. Ending one, yes, but not beginning one.

Egisto iced a bottle of Korbel's brut, one of the better California wines, and put a chilled champagne glass on the bar. Morgan asked the bartender to join him, so another glass was chilled and they drank to each other's health. They had a few more drinks together and Morgan was surprised to find the bottle empty. He ordered another and Egisto drank with him and started talking about horse racing and Morgan spoke of some of the races he had seen at Santa Anita, on most of which Egisto had lost money, and when other customers began drifting in at noontime the second bottle was finished.

Morgan shook hands with Egisto and went out of the bar feeling very good. He walked a few blocks down Fillmore and turned onto Chestnut, the business street of the Marina District, with two or more bars to every block. He paused in front of one, feeling thirsty again. He wondered about the champagne he had been drinking and concluded that when it came to wine a man could take it or leave it alone. He turned into the bar and ordered another bottle of Korbel. The bartender, however, was a rather surly sort, so Morgan did not ask the man to drink with him. It took him an hour or more to finish the bottle and then he left.

He walked down to the end of Chestnut Street, still feeling very good, and came to a halt at the Lombard approach to the Golden Gate Bridge. He turned off to the north, toward the yacht harbor, and soon found himself walking by the gates of the army's vast Presidio. He stopped to stare at the uniformed guards and the army trucks going in and out and felt a bitter taste in his mouth. The mere sight of uniforms was enough to turn his stomach over. He spun about on his heel and walked quickly away.

He thought that he should get back to the house and rest, so he headed in that direction. He crossed Chestnut again and almost turned toward another bar, but decided that he had had his little celebration and enough was enough. He walked up to Lombard and started down that street, no longer feeling very good. He was thinking of the Army, and he felt the old burning sensation starting in his stomach and the flames creeping out into his blood stream and into his brain.

He came to a bar decorated with modern brick and redwood and turned in without hesitation. Coming in out of the sun he could barely see and groped his way to a stool at the bar. The bartender waited patiently as Morgan wrestled with the problem of what to drink. He started to get up once, wanting to walk out, but then sank back to the stool and ordered a bottle of beer. No harm in that. After a bottle or two he would go home and take a nap and be in fine shape for Irene's cocktail party.

He sipped at his beer and his eyes became accustomed to the dimness of the room and he got interested in the conversation of the man on the stool at his side. The other customer was talking with the bartender about some adventure that he had had some time before. Morgan learned that his name was Mac and the bartender, who seemed to be an old friend, was Ken.

Mac was saying, "I had a new C-Forty-seven, you see, right out of the factory, that had to be delivered to Adak up in the Aleutian chain. Man, you have no idea what those new ships were like. They were turning 'em out so fast that nothing ever worked right and this baby was no exception. Out off the coast of Alaska half of my clocks were out, the damned RDF was all screwed and manifold pressure was haywire in the number-one engine. I couldn't figure out if it was just the clock or the engine or what. It was plenty rough and that crate was pounding like to tear its wings off and back in the cabin we had eighteen sailor boys deadheading and puking all over the joint. Jees, but those kids were sick, believe me."

Ken nodded and said, "Yeah, I remember when I was on a can making the Canal run—"

"And besides," Mac continued, ignoring the interruption, "this co-pilot I had was a pink-cheeked second looie who hadn't even had a cockpit check in a forty-seven. What he knew about that ship was for the birds. Every move he made I had to tell him and I practically wore my throat out just yelling at him. How we ever hit that chain I'll never figure out, but we get to Adak okay and then I learn there's what they call a williwaw blowing and the wind is dead on my nose at seventy miles an hour right as I come in over the fence. You ever had anything to do with a williwaw?"

"Well, we had that typhoon there at Wake that time—"

"Pretty much the same thing, Ken. A williwaw is a circular wind, too, but small in diameter. What I didn't know about it, though, was how fast you could cross from one section of the circle into the other. So I got seventy miles of wind smack on the nose as I roll the wheels and the next thing I know I got that same seventy miles of wind smack on my ass. That's what's known in flying circles as a mighty interesting situation. I got on those brakes like I'm crazy, there's not enough time or room to take off again, you see, and my brakes burn out and I'm running out of runway so damned fast it's like someone pulling the rug out from under my feet. There's nothing I can do with that williwaw shoving me along and we go off the end of the runway and into the drink. Man, believe me, that water up there at the chain is cold enough to freeze hell. I don't even notice it. It's a funny thing about shock. You react in such crazy ways. You know what happened to me? Well, how I got out there I don't know, but the wreck is nose down in the water and muck and I find myself standing out on the wing waist-deep in water and characters in asbestos suits up above yelling at me to get my tail out of there before something blows. The water's all covered with gas and oil, and with two red-hot engines steaming away anything can go. But not me. Oh, no. I had a blue baseball cap I used to wear flying and I notice it's not on my head and, by God, I gotta find that cap or I don't go. It's a fact. I start thrashing around after it and to hell with everything else." He laughed. "So these crash boys gotta get down in the water themselves and put the strong arm on me and drag me to hell out of there. That's how you react when you go into shock. Just crazy."

Ken asked, "Did anything blow?"

"Oh, sure, after they got me out. Everything let go. The stuff on the water burned all that day and all night. It was quite a sight. My plane wasn't the only one in the drink. Plenty of others before me had run off the same way. It was a right smart bonfire."

He chuckled and subsided into his glass. Morgan frowned and asked him,

"How about your co-pilot and the passengers?"

Mac turned his head to squint at Morgan and after a moment he shrugged. "They didn't make it."

Morgan said coldly, "Then their bodies must have been contributing to the right smart bonfire."

"Well, I don't know. You just don't think about those things."

"The way you were talking, I assume you were flying for the old ATC?"

"That's right."

"With the airlines now?"

"Oh, no. I got out for a while, but I didn't like it, so I went back in." He chuckled and winked. "I'm still driving for the Air Force. But I got my majority last year, so it's worked out pretty well."

Ken chuckled with him and said, "Best I ever made was seaman, second class, and then I got busted."

"Drag, Ken, it's all drag. You lay the general's daughter and you got it made."

Morgan thought of his general, who had also had a daughter, a frightened, shy little girl with long pigtails and the wide eyes of a beaten cocker spaniel, and the fire in his stomach burned even more fiercely.

Morgan asked icily, "What was wrong, Major? Didn't you have what it takes to make the airlines?"

The major glanced at him, still smiling, but the smile was thin. "What's your problem, mister? I don't remember asking you to butt into our conversation."

"I'm nosy that way."

"It's a good way to get your nose flattened all over your face."

"And you're just the boy who can do it?"

"Right."

"In that case, I'll retract my nose. I like it the way it is." He looked away and told the bartender, "Set 'em up for the two of us, Ken, and yourself, as well. Better make it doubles all around. Put mine on the rocks."

The major stared at Morgan, obviously wondering whether or not to drink with him, but then he shrugged and his smile broadened again. Just a goof ball, he thought. Harmless. And yellow, besides.

Morgan took out his wallet and saw that he was down to three dollars, exactly the price of the three double drinks. He put the money on the bar and felt panic beginning and then suddenly he remembered the money in his coat pocket. He took out the envelope Glenna had given him and slipped the ten bills into his wallet. Then he stared at the double shot of bourbon that Ken placed before him.

He knew what would happen if he lifted the glass, but he told himself that this time it was different and as soon as the fires were put out and he had taken care of the major he would go home and go to bed and everything would be all right. He also knew that he was lying to himself. On the other hand, it was about time to find out if he really could drink socially without going off on a wild binge. He lifted the glass with a shaking hand, pulled his stomach in and downed the heavy drink with one swallow and a long sigh.

He shuddered, coughed and gasped, then smiled at the bartender and told him happily, "Better set 'em up again."

The bartender frowned, knowing instantly that he had a lush on his hands, but he was glad to oblige and make music with the cash register.

The bartender was smart enough to switch to weak tea after the first few drinks, but the major went on matching them with Morgan. He was faintly suspicious at first and had a slight hunch that all was not as it seemed, but then he thought that Morgan was strictly a sucker wanting to make a big wheel of himself, and he relaxed. By the time the cocktail hour rolled around the major was so drunk he couldn't stand without assistance. Morgan even had to help him into the men's room.

Morgan learned a few facts about the major, all to his liking. He had the greatest little old wife in the world, they had just moved into a new apartment and that night they were having a big housewarming. Half the brass of Hamilton Field had apparently been invited. The major was supposed to be home at six sharp and the party would begin soon thereafter.

At six sharp the major could no longer read the time and Morgan lied that it was a few minutes before five. The bartender, about to go off shift, was beginning to worry about his friend and told the major that he would personally take him home as soon as he could leave. He got busy with a number of other customers, however, and Morgan had no difficulty steering the major outside and into a passing taxi. Morgan held a whispered consultation with the cab driver, wanting to know which bar in town was an exclusive hangout for fairies and Lesbians. The driver told him of a place in North Beach, so Morgan ordered that they be driven there.

It was a small bar on a side street off Columbus Avenue, with sawdust on the floor, padded barrels for stools and empty brandy bottles stuck with candles littering the few tables. The place was packed with homosexuals, all talking excitedly and eying the "trade" as they came in. Morgan had trouble keeping the major on his feet and shoving his way through the crowd to space at the bar. He nudged a redheaded fairy from a stool, sat the major down and ordered drinks for the major, himself and the fairies to either side of them.

The bartender took a dim view of the major's condition, but when Morgan placed a hundred-dollar bill on the bar the man was happy to oblige. Morgan ordered two more rounds of drinks, engaged the fairies in conversation and let it be known that the major was quite a lover and was looking for excitement. He stacked two extra drinks in front of the major, who was by then hardly capable of speech, quietly collected his change and backed away from the bar. He walked away as if going to the men's room, but turned and headed toward the door. He paused once and looked back. The last he saw of the major was a covey of fairies hanging onto his broad shoulders.

Morgan went out to the sidewalk and almost collapsed with laughter. It was eight o'clock and the major was already two hours late for his arrival at home. If he got home at all that evening he would certainly be in the dog house. Morgan doubted, however, that he would get home. The odds were a hundred to one in his mind that, sooner or later, one or more of the fairies would offer to take the major home and he would wind up either in a strange apartment or a hotel room. Morgan thought of the reception he would get when he finally did make it home and howled with laughter. The son of a bitch, he thought.

He walked down Columbus Avenue a block or so and crossed the street to another bar, where virtually nothing but Italian was spoken. He tired of having no one to talk to and made his way on down the street from bar to bar. In spite of the quantities of alcohol he had consumed and the high flush in his thin cheeks, he looked fairly sober, his step was firm and, except for a slight thickness, his speech was as good as ever. His brain, however, had stopped on dead center. Nothing meant anything to him except the next drink, the money to pay for it and a place to consume it. The past was dead, there was no future and he existed only in the immediate present. He drank quietly, he behaved himself in the places he visited and no one bothered him. He could continue in that manner for three or four days. It was not until he ran low on money and switched to cheap wine that he began getting into trouble.

Fifteen minutes before two A.M., closing time, Morgan left the last bar he was in and walked into a liquor store, where he bought a quart of good bourbon and a bag of potato chips. Returning to his apartment at Irene's home never entered his mind. He stopped a taxi and was taken to a cheap but fairly clean hotel in the downtown tenderloin district. The clerk regarded him suspiciously, but shrugged philosophically and accepted payment for a room in advance. An elderly bellboy took him up to a room and bath on the fourth floor overlooking the street. Morgan had been in hundreds just like it, and didn't even bother to look around.

He stood in the middle of the floor and blinked at the bellhop. "Know any good whores?" he asked.

The bellhop sighed. "Sure wish I did, mister."

"None around?"

"None right now. The lid's on. Give things a month or two to cool off and the girls will be back, but right now it's dead. Last call girl I knew took off a couple weeks ago for L.A. I told her she was nuts. How can a gal make a living with all that free stuff down there?"

"Maybe it's—it's just as well. Shape I'm in I couldn't do—do much—any— anyway." He handed the bellhop a dollar bill. "Good night."

"Thank you, sir. Good night. Just call, anything you need. Glad to oblige."

"Sure."

As soon as he was gone, Morgan placed his package on the dresser, ripped open the bag of potato chips and crammed some of them into his mouth. He took off his coat and tie and kicked his shoes into a corner and padded into the bathroom. He got an empty glass and filled two others with water and took them back to the dresser. He had trouble getting the bottle open and was cursing and perspiring when he finally poured some bourbon into the empty glass and got it to his mouth. He downed the drink in two gulps and stood there staring at the white wall for a long while, thinking of nothing. He poured more whisky into the glass and as he raised it to his lips he staggered a bit and felt a wave of faintness sweep him. He grinned. He was smart. He had a bed to rest in for a while and when he was refreshed there was the bottle on the dresser and next morning the bars would open again.

He opened his eyes just before dawn, still dressed and flat on his back on the bed. He blinked owlishly at the ceiling light, then rolled to his side to see where he was. He saw the bottle and lurched to the dresser and tilted it. For a chaser, he used the lukewarm water on the dresser. He had another long drink and grinned foolishly and again flopped on the bed and in a moment was fast asleep.

Twice he awakened during the morning and helped himself to the bottle. But the last time he closed his eyes he slept until noon and when he awakened his brain was not quite functioning. He sat up and looked at the few fingers of whisky still in the bottle. He knew that he needed the drink, yet for a moment he was incapable of making a move to get it. He frowned and buried his face in his hands and shook his head and then realized that as he had awakened he had thought he was in Irene's home for a fraction of a second and that it was time to get up and meet her for breakfast.

He dropped his feet to the floor and sat there staring at the bottle. The past had come alive again and something about a cocktail party was bothering him and then he remembered that the party had been the night before. He ran his fingers through his tousled hair and bit at his lower lip and wondered what Irene was thinking. Obviously, she would know by now that he had not returned during the night and the next guess would be a simple one to make.

He got to his feet and raised the blind at the window and looked down at the busy street and at the clear sky and then at his watch. Irene would be having lunch about now, probably out on the terrace. He could picture her seated at a glass-topped table, the long slim legs, the thin waist, a cotton dress billowing about her knees, the smooth, well-rounded shoulders, the fine dark eyes— He frowned and shook his head. Those fine dark eyes would be staring blankly into space, sight turned inward. She would be wondering, and knowing, what had happened to Morgan O'Keefe, drunk.

He jerked his head angrily and turned to the dresser. He poured the contents of the bottle into a water glass. As he raised it to his lips he stopped and stared at his hand. He was still drunk and knew that at that point his hand should be shaking with eagerness to get the whisky down his throat. Yet his hand was not shaking, nor could he feel the usual perspiration on his forehead. He was drunk, and he needed the drink badly, yet the always-before insane craving for that drink had somehow lessened. He wondered if he could put the glass back on the dresser. He tried it. His stomach almost turned over and there was a hammering in his brain, but he forced his arm out and placed the glass on the dresser. Then he felt perspiration heavy on his forehead and had to turn away quickly and drop into a chair.

He stared at the wall and wondered what had happened and knew that it had something to do with the moment he had awakened. Where before nothing had ever interfered with his total concentration on the next drink, this time he had come awake with something else on his mind and therefore the pattern was not quite the same. There was something else to think about, not just himself and a thirst that craved to be satisfied instantly. The thirst was there and demanded satisfaction as it always had, but it was no longer the sum of his thinking.

There was something tugging at his mind exactly as it had the day before, after leaving Irene's room. He closed his eyes and pounded lightly at his forehead with his fists and his mind's eye was again upon the knot he had held in his hand and the hole in the baseboard.

He sighed and got to his feet and stood before the dresser, staring at the clear amber liquor in the glass. Already he had waited five minutes, perhaps ten or fifteen. He wondered how much longer he could go.

He went to the telephone and learned from the desk clerk that the hotel had a small coffee shop. He asked to have a decanter of coffee sent up to his room with some buttered rolls and a glass of orange juice. He could not touch the food when it first arrived, but he was able to drink two cups of hot black coffee. Then he got the orange juice down and with the next cup of coffee he ate the two rolls.

He went into the bathroom and showered and dressed again and came out to stand before the glass on the dresser. He needed the drink so badly that he had to pull in his stomach tightly and suddenly he wondered whom he was trying to fool. He reached jerkily for the glass, but in mid-flight his hand paused and he looked at the palm of his hand and again he saw the knot lying there and knew finally, with a shock so deep that it almost sobered him, what it was that had been bothering him.

His hands closed into tight fists, he spun about on his heel and a few minutes later found himself standing in the sun on the street. He started walking fast, as fast as possible, in a hurry to get away from the room and the glass. But three blocks away from the hotel he turned into a bar and ordered a shot of whisky. He stared at it and balanced it with what was in his mind and ordered a cup of coffee and drank that instead. He sat there for half an hour staring at the shot glass and in the end got up and walked out without touching it.

He wondered if he could eat something substantial, which he had never been able to do while on a binge, and he wandered into a small restaurant. He had no difficulty whatever consuming an order of ham and eggs and potatoes. He relished the meal. He was cold sober. He was so amazed that he walked for block after block in a mental fog.

He came to a halt finally in the middle of Union Square and looked around at the plush hotels and the big department stores and the long strings of cars creeping down into the garage under the square and the men hurrying along the sidewalks and the good-looking, smartly dressed San Francisco women. He had a tremendous sense of well being. If he could hold on a little longer he would at last be a respected part of the life surging about him.

All because he had once made a present for his mother. He closed his eyes and was again a young boy putting together a handsome chopping block in the high school shop. It was there that he learned about the various kinds of hard woods and their distinctive characteristics. He had never made anything in wood since, yet the knowledge he had acquired then had been stored far back in his mind and had at last come forward to plague him and to inform him that the knot he had held in his hand was walnut and did not belong in the hole in which it was fitted. The baseboard was of oak.

Chapter Eleven

Morgan ran across Post Street to hail a taxi in front of the Drake and had the driver go to Irene's home. When he let himself in through the front door he encountered Carl in the main hallway. The butler studied him coldly, his lips thinned to an angry line, but when he saw that Morgan was obviously sober, though excited, he blinked his surprise.

Morgan asked him, "Is Mrs. Wilson home?"

"Yes, sir. She is—ah—not feeling well, so she is in her room. Shall I—"

"No, thanks, Carl. I'll tell her myself."

"Very good, sir. By the way, an airmail letter arrived for you this morning. I put it in your apartment."

"That's from my agent. Thanks again, Carl."

He looked toward the stairs, hesitated a moment, then ran up the steps. His whole being was concentrated on a single idea. He did not even think of knocking. He opened Irene's door and stepped into the bedroom. He heard her gasp of shock and saw her half dressed in the dressing room with her black hair tucked neatly under a white bathing cap, apparently about to take a shower. He was not interested in her condition, or even conscious of it, as he turned away.

He dropped to his heels and squatted close by the baseboard near the door. Carl had not yet glued the knot, so Morgan was about to work it loose and lift it out to examine it closely. It was definitely walnut, and the baseboard was just as definitely oak. He got down on his knees and elbows and examined the hole in the baseboard and felt the edges with his fingers. There was no doubt that the hole had been cut in the baseboard with tools and then painstakingly and cleverly filed to make the knot fit.

He lifted his head and called excitedly, "Irene, come here. For God's sake, come here."

"Morgan," she cried, "you're drunk."

"I am not drunk, damn it. I was drunk last night, but not today. I'm cold sober."

"But have you lost your mind? Just to come bursting—"

"God damn it, come here, I say."

The urgency in his voice was too compelling to be denied and she hurried to his side. She was in bra and panties, but held a petticoat before her body. He straightened and got to his feet and smiled lightly at the flush in her cheeks. She stared at him unbelievingly, but there was no doubting his statement that he was cold sober.

"But last night," she said, "when you didn't show up for the party—and then at midnight when Carl told me you were still not home—"

"I know. I know. Sure, I was out on a binge. I thought I could celebrate a little and that champagne would be all right. I was just kidding myself. I got plastered and everything went the same way it's always gone. But then something happened. You got in the way."

Her shoulders quivered and she looked into his eyes. "I got in the way?"

"That's right. I woke up today thinking about you and for a few minutes I held off taking that first drink I always need so badly. Then there was something else in my mind bothering me and I never did get that drink. Do you know what it was?"

"How could I?"

He held the knot before her eyes. "Do you know what this is?"

She frowned. "Well—"

"It's a walnut knot. The baseboard is oak. It's also a damned clever fit, stained the same as the baseboard it was in." He turned it over and showed her the reverse side. "But this side hasn't been stained, and you can tell that it's walnut."

She blinked and shook her head. "I don't know the difference."

"Then be happy that I was once a small boy, because I do know the difference. Each is a hard wood, but there's a difference in appearance and feel. I must have noticed it when I picked up the knot yesterday, yet it didn't register until today. Believe me, Irene, limbs of walnut trees do not grow out of oak trunks."

"I don't understand."

He dropped a hand to her shoulder and bit into the flesh with his fingers. "I think I do, though. Let's hope to God I'm right. Now, how about your bed? Is it in the same position it was in that night ten years ago?"

"Well, yes—"

"And where were you when you fired the gun? Had you gotten out of bed?"

"No. I was sitting up when—when I pulled the trigger. For heaven's sake, Morgan, what's this all about?"

He walked away from her and sat in the middle of the bed and looked toward the doorway. He lifted his right arm out straight and sighted toward the hole in the baseboard. A wild bullet could have hit exactly in that hole. It was all so simple.

Irene was still staring at him. He got up and stood before her. He said gently, "There were two guns involved that night, Irene. One was the pistol your husband gave you and the other was a Colt belonging to the prowler. You did fire a gun, but you sure as hell never hit your husband." He pointed and said, "The bullet you fired crashed into this baseboard. Someone later carved out the bullet hole and fitted in the knot. That someone is a man named Casey, a carpenter. And your sympathetic, brokenhearted brother-in-law has been paying him off ever since. Do you understand?"

She dropped the petticoat to the floor and stumbled back a few steps to fall into a chair and stare wide-eyed at Morgan. "No!" she cried. "It's impossible. It couldn't have happened that way."

"But that's precisely the way it did happen. You thought you had fired twice because you did hear two shots. It was undoubtedly Scapini who was standing in your doorway, and not your husband. Your husband heard something and came out of his room and perhaps rushed the prowler and Scapini got excited and shot him and dropped him a little farther down the hallway, where he was found. It was Scapini who killed Jay Wilson, not you. Your bullet went through the baseboard. Now do you understand?"

All color had drained from her face and she gasped, "No, no!"

Morgan went on relentlessly, "Frank found Scapini downstairs and probably picked up his gun off the floor. Then when he saw what had happened up here he switched guns with you in an attempt to pin the whole thing on you."

She shook her head slowly. "No, Morgan. He would have had to know which gun—"

Morgan interrupted, "Sure. But he knew. Obviously he came into your bedroom and looked around and saw the bullet hole in the baseboard. That hole could only have been made by a gun fired from this room, which meant your gun. So he knew that it was Scapini's weapon that killed his brother, but he tried to pin the murder on you."

Her hands went to her face and she cried, "I can't believe it! It's too ghastly! I can't believe it!"

Morgan left her and ran down the stairs and through the house back to the kitchen, where he found Carl and Anna talking together. He learned that tools were kept in a small room behind the garages and went down the stairs to the basement and to the storage room. He found two claw hammers and a large crowbar. He hurried back through the house and up to Irene's bedroom. She was still seated where he had left her, staring at the hole in the baseboard.

Morgan wasted no time and tackled the baseboard at once. He tore at it with the claws of the hammers and opened a small slit along the upper edge. He pried the crowbar into the slit and worked it back and forth until he had a good purchase. Then he proceeded to rip the baseboard from the wall. He sat down on the floor finally, braced his feet against the wall and pulled the baseboard completely away with his hands. He got down on his elbows and knees and looked into the long opening. Behind where the knot had been was an upright two-by-four that had been smashed by the impact of a lead bullet. He examined the broken gash with his hands and felt into it with his fingers and almost shouted.

He sat back and turned to look at Irene. "The slug is still in there. I could feel the lead."

She wet her lips with the tip of her tongue and swallowed and said harshly, "The—the bullet?"

"Yes. Your bullet. The one you fired. The one that did not kill your husband."

"You—you're positive?"

"It's a bullet, all right. And it isn't common to find bullets in bedroom walls."

"But the police—"

"Well," he said, "that I can't figure out. But we'll know soon enough." He got to his feet and went to the extension telephone at the side of her bed. "I'm going to call Lieutenant Scanlon. He can shed a lot of light on this."

But then he thought of Frank Wilson and felt that he should at least have the pleasure of facing the man himself. He asked Irene for the Wilsons' telephone number. She was slumped over and staring blankly into space and he had to ask her again before she understood and mumbled the number. Morgan got a maid on the wire and gave his name and asked for Frank Wilson, but after a minute Glenna answered.

"Morgan?" she asked. "Why are you calling Frank?"

"Is he there? Is he home?"

"Why, yes, he is. The maid just happened to tell me on her way upstairs—Morgan, what is it you want?"

"I want to speak to your husband. Isn't that simple enough?"

"Well, not exactly, in view of the circumstances. Can't you tell me what it's all about?"

"Just tell him for me that I want him to get over here to Irene's right away."

Glenna laughed shortly. "That sounds rather highhanded. Since when is he jumping when you snap your fingers? Look here, Morgan—"

"You look here," he snapped. "Tell him I'm giving him fifteen minutes to get over here, or I'm calling Lieutenant Scanlon." He slammed the phone down into its cradle.

He went to Irene and helped her to her feet and steered her into the dressing room. When he told her, "Put some clothes on," she nodded numbly and turned to the crowded racks. Morgan stepped out of the dressing room and closed the door.

He went downstairs and told Carl to send Frank Wilson directly up to Irene's room when he arrived. He turned back up the stairs and left the door to Irene's room open and sat on the edge of the bed to stare again at the long gash where the baseboard had been. He took the knot from his pocket and turned it over and over in his hand. So simple, he was thinking. So damned simple. And because of its simplicity Irene had suffered for ten long years. Nothing could turn back those years, but, by God, he was thinking, someone else was going to sweat for them now.

As Irene came out of the dressing room in a cotton frock there were steps in the hallway and then Glenna was standing in the doorway staring in and Frank was frowning curiously at Morgan over her shoulder. Glenna was smiling oddly, a tight little smile that was meant to be brave, or arrogant. She paid no attention to Irene, but had her eyes fixed steadily on Morgan, as if she were trying to read his mind. He turned and looked at Irene. She stood stiffly at his side, pale and nervous, but apparently recovered from the original shock of Morgan's discoveries.

Frank glanced from one to the other, cleared his throat and growled, "Well, O'Keefe?"

Morgan held his temper in check and said quietly, "Come in. I have something to show you."

He watched Frank closely as the two of them entered the room, and he saw the older man's eyes swing down to the gash in the wall and the ripped baseboard lying on the floor. There was no need for Morgan to say anything. Frank came to an abrupt halt. All color drained from his face, and his heavy shoulders sagged. It was as if a balloon had been punctured and all the air was running out. He turned his head slowly to look at his wife, who was also staring at the baseboard, then groped his way blindly toward a chair by the dresser and dropped into it heavily. The eyes he turned upon Morgan were almost literally dead.

"I was afraid," he said. "A man of your imagination—in this house—"

"So you wanted me out of town. Do you know that the slug is still in there, embedded in a two-by-four?"

Frank let out a huge breath of air. "I wouldn't know. You see, I wasn't—"

Glenna cried, "Frank, you fool! Don't say anything. Don't say another word! You hear me?"

Morgan was startled by her outburst and looked at her with surprise. Her face was suddenly as pale as Frank's, the lipstick on her mouth stood out as a bloody slash, and her hands were shaking so badly that she dropped her purse to the floor.

Frank turned his dead eyes upon his wife and the suggestion of a bitter smile crept about his lips. "Why not?" he said. "O'Keefe knows. And why should I hold back now because of you? You're all packed. You're ready to leave. I have nothing to lose any more. I lost my self-respect years ago and now I've lost you, too. What else is there?"

She cried again, "Don't say a word! He can't prove anything! No one can!"

"I'm afraid you're wrong. He knows about the carpenter. Casey told me what O'Keefe said to him at the bar. All Scanlon has to do is question that loud-mouthed Irishman once and he'll tell everything he knows."

"No, Frank. Please, don't say anything. Please. I beg you."

"It's too late, Glenna. It's much too late. Everything is too late." He turned to look at Irene, but his eyes could not quite meet hers. He stared down at the carpet for a moment, then looked across at Morgan. "I guess I seem pretty loath-some to you, don't I?"

Morgan stared at him through narrowed eyes. "That's an understatement, Wilson. For what you've done to Irene—"

"I know. I almost destroyed one to save another and I've lost everything now. What I've done to myself, as well— It was never worth it. Never at any time was it worth it. But a man never seems to know that until it's too late. Well," he sighed, "what do you intend doing about all this?"

Glenna moved quickly to Morgan and put a hand on his shoulder and forced a smile. "You don't really intend doing anything, do you, darling? And, besides, there isn't really anything that can be done. You realize that, don't you?"

Morgan asked, "How about aiding and abetting a criminal and obstructing justice?"

She cried hysterically, "You wouldn't dare!"

Irene looked at her steadily and said, "It isn't required of Mr. O'Keefe to take any action. Have you forgotten me, Glenna?"

"No, I haven't," she snarled. "And of course you would do something and rake it all up again to hurt someone else. You've always hated me. Always. You hated me because I was more beautiful and you hated the attention I always had. You've always hated me."

Irene said quietly, "No, Glenna, you're wrong. I was once very fond of you."

"You're lying!"

Frank said, "Stop it, Glenna. She's telling the truth. You were the one who al-ways hated. You hated Irene because of her youth and position and her greater inheritances—"

"You're lying, too."

Frank looked away.

Morgan said, "One thing puzzles me. The bullet hole in the baseboard could not have been plugged with the knot before the police got here that night. It had to be done later."

Frank looked toward Glenna, as if asking her a question, but she was still glar-ing murderously at Irene. He explained, "The job was done later, after the po-lice had left the house for the last time and before Irene returned home from the hospital. Casey got a knot somewhere, carved out the bullet hole and then shaped it to fit the knot. I guess he stained it over, too." He asked Glenna, "Why didn't he replace the whole baseboard?"

"He couldn't find anything to match," she snapped.

Morgan missed the implications of their exchange and said, "That isn't what puzzles me. That bullet hole must have been in the baseboard all the time the police were in the house. It's unbelievable to me that they wouldn't have found it."

Frank glanced again at Glenna, then explained, "All that Glenna did, after she spotted the bullet hole, was to put a suitcase under the dresser to hide it. A man would never think of hiding a thing in that manner. It's so obvious and so childish. And yet it worked. When the police arrived the first thing they asked me was whether or not anything had been moved and I said no, which was the truth as I knew it. So naturally they assumed the suitcase had been under the dresser all along and wouldn't allow anything to be touched or moved, including the case, while they made their examinations. The hole was hidden effectively by a ruse as simple as that."

Morgan blinked. "I'm not following you at all. Don't you mean that you were the one who put the suitcase under the dresser?"

Glenna cried out, her voice cracking, "You see, Frank? He doesn't know what happened. He's just guessing and you're telling him everything. My God, you fool, shut up!"

Frank shook his head like a sick animal. "It's just a matter of detail, my dear. Which of us did what is not important." Then he looked at Morgan and said, "I wasn't the first to arrive at the house. Glenna got here first."

Irene gasped, "You, Glenna? You were the one—"

Glenna glanced from one to the other and tears of self-pity welled into her eyes. She screamed something incoherent and threw herself face down on the bed and began sobbing hysterically.

Frank stared at her for a moment without expression, then looked back at Morgan. "You may as well know all about it," he said in a dull, dead voice. "Unbelievable as it may seem now, O'Keefe, I used to enjoy tinkering with automobiles. That night I was down in our garage working late on one of the engines. It was Glenna who took the call from Irene immediately after the accident. Irene was suffering so badly from shock she didn't know who she was talking to. And when Glenna understood what had happened she left our house and ran over here without letting me know. Perhaps she didn't mean to do it that way. I don't know."

"But there was no mention in the papers of your wife's being here."

"I know. I didn't even know it myself. So when she got here she saw the prowler lying in the lower hallway and grabbed his gun from the floor. She then came upstairs and found Irene unconscious in the hallway. She turned on all the lights around and spotted the bullet hole over there near the door. Glenna had handled guns before and she knew that each one had been fired. It was just as obvious to her, because of that bullet hole, that it was Scapini who had killed Jay and not Irene. I don't think she really believed at the time that she could make the situation look like murder, but she hated Irene and here was a way to make her suffer. So she took Jay's gun away and wiped the real death weapon clean and placed it in Irene's hand. All this, of course, I learned about much later."

Glenna twisted about to cry at him, "Don't be so innocent! You must have guessed even before I told you!"

Frank pressed his fingertips to his eyelids for a moment, as if in pain, and then said, "I guessed nothing. Anyway," he continued, "she then left the house and returned to our home. She had just placed Jay's gun under some clothes in her dresser when I came up from the garages. She pretended that she had just that moment received the call from Irene and told me that something tragic had occurred over here. So—well—I ran over here."

Morgan asked, "You had no idea that Glenna had already been here?"

"None whatever. And after I arrived here I was so upset and grief-stricken that I simply was not capable of lucid thinking."

Morgan asked sharply, "What did you think at first? Did you think the shooting was purely an accident?"

His deep sigh was almost a groan as he replied, "Frankly, as I say, my mind just was not working. The only thing that meant anything to me was that my brother was dead. Who had shot him was immaterial, at the moment."

"What about later?"

"Well, starting the next day, Glenna kept pounding away at me that the death weapon wasn't the type of gun Jay would have bought and that Irene had bought it herself somewhere and had grasped that particularly opportune moment to get rid of Jay and add his inheritance to her own. I should have known better, but I was in such a daze that after a while I began thinking the same way. So I tried to have Irene indicted."

Morgan frowned. "Wait a minute. You mean to say you had no idea what had taken place here that night?"

"No. Not until much later. It was Glenna who looked up Casey, the carpenter—he had worked for us once—and paid him a thousand dollars to conceal the bullet hole. Casey was reading the papers, of course, so knew exactly what he was doing and could guess at the reasons for it. A few months later he decided that a thousand wasn't enough and tried to blackmail Glenna for more. She proved to be a little too tough to handle and warned him that exposing her would also mean exposure for himself. She refused to pay him another dime. That—that's when he came to me. I wasn't quite as tough as my wife. I've been paying Casey two hundred a month ever since."

"I see. So then you knew the whole story."

"Yes. I was horrified. Also, unfortunately for Irene, I was terrified, as well. Glenna had obstructed justice. She had aided and abetted a criminal. She was, in a way, accessory to a murder. Public exposure would mean destroying her. I couldn't do it. I have always loved my wife, O'Keefe. Maybe that's hard to understand, but— Anyway, I couldn't destroy her, even though I knew what it was doing to Irene. But now—well—what is there left?"

Morgan was thinking of Irene's ten years and there was no pity in his voice as he said, "Nothing. Absolutely nothing. And it makes me happy to say it."

Glenna raised herself on her hands and turned toward Morgan with a tear-streaked face. "Why didn't you leave town?" she sobbed. "Why didn't you get out? I gave you the money. Why didn't you go? And those thugs—"

"You knew about them?"

"Oh, you fool," she sneered. "You didn't think Frank hired them, did you? He hasn't guts enough for that. I was the one who told Casey what to do. That's why I had you meet me at the bar, so he could follow you. But I told him I didn't want you hurt. I just wanted you scared a little." She asked foolishly, tenderly, "They didn't hurt you, did they? Tell me they didn't hurt you."

Morgan felt sick and had to swallow hard to control his stomach. He looked around at Irene and saw the hot tears in her eyes and the way she was looking at Frank, as if seeing him clearly for the first time, knowing his weakness and the thing he had done and yet knowing, too, what he had gone through and why and what it had done to him. She was not thinking of herself, of all that she had gone through. She would think of that later and accept the true situation finally, but at the moment her sympathies were all for Frank.

Morgan shook his head in wonder and looked back at the older man. "One thing more," he said. "What ever happened to the other gun?"

Frank's head came up and his eyes were no longer dull, but shining with a strange light. "I took that away from Glenna," he replied, "after I got the whole story from her. I've kept it ever since." He paused a moment to rub the back of his hand over his lips, then said, "In fact, when Glenna told me that you wanted me over here at once or you would call Lieutenant Scanlon, I knew that you had learned something important. So I came prepared. This is the same gun."

He took the gun from his pocket and Morgan stared at the cold, blue-steel barrel and felt his stomach tighten into a knot. Glenna sat up too and turned slowly to face her husband, her eyes wide with fear. Irene gasped and put a hand to her mouth. Morgan groaned inwardly, cursing himself for a fool and telling himself that he should have known long before that the pressures so long generated would have to find release in some sort of explosion. Characters could be shoved about in a novel with impunity, but one had to answer to a living character with his back to the wall and nothing more to lose.

Frank stared into his eyes and said, "There's only one course to follow now, and that means the final loss of everything. I can't take any more, O'Keefe. Maybe Glenna can, she has much more strength than I, but I can't. I—I'm sorry to do it this way, but—"

He raised the gun slowly. Every muscle in Morgan's body tightened, but the gun kept rising and the hand turned and the barrel swung toward Frank's temple and his finger tightened on the trigger. Morgan threw himself from the bed and dived across the room like a human projectile. He slammed into Frank and knocked him backward from the chair to the floor, then wrenched the pistol from his hand and threw it across the room.

"Oh, no, you don't," he cried. "You don't get out that easy." He lifted Frank to his feet and shoved him against a wall and called to Irene over his shoulder, "Call the police. Call Scanlon."

Irene walked stiffly toward them and gently but firmly drew Morgan's hands away from Frank's shoulders. "Frank," she said.

He met her eyes then for the first time and said hoarsely, "Yes, Irene?"

"Take Glenna home."

Frank was hardly conscious of what she was saying, but Glenna was on her feet at once and hurried across the room. She asked wildly, "We can go, Irene? You're letting us go? What about the police? Are you going to call the police?"

Irene looked at her coldly and shook her head. "No, I don't intend calling the police. Not right now."

"Later?"

"That depends."

"On what?"

An odd light of vengeance appeared in Irene's eyes. "It depends on how long you remain with Frank. The day you leave him I shall call Scanlon and personally press charges against you. I will also see to it that my attorneys pick every ounce of flesh from your bones."

"No," Glenna gasped. "You can't do that. You aren't God. You can't dictate our lives."

"You dictated the course of my life for ten years. Now it's my turn. But it's entirely up to you. Remain with Frank and I shall press no charges. Leave him and I shall press charges immediately. There's nothing more to say. Now, if you don't mind, I should like you to leave my home—at once."

Glenna looked at the sagging bulk of her husband and suddenly she, too, seemed to age. Morgan knew the biggest thing in her life at the moment was to break loose of the past and her aging husband and recapture her youth. More than anything in the world, she wanted to make full use of the last of her unusual beauty before it faded, as it must, eventually. But now she had to stay and she had to pay. He wondered how well she would stand up under it and suddenly looked at Irene with grudging admiration. She did have a bit of calculating bitch in her, after all.

Frank was also beginning to grasp the implications of Irene's decision. He blinked at Irene, and then he looked at his wife and his eyes were again alive and cleared of the shadow of death. His back straightened and his shoulders squared. He started to say something to Irene, but thought better of it and turned away. He took Glenna's arm, turned her toward the door and walked out of the room.

Morgan placed his hands on Irene's shoulders and said gently, "But now no one will know. You still have the same people to face who will continue thinking the same way about you."

"I've been doing that for years without strength," she said. "But now I have strength and I know and you know. I don't think I shall mind any longer whom I have to face or what they think of me."

"You think you're strong enough for that?"

"Yes. My weakness was in my own doubts about myself. That's why I couldn't face the world. But now that weakness is gone. What others think of me now is really of no importance."

"You're a brave woman, Irene."

She smiled softly and said, "Now I can give myself, Morgan, with no barriers, no doubts and no reservations."

"No problems?"

"Gone. All gone."

"I seem to have lost a few myself." His fingers tightened on her shoulders. "But do you think it could work with us, the lady and the drunk?"

She leaned into his arms and pressed a cheek against his and whispered, "I am sure of it. Besides," she added, "I never was a lady. Not really."

THE END

H. VERNOR DIXON BIBLIOGRAPHY
(1908-1984)

NOVELS

Laughing Gods (1935)
Something for Nothing (1950)
To Hell Together (1951; abridged edition, 1959)
Deep is the Pit (1952)
The Marriage Bed (1952)
Too Rich to Die (1953)
Up a Winding Stair (1953)
A Lover for Cindy (1954)
The Hunger and the Hate (1955)
Cry Blood (1956)
Killer in Silk (1956)
That Girl Marian (1962)
Guerrilla (1963)
The Pleasure Seekers (1963)
The Rag Pickers (1966)
The Moon is Green (unpublished)

STORIES

The Experimenter (*Collier's*, July 25 1936)
Not in the Book (*Collier's*, Sept 26 1936)
Experience Not Necessary (*Collier's*, Aug 7 1937)
Tennis Bum (*The American Magazine*, Feb 1939)
The Captains Bride (*The American Magazine*, Mar 1939)
One Was Enough (*The American Magazine*, Aug 1939)
Clear and Unlimited (*Collier's*, Aug 12 1939)
Inquire of the Sea (*The American Magazine*, Sept 1939)
Poodle on a Leash (*The American Magazine*, Nov 1939)
Bali Love Song (*The American Magazine*, Apr 1940)
The Sharks of Hihimanu (*Cosmopolitan*, June 1940)
The Siren Smiled (*The American Magazine*, July, Aug, Sept, Oct, Nov 1940)
Manhattan Jungle (*The American Magazine*, Mar 1941)
Generals Make Promises (*The American Magazine*, May 1941; *Argosy* (UK), Feb 1942)
Call Me Edie, Honey! (*The American Magazine*, Aug 1941)
Test Flight (*Cosmopolitan*, July 1942)
Women Like a Beating (*The American Magazine*, July 1942)

The Game Is for Mary (*The American Magazine*, Sept 1942)
Built for a Pilot (*Collier's*, Dec 12 1942)
Civilian Pilot (*Collier's*, Jan 30 1943)
Follow the Leader (*Collier's*, Mar 6 1943)
Flat-Top Jenny (*Cosmopolitan*, Oct 1943)
The Eager Beaver (*Collier's*, Dec 11 1943)
Only Bats Fly Blind (*Argosy*, Jan 1944)
Via the Horn and Hell (*Argosy*, Feb 1944)
Harpooner's Lady (*Argosy*, Mar 1944)
There Was a Girl— (*The American Magazine*, Apr 1944)
A Guy Like Red (*Collier's*, Apr 15 1944)
Come in Like a Yankee! (*Argosy*, June 1944)
No Imagination (*Liberty*, July 1 1944)
Grandstand Flyer (*Argosy*, Sept 1944)
The Better Things (*Liberty*, Sept 9 1944)
How to Fight a War (*Argosy*, Oct 1944)
The Bobby-Sock Bride (*Liberty*, Nov 11 1944)
A Dog of Character (*Argosy*, Feb 1945; *Argosy* (Canada), Nov 1945)
Navigator to Colonel (*Argosy*, Mar 1945)
'Round the Horn to Hell (*Argosy*, Apr 1945)
Overnight Diver (*Argosy*, May 1945)
A Downright Peaceful Man! (*Argosy*, June 1945)
The Go-Devil (*The Blue Book Magazine*, July 1945)
You Can't Win (*Cosmopolitan*, Sept 1945)
To Act As God (*Liberty*, Dec 22 1945)
Moonlight (*Cosmopolitan*, Jan 1946)
Is This to Be Our Tomorrow? (*The Blue Book Magazine*, Apr 1946)
The Cub (*Collier's*, Apr 27 1946)
The Black-Haired Widow (*Liberty*, May 25 1946)
The Little Woman (*Liberty*, Aug 17 1946)
The Artist and the Heiress (*The American Magazine*, Mar 1947)
The Pitch to Rio (*The Saturday Evening Post*, Sept 6 1947)
100 Fathoms (*Liberty*, May 1949)
Deep Salvage (*Liberty*, Dec 1949, Jan, Feb, Mar 1950)
Trapped! (*This Week*, 1950; *Suspense* (UK), Apr 1960)
This Is Jo— (*Argosy*, Jan 1950)
The Reef (*Argosy* (UK), May 1950)
Murder Flies High (*The American Magazine*, July 1956)
The Bartender Bit (*Cosmopolitan*, Nov 1957)

STORY COLLECTION
Come in Like a Yankee and Other Stories (1944)